Queen of the Court

A Novel

Melanie Howard and Andrea Leidolf

Match Point Press

This book is a work of fiction. Characters, organizations, events and incidents are the product of the authors' imagination. Any resemblance to actual persons and places is entirely coincidental.

ISBN: 0989560694
ISBN-13: 9780989560696

For Dottie Howard and Kerry Rider, who would have loved this book

Tennis is a perfect combination of violent action taking place in an atmosphere of total tranquility.

-Billy Jean King

1

"I cannot believe that behemoth, that monstrosity," said Lavinia Endicott Winter, clenching her teeth as she gripped the steering wheel of her silver 1990 diesel Mercedes (121,000 miles, mint condition).

She stared out the windshield up the winding drive that led to a massive, mostly Georgian-style club house. Although still out of sight, it was never out of Lavinia's mind. "It has driven this club into bankruptcy. Your father, the senator, is probably rolling in his grave." Lavinia turned slightly toward her daughter, Allie Beech, and shook her head.

"Only if his secretary is in there with him, Mother," Allie replied. At forty-two, she'd been raised on her mother's tirades.

"I am going to ignore that," Lavinia said, arching one perfectly penciled eyebrow. "Dear God, the trash that we have admitted into this club; Wayne Jones, that horrid redneck strip club owner, and his tacky ex-stripper wife." Lavinia wiped her brow with a crisp white handkerchief, piloting the Mercedes one-handed. The route was so familiar the car could have driven it itself.

A tiger-striped cat, a member of Belle Vista's substantial feral cat colony, darted across the road.

"Damn it," said Allie as Lavinia hit the brakes, jolting them both.

"Vermin! We should exterminate them," said Lavinia, leaving Allie to wonder whether she was referring to the cats, the Joneses or both.

"Mr. Jones apparently owns some legitimate businesses, like, um, car washes, and they claim Shana was his bookkeeper, not a stripper," said Allie, flipping down the passenger-side visor and smoothing back her sleek dark brown hair. "I just hope she found time to learn some tennis during her *bookkeeping* career, since her husband essentially bought her a spot on my team."

Lavinia snorted and shook her head. Her silver bob did not move. It never did. "Belle Vista Country Club builds a new clubhouse, can't pay its bills, and along comes Wayne Jones with an offer we can't refuse." Lavinia spoke more to herself than to her daughter.

"Well we had to save the club somehow, Mother." Allie reached to check her iPhone, a habit that profoundly annoyed Lavinia. "Anyway, it's not as if anything really ever changes at Belle Vista."

The winding, tree-lined road the women drove traversed the heart of the historic Belle Vista Country Club, slicing through land settled by Tazewell Edgemoor, an eccentric packed off to the colonies by his aristocratic family. Along with various family heirlooms, Tazewell brought a pair of cats, who survived the journey and multiplied enthusiastically in their new environs.

By the start of the Civil War, his heir, Ezekiel, grew cotton and tobacco on the family's plantation, called Belle Vista. The original mansion was burned to the ground during the Civil War by federal troops in retaliation for Edgemoor's service on General Robert E. Lee's senior staff (and because no one on either side liked him).

Civil engineer and golf enthusiast Thomas Jardine gained control of Belle Vista in 1920, when he married the last of the Edgemoors, the slightly unhinged Elizabeth. The peculiar young woman asked him to change his name to Edgemoor, and her vast fortune persuaded him to agree.

Jardine (now Edgemoor) built the original clubhouse and a nine-hole golf course on the former plantation grounds. On the main patio, he erected a monument to himself; a bronze fountain where water eternally springs from his "mashie" (five iron), as he overlooks the verdant golf course.

Today, the Belle Vista website paints an idyllic picture of the club:

"Belle Vista boasts the finest amenities of any country club in the region. There is an eighteen-hole golf course on 300 landscaped acres designed by renowned architect Franz Mulligan. The state-of-the-art tennis complex has

eight outdoor clay courts and five indoor courts. The newly renovated fitness center is equipped with sauna and steam rooms. There is an Olympic swimming pool surrounded by baby pools, and an outdoor tiki bar. The golf and tennis shops stock the latest athletic fashions and the kitchen is known for its light, healthy cuisine. Many families who joined the club in 1922 still hold memberships today. The centerpiece of the club is the new 65,000-square-foot clubhouse featuring formal and casual dining, bars, terrace and patio settings, a ballroom and meeting rooms, twelve fireplaces and the 19th Hole Bar and Grille. The views of the river and city are unparalleled."

What the website does not reveal is that construction of the new clubhouse has disrupted this haven of serenity for the upper classes. The extravagant structure looms over the grounds, its columns and stonework a confused mixture of several architectural styles that perfectly capture the original plantation's spirit of oppressive grandiosity. The board approved its construction despite the objections of many senior members, including Lavinia Winter.

Unfortunately, many of Lavinia's dire predictions came true: the spectacular new clubhouse was so far over budget that Belle Vista was forced to the brink of bankruptcy. There was plenty of blame to go around, from the Board of Governors to the shady builder. But in the end, members were faced with a choice, lose the club or sell fifty-one percent of the ownership to the only interested buyer; Big Wayne Jones, entrepreneur, strip club owner and ex-convict whose wife, it seems, wants to play tennis.

The Belle Vista Country Club Vision Statement, which hangs in an ornate gold frame in the foyer of the clubhouse, reads:

"The Belle Vista Country Club strives to be a lifelong haven for our exclusive members, their families and their guests. In our superb setting, one can relax and enjoy recreational and social activities with people who share values and traditions."

The membership is entirely upper class and white. The initiation fee is $100,000. Monthly dues are $900 and there is an annual food minimum. Currently, there is no waiting list.

Lavinia hit the brakes hard again, and she and Allie whipped forward.

"My Lord, Mother, you are going to give me whiplash."

Lavinia's bumper stopped only inches from the dark blue Jaguar in front of her. A line of cars was backed up from the parking lot, down the hill onto Clubhouse Drive (Members and Guests Only).

"Just look at this horrible traffic. I just know it has something to do with that reality show. As if things weren't dire enough." Lavinia sighed and rested her papery thin cheek on the steering wheel as if signaling defeat.

Allie looked over and felt a bit guilty. Not that she approved of the Joneses filming *Queen of the Court* – what a ridiculous title – at the club, but since it was to be about her beloved tennis team she felt obligated to participate. In fact, she'd never tell Lavinia, but she'd already scheduled an individual interview with the director.

"I must step out and see what the delay is," Lavinia said impatiently, jamming her old Benz into park.

The parking lot surrounding the clubhouse was a circus. Crew members were unloading camera equipment and lights from large trucks with "Vixen Video Productions" in purple script on the side. A large wrecking crane sat directly in front of the clubhouse, and men in neon orange vests blocked the entrance to the parking lot. Lead cameraman Jamal Whitley trained his shoulder-mounted camera on a large stone sign engraved with the words BELLE VISTA COUNTRY CLUB, EST. 1922.

Rex Range, the director, wearing a turtleneck and tweed blazer despite the warmth of the morning, stood beside him holding a clipboard and gestured with his pen. "Make sure you get this," he said, nodding towards the crane.

"What do you see, Mother?" asked Allie, whose vision was blocked by a van two cars ahead.

Lavinia peered around the line of traffic, just in time to see the wrecking ball swing in a slow, relentless arc toward the sign, striking and shattering it into rubble. She let loose a horror movie scream that rang in Allie's ears.

"Do you believe this place?" asked Jamal, shaking his head as he struggled to set up lighting equipment on the patio adjacent to the outdoor tennis courts.

"Beats the hell out of the last show I styled, *The Cat Collectors*. I still can't get the smell of cat piss out of my clothes." Stylist Byron Lord grimaced as he dropped an armload of women's tennis clothes on a glass-and-wrought iron courtside table. At 110 pounds soaking wet, even lifting tennis clothes was a strain for the elfin Byron.

"This, I'm afraid, promises to be even more boring than old cat ladies; *Queen of the Court*, the spellbinding saga of a country club tennis team. We have hit rock bottom, gentlemen. To think I started in serious documentaries," lamented Rex in the posh British accent he used to disguise his East London council flat upbringing. Jamal and Byron shared a look. Their director tended to gas on about his career in documentaries, but as far as they knew, his one effort, *Zelda Fitzgerald and her Eczema: More Than Skin Deep*, had never aired. He checked off items on his clipboard as he reviewed the camera and lighting set up. "I should have an assistant."

"As long as we get paid. Your buddy Jones is making sure of that, right Rex?" Jamal eyed Rex suspiciously. He had been stiffed on more than one Vixen job.

"Wayne Jones is not my buddy. You'll get paid, unless I decide to give your job to one of the thousands of unemployed cameramen who don't make smartass comments. And furthermore…"

Rex never got to finish his sentence. With a banshee wail, a red-headed blur hurtled through the courtyard wielding a super soaker, tripped over a cord, and fell at Jamal's feet while still managing to get off a good squirt that thoroughly soaked Rex.

"Why do I feel the indignities are only just beginning?" said Rex, shaking his clipboard in a useless effort to salvage his list.

Unfazed, a small, red-headed boy got up and rubbed his knee, grinning up at his handiwork.

"Lil Wayne, get over here *right now*!"

A statuesque redhead, her perfectly sculpted breasts barely concealed by a very small, wet white tank top, hurried onto the courtside patio. She held the hand of a pale little girl with wispy brown hair whose white tennis dress hung on her thin frame.

Jamal looked down at the freckled red-headed boy who was checking his water gun for damage. "Your name is Lil Wayne? For real?"

"Hi Rex, I'm so excited to meet your crew. I'm Shana Lee Jones, and this is Destiny and Lil Wayne," the redhead said, holding up the girl's hand and pointing at the boy. "I'm real sorry about Lil Wayne," Shana added with a big smile that showed a row of white teeth slightly stained with red lipstick. "He didn't break anything, did he?"

Jamal smiled goofily at Shana. "No problem. So how come you got a kid named Lil Wayne?"

"Oh, he's named after his daddy," Shana said, hugging the squirming boy.

Jamal and Rex exchanged a glance as Dick Evans, the gray-haired tennis shop manager, limped over, a stern look on his face.

"I hope you fellas realize that you cannot go out on the courts without regulation shoes. We also have an all white rule."

"Can't say I'm surprised," Jamal said, shaking his head.

"Oh no, honey. He don't mean that only white people are allowed. You have to wear white when you play tennis." Shana smiled and pointed to the rows of immaculately groomed clay courts, where old white rich people were playing tennis with varying degrees of success.

"I can't say I'm seeing the difference," said Jamal with a shrug.

At that moment, Allie Beech strode onto the patio, her black-and-white patterned tennis bag slung over her shoulder and her pale, high-boned cheeks flushed with anger. Shana had never met Allie, or any of the other tennis team members. Rex felt it would be more "authentic" if they encountered each other for the first time on camera.

"Our club sign has been destroyed – *destroyed*! I demand to know who is responsible."

Shana stared in awe at Allie, whose boarding-school posture made her seem taller than five foot seven inches, even in her flats. She looked like the women in ads for sable coats or high-end vodkas; her chestnut hair smoothed into a glossy pony-tail, her pale skin perfect and either make-up free, or covered in some makeup so expensive it didn't even show. Her dress was simple white poplin trimmed in navy and her only jewelry pearl studs and a gold Cartier tank watch. Shana wished she'd left off her false eyelashes and green eye shadow, not to mention all that hair spray and her big diamond "S" pendant.

"Hi, I'm Shana Lee Jones," said Shana, with a tentative smile, offering Allie her free hand, her long red nails suddenly seeming just a bit too bright. "Please don't worry about the sign. Me and my husband had a new one made. It's going up later today. You'll love it, it's way more modern."

"Allie Beech, ladies tennis team co-captain." Allie took Shana's hand reluctantly and released it quickly. She had hoped that Shana would look a bit more like a bookkeeper and a little less like a stripper. "Do you realize that sign was carved by Italian stone masons in 1922?"

"Oh, I know honey." Shana nodded sympathetically. "But ya'll won't have to put up with all this old stuff now that the Joneses are here! And you'll be relieved to know that our new sign was made right here in America."

Allie stared at Shana in disbelief and then regained her composure. She forced herself to remember that this woman owned most of the club. At least for now. "Our team lunch begins shortly. We'll be at the long table on the second floor terrace. Don't be late." She turned abruptly and walked away, head held high, before Shana could utter another word.

"Me*ow*" whispered Byron.

In the bowels of the Belle Vista kitchen, Maria Delgado, Consuela Guzman, and Carmen Lopez prepared lunch in their crisp green and blue uniforms.

"Consuela, let's get moving. I need to get to the mall for my restaurant shift," said Maria, exasperated with Consuela's lethargic pace.

"As if these tennis ladies are actually going to eat," Consuela replied in Spanish as she topped a salad with a salmon filet. "Well, maybe Caroline Walinsky. She's been packing it on since her divorce."

"You better hope that these women never learn Spanish," Maria admonished.

"Oh, I always speak English around them. I like the way 'Mrs. Beech' sounds the same as 'Mrs. Bitch' in my accent."

Maria laughed in spite of herself. "I'm going to go pour the wine. They may only eat air, but they like to wash it down with a whole lot of Chardonnay."

The Belle Vista ladies tennis team gathered at its usual terrace table overlooking the tennis courts and immaculately groomed hills of the golf course beyond. Allie sat near the head of the table, next to team captain Lou Butts, their heads lowered as they conversed quietly. Taylor Thomas saw Maria from across the room and lifted her glass toward her, as if to get the wine into it faster. Karen Davis eyed the hovering camera crew suspiciously. At the very end of the table, in accordance with their status as lower court players, sat the Donaldson twins (now Mitsy Donaldson Schwarz and Bitsy Donaldson Gargiano), Kendall Pedersen and Hayes Grant. They pointed at Jamal and laughed nervously.

"Just ignore us," Rex assured them soothingly. "I know it's awkward at first, but believe me, you'll get used to it."

Lou turned and gave the camera a withering stare. Louisa Edgemoor Spencer Butts, fifty, with her short, no-nonsense naturally graying hair, minimal makeup and patrician bearing didn't fear Rex's cameras. She felt only disdain.

"Ahem," Lou cleared her lovely, long, slightly wrinkled throat. She opened a paisley binder and was about to speak when Allie's iPhone chimed.

"Excuse me," Allie said. "No, I will not take you to the mall. No, absolutely not. Figure it out," she whispered into her phone.

"Allison," said Lou in a warning tone. Although she didn't wish to create a scene on camera, phone calls were strictly forbidden at meetings and practice, not to mention matches.

"Welcome to the fifty-second season of Belle Vista Ladies' Team Tennis." Lou smiled and lifted her wine glass to the table, and the rest of the ladies followed suit, although Karen toasted with water. "This is a transition year for us. Dottie McCoy has retired and Lorna Smythe has decided to leave the team to spend more time with her family."

Ha, thought Allie, though she smiled along with the rest. Typical. She knew Lou had decided that Dottie was too old for competitive play, and she'd seen the old bird whack their pro, Justin Reynolds, on the head with her oversized Prince racquet when he delivered the news. As for Lorna, well, gossip had it she was in a mental hospital, in part because of pressure from Lou to "step it up or get off the court".

"In their place, I want to welcome new members Karen Davis and Shana Jones. I notice Shana and Caroline Walinsky are," Lou paused and looked down at her watch, "seven minutes late. We don't wait for latecomers. Maria, go ahead and serve the salmon Caesar salad." Maria nodded and headed for the kitchen.

"Can I see a menu?" Karen asked. She was avoiding farmed salmon, which contained dyes, while she tried to get pregnant. Lou shot her a look.

"We pre-order lunch," Allie replied. "Everyone has the salmon."

"But, I…," Karen sputtered.

"Oh, just have the flipping salmon," Taylor snapped, oblivious to both the cameras and Lou's warning look. She took another slug of wine.

Caroline Walinsky, voluptuous and punctuality-challenged, approached the table with a stiff, strange gait. The camera focused on her as she slid into a chair beside Taylor.

"Oh Lou, Allie, I'm so sorry to be late." She smiled sheepishly. Caroline was terrified of Lou, Allie, and for totally different reasons, Taylor. Divorce had left Caroline as socially vulnerable as a wounded she wolf in a hungry pack.

"You're always late," snapped Lou. "Why should today be any different? Why are you limping? If you're injured, we'll have to replace you."

Caroline straightened her back. "Oh, no, it's nothing. It was free Brazilian day at the new spa."

The other women's mouths opened in perfectly lipsticked Os. Lou pointed to the camera.

"Oh gawd Caroline," Taylor said, nearly spitting out her wine. "You just told everyone out in TV Land that you fried your… " Allie reached across the table and sunk her fingernails into Taylor's forearm.

"Owww!"

"Stop," Allie whispered to her, digging her nails in deeper.

"If we're done with all of our interruptions and personal hygiene disasters - really Caroline - let's proceed. Where was I?" She peered at her binder. "Oh yes, first, I'd like to welcome Taylor back to the team." Lou forced a smile.

"I'd like to thank Congressman Butts for intervening with the Rules Committee on her behalf," Allie interjected, as Lou preened.

"Excuse me," said Karen, raising her hand slightly. "But how does this work?"

"How does *what* work?" asked Lou.

"Team tennis."

There was a general intake of breath. This was akin to admitting one did not know the date, the name of the president, or the location of the area's best nail salon.

"Five doubles teams, ranked from court one down to court five, play best of three sets. We play other Dominion League clubs on Friday mornings at nine. I'll get you a rulebook," Lou said, spacing her words carefully, as if speaking to a particularly slow child.

"Who decides which players play on which court? I mean, how we're ranked," Karen continued, oblivious to the fact that Lou's mouth had thinned into a disapproving line.

"I do, of course," Lou replied curtly.

Jamal lowered the camera and turned to Rex. "Isn't this enough of the ladies who lunch?"

Rex winked. "Things are about to get interesting. I found a bitch-seeking Russian missile in the parking lot earlier. It should launch anytime now."

Rex gave Jamal a nudge as a tall woman in spandex shorts and stomach-baring hot pink sports bra charged onto the terrace, her long white-blonde braid swinging behind her.

"Boom," Rex said under his breath as Caroline jumped up from the table.

"No! Not her," Caroline shrieked. "This is *so* much worse than hot wax."

Elena Walinsky, the fit and fierce Russian athlete who broke up Caroline's marriage, stopped short at the table and turned to Jamal. "Try to film left side," she said in a thick spy movie accent that made Taylor snort. "When I pose for Russian *Playboy*, naked of course, photographer said it was best." Elena put a hand on her hip and thrust it forward.

"Excuse me, but that attire is not allowed in the Grille or on the terrace," Lou lectured.

Elena turned on her with an icy blue stare. "Why am I not on team? I was Uzbek Junior champion at fifteen, then quarter finalist in junior doubles at Australian Open. Now I am not good enough for ridiculous club team?"

Allie looked up at Elena, interested.

"You played on the tour?"

"Allie," Lou hissed. She turned back to Elena. "I'm sorry, this team is full."

"Ha! They call this democracy!" Elena threw her head back. "Even in communist days, we have tryouts. Okay, sometimes people get shot, but still, tryouts." She whipped her braid around and marched away.

Caroline sat back down. She was shaking. "Thank you so much, Lou."

"A world ranked junior player," Allie mused under her breath. She really wanted to beat River's Edge this year; that Lauren Lippert was getting way too smug since becoming captain. Lou gave her a sharp look, and Allie felt her face flush. Once Lou made a decision, it was final.

"Caroline, don't worry. Your ex-husband's trophy wife will play on this team over my dead body." Lou slammed her paisley binder shut and rose to leave. "I think we've had enough excitement for one meeting. I'll see all of you on the courts for practice at three o'clock sharp. Hopefully, Mrs. Jones will decide to grace us with her presence."

As if Lou had conjured her, Shana appeared on the terrace, lugging a huge shopping bag, an equally oversized smile on her face. "You must be Lou Butts," she said, giving Lou, who froze on contact, a big hug, then pulling up a chair and scooting in between her and Allie.

Shana turned to the rest of the table as Jamal focused his camera on her. "Hi ya'll, I'm so sorry I missed lunch, but I just had to run out and pick these up when I heard they were ready." She pointed at the bag resting at her feet.

"I'm your new teammate, Shana LEE Jones," she continued, "I like the Lee, gives my name a little spark. And speaking of spark!" Shana reached down and opened the shopping bag. She pulled out a slinky white spandex tennis dress, its plunging neckline and skirt bordered in sparkling teal.

"My lord," gasped Lou. "What is that? It looks like a majorette costume."

"Lou, me and you are on the same page! That is just what I said to the designer – make our new tennis uniforms sexy and fun, like majorette costumes."

"*Our new tennis uniforms?*" Allie asked in disbelief.

"Shit," said Taylor, draining her wine glass. "We're all going to need Brazilians to wear those things."

"Aren't they sweet? Here's the best part. They sewed each of our names over the right boob; so classy." Shana held up the uniform and pointed, Vanna-style. "The new club name is on the left."

"*New club name?*" repeated Allie.

"Uh huh, Jones Belle Vista," said Shana, holding the uniform up so Jamal could zoom in.

"Oh, dear God." Lou began to choke uncontrollably.

SHANA LEE JONES INTERVIEW

In a corner of the tennis shop converted to a studio, Shana Lee Jones admired a tangled pile of jewelry. Her fingers lingered over a flashy diamond pendant. She had two hours to record her individual interview before practice began.

"I really like this one, Byron. It could be my signature piece." Shana looked up and smiled.

Byron scratched his chin, where a few thin blonde hairs were making an attempt at a goatee. "I don't know; Number One Mama was really speaking to me. Why not wear both?"

"I don't want to look too flashy," Shana said. She frowned, thinking of Allie Beech, her sleek pony tail and her simple pearl studs. "When people see Jones Belle Vista on TV, I want them to see classy and tasteful."

Behind the camera, Jamal laughed, and then struggled to cover it with a cough.

"You okay over there, Jamal?"

"Jamal just has a little asthma. In fact, if he isn't careful he may *choke to death*," said Byron, glaring over his should at Jamal. "Shana, I think you should just be yourself. If tasteful were a disease, this place would be quarantined. That Butts woman wouldn't even let me put a little blush on her. I won't be held responsible when she hits the screen in high definition."

Shana picked up one of the makeup brushes and eyed herself in the mirror, then applied blush to her cheeks and décolletage. "Maybe I'll host a makeover party for the team and we can introduce Lou to some color," she said, triggering another of Jamal's 'coughing spells'.

"I guess the first thing I want our viewers, and my new friends at Jones Belle Vista, to know is that Wayne and I may have bought us a country club, but we're not gonna go around acting like big shots. See, it's hard to believe when you meet us and see our lifestyle; but me and Wayne come from very humble beginnings.

I grew up in a close-knit family, in a small town in West Virginia."

Shana Lee Jones had come a long way – farther than she wanted to admit on camera. She was raised in a tired, cramped trailer at the foot of a mountain in Croaker Hollow, near Moneton. Shana, her mother, Lurleen, and brother Billy had shared the rusty double-wide with Grandma Rose and shifty, unemployed Uncle Ray.

"Now I knew from an early age I wanted to be on TV, but my family didn't think acting was a sensible career."

Lurleen and Grandma Rose watched *Wheel of Fortune* every day on a small black-and-white television precariously balanced on the grimy Formica counter. Shana was transfixed by the glamorous Vanna White. "Someday, I'll be on TV," Shana would say while Vanna turned the letters.

"You can always dream," Lurleen would reply, patting Shana on the head with her free hand and flicking ashes into a beer can with the other. Lurleen, who'd had Billy at sixteen and Shana at twenty, knew that most dreams in Croaker Holler went up in smoke.

"We went to church every Sunday and learned those good Bible-based values that built America."

The World's End Apocalyptic Church of Signs was a plain wooden church with a small but fanatical congregation. Members would speak in tongues as the preacher, Pastor John, wrapped poisonous snakes around his neck, just like the Bible commanded. One warm summer afternoon, a large rattlesnake bit Pastor John and he was called home to the Lord, prompting the Fish and Game Commission to shut down the church. Shana didn't lose faith, but she developed a lifelong terror of snakes.

"Now I left West Virginia to find a career. I became a bookkeeper in the entertainment industry, which is how I met the love of my life and my husband, Big Wayne Jones."

Shana ran away before finishing high school and ended up as a stripper at the Do It All Night nightclub on Route 1. One of her acts required her to dress up as Eve and dance seductively around a pole, a large fake snake draped around her shoulders. This always made her think of poor Pastor John and his handsome, doomed son, Levi. But it also caught the eye of the man who would change her life forever: Wayne Jones.

"Now Wayne was my Prince Charming, but truth was, he'd been a little wild in his past life."

Wayne had been a member of the biker gang Redneck Royals, and a series of brawls had landed him in prison. Wayne was grateful for his time behind bars, because that was where he found the Lord.

Wayne faithfully attended Bible study, where the prison chaplain urged him to contemplate the Ten Commandments. Many nights Wayne lay awake, one eye on his homicidal cellmate, wondering if a man had to love his neighbor even after the bastard stole his drugs and old lady, or if "Thou shalt not kill" covered manslaughter, as well as murder one.

One day, Reverend Paul, who resembled a frail Mr. Rogers, was reading from the huge Bible on his desk when a muscular, tattooed convict pulled a shiv from his sock and grabbed the old man as a hostage. The prayer group morphed into a riot, but Wayne remained calm. He lifted the heavy Bible from the reverend's desk and brought it down on the skull of the hostage taker, earning early parole and leaving him with no doubt that the Bible saves.

Wayne went to work as a bouncer at the Do It All Night, where Shana admired Wayne's skill at removing unruly customers and he admired her skill at removing clothing. Their relationship blossomed into love, and they decided to open their own gentlemen's club, Big Wayne's, where Shana could give up the pole for bookkeeping.

"Now a lot of folks criticize me and Wayne for owning gentlemen's clubs, but at Big Wayne's we always treated our strippers with respect. We made lots of money, but so did the girls. We also offered the first comprehensive health plan for strippers on the East Coast, including dental. Not to mention a 401k. And when Wayne and I got married in Vegas, two of our dancers, Crystal and Shontae, came as witnesses. All expenses paid."

"Destiny was born, and two years later, I had Lil Wayne. We were living the American Dream, with a big house and a pool, but something was missing."

Shana was lonely once she wasn't working anymore. Her suburban neighbors didn't fancy hanging out with the owners of Big

Wayne's, no matter how much money they had or how many plates of homemade muffins Shana brought over.

"Well, I didn't know what exactly was missing until I had a vision. Women in my family have had visions for generations. They call it Second Sight. One night, my Mama had a dream that my brother Billy was in trouble down by the river, where people drown all the time, and she saved him."

Lurleen had raced down to the river bank, where the town's worst teenagers hung out, just as a police officer was pouring Billy's last beer into the sand. The officer agreed not to charge Billy if Lurleen took him directly home. Billy threw up in his mother's car, but as this incident was not added to his rather substantial juvenile record, it was still considered a win for the Sight.

Shana didn't tell Rex that Grandma Rose often saw spirits and heard voices, usually those of Civil War soldiers. Shana's Sight came later, mostly in small visions, like the one that told her to paint their triple garage doors purple. That got them fined by the Enclave Homeowners' Association, but Shana was not discouraged. She felt something big was coming.

"I was working out on the Stairmaster in our home gym, and Big Wayne was lifting weights and smoking his cigar. Suddenly, I saw a big brick building on a hill. It was as clear as if I was there, then it vanished. That night, we saw Belle Vista's foreclosure on the news and I knew in my heart that we had to save that club. I also thought it would be the perfect place to film a TV show – with me as the star – just like I always dreamed. Wayne wasn't convinced at first, but my honey bear always wants me to have whatever I want. He said to me, 'I'll bail out a bunch of rich assholes if it will make you happy.'"

Shana stopped and clapped her hand over her mouth. "Oh, I shouldn't a said that!"

"Don't worry," Rex assured her. "Most of what we film gets cut."

But not the bits where you call rich people assholes, Jamal thought, feeling a bit sorry for Shana.

After the cameras stopped, and Rex and Jamal stepped outside to discuss the next shoot, Shana remained in her chair, thinking.

Sometimes, Shana felt that her life was like a river; always changing, unpredictable. The Moneton River ran behind the trailer park where she grew up. Grandma Rose often saw long dead soldiers bathing there. Shana learned in school that Moneton meant "Big Water". She found that funny, because sometimes the river was just a trickle. Then other times, it ran hard and fast. It was brown. It was green. It was blue. There were turtles, stacked up on logs like dominoes, and herons, frogs and bald eagles. There were also tires and beer cans, and once, a dead body. The river twisted and turned, with shallow rapids and deep, cool pools. Coves and tributaries shot off from the river like secrets. When Shana was a girl, she liked to explore these hidden places. As she grew older, she kept certain memories there, buried beneath the thick, silky mud.

2

Shana watched as Byron sorted through a pile of tennis outfits stacked on a table outside the tennis shop. "This one would be perfect on Taylor," Shana said as she held up a tiny Adidas skirt. "She is stunning, don't you think?"

"Honey, her husband is a plastic surgeon. For all we know, she used to be a man," Byron replied, tossing Shana's choice into his 'yes' pile.

"You are terrible," Shana said, laughing. "I didn't say anything I shouldn't have on camera, did I?"

"I never listen to what anyone says on these shows. It's all about the look," said Byron. "Unless you're throwing tables, you're well within the bounds of reality show propriety."

"Sounds a lot like holiday dinners where I'm from," Shana said as Allie entered the tennis shop to pick up her new Dunlop racquet. She looked over at Shana and Byron and frowned.

"Shana, you need to get to the locker room and change for practice. In case you didn't get her point at lunch, Lou values promptness." Allie picked her racquet up off the counter and turned to go.

"Did you see the new sign when you came in?" Shana asked Allie eagerly. She and Wayne had picked out a vintage Vegas-style sign with "Jones Belle Vista" in neon with flashing white lights surrounding it. Allie opened her mouth to say something, but quickly closed it.

Byron approached Allie with a handful of tennis clothes on hangers. "Here, Ms. Co-Captain, take these with you. I've marked who should wear what for practice." Allie made no move to take the clothes.

"Excuse me, whoever you are, but first, don't order me around like the help, and second, we wear our own clothes around here," Allie snapped, holding her racquet defensively across her chest.

"First, ordering the help around is your area, and second, don't get me started on your clothes," Byron shot back.

Allie turned and walked out of the shop, leaving Byron and the clothes behind. She was still steaming when she ran into her teenage daughter Bethany.

"Mother, you *need* to take me to the mall. I'm supposed to meet Katie and Reese; Nordstrom is having a makeup event," Bethany demanded, tossing her artfully highlighted hair.

"I have practice," Allie replied. Bethany was a darling, but she did suck all the oxygen out of a room or, in this case, the great outdoors.

"Busy," Bethany huffed. "Batting balls around. That's all this family ever does."

Allie marched past Bethany towards the locker room entrance. "No one told you to get your license suspended again," Allie called over her shoulder. "Ask Maria to take you."

"News flash, Maria hasn't been our nanny for six years," Bethany shouted at her retreating mother's taut back. She flopped down on a bench just as Shana came out of the tennis shop with an armful of plastic-covered clothes. With a crash, one of the courtyard tables tumbled over as Lil Wayne hurled himself at Shana, sending clothes everywhere.

"I give up!" said Byron, throwing his hands in the air. Justin Reynolds, head tennis pro, stumbled after Lil Wayne, Destiny by his side and a broken tennis racquet in his hand.

"Mrs. Jones," Justin pleaded. "You've got to take these kids. I'm supposed to be coaching the juniors, and then your team, on camera. I'm begging you, find a babysitter."

"I'm so sorry," Shana said to Justin. She quickly turned to Bethany. "Excuse me, miss? Are you interested in a babysitting job?"

"Are you kidding?" Bethany looked at Shana as if she were a bug. "I'm going to the mall."

"Perfect! Lil Wayne and Destiny love the mall." Shana fished several hundred dollar bills out of her bra. "Here's $300. If that doesn't cover it, let me know. What's your name anyway?"

"Bethany Beech. If you play tennis you must know my mom." The girl smiled sweetly, her whole demeanor altered. "I'll take great care of Dwayne and Tiffany." Bethany stuffed the money into her purse and dragged the children towards the parking lot.

"It's Destiny and Lil Wayne," Shana called after them. "Oh well." If Bethany was Allie's daughter, surely her kids were in the best of hands. She helped Byron gather up the tennis clothes and carried them toward the locker room.

Caroline, Lou, Karen and Taylor were already in the plush ladies locker room, in various states of undress. Taylor and Lou had brass nameplates on their cherry-paneled lockers, while Caroline had taken over the locker of a recently deceased member to avoid the $500 annual fee. Karen kept her sports clothes in her Nike tennis bag.

"Are we supposed to wear our own tennis clothes?" asked Caroline. "They get free clothes on *The Real Housewives*."

"We can ask that gay guy," said Taylor.

"Are you sure he's … well, you know?" asked Lou uncomfortably. Lou did not dislike gays; that would be an unseemly prejudice. She just preferred a world where she didn't ask, and they didn't tell.

"You're kidding, right? I always know, even when it's not obvious." Taylor tapped her head. "Excellent gaydar."

"They can't make us wear Shana's trashy uniform. Can you imagine?" Lou shivered. "Where is she from, anyway?"

"West Virginia," answered Caroline solemnly. "It's so embarrassing. Jones Belle Vista! The other teams will be laughing at us."

"They probably won't even notice," said Karen, who was a bit put off by all the drama.

"Oh please," said Lou. "How could they *possibly* not notice? We have a new name, a hideous new sign, trampy uniforms, and we're the subject of a *reality* show."

"My mother always said 'There's nothing worse than a redneck with money'," said Taylor. "Exactly where did all their money come from?"

"Strip clubs," Lou coughed out. She reminded herself to drink some water before practice. "The Board of Governors drove Belle Vista to the brink of financial ruin. When that happens, people like Wayne Jones always show up."

"All this talk about the damn Joneses is making my back tight," Taylor said, stretching from side to side. She reached into her tennis bag and pulled out a large prescription bottle, popped the lid, and swallowed two pills dry.

"I thought it was your shoulder that bothered you?" Caroline asked. "What are you taking?"

"Vicodin," Taylor answered.

"What about all that wine you had at lunch?" Lou looked over with concern, remembering last year's "Taylor Incident".

Taylor looked down at the bottle and read the warning label.

"Looks like unless I plan to operate heavy machinery, I'm good."

"That's an awfully large bottle," said Karen dubiously.

"Not that it's any of your business, Little Miss Prosecutor, but my husband is a plastic surgeon. I have chronic back, shoulder and neck pain, so he writes me prescriptions. You don't want me in pain. If I'm in pain, I make sure everyone else feels it too."

"Speaking of plastic surgery," said Caroline, "how many boob jobs do you think Shana has had?"

"Those suckers definitely aren't real," said Taylor, who considered herself an expert by marriage. "Watch her run. Her boobs will remain perfectly frozen."

"Do you think Elena has had any work done?" Caroline asked, wriggling into an Adidas tennis dress.

"Just stop thinking about her," said Taylor. Caroline's obsession with her replacement was starting to get on Taylor's nerves.

"Because she basically ruined my life, I think about her all the time," Caroline said angrily, looking at her reflection. She didn't remember having a muffin top last time she'd worn this. Or that roll *over* the muffin top.

"Elena really gives me the creeps," Taylor announced, sliding into tight white Nike shorts. "It's the angry foreigner thing. Is she even an American citizen?"

"Of course she is," said Lou. "She is married to Caroline's ex-husband."

Caroline pulled a hair brush out of her bag and began brushing her hair with short, angry strokes. "Please Lou, just make sure she doesn't get on the team."

"I already told you, over my dead body," Lou reassured her.

Allie entered the locker room, closing the door behind her. "Over your dead body what, Lou?"

"I was just reassuring Caroline that under no circumstances will Elena be on this team."

"She was a junior champion. I'd love to see her play," Allie said. "Justin told me she used to practice in empty swimming pools in sub-zero temperatures back in Uzbekistan."

"Can we please stop admiring the woman who stole my husband?" Caroline slammed the brush onto the counter top. "I liked it better when we were gossiping about trailer tr… "

Allie reached over and shoved a wrist sweatband in Caroline's open mouth just as Shana pushed open the door and entered the room with her armload of tennis wear.

"Hi, y'all," said Shana, oblivious to the awkward silence. "Who wants to try on some new outfits?"

Bethany leaned against a late model black Lexus SUV, a death grip on the wrist of a wriggling Lil Wayne. "Look, Dwayne, don't think you can pull any crap on me."

"It's Wayne," whispered Destiny, holding tightly to the hem of Bethany's skirt.

"And you, Tiffany, let go of my skirt. It's Prada, not some rag from Forever 21."

"Destiny."

"Oh, like there's any difference." Bethany deftly worked her iPhone with her left hand. "Hey, Reese, it's Bethany. I need you to pick me up at the club. Well, fine, whatever. Kiss kiss." Bethany angrily tossed the phone into the handbag resting near her feet. "Bitch!"

"You said the B-word! You said the B-word!" shouted Lil Wayne, jumping up and down.

"Shut up, Dwayne, I have duct tape you know."

Just then, Bethany spied Maria crossing the Belle Vista parking lot. "Maria! Maria! Over here!"

Maria's shoulders drooped. Bethany never spoke to her unless she wanted something.

"Maria, I need you to take me to the mall. Now."

Maria bit back a rebuke.

"Sorry, Bethany, I can't."

"Look, Maria, I know you're going to the mall for your other job, so just take me and these stupid kids with you."

Maria's face hardened. She'd had enough. "Fine, Bethany. You want to go to the mall, follow me."

Bethany tried to breathe through her mouth. She could literally feel her mascara melting. If she believed in hell, which of course was a totally lame idea, it would be something like this; an overheated bus filled with, like, the entire third word and that psycho little Dwayne bouncing up and down, singing some country crap.

Bethany felt a sudden cool breeze on her neck, which was nice. Until she realized the weird vagrant in the seat behind her was holding her hair up to his nose and - ugh, gross - *sniffing* it.

"Ewww!" Bethany whipped her hair out of his reach. "Why didn't you tell me you didn't have a car?" she asked Maria accusingly.

"You didn't ask. You never listen to what other people are trying to tell you, Bethany," said Maria, who was seated across thc aisle with Destiny.

On the seat beside Bethany, Lil Wayne screeched another chorus of "Friends in Low Places," bouncing in time with the music. Behind her, the vagrant clapped along.

Bethany gritted her teeth and pulled out her iPhone.

"Great," she complained. "Now I'll be late and miss my friends." She turned to Lil Wayne and yelled "Will you PLEASE pipe down?"

Lil Wayne snatched the phone out of Bethany's manicured hand and hurled it out the bus window. A cement truck in the next lane crushed it under a front tire, and Bethany shrieked as if she were being crushed with it.

Ten agonizing minutes later, Bethany exited the bus behind Maria and the children, teetering precariously on her Guiseppe Zanotti platform sandals, and displaying the usual expanse of tanned, toned leg.

That leg caught the attention of a darkly handsome young man in a tight white t-shirt and jeans, leaning against a pickup truck parked at the edge of the mall parking lot. As he was admiring Bethany, Enrique Flores took notice of the little group with her and laughed to himself. This was turning out to be a good day.

"Hey, Aunt Maria," he said, strolling over.

"Enrique, what are you doing here?" Maria replied warily in Spanish.

"Just finished work." Enrique kissed Maria on the cheek. "Aren't you going to introduce me to your friends?"

Maria looked darkly from Enrique to Bethany, whose sour, angry face had suddenly, miraculously, produced a flirtatious smile. A smile Enrique returned.

"Enrique, this girl is off limits, do you hear," said Maria in Spanish. "Her parents are very powerful and I don't need any trouble."

"Excuse me," interrupted Bethany. "It's, like, rude to speak Spanish in front of regular people."

Enrique turned to Bethany and held out his hand.

"I am Enrique Flores and am very pleased to meet you, Miss…?"

Bethany placed her free left hand in Enrique's, as Lil Wayne continued twisting her right.

"Bethany, Bethany Beech. And these kids," she shot Wayne and Destiny a look of disgust, "really belong to someone named Jones, but I'm stuck babysitting."

"Looks like you could use some help, want me to tag along?"

Bethany gave Enrique a look usually reserved for a firefighter at the moment he pulls a woman from a blazing building.

"Oh, God, I would be grateful. I mean, like, really, really grateful."

That sounded, like, really, really promising. Enrique turned his charm on the little Joneses.

"Hey kids, what do you say we hit the food court?"

Lou, pointedly wearing her own clothes and pointedly ignoring the cameras, rallied with Justin as the rest of the team trickled onto the court.

"Can we keep these?" asked Caroline eagerly as she smoothed down a Tail skirt and top trimmed in pink that almost concealed her muffin top. She'd already jammed two tops in her bag when Shana wasn't looking.

"You'll have to ask Rex, but I don't think so," said Shana, giving the director a little wave as she put her tennis bag down on a court-side bench.

"Ladies, no waving at the cameras," Rex admonished. "Act naturally."

"When did y'all take up tennis?" Shana turned and asked the others, pulling out her Wilson One BLX2. Her first beat-up, used racquet had been a Wilson, and Shana was loyal.

"I've been playing since I was five," answered Allie smugly, adjusting her black Nike visor. She wondered how it would look on camera. "Caroline and Taylor played in high school."

"Me too," volunteered Karen, pointing to her Academy of the Sacred Heart t-shirt. "Captain."

"Of the *What Not to Wear* team," snarked Taylor, who'd paired a tight Nike top trimmed in Day-Glo yellow from Byron's stash with her tiny shorts. Caroline noted wistfully that even when Taylor lifted her arms to pull back her hair, her tanned torso was perfectly smooth.

"My high school didn't have a tennis team, but I took lessons at the Briarwood Resort." Shana smiled sweetly, adjusting her strings with her chili-red nails.

"The *Briarwood*?" Allie asked incredulously, strapping a pressure band on her right forearm. "Where the president stays?"

"My mama was a close personal friend of one of the pros," said Shana, lowering her eyes. In fact, Lurleen had been a laundress who'd gotten up close and personal with the head pro on stacks of clean towels in the Briarwood laundry. "I haven't played much since, but I like to keep in shape."

And show it, thought Allie, eyeing Shana's ruffled Stella McCartney tennis dress with spaghetti straps and a cutout back. How did one wear a bra with that?

Caroline pulled a bottle of sunscreen from her bag and slathered it liberally over her arms and legs.

"That smells good," said Karen, stretching and touching her toes.

"It's made by monks at this little monastery in Provence." Caroline looked down at the label. "They use organic honey and lavender."

"Where did you get it?" Karen asked, second guessing her decision to wear her beloved but somewhat ratty t-shirt on camera.

"Has to be QVC," said Taylor, shaking her head.

"I thought you weren't ordering from QVC anymore," said Allie. "Isn't that part of your alimony agreement?"

"I have to have sunscreen. Is a judge going to deny me that?" Caroline answered, striking her Wilson Steam against the bench.

"Wow, I can really smell that honey," Shana said.

Lou had approached the net and was lecturing Justin, tapping her watch pointedly.

"Uh, ladies," Justin hollered. "We're running five minutes late. Pair up for a quick warm up, then we'll do a round of Queen of the Court."

"That's my favorite drill, it's how I named my show," said Shana to the group, hoping for some shared enthusiasm. So far these women seemed kind of angry about everything.

"How very clever," said Allie, turning her back on Shana and walking off to hit with Lou.

Enrique and Bethany sat side by side on a bench by the Food Court fountain, drinking smoothies as Lil Wayne ran in manic circles. Slightly behind them, Destiny stood outside Build-a-Bear longingly watching the children inside. Destiny glanced over at Bethany. She was a hopeful child by nature, but she realized her chances of getting Bethany to take her in Build-a-Bear were zero. Now, if she were with Maria....

Bethany did her best to ignore the airplane and explosion noises Lil Wayne was making, as well as the dirty looks from a nearby group of mothers with strollers sipping Starbucks decaf lattes.

"So where are you in school?" she asked Enrique.

"I'm studying independently."

"Really? Studying what?"

"Right now? A beautiful blonde with an amazing smile."

Bethany smiled some more.

"How about you?"

"Well, my mother wants me to go to her old school, Vassar, and it's like filled with country club wives in training, hippie feminist poets, and lesbian field hockey players."

"I'm guessing that's not your plan?"

Suddenly animated, Bethany put down her smoothie.

"No! I want to be like a Kardashian, only with talent. I want to design clothes and sell them on TV and the Internet."

Enrique didn't give a shit about the Kardashians or fashion, but he did love the way Bethany bounced up and down when she got excited. He gave Bethany what he hoped was an encouraging smile and took her hand. They leaned closer to each other.

"Splash zone, splash zone, you're in the Sea World splash zone!!!! Yeeeeeeee!"

A huge splash inundated them as Lil Wayne jumped into the fountain.

Mothers grabbed their toddlers and lattes and hustled away.

"Get out of there now, you little monster," shrieked Bethany.

Enrique had to admit that while Lil Wayne had ruined the moment Bethany looked even more fetching soaked to the skin.

"Calm down," he said. "I'm going to grab him before the mall cops throw us out."

Enrique stood on the edge of the fountain and made a grab for Lil Wayne, who dived out of his reach and sent Enrique plunging into the fountain. He came up sputtering and cursing, grabbed Lil Wayne, and dragged him out kicking and screaming.

Bethany choked with real laughter. "Oh my God, I have not had this much fun at the mall since I was, like, six. I know you're pissed, but, it's like, hysterical."

Enrique sat down, a soaked Lil Wayne held firmly on his lap. "I guess this is where I get to prove I'm a good sport by not drowning him, but I wish he'd just be quiet like his sister."

Bethany and Enrique stared at each other, horror struck. Destiny!

Bethany looked frantically around them, but the wispy haired little girl in the Tinkerbell t-shirt was nowhere to be seen.

Lou watched disapprovingly as her team began warming up in their new outfits. "Where has everyone been? Having a fashion show? I am considering penalties for tardiness," she snapped. "No time for short court, move back to the baseline."

After five minutes, Lou was somewhat mollified by the fact that both Shana and Karen, despite their vastly different yet equally inappropriate outfits, seemed to have strong ground strokes and good movement. She was particularly impressed by Shana's crosscourt forehand.

"Caroline," said Lou in her drill-sergeant tone, noticing her talking to Justin. "Keep the chatting to a minimum. It slows down practice."

"Okay," said Justin. "Let's get started with Queen of the Court. Pair off in teams, four playing and one waiting on the sideline. I'll feed in a ball and you'll play out the point. First two on each court with five points are the queens."

(The Donaldson twins and other lower-ranked players, who avoided Lou and Allie whenever possible, had already assembled on the far court.)

Allie walked over to Lou. "Should we start?"

"Actually, Allie, I was thinking it would be a nice gesture for me to partner with Shana. To make her feel welcome."

"Lou, you're not thinking of being her partner for the season? Don't stick me with Taylor again."

Taylor missed a practice volley and dropped her racquet. "Shit!"

"Stop swearing," said Lou, fixing her laser stare on Taylor. "We are on camera."

In this case, Lou had little to worry about. Jamal, under attack by a determined bee, was jumping up and down, swatting away, his camera swinging wildly. Rex grabbed the camera and steadied it as the bee flew up and away.

"Is that cameraman having a seizure?" asked Karen.

"Jamal seems to have a lot of health issues," replied Shana with concern.

Lou turned back to Allie and was about to speak when a phone rang courtside. Allie recognized her chime and looked over.

"I should get that; it could be one of the twins."

"Allison, you know the rules."

"Yes, well there's no rule I have to babysit Taylor every year," she spat back, storming off court. She fished her phone out of her bag. "Hello?"

"Look, Mom. We've got a situation here," said Bethany. They had trudged the length of the mall, Enrique dragging Lil Wayne behind. No Destiny.

"The phone? It's like Enrique's. Mom, forget Enrique. Focus. We need you down here right away. So then send someone else. How about one of Daddy's lawyers? Of course I'm not in trouble. Yet. Hold on, there's a call coming through."

"Hello, Enrique's phone. Oh, you have her. Thank God!" Bethany turned to Enrique. "Destiny's with Maria, something about Build-a-Bear."

But Enrique had stopped dead. He was staring at three hard-faced men with tattooed arms in baggy jeans and muscle shirts headed in their direction.

"Shit."

Bethany had many flaws, but she was very good at sensing when it was time to escape, a talent that had come in handy at many an underage party bust.

She grabbed Enrique's hand.

"Quick. Into Nordstrom. They're having a makeup event. It will be a zoo."

Bethany, Enrique and Lil Wayne hustled into the makeup maze at Nordstrom, which was re-imagined as a disco and filled with chattering women having their faces made up by "consultants" in black priestess-like tunics. Bethany headed straight for the M.A.C. counter. Ignoring the crush of customers, she dragged Enrique and Lil Wayne behind the counter, where all three crouched on the floor.

An elegant African American woman with cropped hair and severe penciled eyebrows looked down in dismay.

"Bethany? You can't bring your, uh, guests behind the counter. We're previewing next season's color collection."

"Soraya, I've bought enough makeup from you to pay off a mortgage." Bethany dug Shana's $300 out of her handbag and handed it to her. "Now just give me $300 of whatever and let us hang here a few moments, okay."

Soraya fingered the cash and raised an arched brow. "I'm not sure..."

"Okay, add another $200 of products on my charge."

Soraya smiled. "Sure, hon. Will you be taking it with you, or should we deliver?"

"Whatever, just pretend like we are not here, okay?"

Enrique cowered next to Lil Wayne (who for once was quiet – he'd seen enough episodes of *Cops* to realize he was now on the lam) and faced Bethany.

"So?" she said.

"It's Hector Ortiz and some of the Latin Locos. They must have seen my truck outside. I refused an invitation to join his little organization, and he's pretty pissed."

Bethany nodded.

"My grandmother gets the same way when anyone RSVPs no."

"I doubt your grandmother has a gang of goons with machetes."

"She doesn't need them."

"Look, it's no use, they are just going to stand by the exits and wait for me to bolt."

"Are they going to wipe you out?" whispered Lil Wayne excitedly. "Or is it just gonna be a beat down?"

Enrique looked as if he were going to throw up.

"Dwayne, you are not helping," said Bethany. "If we want to save our friend Enrique," Lil Wayne nodded yes furiously, "you and I are going to have to create a distraction. First, you take my watch." She slipped a Cartier gold tank off her wrist and handed it to Lil Wayne.

Enrique shook his head. "I don't want you involved in this."

Bethany turned to him. "No worries. I never thought I would say this, but saving your life is more important than me being inconvenienced. You wait till you hear me scream – believe me, you'll hear it – then run."

Enrique looked into Bethany's eyes, took her by the shoulders, and kissed her.

"Gross," said Lil Wayne.

Allie hit redial again, but Bethany – or Enrique, whoever he was – couldn't or wouldn't pick up. She knew from experience she had better head for the mall like lightning after practice. In front of the cameras, she'd try to look unconcerned.

She stood up and walked over to Karen to wait their turn on court. She didn't have to play with Taylor after all. Taylor and Caroline had challenged Lou and Shana, and it was not going well.

Caroline, huffing, failed to make it to another ball, putting them down 0-5.

"Mrs. Butts and Mrs. Jones remain as queens; next challengers," said Justin.

"Looks like those post-divorce ice cream binges have slowed you down a bit, Caroline," said Taylor as they walked to the sidelines.

"Oh, shut up Taylor and take another Vicodin. We all know why you're in such a foul mood. Last Friday, after your third margarita, you announced that you and doctor perfect hadn't done it in six months." Despite Rex's instructions, Caroline looked directly at the camera and smiled, then walked over to her bag and pulled out her sunscreen. Taylor followed her.

"Why don't you keep your big mouth, which now fits the rest of you, shut? And stop smearing that smelly gunk on."

"I like the smell," said Karen as she walked by.

"Who asked you?" said Taylor.

Justin knew where this was going and he didn't like it. "Less chatting and more tennis, ladies."

Ignoring him, Caroline walked on court to complain to Lou. "Taylor's so spiteful," she said, in the irritating whine of a child whose toy has just been snatched away.

"Let's discuss this later. On the phone. We've embarrassed ourselves enough for one day," Lou replied. Lou despised whiners. "Now move off the court so the rest of us can practice."

But Caroline stubbornly stood her ground. "She's a menace. You remember last year. And she's a *bitch*!"

Unnoticed, the bee that had attacked Jamal hovered over the court seeking another target. Intoxicated by Caroline's honey and lavender sunscreen, it dove hard for her just as Lou, in an attempt at damage control, stepped in between a raving Caroline and the camera. The bee missed its intended target and stung Lou just above her clavicle. The rest of the team froze as their esteemed leader gripped her shoulder and fell to the ground. "Bee sting!" she yelled.

"Oh, no, she's deathly allergic," cried Allie, running to Lou. "She needs medication. Lou, where is your Epipen?"

"Someone dial 911, I'll get help," Justin said, breaking into a sweat. "There must be doctors on the golf course." He sprinted toward the driving range.

Allie ran to the bench and began to rummage frantically through Lou's tennis bag, pushing aside hair elastics, Neutrogena sunscreen and sweatbands in search of the lifesaving Epipen.

Lou lay on her back moaning as Shana cradled her head in her lap, while Karen called 911. Caroline and Taylor, their fight forgotten, clutched each other while shrieking hysterically.

"Allie! Lou says her medicine is in her Coach bag, in the car," Shana yelled.

Allie ran towards the parking lot, while Shana and Karen started CPR. Shana pounded vigorously on Lou's chest, while Karen breathed into her mouth.

Jamal lowered his camera, but Rex pushed it back up.

"Are you crazy? Keep it going. This is great!"

"She's hurt. This doesn't feel right. We should get help." Jamal looked at Rex and shook his head.

"I'm sure she'll be fine, these women are real drama queens. Byron, go get some more help," Rex barked as Byron scurried toward the tennis shop. "You get every minute of this or you're fired. You're not a doctor just because you filmed *Real Hospital Hunks*."

On the court, Lou managed to choke out a few words. "Not my car ... husband's Porsche ... playing golf here ... with Roy Beech." With a final choking breath, she closed her eyes for the last time. Shana, who'd seen death by venom up close and personal before, although never on well-groomed clay, let out a piercing wail.

Big Wayne, Roy Beech, Spencer Thomas and Greg Davis had just finished eighteen holes, and were watching Fox News in the main clubhouse bar.

"Thanks for being our fourth, Greg. I can't believe Dan Butts got called into a meeting on the Hill on a Saturday. Congressmen must work harder than I thought," said Big Wayne, sucking the foam off his Bud.

"I'm going to switch that to ESPN, the Nats are playing," said Roy, grabbing the remote. He froze in mid click. "Holy shit."

On screen, two police officers were leading Congressman Dan Butts to a waiting patrol car. In the background was a seedy, one-story building on a sordid commercial strip with a flashing neon sign: "*HERE KITTY KITTY MASSAGE PARLOR - Cash Only*".

Reporter Kelley Morgan, looking as grave as she could in hot pink, announced, "Among those arrested in today's prostitution raid was Congressman Dan Butts." As the camera pulled back, the men could see Dan Butt's black Porsche with its congressional plates in the massage parlor parking lot. What they could not see was Lou's Coach bag under the passenger seat, her Epipen tucked neatly in the side pocket.

KAREN DAVIS INTERVIEW

Karen Davis sat between Bethany and Lil Wayne on the hard orange plastic chairs in the Nordstrom security office and tried to project her Serious Courtroom Look as she faced Karl Eggers, head of security. This was made difficult by the fact she was still in tennis clothes, not to mention Karl Eggers was sweating profusely and had no discernible neck.

Plus, she felt physically ill – seeing someone actually die on the tennis court. Of course, as a prosecutor Karen had seen plenty of photos of murder victims. That had been in the course of work, which, as she'd told Rex in her interview this morning, she'd quit because of the stress.

"I always thought that hard work would get me everything I wanted. And it really did until last year."

As a child, in her gray, gothic Catholic school, she'd focused on academics while the other girls whispered and gossiped about clothes and boys. Even the tennis team was all about competition. That had gotten her into Yale, then into Harvard Law School, where she'd met Greg, her first and only boyfriend (unless you count her prom date, who entered the seminary a month later).

But what was a social life compared to editing Law Review and becoming an assistant US attorney? One that was trusted with prosecuting some of the toughest criminals out there, like the infamous drug dealer, Jamaican Jimmy. Karen smiled as she thought of the judge intoning "Twenty five years in prison," as Jimmy glared at Karen.

"But then, when Greg and I couldn't get pregnant, we thought maybe I was working TOO hard. Of course, we considered other options before I quit work."

"What do you mean, adoption?" Georgianna Davis had exclaimed when she and Greg had mentioned the possibility during an excruciating Sunday dinner. Georgianna looked shocked, no mean feat since her age-defying unlined forehead and eyebrows could barely move. "The Davis family is one of the oldest in this area – directly related to two presidents. Surely you'll want to carry on the family name by having real children?"

Greg had sat silently and stared into his gazpacho. He rarely spoke up to Georgianna.

"Well, we would certainly adopt only 'real children', since as far as I'm aware they haven't invented any other kind. And I'm not sure you can count Jefferson Davis as a 'real' president. I believe outside the South he's thought of as more of a trait..."

"Karen," Greg interrupted. "I've got a great idea. Why don't we put off any decision till after vacation? Mom and Dad are giving us a trip to Jamaica."

"First, we tried a second honeymoon, but somehow I still felt stressed."

Jamaica, as it turned out, was filled with Jamaican Jimmy's bloodthirsty relatives. As she and Greg had embraced in the small, vine covered bungalow on the beach, two men with clubs burst through the front door. Greg dived under the bed, and Karen picked up the nearest object, her Babolat racquet, and knocked out one assailant with a two-handed backhand, then the other with a crushing overhead stroke.

"But while vacationing I had this wonderful idea – why not take time off and play a little tennis? Something told me even though I hadn't played much since college, my backhand and smash were still pretty good."

Well, so far, Karen's new life of leisure had triggered a massive attack of TMJ. After Lou's horrible death, she'd been more than glad to help Allie out by going to the mall to fetch her teenage daughter and Shana's children. Allie had murmured something about "a slight problem". She'd thought maybe they'd had car trouble. Instead, here she was representing Belle Vista's Lindsay Lohan, up for aggravated assault.

"Bethany salts lots of people!" Lil Wayne had informed Karen cheerfully when she arrived.

Karen fought the urge to massage her aching jaw, took a deep breath, and spoke.

"Now, Mr. Eggers, I understand you are accusing Miss Beech of pushing a display rack of Chanel handbags over on some of your customers."

Bethany held up a French manicured index finger. "Excuse me, they were Kate Spade. On sale. And those aren't customers, they are wanted criminals. I was making a citizen's arrest."

Mr. Eggers looked puzzled. "How do you know this Miss Beech?"

Bethany thought quickly.

"I saw it on Twitter."

She guessed correctly that Eggers knew jack about Twitter.

At the sound of a knock, Eggers heaved himself up, waddled across the room, and opened the door. Outside, three uniformed police officers held Hector Ortiz and his two flunkies in cuffs.

"We just want to thank that young lady," said the officer in front, smiling at Bethany, whose skirt, Karen thought, was showing an unreasonable amount of thigh.

"We've been after these guys for a while. Oh, and we found this in Hector's pocket – it has your name engraved on the back, Miss."

Bethany's big blue eyes grew even bigger. "My Cartier watch! He must have stolen it RIGHT OFF MY WRIST!"

Lil Wayne grinned. Sticking that watch in that guy's pocket had been easy once Bethany salted him with those purses. He hoped his mother would let her babysit all the time.

Karen swore she saw Bethany give Lil Wayne a wink.

Eggers shrugged his shoulders. "Miss Beech, you're free to go. Oh, and stop by customer service and pick up a $100 gift certificate as an apology from Nordstrom."

Bethany beamed. "All is forgiven Mr. Eggers."

"Tell Enrique this isn't over," Hector snarled in Spanish over his shoulder as the police led him away.

Bethany had no idea what he'd said, but she recognized the tone of a threat, and that bastard was not getting in the last foreign word. She shouted back the only phrase she remembered from French I.

"Le chat de ma tante est noir avec quatre pattes blanche!"

Accompanied by her raised middle finger, "The cat of my aunt is gray with four white paws," sounded pretty scary.

3

Outside historic St. Bede's church, the media horde's collective head turned as a late-model black Mercedes sedan squealed into the parking lot and nearly took out Channel 4's van.

"Quint!" squealed Allie in time with the tires.

"Chillax Mama, it's all good," replied Bethany's twin brother, Quint, as he slipped into a parking space marked "Rector Only".

"You cannot park here!"

"Again, chill. Reverend Tim is afraid to park his old beemer here since Bethany smashed into it last Christmas Eve."

Quint – short for Roy Forrest Beech V – checked his reflection in the sun flap mirror. He could definitely use some Visine, but he liked the way his blond lettuce flowed perfectly over the collar of his Ralph Lauren navy blazer.

"Tim is hot for an old guy, but what kind of moron leaves Hollywood for priesting?" commented Bethany from the back seat, where she unbuttoned the top three buttons on the tasteful black Chanel blouse her mother had bought her, and adjusted her black lace bra for maximum camera-ready cleavage.

"Bethany! Language! Respect!"

"I still don't get why Dad didn't come. He and Congressman Butts are, like, best buds," said Quint, killing the engine.

"Your father cannot afford to be associated in the media with Congressman … I mean *Mr.* Butts and his current troubles. On the other hand, as Lou's oldest friend, it is appropriate that I – and you two – bid her farewell. I have a planned a wonderful service and eulogy. And you, Quint, will take his place as pallbearer."

That made Quint wish he hadn't smoked half a joint before leaving home.

Inside St. Bede's, Reverend Tim Channing enjoyed the last few moments of silence before his church filled with congregants gathered to mourn the untimely passing of Louisa Edgemoor Spencer Butts, whose tasteful mahogany casket, closed and covered with flowers, rested at the foot of the Holy Table. Episcopalians do not use the word altar.

St. Bede's, an historic church proud of its colonial simplicity, disdained both the weeping virgins and guilt of Catholicism and the personal Jesus of evangelical Protestants. As a result of all this good taste, Channing often found himself lowering his voice to avoid having it echo through the mostly empty church.

Channing sighed. This was not what he imagined when he abandoned his acting career for the Episcopal priesthood. He'd felt the calling while playing the Reverend Terrance Treadwell in *The Rector's Romance*, a failed Hallmark Channel attempt to capture the *Masterpiece Theater* audience. Unfortunately, St. Bede's was nothing like a fictitious English parish; it was more like Los Angeles. Channing had received just two dinner invitations in five years, and one of those was for Thai takeout.

Thanks to Quint's *Grand Theft Auto* driving style, the Beeches had been among the first to arrive. As they entered the church, luxury vehicles continued to file into the parking lot, where a shiny black hearse waited in the misty damp, incongruously surrounded by media vans with satellite dishes. A clutch of reporters gathered off to the side of the church steps, along with the Vixen crew.

Shana and Wayne Jones waited in their church car, a pearly white Cadillac sedan. They watched Dan Butts exit a black Ford Explorer with tinted windows flanked by two fit, dark-suited men in their late twenties who held off the media horde as he quickly ducked into the church.

"Oh my God," said Shana. "Those must be Lou's handsome grown sons – oh, and honey look, they're both deaf."

She choked back a sob, having already gone through a box of Kleenex on the ride over. Wayne reflected that funerals, weddings and Lifetime movies always brought out the waterworks in his tenderhearted wife.

"Shana, sweetheart, those are U.S. marshals wearing earpieces. You gotta watch the news, honey. Dan's got himself in a mess. He was fixing visa troubles for Nancy Kim, the 'Here Kitty Kitty Madame,' plus setting up other congressmen for blackmail."

Wayne tried to turn toward Shana, but his 44 long black Hugo Boss suit (a steal at Men's Warehouse) was tight enough to make it tough. A mountain of a man, Wayne still had quite a bit of bouncer muscle, but his stomach had expanded along with his bank account.

"Wayne, don't talk bad about our friends in front of the little ones."

Lil Wayne and Destiny sat in the back watching a video on their iPad. Both Shana and Wayne had been raised in families where funerals were as much a part of growing up as playing tag and hunting squirrels. The Jones kids were funeral veterans, having already lost a grandparent (black lung), an uncle (overdose) and godparent (biker shootout).

"Sorry sweetie," Wayne leaned toward Shana and took her hand. "Now dry your eyes. Just remember, Lou has gone to Jesus and a better place. The Lord spared her seeing her husband disgraced."

Shana held a finger to her lips, but Wayne continued. Funerals made him wax philosophical. "You know honey, I can't judge a man for running afoul of the law; Lord knows I did before I found Jesus and my Shana. But I hate how you-know-who lied to his good wife of twenty-five years. ("He means Dirty Dan," Lil Wayne whispered to Destiny. He was too young to read the tabloids but had finely honed eavesdropping skills.)You and me, we ain't perfect, but our marriage is built on faith and the rock of honesty."

Shana blinked rapidly, and Wayne wondered if she'd cried off the adhesive on her eyelashes again. At his pappy's funeral one had dropped right into the casket.

"I'm sorry Wayne, but I have to…I have to…it's time for me to…" Shana's words tumbled out as fast as dice at a craps game. "Go to the ladies room!" And with that she bolted from the car, past the cameras and into the church as fast as her black patent Diba stilettos could carry her.

Jamal Whitley used his broad shoulders to keep MSNBC and News Channel 7 from crowding his camera. "Down in front," he chided a photographer from the Post who blocked his view of the church steps.

"Since when are you giving orders around here?" interjected Max Mavis from Fox News. "This isn't an episode of *Cupcake Wars*."

Jamal was not fussed, as his grandmother used to say. He'd just learned from Rex that Bravo, TLC and the Tennis Channel were all interested in *Queen of the Court*. That would mean real money when Big Wayne's investment was spent. Last week they'd just had the reality show basics of boobs and bitches. Now they had all that, *plus* death, scandal, politics and Korean hookers. Suddenly, they were hot.

Rex stepped up beside Jamal in a dark brown corduroy three-piece suit that had seen better days. He finished the look with a mustard-colored ascot.

"Damn, man, what'd you do, rob the wardrobe girl from *That 70's Show?*"

Rex pulled Jamal aside and lowered his voice.

"You keep the cameras going out here and I'll take care of inside."

The media were banned from the service, but Rex was permitted as long as his cameras remained outside. He'd splurged on an iPhone rather than a new suit so he could surreptitiously record the entire service.

As it turned out, Roy Beech was not the only man missing in action. Golf buddies, colleagues, even Dan Butts' proctologist, thought it wiser not to be filmed shaking hands with current tabloid favorite "Dirty Dan". Notable exceptions were Greg Davis and his father Lloyd, who as defense attorneys found it both acceptable and lucrative to mingle with the indicted.

Karen cringed and tried to hide under her wide-brimmed black straw hat as she walked into church with Greg and his parents. She'd spent more than a few hours during her career reviewing media and surveillance tapes of criminals' funerals to see who their friends and associates were. She felt even worse when she saw Sean Flannery at Dan's side. She'd last seen the handsome U.S. marshal pushing Jamaican Jimmy none too gently out the door of the Federal District Courthouse. She just *knew* he was thinking she'd gone over to the dark side.

In reality, Sean was a simple guy who loved sports, beer, his dog and good looking women. His only thought, as Karen slid into a pew, was that he missed staring at her rather spectacular ass during closing arguments.

Caroline was predictably the last to arrive at the service, having missed the prelude, the Psalms and the Old Testament reading. Taylor fidgeted beside her as Caroline angled her giant black Escalade across the grass in front of the church.

"Why are you always so late?"

"Once the parking lot is full, I have an excuse for taking a really good spot. Besides, we only missed the boring part."

"It's church," complained Taylor as she slid out of the massive vehicle, her skirt riding up dangerously. Taylor, who hated panty lines, seldom bothered with underwear. "It's all boring."

"You should be thanking me for picking you up after Dr. Perfect bailed," replied Caroline, locking the Escalade with a noisy double beep that could be heard over the choir inside.

"My husband had an emergency. Glenna Peters got a cheapo boob job in Brazil and one of them exploded." Taylor fished in her purse and picked out a vial of pills as she walked, unscrewing the top and tossing several in her mouth.

"Taylor, can you stop popping your goddamned pills for once and think about Lou," Caroline stage-whispered as they click-clacked up the steps and past the cameras.

"Me? Why don't *you* think about her," Taylor replied at top volume. "You practically murdered her with that bee bait you call sunscreen."

Max Mavis shook his head and lit a cigarette as he watched the two bickering blondes sashay by. He might not be Katie Couric or Anderson Cooper, but surely he deserved better than being stuck outside Barbie's Dream Church, waiting to interview the latest in a long line of politicians who couldn't keep it in his pants.

ALLIE BEECH INTERVIEW

During the Gospel, Allie contemplated the eulogy she was about to deliver. It didn't really capture her relationship with Lou. She'd been a little evasive with Rex in the interview she gave after Lou's death as well. In her heart of hearts, she hated her oldest, dearest friend.

"We couldn't have been closer if we were sisters."

Ha. Maybe the sisters in *Whatever Happened to Baby Jane.*

"When I was a child, Lou would babysit me. We always had such fun."

She vividly recalled a beautiful summer evening when she was about six. Lou had told Lavinia she planned to let Allie stay up late, have ice cream and catch fireflies. But as soon as the front door slammed shut, Lou yelled, "Go to bed you little brat."

"You are not the boss of me," Allie screamed back, making a mad dash for the back door, firefly jar in hand.

"Oh yes I am," said Lou, grabbing Allie by the wrist, "and I always will be." Lou pushed her into her room, closed the door, and turned the lock.

And it was true. Lou married the handsome Dan Butts,(oh how Allie hoped Lou could see Dirty Dan now), a graduate of the University of Virginia and Yale Law School, while Allie settled for Roy Beech, who'd dropped out after three years at Hampden Sydney.

True, Roy had made a fortune in real estate, but Lou never failed to use Dan's prestige to get every social position Allie wanted.

"Lou was our social leader, Chairwoman of the Jardine Academy gala, the Kidney Foundation Casino Night, the Leukemia Fun Fair, the Bounce for Brain Tumors trampoline marathon and, well pretty much everything. Some people felt she should have shared responsibility with...others. But that was Lou. So dedicated."

"And what about your relationship on court?" Rex had asked.

Ah. Tennis.

How many times had she watched Lavinia hand the club women's singles trophy, the Edgemoor Cup, to Lou? And ten straight years of being relegated to co-captain.

"We got along splendidly on court as well. Now that she's gone, as the new captain, I plan to lead the team to victory this season in her memory."

4

Allie knelt to pray. She was terribly distraught that Lou had died of course, but, on the bright side, it could finally be her moment. Roy, who had faithfully fundraised for the Republicans for years and still had a full head of hair at forty-eight, was a natural to fill Dan's vacated House seat. Then Allie would take her rightful place at the head of the Belle Vista community. Or would she? Fate, in the unseemly persona of Shana Jones, had thrown yet another roadblock in her way.

Shana owned the club. *Owned*. Even Lou hadn't managed that. As impossible as it seemed, she also appeared to have an amazing tennis game. Allie had rather enjoyed seeing Lou squirm as Shana unwittingly and enthusiastically spoiled her perfect life. But now that it was potentially *Allie's* perfect life, Shana had to be stopped.

"Dear Lord," Allie prayed, hands clasped together, "please, help me find a way to defeat this interloper."

Jesus and his Golden Rule were well and good, but Allie had always preferred the vengeful, smiting God of the Old Testament.

Kneeling next to Allie, Lavinia looked at the beatific smile on her daughter's face, and wished she could be so untroubled. Lavinia was well aware that, in the sight of the Lord, she was more of a sinner than Dirty Dan could ever be. She knew she should feel guilt, but all she felt was the arthritis in her knees and an unsettling fear of discovery. If the venerable stone Belle Vista sign and Dan Butts could be pulled down in the same week, no one was safe, not even Lavinia Endicott Winter.

"The Gospel of the Lord," intoned the Reverend Channing in his best priestly baritone.

"Praise be to thee, Oh Christ," replied the congregants solemnly.

Allie rose and took the small staircase up to the raised lectern, where the congregants could admire her new black Chanel suit, and she could look down on her friends and family. She found the sensation not at all unpleasant. For a moment her eye caught on something jarring in a sea of tasteful black. There was Shana Jones seated next to an enormous Black woman, both in white dresses of some viscous shiny material. Allie was momentarily rendered speechless, until Reverend Channing pointedly cleared his throat.

"Lou was many things. Loyal wife," Allie allowed herself a scathing look at Dan, "Chair of the Belle Vista garden club, head of the club employee gift fund and captain of our wonderful ladies tennis team..."

Shana shifted uncomfortably in her seat. She figured an Episcopal eulogy might be short on sin and hell, but it seemed like Allie was going to leave out joy and Jesus too. And the funeral! No flower girls to seat the family, no procession by the casket to wish Lou farewell – in fact, the casket was closed. How on earth was Dan supposed to beg Lou's forgiveness if he couldn't even see her dear face? It was all so formal and cold. Shana believed that funerals should be a spiritual cleansing and a balm to those left behind. Of course, she reflected guiltily, she had a bad history of going overboard when it came to comforting the bereaved.

She drifted back to the funeral of Pastor John, and remembered how brave his son Levi looked as he passed the serpents over the open casket, only dropping one (which was never found and presumably went to its reward with the pastor). After the singing and the shouting, rolling in the aisles and speaking in tongues, Shana, only seventeen, was in a frenzy of love for Jesus. Which later, behind the church, got all confused with love for Levi. Funerals were a bit like prom night where she came from.

Shana squeezed her eyes tight and prayed to Jesus, who she talked to just like a good friend. "Jesus, I never lost faith, even when you called Levi home, leaving my heart broken."

"I knew you would make it right again, and now you've given me this good husband and wonderful family. I know I've got to unburden myself to Wayne and tell him, well, you know Lord."

Shana could almost hear Jesus say "It's about time!" She did not want to disappoint her Lord, but with her new TV show and Jones Belle Vista, well, the timing was kinda bad. And she hated to admit it, but she was afraid. Wayne was getting more and more righteous.

Only yesterday he'd told her he wanted to sell his gentlemen's clubs and invest in something "family-oriented". What if sharing her past with Wayne meant she'd lose her husband, her family – everything?

"If it's okay with you, Jesus, I'd like to keep this between us for just a bit longer. Maybe till after the show is done shooting?" Shana waited for a sign of divine impatience, like maybe lightning striking the church. Nothing. Clearly Jesus was okay with her plan. She waved to attract Allie's attention.

Allie was wrapping up when she noticed Shana Jones' upraised hand. What on earth? She decided to ignore her. But Shana was not one to take a hint.

"'Scuse me! Allie! 'Scuse me!" Shana jumped up, and she and the large woman seated beside her headed into the aisle and toward the front of the church. Both, improbably, carried cordless microphones.

"Thank you, God," murmured Rex, who'd started to think his secret funeral footage was a bust.

"Allie, Reverend Treadwell," Shana began.

Channing beamed. He'd been recognized!

"This is Bishop Charnisse Jones, no relation, from my regular church, the Tabernacle of Prayer and Praise on Route 1. Bishop Charnisse and me prepared a little tribute to Lou in the Pentecostal tradition."

Allie recoiled.

"I really don't think..."

But to her dismay, that grinning idiot Channing interrupted her.

"We'd be delighted," he said.

Shana began, gesturing at her clingy white dress. "Well, you see me and Bishop Jones are wearing white. That's because we believe today is a day of joy, because Lou has gone home to Jesus." She held the microphone toward the crowd where Wayne, Destiny and Lil Wayne shouted "Amen". The rest of the congregation appeared to be in shock. WASP shock, meaning they remained expressionless.

"WTF?" whispered Taylor to Caroline, who was busy trying to surreptitiously unclasp the hooks at the waist of last year's size eight St. John skirt, which was not accommodating this year's waistline.

Who said knits were forgiving? She wished she hadn't made that stop for donuts on the way to church.

Shana began to clap rhythmically as Bishop Jones (no relation) paced up and down in front of the congregation.

"Now I'm here to talk about Lou!"

"Yes Lou!" shouted Wayne.

"Lou loved tennis! Lou loved flowers, making them all grow for the Lord!"

"Amen!" This from Quint, who began to clap enthusiastically, if not exactly in time, as his mother glared from above.

"What else did Lou love?"

Silence. Charnisse frowned.

Quint raised his hand timidly.

"This ain't math class, son, just shout it out!"

"Uh, she loved, like, Mr. Butts?"

"Yes she loved her husband. He did her wrong, but she loved him strong!"

"Amen!" screamed Lil Wayne.

"Who else did she love?" chimed in Shana.

Silence.

Charnisse's frown deepened. She'd always suspected most rich white people were dimwitted, despite the fact they seemed to be in charge of everything.

Reverend Channing took the mike out of Shana's hand. "I believe the response the Misses Jones are seeking is *Jesus*. Let's try this again. Bishop?"

"Who else did she *loooove*?" shouted Charnisse, glaring at the front row till they choked out a muted "Jesus?"

"Tell me again, I can't HEAR you!"

"Jesus!" shouted Karen, who disliked the way her snotty mother-in-law was glaring at Shana, who unlike everyone else at Belle Vista, had actually been nice to her.

In the next pew, Caroline began sweating profusely and gripped Taylor's arm as the church swam before her eyes.

"Owww. Let go," snapped Taylor, prying off Caroline's hand.

"Yes, she loved Jeeeeezus," called out Bishop Jones. "Now on your feet, and stomp those feet and clap those hands to praise the Lord!"

To Allie's amazement, Dan Butts stood up, tears streaming from his eyes, and began to clap, followed by his guards, her idiot son, the entire Jones clan and that self-righteous Catholic bitch with the slice backhand, Karen. Slowly, the entire congregation stood and followed their lead, clapping (although as Charnisse noted later, with as little movement and noise as possible) as Shana and her Bishop lead them in "I'll Fly Away".

In the middle of the chorus, Caroline pushed her way past Taylor into the aisle and, with a wail, fell forward and began writhing on the ground.

"Oh, yes, she is FILLED with the spirit!" shouted Charnisse.

"She's just filled with Dunkin Donuts," Taylor yelled back.

Karen, thinking her new lifestyle required a lot of first aid training, rushed to Caroline's assistance just as she lost her entire breakfast.

In the ensuing chaos, many parishioners broke for daylight, fleeing past the media to the sanctuary of their cars.

Only Allie, frozen with fury, stood stock still and silent in her perch on high.

5

Sage Silverfox Shapiro did not want to play tennis. She had agreed to meet her friend Zoe at the public courts near Saint Ann's, but she was tired and had a big poetry seminar project due the next day. Zoe loved to play tennis, but there was no tennis team at their progressive Brooklyn Heights high school. There was no Recreational Arts offering for tennis either, though there was one for table tennis and squash, as well as ultimate Frisbee and yoga. Zoe had created her own course, which involved finding other students to play with her. Sage stretched her long legs out in the April sun and closed her eyes.

A shadow blocked the sun and Sage opened her eyes. Zoe was smiling, tennis racquet in hand.

"Wake up, it's tennis time," she said.

"You're blocking my sun," Sage sighed. "I was hoping you wouldn't show up. I have so much homework."

Sage flipped her red hair forward and then back, and secured it in a ponytail.

"No such luck," Zoe laughed. She reached down and picked up Sage's tattered L.L. Bean backpack. Her monogram was embroidered on the front. sSs. "I love that your initials look like snakes."

Sage had a pet snake named Sylvia, after Sylvia Plath, and two red-eared slider turtles named Mary Kate and Ashley. They shared a cluttered but cozy brownstone with two cats and a rescued greyhound named Pokey, not to mention Sage's moms, Galen and Fern Shapiro. The Shapiros owned and operated The Moon Goddess, a vegan bakery in Park Slope.

The moms had initially been reluctant to let Sage get Sylvia because of the natural snake diet, which would mean sacrificing scared little rodents on a regular basis. But Sage persisted. She even found a cruelty free pet food company in Oregon that sold "faux mice" online.

"Let's get this over with," Sage said. She reached for her racquet. "At least the weather is good." It had been a particularly cold wet spring.

"Try to show a little enthusiasm; this is supposed to be fun," Zoe said.

"Go easy on me. I need to conserve some energy for Poetry Seminar."

Sage was trying to finish her junior year strong. There were no grades at Saint Ann's, but teachers wrote lengthy student evaluations and many graduates were accepted at Ivy League schools. Sage really wanted to study poetry at Brown.

After a particularly uninspired two sets, Sage headed home down her quiet, tree-lined street just blocks from Prospect Park. She knew at least one of her moms would be waiting for her with dinner on the stove. It was a nice feeling.

Fern had been born Rebecca Shapiro in Flatbush, but the patriarchal nature of traditional Judaism held little appeal for her. She took a Wiccan name during a sacred circle naming ceremony in 1982, but always honored certain Jewish traditions (mainly the ones involving food).

Galen started life as Margaret Fitzsimmons in Brookline, Massachusetts, one of seven children in an Irish Catholic family ruled by a drunken father who could never accept her orientation. Margaret refused to bend to his will and left home at seventeen, without regrets.

When Margaret met Fern at a food co-op, a shared interest in veganism, cooking and animal rights grew into love. At their Wiccan handfasting ceremony, Galen (she had ditched Margaret when she began practicing Wicca) took the name Shapiro out of respect for Fern's desire to retain her Jewish roots.

After a stint on an organic farm in Maine, the Shapiros settled in Park Slope with their adopted daughter Sage. They opened The Moon Goddess in 1996 and took turns running the bakery and caring for Sage, who spent much of her toddlerhood covered with flour behind the bakery counter. They were an unconventional but happy family, and the tall, green-eyed, intellectually curious Sage was the light of both mothers' lives.

"What's for dinner?" Sage asked as she entered the kitchen. Pokey left his warm bed in the corner of the kitchen, greeting Sage with a wagging tail and a cold nose pressed into her hand.

"Kung Pao Tofu," Galen said, smiling. It was one of Sage's favorites. "How was your day, Snow Pea?" Galen's freckled brow and frizzy strawberry blonde hair were damp with sweat.

"OK, but I have a ton of work to do for Poetry Seminar." Sage dropped her backpack. What she really wanted to do was watch *Keeping Up with the Kardashians*, but that was not going to happen.

Galen was thrilled that Sage was so interested in poetry; she'd majored in poetry at Bennington. "Come and give me a hug and I'll feed you and you can get to work."

Galen approached Sage with open arms. Bliss, one of the cats, rubbed against Sage's leg, as her mother engulfed her. Galen smelled like patchouli and sweat and lemons. Sage leaned into her mother's ample bosom and took a deep breath. Home.

Home, thought Roy Beech as he stepped into his study, the one room in the Beech house off limits to Allie and her decorating talents. He dropped into his worn leather desk chair and absentmindedly picked up the pewter julep cup that held his pens (his mother had bought it for his college graduation, and since it was monogrammed couldn't return it when he fell several credits short). Roy had known what he had to do the second he saw Congressman Dan Butts led out of the Here Kitty Kitty Massage Parlor in handcuffs.

Poor Dan! Poor Roy!

He knew Allie would want him to run for Dan's seat. Being a real estate developer suited him just fine. As far as he could tell, Congress didn't do much, and he liked action, like buying the Talbot farm and convincing the planning commission to approve Serenity Knolls, a planned community of 200 luxury homes and townhomes jammed onto space originally zoned for fifty. Roy had made a fortune on that deal alone, and there had been so many others.

Most country club wives would be thrilled with that. But *his* wife, a senator's daughter, wanted at the very least to be a congressman's wife.

Sometimes Roy regretted that Allie had dropped out of the Corcoran masters program to work as a decorator, and had quit altogether when she had the twins. For the last two decades, Allie's considerable drive had been focused on nothing but Belle Vista, tennis, and to a lesser extent the twins. Now, the Allie laser beam had turned in his direction.

Although it had only been two weeks since Lou's death and Dan's resignation, Roy had already hired a smart young campaign manager, Ian Thorne. Ian was boyish looking, with a mop of wavy hair and serious brown eyes. He rarely laughed, but was quick to smile. He had worked for Sarah Palin in '08, and while that hadn't gone extremely well, he had made some excellent contacts and had since worked on successful Tea Party campaigns in the House. He was hard working and direct, and Roy had liked him immediately.

Roy told Ian upfront that he wanted nothing to do with the Tea Party. The upper middle class voters in Roy's circles found that segment of the party too lowbrow. Allie said the women looked like Wal-Mart shoppers, all bad perms and sweatpants.

Ian had simply shrugged. One visit to the Beech's imposing hilltop Tudor told him all he needed to know; his paycheck would be substantial.

Sage wanted a cup of tea before she tackled her Poetry Seminar project. While Galen puttered nearby, watering their window box herb garden, she opened the cabinet and stared at her choices, which included Blue Mountain Nilgiri, Iron Goddess Oolong, Jasmine Petals, Lapsang Souchong and New Moon Darjeeling. She furrowed her brow slightly and reached for the Lipton.

She loved that Fern and Galen, despite their avid vegan Wiccaness, supported her right to make her own choices, even if those choices were not certified organic. They let her watch *Teen Mom*, even though they found it appalling. When she wanted to go to McDonald's in seventh grade, they let her, shaking their heads as she had marched defiantly towards the golden arches.

Fern entered the kitchen just as the kettle whistled. She was stocky and dark, with mischievous blue eyes and a slow, warm smile. Her Wiccan pentagram, which she never took off, hung around her neck.

"Hello Star Light," she said upon seeing her daughter. "How was your day?"

"Fine Mama," Sage answered. "How was The Moon Goddess?"

"Pretty good." Fern pulled up a stool at the counter while Galen began to reheat the Kung Pao Tofu. "I'm thinking of having the goddess mural repainted. It's lacking in luster."

"Do we have any honey?" Sage asked as she plunged her tea bag into the steaming water.

"Somewhere," said Galen, looking around the cluttered kitchen.

"Love, do you remember that fantastic organic honey we used to get from California?"

Fern smiled at Galen.

"Oh yes," Galen answered, handing a jar of honey to Sage. "It was made by The Universal Family of Truth, a cult."

Sage's eyes widened.

"How come they don't make honey anymore?" Sage asked.

"The leader, Father Yaweh, jumped off a cliff near Santa Cruz. He was under the impression that he could fly and it really ended badly," Galen said, sending her right hand into a mock swan dive that ended with a resounding smack in her left palm.

"No Yaweh, no honey."

"Jeez!" Sage laughed. "That's crazy. This honey is fine," she said, looking at the label. "I really need to start working."

She gathered her tea and her backpack and headed up the creaky stairs to her bedroom. Her mothers watched her glide out of sight, always amazed by her beauty and poise, her breezy self confidence and good humor. They still remembered the first time they saw her, seventeen years ago. How could they ever forget? Her small hand had grasped Galen's finger tightly. She had the softest red hair, and blue eyes that over time became a piercing emerald green.

Sage tossed her backpack on her bed and opened her Mac Book. She fed Mary Kate and Ashley a handful of dried shrimp and turned towards Sylvia.

"Hey girl," Sage lifted the Corn snake from her habitat and draped her over her shoulders. She sat at her desk and stared at the computer screen. Time to write. She had titled her project "Roots". This allowed for many interpretations, from the physical to the spiritual and emotional. She had already written several strong poems but was struggling with an attempt to explore her personal roots. She loved her two moms, but she knew nothing about her birth parents and, lately, that had begun to nag at her.

Sage placed her fingers on the keyboard and closed her eyes, summoning an image in her mind. She rested her cheek against Sylvia's scaly skin. The snake's forked tongue gently flicked a loose strand of dark red hair and the words, fast and beautiful, flew from her fingertips.

Ian Thorne drove his blue BMW coupe up Belle Vista Drive and mused that he never knew what to expect when he signed on to manage a campaign. Roy Beech looked good on paper. He had the successful career and the beautiful family. He was good looking in a Ken doll way, with a square jaw and Kennedy hair, and he donated to the correct causes and candidates. Still, the team of opposition researchers Ian hired to dig up dirt on Roy and his family had revealed some serious concerns.

First, Allie Beech was participating in *Queen of the Court*, a country club reality show, which could only mean publicity of the worst kind. Ian found Allie cold and unlikable, and he didn't need a poll to tell him viewers and voters would too.

The teenage twins were also potential embarrassments, especially Bethany. Her Facebook page was a minefield and her Twitter account inappropriate at best. Quint was less prolific on social media, but his heavy lidded eyes and dismal grades were a red flag.

Ian pulled into the Beech's driveway behind Allie's black Mercedes. Time to deliver some unwelcome recommendations: no reality shows or social media for the duration of the campaign. He was only glad that this was twenty-first century America, not medieval Florence or ancient Rome. Allie Beech definitely had a "kill the messenger" look about her.

"There were some things we should go over before the campaign kicks off," Ian said, trying to get comfortable in a stiff club chair upholstered in white Scalamandre silk. Allie's elegant living room was as cold and formal as she was.

"My father was a senator." Allie smiled tensely at Ian from her perch on the pale blue silk settee. "I know all about campaigning." Roy, who sat next to Allie, gave Ian an encouraging smile, but remained silent.

Bethany sat in the other club chair idly picking at her nails, while Quint sat on the floor, earbuds in, head nodding to a tune. Allie frowned, noticing Ian's loafers had tracked dirt onto her buff petit point rug.

"Well, things have changed since your dad ran for office," said Ian, taking Roy's lead and smiling pleasantly at Allie.

Allie did not return his smile. Was he implying she was *old*?

"This brings me to my first topic, the reality show. I don't think it's a good idea."

Silence.

"I *have* to do the show," Allie said, sitting up straight and pressing her palms into the sofa cushion. "*Queen of the Court* is part of the agreement with Wayne and Shana Jones, who now own a majority interest in our club."

"I understand that," Ian said patiently. "But where does it say that you have to participate?"

"I have to participate because I am the captain of the Belle Vista tennis team. I think it will demonstrate that I am a community leader."

"Uh, I don't think so. Country clubs are elitist, and in this economy we really need to avoid that message. Also, reality shows are silly and embarrassing."

Allie looked at Roy sharply. "Roy?"

"I'm sure we can come to some kind of compromise," Roy said, looking at Ian hopefully. In the Beech house "compromise" meant doing things Allie's way.

"I'm just telling you what I think. It's what Roy is paying me for." Ian stretched his legs. Allie looked disapprovingly at his shoes, which were still shedding dirt.

"If only we could find some way to buy the club back from the Joneses. That would solve everything." Allie twisted her Tiffany circlet diamond and platinum wedding band.

"I'm not following you." Ian shifted in the unyielding chair. Really, who sat in these things?

"The *Joneses*. The tacky people who now own most of Belle Vista. Shana is from West Virginia…"

"We seem to have gotten off topic," interrupted Ian with a strained smile. "I'll just let you think about the political risks this reality show entails. Next: Quint and Bethany. Your Facebook and Twitter accounts need to basically disappear."

"Are you fucking kidding me?" Bethany said, jolted out of her stupor. "No way!"

"Bethany. *Language!*" said Allie.

Roy remained silent, although, Ian noted, his smile was fading.

"Come on, Ian." Bethany stomped one pretty foot, sheathed in a bright orange Tory Burch flat. "You can't make me give up Twitter. My followers will be so pissed off."

Ian wondered what was holding up her matching romper. If it was duct tape, he wanted some of the extra for her mouth.

"I'm actually fine with that," Quint said sheepishly, refusing to meet his sister's angry stare. Updating Facebook and Twitter was hard work.

"You are *so* overreacting," said Bethany.

"Oh? Really?" Ian had been waiting for this moment. He stood and pulled his iPhone from the pocket of his navy blazer, and scrolled around for a few tense seconds. When he found what he was looking for, he held the screen close to Bethany's startled face.

Sage Silverfox Shapiro received stellar comments from her instructor, and positive feedback from her classmates on her Poetry Seminar project. The poem "Searching" was selected to be published in the school's prestigious literary magazine later that spring.

Searching
By Sage Silverfox Shapiro

It is human nature to Search-
says Psychology: Today
searching is not a quest-
it is a test
of ourselves.
an evolutionary
coping mechanism,
a cyclic mismatch-
a face
that should invoke
a feeling and doesn't
a feeling
that cannot bring to mind
a face.

6

Belted tightly into her plush terry robe, Allie sat on the floral chintz loveseat in her sunroom and sipped delicately at her coffee, while trying to read the Post. Really, she was just counting the minutes till 8 a.m., after which she could call her mother (Lavinia had a strict morning routine, including a 7:30 walk, and did not take kindly to interruptions). She was so excited she kept reading the first sentence of the top story, something about debt ceilings, over and over.

It had hit her as she'd walked past the trophy case on the way to the club grille for lunch with Roy yesterday. The case was littered with old black-and-white pictures of Phillippa "Pippa" Edgemoor, the peculiar heiress who vanished decades ago from Belle Vista.

One Christmas, after too much eggnog, Lavinia had told Allie that if Pippa died and left no heirs, Belle Vista would inherit the millions in the Edgemoor Trust. The family wanted to ensure that their land and their lifestyle endured, even if they did not.

As far as anyone knew, Pippa's only living and very distant relative had been *Lou Butts*. And now that Lou was dead, only Pippa stood between the club and money that could free them from Wayne and Shana Jones.

If she could prove Pippa was dead, that is. Allie frowned and dropped the front page. Pippa had not been seen in over forty years, but Lavinia had received postcards from her periodically from exotic parts of the globe. That was problematic, but Lavinia hadn't mentioned any missives lately. If you believed old Edgar Chastain, Pippa's attorney, who was all too easy to sweet talk, she hadn't touched her trust. Surely, if she were alive, she'd have accessed those funds by now. Of course, the Edgemoors had always been eccentric, which was a polite term for crazy, so that was not proof positive either.

Allie had decided to hire a private detective. Worst case scenario, if they found Pippa alive and well, perhaps she could be persuaded to purchase the club from the Joneses. Allie would rather be at the mercy of an erratic aristocrat than a social-climbing stripper. She planned to meet Clare Buxton, who Bitsy Donaldson had used to investigate her husband's "late hours," on Tuesday. But first, she'd do a little investigating on her own.

Allie checked her watch. 8:01. She picked up her iPhone phone and listened to the ringing on the other end.

"Hello," Lavinia answered.

"Mother, how are you? I thought maybe you might be free for lunch this afternoon."

"Certainly, dear." Lavinia sounded pleased. "Shall we meet at the club? Noon?"

After a few minutes more of small talk, Allie pretended she heard the lawn service arriving and hung up. She loved her mother, of course, hating one's parents and blaming them for everything was so tiresome and middle class, but one long conversation with her today definitely would be enough.

Allie sometimes wondered if her life would have been different if she hadn't been an only child. Lavinia's pregnancy had been difficult and her delivery life-threatening. "Of course, I nearly died having Allison," her mother would often remark to friends and family. Not that Lavinia ever made her feel guilty, exactly. At the same time, Allie felt obligated to be as close to a model child as possible, and Lavinia did nothing to discourage her.

The problem was Lavinia, being Lavinia, had such definite ideas about *everything*. At age five, Allie recalled her mother wrinkling her nose in distaste when she'd wanted chocolate ice cream. "So messy! I'm sure if you think hard about it, Allison, you'll realize you prefer vanilla." She'd kept Allie in pastel smocked dresses and bows until nearly middle school. "If those girls tease you about your clothes, it's their problem," Lavinia would insist. But actually, it was Allie's problem, at least until she'd bribed a friend to bring her normal clothes, so she could change in the bathroom before school.

Then in high school, Lavinia had pulled Allie off the lacrosse team to play year-round tennis. "Lacrosse parents are pushy parvenus," Lavinia had said. "I'm not dealing with four years of that."

Perhaps the only time Allie had stood up to her mother was when she insisted on going to Vassar instead of a southern school. Lavinia had spent four years grumbling that Allie would end up marrying a Jewish Democrat from Harvard. Then, after Allie's college boyfriend (who was all of those things) dumped her and she began dating Roy, Lavinia had constantly complained that he was "not nearly as bright as that Harvard boy".

Allie had told Roy it was her decision to quit graduate school and work in a family friend's interior design business. In reality, Lavinia had convinced her that another art degree was pointless. "If you end up in a high stress career and get pregnant, it might end tragically," Lavinia had warned. "After all, I almost died having you, Allison. Wouldn't it be better if you had a simple job you could quit without regret, and just enjoy life at Belle Vista?"

Allie sighed. She knew that many of her "mom" friends felt she should take more control of her children, particularly Bethany. Those women obviously didn't know how it felt to be controlled.

She drained her cup of coffee, which had gone cold. Lavinia might have steered her into country club life, but once she pried the information about Pippa out of her, it would be Allie who would finally be in control at Belle Vista.

They chose their usual table by the window, which looked out over the doglegged eighteenth hole and trees beyond. Both mother and daughter ordered Cobb salads, with house dressing on the side and, just as the waitress was turning to leave, Allie reached out and touched her elbow. "Could we also get a bottle of Chardonnay?"

Lavinia raised her eyebrows. "Wine at lunch? You're not turning into Taylor Thomas are you?"

"No mother," Allie said, "I just thought it would be nice if we toasted Roy's campaign. It's really taking off, and he's even hired a terrific young campaign manager, Ian Thorne. He worked for Sarah Palin."

"Well, that didn't go too well, did it?" Lavinia placed her starched white napkin in her lap and pursed her lips ever so slightly.

Allie refused to let her mother drag her down. The wine was delivered, opened and poured. They toasted Roy's campaign, and when Lavinia had finished her glass, Allie shifted in her seat.

"It's so nice spending time with you Mother." Allie smiled across the table, dabbed the corners of her mouth with her napkin, and took one deep breath. "I was just looking at all the old trophies and photos outside; you've won so many league and club championships."

"Yes, well, I am hoping to see your name on the Edgemoor Cup this year. Don't neglect your singles practice during team season."

Allie hid her irritation under a tight smile. Lavinia certainly did know how to pick at emotional scabs. "Actually, Phillippa Edgemoor's photo caught my eye. I've always wondered what happened to her. Such a mystery. You were friends, right?"

"I suppose we were, after a fashion. It was a long time ago." Lavinia reached for the wine bottle and poured herself an atypical second glass. "Why on earth are you bringing her up? She's been gone for decades."

"I think if we can find out what happened to Pippa, we may find a way out of this mess." Allie lowered her voice and looked around. "You know, the Jones situation."

"What on earth are you getting at? Stop being evasive and say what you mean."

"I think you know what I mean, Mother," said Allie, dropping her pleasant "two girls at lunch" tone. "If Pippa is dead and we can prove it, her money will revert to Belle Vista, and the board can buy out the…" she reverted to a whisper, "… Joneses."

"*If* the Edgemoor trust still exists," Lavinia replied, lowering her voice as well. "Pippa probably gambled away the money years ago, or changed her will." Lavinia swilled her wine in a very un-Lavinia way.

"*No, she didn't*," Allie said, a triumphant smile spreading across her face. She relished the rare occasions she knew more Belle Vista dirt than her mother. "I called old Edgar Chastain. Of course he's not supposed to even admit there is a trust, but Edgar is *so* fond of me. He told me Pippa Edgemoor has never touched *a penny* of that money.

And she has, or had, no power to alter the beneficiaries. With Lou dead, that money would go to the club."

"Oh Allie, I wish you would just stop with this." Lavinia was flushed from the wine. She waved a pale hand across the table with flourish. "Who knows where Pippa is? She could be anywhere."

"Or she could be *dead*. That's what I'm counting on," Allie said. "Where do you think she might have ended up?"

"I haven't thought about her in years," Lavinia said. She was shaking slightly. She put down her fork and abandoned her half-eaten salad.

"But I remember you mentioning a postcard from her. Do you remember the date, and where it was from?" Allie pressed forward despite Lavinia's discomfort.

"It was from Barcelona, about four years ago. I think. I don't know." Lavinia finished her wine and stared directly at her daughter. "We were not that close. Pippa was a golfer."

A brief description, yet one that carried substantial weight. Women golfers at Belle Vista considered themselves superior to tennis players. They had better lockers and more of the budget, which led to much rivalry and little mixing.

"I've always been leery of the Edgemoors," Lavinia said, finally opening up a little. "There is a long, bloody, murderous history between our families, as you know. Ezekiel Edgemoor shot and killed my great grandfather, Major Francis Endicott, at the Heath House Hotel in Alexandria. Edgemoor was shot in turn, but, unfortunately, the monster lived. His vile genetic material was passed on to Pippa, the golfer." Lavinia looked out the window at the eighteenth green. More golfers. She shuddered.

"Well, I'm hiring a private investigator to look into Pippa's whereabouts. With the Internet, we should be able to track her down, however, I could use some fresh leads. Did you ever hear of other people getting postcards from Pippa, or phone calls? Did any of your friends ever see her?"

Allie attempted to bring her mother back to the current century, but Lavinia was done with her salad, done with her wine and most certainly done with the conversation. She folded her napkin, crisp and clean except for a muted pink lipstick smudge, on the table in front of her and stood up, signaling the end of lunch.

Sage walked through the sweet spring rain; when it hit the sidewalk in front of her, its fragrance exploded and filled the air around her. She took several deep breaths as she headed to school, her yellow rain boots squeaking with every step. She had been thinking a lot about her birth parents recently. She didn't romanticize them or want to live with them. She knew who she was, the daughter of Fern and Galen, a high school student who liked poetry and animals, and was excited about applying to colleges. She would change nothing in her life. She was just curious.

Sage was honest with her mothers, and they were not hurt by her questions. They just wished they had more answers. Sage had been born in West Virginia. After a series of adoption agencies had rejected Fern and Galen, they'd hired Jack Shirley, an adoption lawyer who promised results for cash, as long as no questions were asked. Fern and Galen were a bit ashamed of the channels they had gone through. But they had desperately wanted a baby and knew that, as gay Wiccans, they had few options.

Jack had told them the baby's birth parents were students at a local college, and not much else. The adoption was closed. They were simply called and told to come to Providence Hospital in Morgantown, and after driving all night, Jack met them in the maternity ward and handed them Sage, swaddled in a pink blanket. They paid cash to cover hospital costs and adoption fees and drove home to Brooklyn. They never heard from Jack Shirley again.

Sage had little to go on, but a quick Google search had showed that Jack Shirley had died in 2000, leaving no heirs and no law partners. Feeling lost and frustrated, she entered the St. Ann's student center and plopped down next to her friend Jasper, who listened sympathetically to her story. One of the most tech-savvy students at Saint Ann's, he took notes as they sat sprawled on a tattered second-hand couch, his heavy fingers tapping away on his keyboard. Jasper was a large boy, almost 6 feet 4, and close to 300 pounds. He liked a good tech challenge, he told Sage, wiping his sweaty brow on the sleeve of his flannel shirt. Sage thought he looked like a lumberjack.

"I've got some ideas," he said with a crooked smile. "I think we can crack this. I think we can find your parents."

Allie wore the same black Chanel suit she had worn to Lou's funeral to meet Clare Buxton. Her wardrobe tended to jump from casual to cocktail, and clearly she was going to have to invest in more business attire as the wife of a congressional candidate. She made a mental note to swing by Neiman Marcus after the meeting.

She sat nervously, notebook and black patent Chanel clutch in her lap, in Clare Buxton's dingy waiting room, which was located in a nondescript 1950s low-rise in a part of Arlington that had escaped gentrification. A middle-aged woman, as squat and forgettable as the building itself, opened a cheaply-veneered door and motioned Allie to enter. She closed the door behind them and extended a fleshy hand with unvarnished nails bitten to the quick.

"Clare Buxton, pleasure to meet you."

Allie took her hand reluctantly. "Allie Beech," Allie replied, sitting down in an old government-issue wooden chair. She quickly summed up the detective. Clare was in her early forties, short and stocky. Her ash-blonde hair was shot through with gray and pulled back with a black hair elastic. No make-up. Her baggy clearance rack pants suit was a dispirited tan, her shoes were black and practical. She wore no jewelry and was chewing gum. Socially, an untouchable.

"Give me the background," Clare said, sitting and opening her laptop.

She listened intently as Allie told the story of Pippa Edgemoor and her mysterious disappearance. That Pippa had supposedly left Belle Vista for Palm Springs the day after Christmas 1972; driving as she always did. There were confirmed reports of her being seen in Las Vegas, with her distinctive red Jaguar, sable coat, and family signet ring; but she never arrived at her final destination. Instead, she sent a brief typed note to her attorneys saying that she would be traveling abroad for an undetermined amount of time. After that, nothing but a few postcards.

Clare made note of the Edgemoor Trust and the lack of surviving relatives. When Allie was done, Claire sat silently for a few seconds, and then stood up.

"What makes you think Ms. Edgemoor is dead?"

"If she were alive, wouldn't she want access to her trust?" Allie said. "No one has seen or heard from her in forty years. It's a logical assumption, don't you think?"

"People vanish every day, Ms. Beech. Some disappear on purpose; others fall off cliffs into the ocean, or are dragged into the woods and never come out. This country is full of missing persons, the intentional and the accidental."

Clare cracked her knuckles loudly and nodded to herself.

"Sometimes they're living in Miami with a new name and a new family, and sometimes their bones are swallowed into the ocean or the earth. They are gone in both situations, just more so in the latter."

Allie had little interest in Clare's musings. "How do we go about having Pippa declared dead? Let's just say that she fell off a cliff and drowned. For example."

"That's death in absentia. In most cases, it takes seven years with no indication of life to have someone legally declared dead. Where major estates are involved, more investigation and proof is required. This case will require additional investigation."

To Allie that sounded like detective-speak for "additional money". Lavinia claimed to have received a postcard recently, but it could have been as long as seven years ago. Her memory was not perfect. Allie was certain Pippa was dead. She just HAD to be. But, finding proof of that demise was daunting with the whole world to cover.

Allie pictured Pippa in a tartan Belle Vista golf kilt, teetering on the edge of a Spanish cliff. She either lost her footing or heaved herself away from the ground beneath her (it didn't really matter which). She fell into the ocean below, hardly making a splash, her spiked golf shoes the last bit of her to be swallowed into the deep green sea.

7

Lavinia carefully piloted her vintage diesel Mercedes down the winding roads of one of Washington's glossier suburbs, past gracious old estates forced to coexist alongside garish new McMansions. She turned onto a private road that meandered through the manicured grounds of a deluxe inn-and-spa complex, a traffic-free route to the match at River's Edge.

She would never miss the first tennis match of the season for Belle Vista (she could not bear to think the words "Jones Belle Vista"), although she no longer played on the team.

But today, her mind drifted away from tennis, and back to the disturbing conversation she'd had with Allie at lunch yesterday. Lavinia's hands gripped the wheel more tightly. Her daughter was so smug, so sure, with her private investigator and that cursed Internet. Could technology actually make it possible to dig up the past? Very few people knew about the trust (oh, why had she ever told Allie?), which like all things Edgemoor, was shrouded in Byzantine secrecy. But the trust was not the real issue. Lavinia shuddered with dread as she contemplated the ultimate horror that might unfold at the hands of her daughter. What if that investigator actually *found* Phillipa?

Lavinia rounded a curve on the wooded road and looked to the left for the little cut through to River's Edge. Out of the corner of her eye, she saw what appeared to be a large pile of colorful rags on the edge of the road. She swerved to miss it, but the pile still went tumbling into the bushes with a disturbing thump.

Lavinia screamed as the Mercedes shuddered to a halt. The rags had a human face and a head of grizzled hair.

Allie hit the accelerator of her black Mercedes sedan, a newer version of her mother's. As captain – finally – she had to arrive early to enter each player's name in the official match book. The scores would come later. Shana and Karen were carpooling with Caroline in her mammoth Escalade, but Allie had demurred. The team was expecting her to bring a sub for Lou, but instead Allie had recruited a permanent replacement; a worthy partner for herself. The team would just have to cooperate.

She only hoped the match went as well as the first part of her morning.

Bethany had surprised her, pleasantly for once.

Allie had been on the verge of marching into Bethany's room to berate her for getting up late when her daughter had sashayed down their central staircase in a lovely Reiss knit dress in peacock blue, her nude LK Bennett pumps and tasteful makeup; a younger, blonde Kate Middleton. A rumpled Quint had stumbled after her.

"Mother," Bethany had said, pecking her on the cheek. "I've invited someone for breakfast. I really want you and Daddy to meet him."

"Your father has already left for a campaign meeting."

Then the doorbell had chimed and Bethany had opened the door to one of the most incredibly handsome young men Allie had ever seen, with dark golden skin set off by a pink LaCoste polo, flashing deep brown eyes and a head of wavy black hair. And that smile.

"Mother, this is Enrique Flores Cuervo de Patron. He's from Spain, and he's studying at Georgetown this year. As a special project for my Spanish class, I've agreed to be his cultural ambassador."

"So pleased to meet you," Enrique had said, taking Allie's hand. "I can certainly see where your beautiful daughter gets her elegance and charm."

Quint had been seized by a sudden fit of coughing.

Bethany had silently mouthed "Spanish Royal Family" behind Enrique's back to Allie, who'd nodded enthusiastically.

"So delighted to meet you. And I must say, your English is perfect; no accent at all. Bethany, I'll just go into the kitchen and pour some juice for all of us, while you introduce Enrique to your brother."

What Allie *hadn't* heard, after the kitchen doors closed behind her, was Quint laughing. "Only our uptight mother wouldn't notice your new royal boyfriend is named after two kinds of tequila."

"Keep it down, butt brain," Bethany had warned, "or I might tell her just what those plants in your 'science terrarium' really are."

"Seriously, Bethany, I don't know shit about Spain," Enrique had whispered, panicked.

"Don't worry, neither do my parents."

"Yeah," Quint had added, "we never travel anywhere with spicy food. It gives my Dad gas."

Allie screeched into the circular drive in front of the seven-story Porto Volpe luxury condominiums just as Elena strode out.

"You are being late," said Elena by way of greeting, as she folded her long, tan legs into the passenger side of Allie's car.

"Good morning to you too. How is Jack?"

"Angry. Old wife call for extra money again."

"Elena," said Allie with a sigh, "that was what we in America call a rhetorical question. The only appropriate answer is fine."

"In Uzbekistan we would call that hippopotamacy."

"Hypocrisy," corrected Allie as she pulled out of the drive and accelerated on to the Parkway.

Lauren Lippert, the River's Edge captain, would be livid if she were late, especially since Lauren had to come in two hours early to supervise Vixen as they set up. Of course, Lauren had auditioned for *The Real Housewives*, so she was clearly not as put out as she implied.

"So who are teams?" asked Elena, settling into her seat and, without asking, switching the radio from NPR to hip hop.

"Need to get pumped!"

"Well you and I will play number one, Shana and Taylor at two, Karen and Caroline at three, and at four and five…"

"Who cares about lower courts and inferior players? So, at two we have rich red-haired stripper and crazy skinny blonde, and at three, frowning lawyer and fat ex-wife."

"Elena, you must make an effort to get along with Caroline. Now I haven't told her you are joining the team yet. I thought that, in a match setting, especially on camera, she would remain calm…"

Elena let out a long, harsh laugh.

Lavinia peered down at the rag person, who fortunately seemed to be breathing.

"Sir, are you alive?"

"That's Miz, or Sister Sunshine." The rag woman struggled to her feet, dusted herself off and gave Lavinia a dirty look. On closer observation, Lavinia noted she was swathed in what appeared to be scarves and yards of dirty sari material. "It's a good thing I took a dive, or you might have destroyed my earthly form. And under all this, it's still a pretty hot one."

"Well, thank goodness you seem to be alright," replied Lavinia, putting on her polite leaving-the-luncheon smile. "I'd linger, but I'm running late. Oh, and by the way, you are on a private road."

"I don't believe in private property. And even if I did, you're on it too."

"That is completely different. Now, I don't want to be late."

"Oh, boo hoo. Wait...I feel dizzy. Maybe you did hit me after all.

The woman began to stagger theatrically.

"Oh, I know where this is going. You are looking for a handout."

Suddenly, Lavinia caught sight of a pendant dangling from the woman's neck. Without thinking, she grabbed it and jerked the woman toward her.

"Owww. What, are you going to steal my jewelry to pay some private road toll?"

Lavinia released the pendant and, germs be damned, grabbed the woman by her arms.

"Where did you get that medal? That's from The Merrywood School. Only graduates are allowed to wear them. You ... you must have stolen it."

"You're right about that," said the woman. "From Headmistress Gertrude Wellstone the day she kicked me out – two weeks before graduation, 1963."

Lavinia's eyes widened.

"Judy? Judy *Simpson*? It can't be."

"Why Lavinia Endicott Winter, you look as if you've seen a ghost," Judy said with a wicked smile.

Caroline's phone, stuck deep in her tennis bag, began to chime. Unfortunately, she had it linked with the "hands free" function, which broadcast her calls on the Escalade's sound system.

"This is Cadillac financial services," the smooth computerized voice announced to the entire car. "Please call about your payment at the earliest convenience."

During the twenty-minute ride, she had already heard from American Express, Potomac Gas and Electric and Marie Osmond Dolls, all with the same message: pay up. Now. At least only Karen and Shana had heard. And Lil Wayne.

"Hey Mrs. Wadinsky, is Marie Osmond gonna salt you if you don't pay for them dolls?"

Shana clapped a hand over Lil Wayne's mouth. "I'm sorry Caroline, he's just overexcited; that's why he couldn't go to school today." Or yesterday. Or the day before. In fact, Lil Wayne's kindergarten teacher had suggested home schooling after he'd been in her class just three hours, and pretty much every week since.

"I don't know what you think you're going to do with that little boy during a match," said Caroline, glad for the diversion.

Shana smiled.

"Oh, Jamal'l watch him. Lil Wayne just loves black people."

"*Shana*," said Karen, appalled. "It's African-American, and you can't say that."

Caroline tuned out Karen's lecture, and focused on something more interesting. Herself. She sighed, wondering why her life had to be so difficult. She'd opened up about it to Rex last week on camera. Well, sort of.

CAROLINE WALINSKY INTERVIEW

"When my husband left me last year, I said I would take less spousal support if it meant I could keep my club membership and keep playing team tennis. Of course, that has caused some minor economic problems."

In truth, Caroline owed so many people money she couldn't even keep track. She'd taken to burning the bills in the sunken outdoor fireplace before her daughter Maggie could find them.

Maggie! There was another difficulty. What normal teenage girl hides her mother's credit cards?

On the plus side, Maggie *was* super responsible. She'd even gotten Marie Osmond herself on the phone to work out Caroline's outstanding bill, and Caroline had dutifully returned all the dolls as required. Except Donny, whom she'd hidden in her closet. Which must be why Marie's thugs were after her again.

"Of course, I've coped with my financial situation by practicing thriftiness and good budgeting."

Actually, numbers had made Caroline's head hurt, and had ever since she'd flunked Algebra I. Twice. Instead, she'd taken to "borrowing" the clothes she needed from Nordstrom or boutiques. It wasn't stealing, as she planned to pay for them at some time in the hazy future, when she was rich again.

"No one can say that Caroline Walinsky doesn't know how to adapt to change."

Change indeed. Actual cash, which you sometimes needed, was a real issue. So she'd taken to combing through old jackets, handbags and the furniture for coins which could be converted to bills, or even credit for groceries, at local machines. She would not, however, be going back to the Coin Star in the lobby of the Belle Vista "Social Safeway" anytime soon. Last Tuesday, just as she started to dump her change into the machine, Elena had appeared, wearing her usual compression shorts with a short beaver jacket. It had been a chilly day.

"What is this? Spare change machine? You ask people on the street for money? Do you ring little bell?"

"It's a Coin Star. You put coins in the machine and it adds them all up, and then you get a receipt for bills or groceries." Caroline had resisted the urge to shove Elena into the machine.

"Coin Czar? Funny name. You need money that bad? I will have to tell Jack. Maybe tell everyone." Elena had put her hands on her slender hips and laughed.

"Caroline," shouted Karen "Watch where you're going!"

Caroline nearly t-boned Allie's Mercedes as she swung blindly into the River's Edge parking lot. She slammed on the brakes, jerking her passengers forward. Shaken, she peered through the windshield. Who was that sitting next to Allie? It couldn't be..."

Shana, Karen and Lil Wayne covered their ears as Caroline emitted a primal scream of rage.

"Well, Vinnie," said Judy, shaking her head. "You can't just leave an old friend and fellow Merrywood girl on the side of the road. You don't have to take me far. Just up the road to Merrywood. I was hoping maybe they were still into that charity thing and would give me a place to stay for a while."

"Not likely," Lavinia scoffed. "The school closed more than thirty years ago. It's a luxury spa now.

"Well then, you can find me a place to stay. You wouldn't want me to call the police and report a hit-and-run? Imagine all those investigators and the press looking into the background of Lavinia Winter, the former Cotillion Queen and sainted senator's wife."

Judy watched with interest as Lavinia turned a sickly shade of green.

"I guess you had better come with me," she said, opening the driver's side door and getting in. "I'll take you to a shelter in town right after this morning's tennis match. And by the way, that is senator's widow. My husband died of a heart attack five years ago."

"Sorry," said Judy, opening the passenger-side door.

"He was in the midst of having sex with his secretary," said Lavinia before she could stop herself.

"Ouch. *Really* sorry."

"Now, when we get to River's Edge, you stay in the car and wait for me. And do not speak to anyone."

"Fine," said Judy, nestling into the leather seat and watching the verdant green lawns go by as they drove toward their destination. In the forty-plus years since Judy had last seen her, Lavinia had, if possible, gotten even bossier. No matter. Judy had no intention of taking orders from Lavinia Winter.

8

"Excuse me, are you the director?"

Rex looked up from his clipboard to see a Xena Warrior Princess clone poured into a tight black halter tennis dress, her matching black hair lacquered into a sleek ponytail. Glossy blood red lips parted in a wide smile to reveal gleaming straight white teeth. God, Rex was sick to death of American teeth.

"I am, yes. Can I help you?"

"I'm Lauren Lippert, captain of the River's Edge tennis team, and I'd like to welcome you to our club," she said, gesturing at the mammoth white frame structure looming unimaginatively over the Potomac River. Lauren wore what appeared to be the Hope Diamond on her ring finger. She beckoned Rex closer.

"You know," she said, lowering her voice, "if you are *really* interested in country club tennis, you should think about filming your show at our club. I mean, Belle Vista is fine in its own way, but River's Edge is *truly* exclusive. Only 300 members, including some of the world's wealthiest people."

Lauren lowered her voice another notch.

"My partner Yasmine, for example," she whispered, pointing at an exotic-looking ash blonde warming up on a perfectly raked and watered green clay court. "Her husband is a descendant of the late Shah of Iran."

"Do you mean tennis partner, or *partner* partner?" It was Byron, who had crept up and insinuated himself between them.

"*Really*," said Lauren. "Rex, you and I will chat after the match." She gave Byron a withering look and stalked off to join Yasmine.

"Thank you, Byron. When I hired you, I had no idea your power to offend the haute bourgeoisie would prove so useful."

"My pleasure. My God, look at them all," Byron added, as the three turned to observe the black-clad River's Edge team rallying vigorously as techno music blared in the background. "Lady Ninjas made more powerful by silicone and Botox."

"Watch yourself, Byron. Those rings could be deadly in a fight," Jamal chimed in as he walked over, camera on his shoulder. "I'm going to take a handheld into the parking lot and get footage of our ladies as they arrive."

"Just make sure you get back quickly," said Rex. "I need you to manage the freelancers we hired for today's shoot. They seem to think their main tasks are filching sandwiches and picking up stray cougars. The idiots could fall in the pool and drown without supervision."

"I am NOT getting out of this car," said Caroline, her voice rising. "Lou promised me that Elena would never be on this team. She said, 'Caroline, over my dead…ohhhhhhh," she groaned. "Maybe Taylor's right; I killed Lou, and this is my payback."

"Now Caroline," said Shana, leaning over from the back seat and patting Caroline's shoulder. "You are gonna get out on that court and play your heart out, and when your ex sees you on camera, he's gonna realize what a fine woman he let go."

"Really?" said Caroline, wiping her tearful eyes, and much of her mascara, on the hem of her Jones Belle Vista uniform.

Karen doubted watching Caroline bounce around in her sausage-tight, mascara-smeared tennis dress would give Jack Walinsky second thoughts, but she remained silent. Her plastic Target sports watch showed only five minutes of warm up time left.

"And as far as Lou goes, honey, it was just her time. You know we Appalachian people believe bees are messengers of death," added Shana.

"Oh, Shana, come on," said Karen. She just could not let this slide. "There are bees everywhere."

"And there are people dying *all the time*," said Shana with finality.

Caroline turned her bloodshot blue eyes on Shana. "Can you tell my future? Because I owe my psychic a shitload of money and she's been no help at all."

"Daddy tells mama to see the lottery numbers, but she says it don't work that way," piped in Lil Wayne.

"Lil Wayne's exactly right, the Sight don't … doesn't work that way. But Caroline, if you get out there on that court and fight for Jones Belle Vista, I will try my best."

"Oh, thank you, Shana. I feel so much better now. I think I'm ready to go."

This time, Karen kept her lips tightly closed. Twenty-first century women blabbing about psychics and The Sight. Ridiculous. As she got out, she made a mental note to call Greg and ask him to come home early, since she was ovulating. She reached into the pocket of her warm-up jacket and caressed her medal of St. Gerard, the patron saint of motherhood.

They emerged from the Escalade, and Shana broke into a huge grin when she saw Jamal waiting for them, camera in hand.

"Hi Jamal! Guess what? Your best little friend is here!" A terrified Jamal just managed to lower his camera before Lil Wayne tackled him at the knees.

Lauren Lippert aimed her scarlet Cheshire grin at the cameras, even though she was speaking to Allie. "Your players for courts two and three seem to be late, are you prepared to forfeit?"

"Absolutely not. They will be here momentarily," insisted Allie with more confidence than she felt.

On court one, Elena was warming up with Yasmine, if you could call it that. It looked more like Yasmine was taking enemy fire. She stomped prettily off the court and pulled Lauren aside.

"We have a slight adjustment to make to the lineup," Lauren told Allie, or rather the cameras (Showboat, Allie thought).

"Yasmine and I will play at two, you and your new partner," she cast a withering look at Elena, "can play Riva and Kristen."

Allie's jaw tightened. She'd looked forward to trouncing Lauren.

"I've just got to make my number one fan comfortable, then let's get started. All courts not present in five minutes will forfeit," Lauren announced. She turned her back on Allie and walked to a courtside table where Lavinia (who'd left Judy in her Mercedes, parked well out of sight behind the golf cart barn) sat chatting with an elderly man tethered to an oxygen tent. Lauren adjusted his wheelchair and tucked a black fleece afghan snugly around his legs.

Allie, meanwhile, nervously checked her watch as Shana, Caroline and Karen appeared courtside, trailed by Taylor. Taylor always drove alone.

"I can't believe you are all so late – we'll have to skip the warm up," Allie said through gritted teeth.

"Hi, captain," replied Shana, all smiles.

Allie noted with disapproval that Shana, Caroline and Taylor were wearing that horrid Jones Belle Vista costume. Shana's cleavage was bad enough, but Caroline's uniform showed so many ripples she looked like a caterpillar, and what were those black stains? To top it off, Taylor's uniform was inside out.

"Taylor, your *dress*," said Allie.

Taylor looked down, and then shrugged.

"I like it this way. It looks deconstructed."

Deconstructed was a good description of Taylor, who had a bad case of bed head, and appeared to be wearing a Nike sneaker on her right foot, and a Babolat on her left. It wouldn't have been so noticeable if the Nike hadn't been bright pink and the Babolat black.

"Okay," said Allie. "Please note that the cameras are now rolling."

Taylor zoned out for the rest of the speech. Allie was always warning her about the damn cameras. So far, she thought, the show was going just fine. Rex had said he thought her individual interview was hot, and his tone had told Taylor he meant it.

TAYLOR THOMAS INTERVIEW

"I go all out on the court. I have a lot of natural energy, and people misinterpret that."

That's what she'd said when Rex asked her about getting suspended last year. Of course, in her more sober moments, even Taylor had to admit that the "Taylor Incident" – jumping over the net and chasing her opponent with her racquet - had been pretty hard to misinterpret. She'd wanted to kill that cheating bitch.

"I've promised that this year I'll keep myself under control and, hopefully, there won't be any more misunderstandings."

Taylor had made that pledge to herself, to Lou and, in writing, to Belle Vista's lawyers. But she felt just a tiny bit edgy this morning. Maybe it was that Adderall she'd popped. Technically it had been prescribed for her neighbor's son, but Margie told Taylor she'd changed her mind about giving the kid drugs and was throwing it out. Taylor didn't normally fish through trash cans, but it had seemed like a waste of perfectly good meds. Still, maybe she should have skipped the vente latte with three extra espresso shots afterward.

"My philosophy this year is to play within myself, to stay very centered, very zen. Like a Buddhist monk, you know? Channeling the calm."

Lauren approached and eyed the recent arrivals. "Such *cute* uniforms. I don't understand *why* Allie isn't wearing one," Lauren cooed. Shana beamed, and Allie wondered what it was like to live in an irony-free world.

"Wouldn't she just look great in it?" enthused Shana. "I'm Shana Jones, with Jones Belle Vista, naturally."

Allie cringed.

"Before we start, Lauren, I just have to say how touched I am by you bringing your grandfather to watch," said Shana.

Lauren's red lips formed a tight line, and without another word she stalked toward the court.

"Oh my God," said Taylor with a high-pitched nervous laugh. "Shana, that's her husband, F. Brand Lippert, the billionaire. Most of the River's Edge women are, like, third wives. It costs twice as much to join this as place as Belle Vista, but it's all new money and foreigners."

"I am foreigner and recent money of Mrs. Jones keeps club open, so maybe it is time you are putting sock on it," said Elena as she strolled up, a sheen of sweat on her pale golden skin. She extended her hand to Caroline. "Ex-wife, we should bury hatcheck and defeat women in black. They are weak and deserve destruction."

Shana smiled and gave Caroline an encouraging nod. She reached out and shook Elena's hand.

"Jones Belle Vista on three," said Karen. Allie grimaced as her teammates broadcasted the abominable new club name for Lauren Lippert, her cronies, and the cameras – indeed the whole world – to hear.

Rex grabbed Byron by the sleeve of his Vineyard Vines aqua-striped button down, (no one could accuse him of not embracing country club style) as Byron pursued the ladies armed with his makeup emergency kit, a fresh shirt for Caroline, and fashion tape for Shana's escaping breasts.

"Are you crazy?" said Rex. "The finest stylist alive couldn't improve on those looks."

"But they're a train wreck," wailed Byron.

"And who wouldn't watch a train wreck?" replied Rex with satisfaction. "Now where is your good friend Jamal?"

"Look, little buddy, I will buy you a five-pound bag of Skittles. All you've gotta do is sit in the nice tennis center lounge and watch sports on the big TV while I work." Jamal hated himself for pleading with a six year old, but he was desperate.

"Uh uh, that's boring. I want Bethany to babysit! I wanna use the camera!" Lil Wayne was working himself into a frenzy, turning red and stomping his feet. Jamal figured that, over by the courts, Rex was doing the same thing, except with a few "f-ing Jamals" thrown in.

"Are you in need of emergency child care?"

Jamal and Lil Wayne looked up to see Judy, her gray hair wild and scarves flowing. Jamal figured she was a fortune teller that probably been hired for a party at the club. Either that, or Rex was finally making good on his threat to have Jamal cursed for eternity.

Judy smiled. "It's okay. I'm a good friend of Lavinia Winter. Do you know Lavinia?"

"Mrs. Winter, sure ... " The idea of this lady being friends with old stick-up-her-ass Winter was strange, but hey, Jamal was in reality TV, where strange was the new normal. And, frankly, if she was here to kidnap Lil Wayne, well, it was her funeral.

"Great idea. You can work out the cash with his mom, she pays really well. Take him in the clubhouse and watch TV, tell them you're with Vixen Video Productions."

Jamal hurried away before Lil Wayne, still staring at Judy, could follow.

"Are you a Gypsy?"

"No, I'm just an old white lady in scarves."

"Boring!"

"Tell me about it. You want to go watch TV?"

"Nah. Boring!"

"Totally," agreed Judy, nodding. "Besides, TV will disrupt the flow of your Qi. What do you say we take one of these nifty golf carts out for a spin?"

A grin split Lil Wayne's face. Now *this* was more like it.

Later, it was hard for Allie to pinpoint when her really good day officially morphed into one of her worst ever. The uniforms, Lauren, Jones Belle Vista, were all merely the overture in a comic opera of horrors. The main event would have to be Shana and Taylor's short-lived match against Lauren and Yasmine.

"Look, I know how to back that snotty bitch Yasmine off the net," Taylor whispered to Shana as they walked on to the court. "You set me up with a big service return, and bam."

"Right at her feet, just like Justin taught us," said Shana nodding conspiratorially.

At her feet. Right. Taylor had thought someone who'd worked in strip clubs would have more balls. Oh, well, as usual, she'd have to do it all herself.

Taylor began pounding net shots at Yasmine immediately, but Yasmine's years of gymnastics (she'd been a cheerleader at Duke) had paid off. She returned nearly everything, and Lauren's serve was deadly.

"I am havin' a really tough time with that serve," Shana said to Taylor, breathing hard. They were tied four all in the first set.

"Well, Lauren gets extra attention from their pro, and most of it involves horizontal workouts," replied Taylor loud enough for Lauren and the film crew to hear. Kevin Engle, the River's Edge pro, was a George Clooney look-a-like working at his third country club job in the past two years. He had "fraternization issues," and had been cited in two divorce filings.

Lauren narrowed her eyes at Taylor from across the court. She wound up and hit Shana a serve down the T at nearly eighty miles per hour. Shana lunged at it with her two-handed backhand, and the strain was just too much for her sweat-soaked, overtaxed built-in bra. She returned the ball down the middle, but her impressive right breast sprang free in the process.

Yasmine should have crushed Shana's weak return at the net, but instead she froze, transfixed by her opponent's wardrobe malfunction. The ball whizzed past her, and Lauren popped it up to Taylor, who smashed it right into Yasmine's pretty, shocked face. Blood spurted from her surgically perfected nose as she ran screaming off the court.

"Well," said Taylor with satisfaction, "I guess that's a forfeit. We win!"

"Win!" shrieked Lauren. *"That,"* she pointed at Shana's hastily re-covered breast," was a distraction."

"You returned the shot, so too bad," said Taylor.

"Then," fumed Lauren, "your shot was a…a… courtesy violation!"

She turned for confirmation to Kevin, who had walked out on the court after seeing Yasmine flee. He wished he hadn't slept with the board chairman's wife at his last club. He'd liked it there. Lauren was scary.

"Uh, well, actually, Lauren, uh, there is no such thing as a courtesy violation, and you have to stop play to call a distraction, so I'm afraid …"

"Fine!" Lauren smashed her $350 custom Babolat against the metal net post and marched off court, as Kevin realized he'd have to update his resume yet one more time.

Allie and Elena were already walking off court one, where Riva had feigned a sprained ankle and forfeited, when Lauren accosted them. But an announcement on the speaker system drowned out her tirade.

"Would the owner of a black Cadillac Escalade with Virginia plates 4DLUV report to the parking lot. Your car is being towed."

With a high pitched shriek, Caroline abandoned her racquet in mid serve and ran toward the parking area.

"Did you script this?" Jamal asked Rex, as Lauren resumed berating Allie.

Before Rex could answer, another announcement blared.

"Would the mother of Lyle Wayne Jones please meet security at the cart barn. Immediately."

Shana, still adjusting her uniform, hurried off in the same direction as Caroline.

"You know I am not good enough to have scripted this," said Rex. "Jamal, what are you waiting for? You've got Shana, the freelancers should follow Caroline."

Abandoned on the court to savor her victory alone, Taylor sat down on the courtside bench and pulled a mini-bottle of champagne out of her tennis bag, popped the top, and sipped. Life was good.

Caroline wailed piteously as a burly man in overalls hooked her car up to his tow truck.

"Oh, please, Edwin," she cried.

"Ms. Walinsky, I'm sorry, but I work for the dealership, and they want the car back. Again. The fact that you know me isn't a good sign, Mrs. Walinsky. Have you thought about a KIA? My wife has one, and the payments are real reasonable."

With that, he got into the cab of the tow truck and pulled away.

As Caroline sobbed, a black limo pulled into the lot. The uniformed driver got out and opened the rear left door for Elena, who slid in.

"Elena," said Caroline, sniffing slightly, "could I have a ride to the Cadillac dealership – for Jones Belle Vista?"

"Sorry, ex-wife. Truce for match only, which you spoil with unnecessary forfeit." Elena slammed the door, and Caroline watched the sleek town car glide away. Karen, who'd been watching from a few yards away, came up and put her hand on Caroline's arm.

"Let's go find Shana; maybe we can all split a cab."

"Taylor will give me a ride," said Caroline, rubbing more mascara on her top as she dried her eyes.

Karen had just watched Taylor peel out of the other end of the parking lot, tossing her mini-champagne bottle out the window as she drove away.

"Uh, she's already gone. And I don't think riding with her today was a good idea anyway. Is she always like this?"

"Like what?" said Caroline, blinking.

On the other side of the parking lot, Shana was offering profuse apologies to the River's Edge security team. They'd wrangled Lil Wayne out of a golf cart after he'd terrorized a foursome of elderly women on the fifteenth hole.

"I'm sorry, Mama. I shouldn't have took off and left Judy. But she had to pee."

"Who is Judy?" asked Shana, confused.

"That would be me."

The entire group – Shana, the security guards, Lil Wayne, the crew, and Caroline and Karen, who'd just walked up – stood transfixed as a figure swathed in multi-colored scarves walked toward them, her arms extended and covered with dozens of buzzing honey bees.

"Aaaaaaaah," squealed Caroline as she fainted into the nearest security guard's arms. Shana and Karen cringed.

"Jesus," said Judy. "They're just sweet little bees."

"You'll have to excuse us," said Shana, holding a hand to her heart. "We've recently experienced a bee-related tragedy. And they *are* messengers of death."

"Huh," said Judy, flapping her arms so the bees flew off, away from the cowering crowd. "Never heard that one. I've always believed they were symbols of fertility."

Mouth open, Karen stepped forward and reverently touched Judy's sleeve.

9

Taylor was flying, singing loudly and tunelessly to Springsteen's "Rosalita", when Officer Roger Rankin clocked her black BMW X5 going fifty-five in a twenty-five mile zone.

"Oh shit," she muttered when she heard the siren and saw the red flashing lights behind her. She continued driving, foot easing off the accelerator, telling herself the guilty motorist's fairy tale; that he was trying to get around her to catch a real criminal.

Rankin pulled up beside her and gestured for Taylor to pull over. She bit her lip and pulled to the side of the road. She was right across from Belle Vista, just a couple of miles from Serenity Knolls. She'd almost made it home.

Officer Rankin sat in his car for a few minutes, entering Taylor's license plate information into a lap top. DR PLSTC. He shook his head, got out of his car and walked up to Taylor, who smiled at him through her open window.

He did not smile back.

"Do you know how fast you were going?"

He cocked his head and glared at her over the top of his sunglasses.

"Uh, thirty?"

Taylor tried the smile again, along with pushing her tennis skirt up farther on her thigh.

Rankin studied her for a moment; all tanned skin and white tennis clothes, her dark blonde hair pulled back messily into a pony tail. Ah, the country club set. They always tried to talk their way out of it, or … He eyed her exposed thigh and sighed.

Even if he weren't ethical, drunken rich housewives were not his type. On the last Friday of every July, he worked this stretch of road after the annual Belle Vista swim team banquet. He gave out ten DUIs last time. The drivers, who for some reason found a kids' party a good excuse for getting wasted, tried talking their way out of it, their children wide eyed and clutching shiny trophies in the back seat.

"Drivers license, please," he said, hand outstretched. As Taylor reached into her Traci jungle jaguar print tennis bag on the passenger seat, Rankin noticed a vial of prescription meds and two mini champagne bottles, one open.

"Get out of the vehicle, Ma'am." He opened Taylor's car door and she turned wildly towards him.

"Why?" she asked.

"Have you been drinking?"

"I had a glass of wine with lunch. But I drank lots of water and coffee afterward."

Right, thought Rankin.

"Just step out here ma'am. Let's start with you standing on one leg."

Caroline's cell phone buzzed and chimed, and she struggled to pull it out of her bag. She was jammed into a cab with Karen, Shana, Lil Wayne and that strange woman, who said her name was Judy.

"Hello," her eyes widened, so that she looked like one of Marie's dolls. "Yes, she's here."

Caroline reached across Shana and Lil Wayne and handed her phone to Karen.

"It's for you."

"Thank God! Where are you?" said Taylor. She sounded panicked.

"In a cab on the way home," Karen responded. She didn't ask why Taylor wanted to speak to her, because she dreaded the answer.

"There's been a terrible misunderstanding."

As Taylor cried into her phone, Officer Rankin glanced at her in his rear view mirror and shook his head.

"Where are you, Taylor? Try to calm down," Karen said. She felt her TMJ kicking in again.

"I am in the back of a police car, on my way to the Duke Street station." Taylor looked forlornly out the window. She hoped no one she knew would see her.

"Why are you in the back of a police car?" Karen asked, even though she knew the answer. Her jaw throbbed.

"Uh, reckless speeding. And maybe something else. I think."

"You *think*?"

"I had a glass of wine to celebrate my win, and now this fuckwad says I'm impaled!"

"That's impaired."

"Just meet me at the station. *Please*."

"Okay." Karen sighed. "I'll have to go home and change first, but I'll try to make it fast. For your own sake, do not refer to law enforcement as," She looked over at Lil Wayne wedged, in between Shana and Judy. "… you know what." She hung up.

"Fuckwad!" hollered Lil Wayne as Shana clapped a hand over his mouth. Taylor was easy to hear, even on a cell phone.

"Taylor's in a bit of, uh, difficulty," Karen said lamely as the other women looked at her. She was not about to say "drunk" and "jail" in front of a child, even Lil Wayne. "I'm going to try and help her out."

Shana leaned over and whispered, "Which police station? I'll meet you there."

Karen raised her eyebrows.

"Wayne'll be home to take the kids and settle our guest Judy in. I think we should show Taylor some team support. You in, Caroline? I'll pick you up."

"Sorry, I have to do something."

Until she returned all those clothes she'd "borrowed" from Nordstrom, Caroline was giving the police a wide berth.

Taylor was led into the police station in handcuffs, the only time she'd worn them for non-recreational purposes. She cut quite a figure in her skimpy tennis uniform and expensive jewelry, her makeup running with tears. Officer Rankin approached the booking officer.

"Maria Sharapova here was doing fifty-five in a twenty-five, and then failed a field sobriety test. Run a breathalyzer on her ASAP."

He handed over his paperwork and, without another glance at Taylor, exited the building.

"Asshole," said Taylor under her breath.

Forty-five minutes later, Taylor had blown a .12, and talked her way out of a holding cell and back onto a hard wooden bench in the main station. What was taking Karen so long? Then she saw her. Shana, not Karen.

"Oh, honey," Shana approached with her arms outstretched. "You poor thing."

"What are you doing here? I called Karen. She's a lawyer. You're a stripper."

Shana's face fell. In her experience, the criminally accused were usually more gracious about assistance.

"I thought that you might need some support," Shana said, looking directly at the handcuffs. Shana's mouth twitched as if she might actually cry.

"I'm sorry, Shana," Taylor apologized. "I'm just a bitch. Everyone says so."

"It's okay," Shana smiled. "I've been called worse." She sat down next to Taylor, and put her hand on her shoulder. "Karen will be here soon. She wanted to go home and put on some lawyer clothes. Have you called Spencer?"

"No!" Taylor jumped to her feet. "Please don't call Spencer." Spencer had cut down on her prescriptions and was watching her drinking, making noises about AA or rehab.

"Don't worry, honey," Shana said. "He doesn't need to know."

They heard the urgent click click of Karen's pumps on the linoleum floor. She had changed into a conservative navy blue suit, and was carrying a smart black leather briefcase.

"Sorry, but I didn't want to show up in tennis clothes." Karen motioned Shana aside, and sat down next to Taylor. She was surprised how good it felt to be back in a suit. "Why don't you start at the beginning?"

Outside, Rex pulled his battered Toyota Celica into the police lot, with Jamal in the passenger seat.

"I can't believe that Caroline actually texted you 'Don't go to the police station, it will embarrass Taylor'," Jamal said, laughing. "They really don't get how this reality show shit works, do they?"

"All we have to do is wait patiently, she should be out soon." Rex glanced at his watch. He thought about Shana's breast popping out from her spandex, the crazy old hippie woman, and, now, an arrest. It had been a good day.

While Karen handled the legal paperwork, Shana sat with the accused in the waiting area.

"I thought you played really good today." Shana was trying to distract an increasingly weepy Taylor, as a blistering hangover and the seriousness of her situation hit her at the same time.

"It felt good to win," Taylor said, a hint of a smile appearing on her face. "You played great too. I can't believe you flashed everyone your tit! That was hysterical. It really messed up Yasmine, and Lauren was so pissed."

"Whatever it takes," Shana said. "I gotta talk to Rex about that. I sure don't want it on TV. Remember what happened to Janet Jackson at the Super Bowl?"

Karen approached with a severe look on her face. The grim fucking reaper, Taylor thought.

"Are you ready for your close up?" Karen asked, setting her briefcase down on the linoleum floor. Taylor stared at her blankly. "Your mug shot," she explained.

Taylor winced. "But I look horrible. Do I have to?"

"Yes," Karen said. "It's mandatory. Just get it over with."

Taylor touched her hair and looked desperately at Shana. Shana reached for her purse. "Can you just give us a minute?" she asked Karen.

Shana opened her white leather Michael Kors satchel and began pulling things out; a round hairbrush full of russet hair, Chanel face powder, various lipsticks.

"It's a mug shot, not a photo shoot for *Town and Country*."

"It will just take a minute," Shana answered, as she took Taylor's hair out of its tangled pony tail and began brushing it. "We'll get you fixed up real good."

Taylor smiled over her shoulder at Shana. She appreciated those who appreciated her beauty. Shana brushed until Taylor's blond hair fell gently and shining on her shoulders. She removed the smudged eyeliner and the blotches of mascara with her emergency moist towlettes, and applied fresh powder to Taylor's splotchy face. Then, she contemplated lip color for several minutes before choosing Petal Pink.

"I just think, considering the situation, we should stay away from the reds," Shana explained, as she handed Taylor a black-and-gold lipstick tube. "Pink screams innocent, dontcha think?"

"Enough already." Karen put her hands on her hips.

"Okay, Jesus fucking Christ, calm the fuck down." Taylor pursed her newly pink lips.

"Now Taylor, I know that you are really upset, but please do not take the Lord's name in vain," Shana admonished, as she gathered up her beauty supplies.

"I'm sorry," said Taylor, hugging Shana. "I really appreciate your help, Shana. I'm also sorry that I called you a hooker."

"*Stripper*. You called me a stripper."

After the mug shot and fingerprinting, (Taylor threatened to bill the police for a new French manicure) it was time to leave. Almost.

"I'm going to need $500 for your bail," said Karen.

"But Spencer will find out if I use our debit or credit cards. I can't exactly pretend I bought a new pair of shoes from the police."

"I don't really know how you can avoid having him find out," said Karen. She looked down at the paperwork in front of her. "You've been arrested and charged with a DUI and reckless driving, you're going to have to appear in court, there will be a fine, community service, and, if we get unlucky, jail time."

"Oh my God," Taylor wailed, threatening to destroy Shana's jailhouse makeover.

"Let's not worry about all that right now. Karen, I'll post bail for Taylor. Big Wayne won't care; he's had his own run-ins with the law." Shana rummaged through her bag for her checkbook.

"Really?" Taylor asked. "You'd do that for me?"

"Of course I would," said Shana. She smiled brightly. "We're on the same team, aren't we?" She reached into her purse, pulled out Red Hot Red, and applied it to her parted lips.

"What the fuck are you doing here?" Taylor said, as she emerged from the station to find Jamal waiting, camera running.

Karen held her hand up, signaling him to stop recording, but Jamal ignored her.

"Please stop filming," Shana pleaded, stepping towards Jamal. Rex, who stood at his side, put a restraining hand on his arm, and Jamal lowered the camera. After all, Big Wayne was bankrolling the production.

Rex smiled, hoping to put Shana at ease. "Great tennis today, ladies. We got the last smash there on film. Blood everywhere! Who knew that tennis could be such a violent sport?"

"They deserved it," Taylor said, looking pleased. Forgetting her aversion to the camera, she reenacted her overhead, her tan arms reaching for the sky. "Don't you want to film that?"

Shana watched, suddenly a bit uneasy about her adventure in reality television. Wayne wouldn't like any of this; the police station, the nip slip, the blood and guts. Not at all.

Taylor, of course, was oblivious to her discomfort and Karen's disapproval. "Now get me out of here," she said, smiling brightly. "I really need a drink."

THE DOMINION CLUB TENNIS LEAGUE ASSOCIATION

TO: ALL LEAGUE CAPTAINS

FROM: THE RULES COMMITTEE

WE HAVE REVIEWED THE CONFLICTING SCORES POSTED BY JONES BELLE VISTA AND RIVER'S EDGE, AS WELL AS LETTERS OF COMPLAINT. THE ASSOCIATION HAS DETERMINED THAT THE MATCH MUST BE REPLAYED WITH DCTLA UMPIRES.

THE ASSOCIATION WOULD LIKE TO INFORM PLAYERS OF THE FOLLOWING:

- PENALTIES CAN BE AWARDED ONLY FOR VIOLATIONS LISTED IN THE DCTLA RULE BOOK.
- RACQUET ABUSE IS FORBIDDEN.
- VERBAL ABUSE IS FORBIDDEN.
- BREASTS ARE TO REMAIN COVERED.
- NO ALCOHOL ON COURT.
- VISITING TEAMS MAY NOT BRING CHILDREN.
- VISITING TEAMS/GUESTS MAY NOT USE GOLF EQUIPMENT OR FACILITIES.
- INAPPROPRIATE PERSONAL RELATIONSHIPS WITH TENNIS STAFF ARE DISCOURAGED.
- VISITING TEAMS/GUESTS MAY NOT ATTRACT DANGEROUS INSECTS TO CLUB PROPERTY.

THE DCTLA CONSIDERS THIS AN OFFICIAL WARNING TO BOTH TEAMS. PLEASE REVIEW THE OFFICIAL DCTLA RULES. A SECOND VIOLATION WILL RESULT IN A TEAM SUSPENSION AND FORFEITURE OF THE ENTIRE SEASON.

Currituck Holmes, President

10

Big Wayne Jones was searching through the triple garage of his four-level stone and stucco McMansion for a bucket and a trout net, when the loud vroom of a motorcycle ripped through the warm Saturday afternoon air.

Wayne looked up to see the bike (Yamaha, he noted with disgust; Wayne was a Harley man) turn into his driveway and glide to a stop. The woman on the back got off, removed her helmet, and shook out her long white-blonde hair. Elena Walinsky stepped into the garage, followed by her husband Jack.

"Hello, husband of Shana," she said, handing Wayne her helmet and stripping off her leather pants, revealing tiny neon green compression shorts underneath. She shrugged off her jacket, baring a tanned, muscled torso, topped by a neon green sports bra. She dumped her leather gear into Wayne's arms as well.

"I am helping Shana with serve; you can talk man stuff with Jack. Private court is out back, no?"

With that she strode out the side door toward the back yard, where the Joneses had a tennis court, pool and Jacuzzi, as well as an outdoor cook center and barbecue pit big enough to roast a mammoth.

Wayne watched her go with an admiring glance. "I hope you won't take this up the wrong way, Jack, but that girl could have had a hell of a career at Big Wayne's."

Jack smiled a tight smile, and Wayne couldn't help but notice his little ferret-like teeth. His trimmed dark brown mustache added to the rodent image, but Wayne shook it off. He didn't like comparing his new friend to a weasel.

"There's no denying my Elena is a fine looking girl," said Jack, taking Elena's gear from Wayne and putting it on the back of the bike. "Never gets cold either. Runs around like that all year long."

"Would you like a beer, Jack? I just got one more little task here for Shana, and then we can talk." Wayne pulled a PBR out of the garage refrigerator and handed it to Jack, then picked up his bucket and net and walked toward the back yard, Jack following.

"I got a little black snake stuck in the Jacuzzi, just got to fish it out. We're havin' that get together tonight, and Shana doesn't think the girls would like it."

Jack shivered. He was not an outdoor guy. "Can't you have your yard man do that?"

Wayne chuckled and slapped Jack on the back, causing him to choke on his beer.

"Big Wayne don't need no yard man. Where we come from, Jack, a man takes pride in taking care of what's his."

"So, you're going to kill the snake?" Jack shuddered.

"Oh, no, Shana won't have that," said Wayne, leaning over the stone-walled Jacuzzi, and dipping his net in. "My lady won't have nothing to do with snakes, but she won't let me kill 'em. Even the poison ones go back into the woods."

Wayne saw Jack turn pale as he pulled the wiggling snake out in his net. "Don't worry; this is just a black snake. Won't do you no harm." Wayne heaved the snake and sent it flying into the woods, as Jack watched in awe.

"Now, what was it you wanted to see me about?"

Bethany and Enrique emerged from the multiplex to find Ian Thorne lounging against the side of Bethany's little red Audi roadster convertible.

"If it isn't my favorite cultural ambassador and her good friend, the Count of Tequila."

"How did you find me?" snarled Bethany.

"Well, let's see, could be mind reading, black magic, or spy satellite technology. Or maybe I just went on that Twitter account you were supposed to shut down."

Enrique knew things were about to go south, because Bethany was tapping her foot and clenching and unclenching her fists. Bethany's temper was legendary, and he had a feeling that this Ian was someone she shouldn't mess with. He had the slick look of a guy who knew more than you did, and always came out on top.

"I'm Enrique Flores," Enrique said, holding out his hand to Ian, who shook it. "I have my own construction business, I'm a citizen – of the United States, not Spain – and I go out with Bethany. End of story."

"I wish that were the end of this story. Can that car fit three people? I caught a cab here and need a ride to your house for a four o'clock campaign meeting."

"If you scrunch in the back," said Bethany. "Not that I want you in my car."

"Oh, I think you do want me in your car. Because your mother has been blabbing this cultural ambassador stuff all over the place, and we have to fix it before it hurts your dad's campaign. And I'm not scrunching in the back, you are. Lover boy is going to drive while he and I have a little talk." Ian looked up at the darkening sky as he held the passenger door open for Bethany. "Keep the top up. Looks like we may get a storm."

Allie tucked her monogrammed blue-and-yellow striped Scout bag under her arm and headed toward the pool. Normally, she avoided the pool on Saturdays, especially when it first opened, but she needed a good swim to relax. The Vixen crew was setting up at Shana's tacky McMansion in The Enclave, so she'd have a camera-free and Shana-free afternoon.

There was no way she or her family would attend the Joneses' barbecue. She'd tried to discourage the rest of the team, but to her annoyance Taylor, Caroline and Karen seemed to have no qualms about being filmed eating vulgar amounts of smoked meat with the Holy Rollers and strip club denizens in the Joneses' social group.

Several weeks had passed since the River's Edge debacle, and things seemed to have calmed down. The team had won matches at Westfield and Dominion Golf without incident. Of course, there was still the River's Edge rematch, but, if she ignored the new club sign, Allie could almost believe things were back to normal. She'd even rescheduled next Monday's meeting with her investigator, Clare Buxton, for the following week. Between Roy's campaign and team tennis, she was exhausted.

Allie walked along the edge of the main pool, a noisy mess of splashing children, nannies and young parents. She passed through a small gate into the adult pool, a lovely, free-form aqua reservoir for those over twenty-one, complete with its own tiki bar and a view of the sixteenth fairway and the city beyond.

On her way in, she was nearly knocked over by Mimi Harrington and Ducky Benson. Mimi and Ducky were golfers, so their relations with Allie were usually cordial, but distant. However, there had been some hard feelings in the golf community ever since Vixen began filming *Queen of the Court*. The golf ladies derided it as tacky, but there was just the tiniest undercurrent of jealousy. Most of them realized that, even in today's reality-crazed world, a show featuring leathery, post-menopausal women stomping around in polos and knee-length skorts would never make prime time.

"Leaving so early?" asked Allie, smiling stiffly.

"Yes," replied Mimi haughtily as she passed by. "It seems to be more your type of crowd today."

Allie frowned as she headed for an umbrella table in the shady far corner. She was still puzzling over Mimi's slight, when she nearly tripped over a pair of excessively bronzed legs extending over the edge of a lounge chair.

"Hey, watch it honey," said a woman in her early thirties with a brassy spiral perm and an all-over tan, made necessary by her hot pink tiny thong bikini. On the lounge next to her sprawled a woman in a lime green bikini who could have been her identical twin, save for the fact that she was African American. Both had enormous breasts that rose straight upward, even though the women were lying on their backs. Pink bikini smoked a cigarette, while lime bikini reached into the large cooler between them, pulled out a PBR, and popped it open.

"Excuse me," said Allie frostily. "But are you guests? Smoking and coolers are prohibited on the Belle Vista pool decks."

"That's *Jones* Belle Vista, honey," said pink bikini. "We're brand new social members. Got a special deal on account of how we work at Big Wayne's. I'm Crystal, and this here's Shontae. Wanna beer?"

"Hey Crystal, you're probably offending her with that forest you got growing down there. Clean up your act, girl," said Shontae, laughing and pointing at Crystal's crotch.

"Huh," said Crystal. As Allie stood open mouthed, she sat up, pulled a razor out of her bedazzled hot pink beach bag, stuck a leg up on the cooler, and proceeded to shave errant hairs from around the tiny pink triangle that posed as her swimsuit bottom.

Allie fled toward the manager's office, dialing her cell phone as she went. "Hello, Clare, this is Allie Beech. We absolutely must meet Monday. The situation has become urgent." As she swept into the clubhouse, Allie saw dark clouds overhead begin to push across the sun.

"You coming to lunch, honey?" Shana shouted from the kitchen.

"In a couple a minutes, darlin'," Wayne hollered back. He often wondered why they'd bothered with the damn intercom; the Joneses weren't the kind of people who had a problem making themselves heard. Except for Destiny. Such a quiet little thing. Destiny was the main reason that Big Wayne was seriously considering Jack Walinsky's investment proposal.

Wayne leaned back in his Easy Boy and contemplated the half dozen antler racks and various game fish on his wall. He wasn't ashamed of how he'd made his money. Still, what had been good enough for him and Shana wasn't good enough for Lil Wayne, and especially Destiny.

Wayne knew that Destiny was surrounded by kids whose daddies were lawyers, doctors and corporate executives. She'd come home crying from her school last week because some little squirt had said, "My Mom says your Daddy is a pimp!" And although it wasn't true, Wayne knew that, in the eyes of the people around here, the truth wasn't any better.

Then there was the country club. He'd taken on fifty-one percent ownership of a money pit. At one hundred grand a piece for the initiation fee, memberships weren't exactly flying off the shelf; there had only been two new members in the past six months. As for the current members, well, now Wayne knew how they all got so rich. They didn't spend shit. Plus, they stole towels from the locker room, toiletries from the bathrooms, salt and pepper shakers, and even silverware. He'd even seen a couple of old golfers load paper bags up with food from the tennis team lunches, like they were shopping at the Safeway.

He'd pushed through social memberships and, at $5,000 ($2500 for Big Wayne's employees) for pool and restaurant privileges, and they were selling briskly. But Jones Belle Vista was still a huge financial drain. The clubhouse was finished, but construction continued on the golf course, indoor tennis center and outdoor gardens. That damned Rex was hounding him for more money too. Wayne sighed. He was one bad month from slipping into the red.

He fingered the slim blue folder with Walinsky's investment proposal. According to these documents, a select group of investors had already made hefty returns from Jack's funds, including F. Brand Lippert, the billionaire. If Wayne sold off the gentlemen's clubs and put that money into Jack's fund, it should make him more than enough to keep up until the Jones Belle Vista construction bills were finally paid, and Rex had finished filming. Plus, Destiny could tell her class that her Dad was Wayne Jones Senior, international financier. He liked the sound of that.

In the Italianate open-plan kitchen, Shana bustled around making a sandwich for Big Wayne. As she pulled some cold cuts out of the Sub-Zero refrigerator, she admitted that life had become so much easier since she'd hired Judy as a live in nanny. She loved her kids, but Lil Wayne could be exhausting.

She had to laugh when she thought back on Judy's "job interview". Shana had already decided, once she'd seen Judy with Lil

Wayne, that she was the right woman for the job. But Karen had nearly gotten hysterical. She insisted that there was a "process," and that Shana could not just pick up a stranger off the street to care for her children. So Shana had agreed to interview Judy, and had let Rex film it.

JUDY SIMPSON JOB INTERVIEW

Shana: *"So Judy, I know you left for California after high school, and Mrs. Winter says you joined up with a religious group. I am a big supporter of faith-based living."*

Judy: *"What my good friend Mrs. Winter meant to say is I joined a cult, the Universal Family of Truth to be precise. I was Father Yaweh Gallileo's thirteenth wife. But before that, I made the sixties scene; concerts, sit-ins, war protests, love-ins, Black Panther rallies. Then, during the Summer of Love, Father spotted me in the Haight, playing tambourine for Jerry Garcia, and I followed the way of Truth for more than ten years."*

Shana: "So you have a wide range of interests, including music! That's good. And truth is such an important family value. What did the Way of Truth involve?"

Judy: *"Mostly having sex with Father, getting high, and chanting. We were also macrobiotic vegetarians, and kept bees. Sold our honey to rich housewives like you. Oh, and we turned over all our worldly goods to Father. Bye-bye trust fund."*

Shana: *"Well, you have a strong background in nutrition, which is great since I'll need you to make lunch sometimes. But I feel badly you were taken advantage of by that Father – did you try to leave?"*

Judy: *"Once. Came back home, but my parents refused to see me. I don't blame them; I'd been what you'd call a problem child."*

Shana: *"That's another point in your favor, you can relate to kids who are high-spirited and have problems with authority. But you did eventually quit your, uh, church, right?"*

Judy: *"Not exactly. One day, Father got some bad acid and jumped off a cliff stark naked; did a beautiful forward somersault, spread his arms wide and … splat. No Father, no Way of Truth."*

Shana: *"My condolences. It's always hard to lose family members, even difficult ones. And then?"*

Judy: *I sold healing crystals for a couple of years in Half Moon Bay, told fortunes on Fourth Street in Berkeley, worked the artichoke harvest, was a groupie for a few bands till I aged out. For a while, I even sold hot pretzels at Sea World in San Diego, but they caught me trying to free the dolphins, and that was pretty much that."*

Shana: *"Awesome – you can teach the kids all about fish AND pretzels. Not many nannies can say that. Now, I got one question Karen really said I gotta ask. So, uh, why do you want this position as our nanny?"*

Judy: *"Well, to be honest I need a place to live and some money; there isn't as much financial security in drugs and promiscuity as one might think. But it's more than that, Mrs. J. I feel a spiritual connection to your family, and believe you and I are meant to help each other on our life journeys."*

Shana: *"Oh, Judy, I feel that too! Please join our family! I mean, let me read this thing Karen wrote out for me: 'Your resume indicates you have the qualifications needed to serve as our live in child-care provider, and pending a reference check, you are hired.'"*

Judy: *"I don't have any references."*

Shana: "Oh, I know that honey. Let's get you moved in."

Shana looked out the window and saw Judy pointing at a cardinal, as Destiny and Lil Wayne watched and listened. In a few minutes, they'd come in and all sit down to a nice, big family lunch. Her heart swelled with love for her children, for her husband, for her new friend, and gratitude for her near-perfect life. Then, Shana burst into tears.

"Know what I've got on here?" said Ian, holding up his iPhone. He'd instructed Enrique to take the long way to the Beech home, which, given Saturday traffic, was pretty much any route.

"The playlist from the Young Republican Douche Bags Ball?" quipped Bethany.

"Nope. The entire life and history of Enrique Flores."

Bethany got serious suddenly. Enrique was the only thing in her life she really cared about. Well, Enrique, and her plan to become famous, and her rather substantial wardrobe. But in that order, which was as close to true love as it came for her. Enrique actually *liked* her. Bethany knew lots of guys who were hot for her, girls who envied her and people in general who were afraid of her. But no one who knew her actually *liked* her. Until now.

"Hey, asshole, I know what you're going to say, like he's from this bad background and has been in some trouble. I just don't care," Bethany snarled.

Ian turned, a sly smile on his handsome face. "Oh, I don't think you have any idea of what I'm going to say, does she Enrique?"

Enrique looked awfully nervous. Bethany wondered for a moment if he'd done something really bad, like armed robbery. Her heart skipped a little, but not in a bad way.

"Look, Ian…,"

"Enrique Flores," recited Ian, reading text on his phone, "president, Jackson High School Debate Society; vice president, Student Council; quarterback of the football team sophomore and junior years; honor society; and, my personal favorite, chairman of the Christmas Toy Drive. Oh, and vice president of Young Democrats, but, hey, nobody's perfect." Ian looked back at Bethany, whose mouth was hanging open.

"If you're not scared yet, Bethany, get ready. 1480 on his SATs."

"You never told me you were smart!" Bethany shouted at Enrique.

"I'm not that smart," pleaded Enrique. "It's not like I got a 1600. I was only a National Merit Semi-Finalist."

"Yeah, well, I don't even know what that is!"

"Turns out your boyfriend, Mr. Badass Bad Boy, dropped out of high school to support his mother and little sister when his Dad skipped town," Ian turned toward Enrique.

"What about his record?" asked Bethany defensively.

"Well, there was leaving 7-11 with a Slurpee and not paying for it," Ian said.

"Oh for fucks sake, I did that at, like, five. But what about... "

"The bad-boy image on Facebook? Pure guesswork, but I think it has something to do with convincing a certain Mr. Hector Ortiz not to mess with him."

Enrique nodded miserably.

"So, you have a completely respectable boyfriend with a great American story. One that would actually help counteract your family's elitist image, and make you more palatable to voters. So what do you say we just tell your parents...? "

"Not my mother. Ian, let me explain this to you," said Bethany, unscrunching herself as much as she could and leaning forward between the seats. "My mother doesn't have an elitist image, she IS elitist. My mom would rather have me date a serial killer with the right pedigree than a saint whose parents had, like, blue collar jobs and accents. You may love this new Enrique 2.0, but one word to my mother, and he's out the door."

The little red car was now climbing the hills of the Belle Vista neighborhood. Although it was still early afternoon, the sky had turned steely gray, and thunder rumbled in the distance. The stately Beech Tudor appeared around the corner, its well-placed crepe myrtles and river beeches bending in the freshening breeze.

"Pull over till we finish this conversation," said Ian. Enrique pulled the car to the curb. "Bethany, Enrique and I are going to step outside and have a little private talk."

The young men exited the car and walked a half block away.

"We better keep walking," said Enrique. "Bethany has like, bat ears."

"First of all, Enrique, I can make part of your little fantasy into the truth. Georgetown University offers a full four-year scholarship to a young person with sterling academic credentials who has been forced to leave school for economic or family reasons. I happen to know a couple of the people who sit on the selection committee, and I've already floated your resume. They are very excited. The scholarship is pretty much yours if you get your paperwork together."

"Really?"

"Really. I talked to your mom and new stepdad. They really want you to go back to school." Ian smiled.

"Yeah," said Enrique. "They're doing okay now. But I still have to make some money."

"That's where the deal comes in," said Ian. "Your girlfriend, or as I like to call her, Gossip Godzilla, needs what we call a handler. Actually, what she needs is a muzzle and tranquilizers, but civil liberties being what they are, I'm going to have to make do with a handler. That's going to be you. Believe me, campaign work pays better than construction."

"No way," said Enrique. "I really, really like Bethany. I know you don't see it, but… "

Ian put up a hand. "Save the love speech, I just ate. All I want is for you to keep her out of trouble until the special election. That's just a few months. You do a good job on this, and who knows? There's always a campaign somewhere, and I always need good staff."

Ian put a hand on Enrique's shoulder. "If you really like her, you'll do this. Do you know what the press will do to her if she, well, acts like herself? The guy with my job on the other side, he's already having a party thinking about it. Think how that mother of hers will treat her if she's the reason Roy loses."

Enrique sighed. Life with Bethany was really complicated. But at least it was never dull. "What do we tell her mother?"

"I hadn't thought that through – these people are a tough one even for me. Keep up the Spanish prince act for Allie for the time being. When the real story leaks out, and it will," Ian smirked again, "you will be such good press for Roy she won't be able to get rid of you."

"And Bethany?"

"You can tell her about Georgetown. But you're strictly an undercover operative on the Beech campaign. You tell her, you go back to being a construction guy whose hobbies are hiding from Hector Ortiz, and letting Bethany buy him fancy shirts."

Enrique looked up at the darkening sky, as if it held the answer. He had a creepy feeling this Ian guy was like the handsome devil character in all those movies – it sounded like he was giving Enrique a good deal, but there would be hell to pay later. Then again, it wasn't every day that he got offered a chance like this, even from the devil. Georgetown!

"Deal," said Enrique, holding out his hand to shake Ian's.

When they got back to the car, Bethany was in the driver's seat.

"Get in, Enrique. Thorne, you take a hike."

It was starting to rain hard, but Ian knew Bethany wasn't kidding. He dashed toward the Beech house as the wind whipped up.

"That was harsh," said Enrique as he got into the passenger seat. Lightning illuminated the sky, and a huge crash sounded.

"You know what's harsh, being lied to by your boyfriend, and finding out all this shit from that sneaky fuck Ian. He doesn't like me."

"He likes you fine. Well, no, that's a lie. He doesn't like you. But I do, which is all that matters."

Enrique turned to Bethany and took her face in his hands.

"Okay. So do you just have a thing for bad Enrique, or can you learn to like good Enrique?"

"Enrique," said Bethany, "You don't have to have a criminal record or bad grades to impress me. I forgive you for everything. Except maybe Debate Society. That's really lame."

As they kissed, a tree came down across the street with a huge crash.

"Holy Shit!" said Enrique as the downed wires popped like fireworks.

"We'd better get out of here and back to my parents' house. Do not tell my mother *anything*," said Bethany, starting the car. "One more thing. Do not lie to me again. Ever."

11

The wind screamed through the neighborhoods surrounding Belle Vista, rampaging like a hoard of vandals with a grudge against the moneyed residents.

The four Beeches, Ian, and Enrique hunkered down in the pitch black wine cellar, where Ian silently wondered how much wine it would take to get through a night with The Beech Bitches. Bethany was already whining, and the AC had only been out for twenty minutes.

"I don't see why we can't go to the Joneses' cookout," she complained. "They live in The Enclave, where everything's new. I'm sure they have power."

"I doubt it. CNN's twitter feed reports two million customers in the mid Atlantic are out," Ian countered. "And I believe we all agreed that this reality show business would be limited to your mother's tennis matches. Which is still a colossal mistake, but Roy is the boss and he has approved it." Ian was glad he couldn't see Roy's face. They both knew who the real boss was.

"When this is over, Roy, you'll need to make a statement about how the power companies aren't responding quickly enough. Maybe we can throw in some stuff about too much government regulation, tree huggers preventing trimming and so on."

"How do you know they're going to screw up?" asked Quint.

"Oh, I always know when someone is going to screw up," said Ian.

Bethany couldn't see shit in the dark, but she could feel Ian staring straight at her.

"Dang, woman, you picked a hell of a night for a barbecue," bellowed Big Wayne from the covered outdoor barbecue pit.

The wind whipped broken branches and debris by Wayne as he stood sentinel over his $7,000 Bull Luxury Q grill island. He had twenty pounds of ribs on the fire and wasn't about to abandon them, although the horizontal rain had soaked him to the skin. Still braving the storm with him was Hound Dog, his twelve-year-old blue tick coon hound. Hound dog was too deaf to mind thunder, and the promise of hot pork scraps more than made up for getting wet.

"What's Wayne shoutin' about?" said Crystal to Shana, who peered nervously out the French doors.

"I don't know, I can't hear him over the wind," said Shana. "But I wish he'd come in, there's so much stick lightning out there."

"Girl, that man ain't gonna leave all that prime pork out in a storm," said Shontae.

"I wish we coulda had better weather and eaten out by the pool," said Shana. "But Judy says this storm is perfect for the séance she's gonna hold later. Wayne wasn't too keen on the idea, but Judy says it's a real fun thing to do at parties, like a social mixer."

Shontae thought that it would take more than an old hippy's party trick to get this odd crowd to mix, but for Shana's sake she kept it to herself. She and Crystal were helping Shana cook burgers and dogs on the indoor cook top, and Shana's little terrier, Skippy, and two of the family's four cats circled Shontae hopefully, like small, furry sharks.

"Shana, you got a regular zoo in this house," she said.

Shana smiled. "And that's not counting Hound Dog, Old Tom Cat, Destiny's new kitty and Lil Wayne's smelly gerbils. Now Judy's gonna be starting an apiary way out back. That's a beehive, so she can make honey. When she first asked, I thought she wanted to keep monkeys, and I still said okay."

Shontae and Crystal laughed. Shana's love for all creatures was a long-standing joke. She'd fed the feral cats outside Big Wayne's and made the exterminator use Have-a-Heart traps for mice.

"Did Wayne tell you that when we bought Belle Vista, the board had plans to poison all the cats on the grounds?"

Shontae gasped. She loved cats so much she'd developed a Catwoman act for Big Wayne's.

"Don't need to tell you I had Wayne put a stop to that."

As the burgers and dogs cooked, Shana bustled around the island setting up bowls of baked beans, potato salad and slaw. She and Wayne had made everything themselves, from the ribs with Wayne's special rub and sauce, to Shana's fried chicken, deviled eggs and white cake with sprinkles.

But they hadn't gotten the turnout Shana had hoped for. A scant handful of Belle Vista members mingled uneasily with a dozen of Big Wayne's work friends, including Mountain, a tattooed bouncer who, like Sting, felt that one name was sufficient. As usual, their neighbors had ignored the invitation.

"I feel bad for Shana," Byron commented to Jamal, who was trying to get footage of Mountain shoveling deviled eggs into his mouth without attracting the big man's notice. Jamal was just guessing, but he figured Mountain would not like the idea of being mocked by a skinny black guy with a degree in film and theater from NYU.

"First of all, she's driving herself crazy trying to dress like that Allie," Byron continued, nodding toward Shana, whose Ralph Lauren white linen shorts and bright green LaCoste polo were way too tight and sexy to ever pass Belle Vista muster, especially with red platform sandals. "No matter what she does, those bitches will still snub her."

"Well, at least those three are here," said Jamal, lowering the camera and pointing toward Karen, Caroline and Taylor. Karen grabbed Taylor's red Solo cup, poured its contents down the sink, filled it with club soda and handed it back to Taylor, who promptly threw it at her. Karen gasped and fled the room, ignored by Shontae and Crystal, who'd seen worse, and by Caroline, who was more concerned about the rapid disappearance of the deviled eggs.

"Shit, I should have got that on film," said Jamal.

"I feel bad for Skinny Bitch too," said Byron, pouring himself a glass of white wine. Technically, he wasn't supposed to drink on the job, but thunderstorms made him nervous.

"I get Shana, but why a pity party for Taylor? She's mean as shit, plus she just got a DUI and she's still pounding down the Chardonnay."

Byron sighed. "I think I might know why she drinks so much. She told me during our last makeup session that her husband doesn't find her attractive."

"Really? Cause she's crazy, but she's smokin' hot."

"Well, it's not going to make any difference, because her husband made a pass at me after Tuesday's shoot."

"Oh man," said Jamal, slapping his leg. "Dr. Perfect's on the downlow! Wait till Rex finds out."

Byron turned to Jamal and fixed him with a thousand yard stare. "Don't you dare say a word. Rex would want him outed on camera with her there, just to get the reaction."

Jamal shook his head. "Byron, we're in reality television, this is the kind of stuff we do. I filmed a lady dying for this show. I'm not sure we can sink any lower."

"Well, J-man, maybe it's time we climbed out of the slime. I am trying to convince Dr. Perfect, whose name is Spencer, by the way, that honesty is the best policy. Maybe I can make him see reason before Taylor completely morphs into Amy Winehouse." Byron laughed a little. "You know, he thinks if he 'becomes gay', he's committing to a life of wearing feather boas and dancing around to 'Born this Way'. So I showed him a picture of Patrick." Patrick O'Malley, Byron's husband, was a New York City detective who had played football at Michigan. He was not the kind of guy you pictured in a feather boa.

Jamal sighed. "Rex is a man of few talents, B-dog, but one of them is ferreting out secrets. If he finds out we've held out on him, he'll get his on camera reaction, *and* we'll be out of a job."

"I'm banking on the fact that there are plenty other of secrets floating around Belle Vista to keep Rex busy," said Byron. "Maybe we can dredge up something on that hideous Beech woman or her evil mother."

Jamal snorted. "Don't count on them getting drunk and spilling their guts to you. When people like that have secrets, they take them to their graves."

As Jamal mouthed the word "graves", a deafening clap of thunder sounded, followed by the boom of the local transformer exploding, plunging The Enclave into darkness. Shontae and Crystal barely had time to shriek before the lights went back on, the AC resumed whirring, and Brad Paisley reprised "Water" on the sound system. Outside, the neighborhood remained dark.

Big Wayne entered the kitchen soaking wet, a huge tray of ribs covered in foil in his hands.

"There's some say a gas-powered generator that can run this whole pile of bricks is a big waste of money. You folks can be thankful Big Wayne ain't one of 'em."

"I'm gonna call Allie so they can all come if their power's out," said Shana. "And they should bring Lavinia. It'll be too hot in her apartment."

Bishop Charnisse Jones had been spooning macaroni salad onto her plate, but now she stopped and turned to Shana.

"That woman ain't coming, Shana. She don't like you," Charnisse said bluntly, but in a kind tone.

All conversation in the room stopped. Jamal aimed his camera at Shana, and thanked God silently that Big Wayne and Mountain had retreated to the garage to fetch more cold beer.

"Oh, Charnisse. Now that's not Christian. Allie means well," said Shana.

"No, she don't," said Charnisse. "Being Christian means you got to turn the other cheek, but I know my Bible, and there's no scripture that says you got to chase someone around yelling 'Please slap me.'" Charnisse patted Shana on the arm and went back to her macaroni salad.

"Well go on everybody, make yourself some plates," said Shana with a forced smile. "I'm gonna go downstairs and tell the kids the food is ready."

"I'll take care of it, Mrs. J," said Judy, who'd come upstairs to get more chips for the kids. She looked at Shana's false smile and teary eyes with concern. "Or maybe you'd like to come with me?" She took hold of Shana's arm and steered her toward the stairs, bag of chips in the other hand.

"Now tell Judy what's wrong," she whispered.

Bethany put her hands on her hips and faced Allie, who stood in an identical pose. By candlelight, the similarity was eerie.

"Look, Maggie Walinsky texted me. The Joneses have some personal power grid or something, and they have lights, air conditioning, TV and food. I am totally going."

"I forbid it, do you hear? You will be buying your clothes at Target for the next decade if you go anywhere near that woman's house."

Enrique looked over at Ian, who shook his head no. Interfering in a Mothra/Godzilla battle was not a good idea. What if Bethany dumped his brand new handler?

"You're just going to have to go with her if she bolts," whispered Ian to Enrique, although he could have shouted and neither Allie nor Bethany would have paid the least bit of attention. Quint and Roy had fled to the game room, where they were playing ping pong by flashlight, mostly smashing the ball at each other and laughing uproariously. Ian sighed. He couldn't stand Allie, but he was beginning to think that she was the Beech with the killer instinct to win a campaign.

Bethany's phone vibrated, interrupting the argument.

"Oh, hello Grandmama. Of course I will come get you. Oh no, the storm's nearly over, I'm sure driving will be fine."

Bethany turned back to Allie with satisfaction. "That was YOUR mother. She is absolutely dying of heat and wants me to take her to the Joneses. Shana couldn't reach you – so rude, not to even answer your phone – so she called Grandmama."

"Mother didn't have air conditioning for most of her *life*. We had to beg her to install it. She wears a sweater when it's below seventy-five," snarled Allie as Bethany stormed out, followed by Enrique, who shrugged his shoulders and waved an apologetic goodbye.

Lavinia smoothed down her plaid Bermuda shorts and tucked a sweater over her arm. She was certain the Joneses' garish manse would be freezing. Why did the nouveau riche seem to think it necessary to keep their vast homes at arctic temperatures?

Lavinia, like most thin WASP women of her class and era, was impervious to weather. Wellies, a broad brimmed-sun hat, a trusty cardigan and a good wax coat were all they needed to survive from Belize to the Bering Sea.

But she had to come up with some excuse to get the family to the Joneses. That wretched Judy Simpson, calling up and demanding they drive through an obstacle course of tree limbs and flooding just to make that Jones woman happy. As it was, she was only delivering part of the goods, herself and Bethany. But Judy would have to be reasonable.

Oh, why hadn't she just run over the woman when she'd had her chance? Instead, she'd done the decent thing and tried to help her. As a result, Judy had ended up meeting that vulgar Jones woman and become, of all ridiculous things, her nanny.

Then, Judy had "bumped into" Lavinia outside Dukes and Duchesses Salon, where Lavinia had had a standing appointment the second Tuesday of each month at 11:15 a.m. for thirty-five years. She had insisted they go for tea and "a little talk". Lavinia shuddered.

Lavinia had been in the midst of giving Judy the brush off when Allie and her private detective (a woman, and not a very attractive one) had marched up. Lavinia's regimented schedule made her all too easy to track.

"Mother, doesn't your hair look lovely," Allie had exclaimed.

Lavinia's helmet of hair had progressed from brunette to gray, but otherwise looked just as it did in the oil portrait of her at age five that hung over her fireplace. Allie had never been good at flattery.

"You have met my old friend, Miss Simpson. We're headed to tea." Suddenly, tea with Judy had seemed the lesser of two evils.

"But mother, I've brought Clare all this way. We'd hoped to go to your townhouse and see if we could find that, uh, item." Allie had obviously not wanted to say anything in front of Judy who, after all, worked for Shana Jones.

"I cannot believe my own daughter doubts my word or my faculties. I'm telling you, I heard from Pippa Edgemoor not more than four years ago. A postcard from Borneo. I'd testify to it in court."

"I thought you said Barcelona. And Mother, this is private family business," Allie had said, looking nervously at Judy.

"Then perhaps you should not conduct it on a public street."

Judy had smiled an angelic smile Lavinia remembered well from her youth. It was the same smile Judy had employed whenever she got caught looking at another girl's paper in class, or sneaking out of the dorm at night.

"Pippa Edgemoor? Funny you should mention her. Ran into her in Half Moon Bay a few years ago. I was working in a shop selling healing crystals, and who should pop in but old Pippa. She was with this guy who couldn't have been more than forty, said they were living on a sailboat."

"Excuse me," Clare had interrupted. "How many years ago?"

"Oh, I don't know. Could be three. Could be five. Could even be *seven*. Is it important? " Judy had asked innocently.

To Lavinia the traffic noise had suddenly become deafening, and the humid air had seemed to suck her breath away; but she had kept her composure.

"If you don't mind, Allison, we have a reservation and you are keeping us," she'd lied. Then, as much as it had pained her, she'd linked her arm through Judy's and headed down St. Asaph Street.

"Women like Pippa Edgemoor don't buy healing crystals," Allie had called angrily after them.

Judy had turned and given Allie her sweetest smile. "You're right about that. She was looking for a sex shop."

Lavinia was jolted back to the present by the brass pineapple knocker on her front door announcing Bethany's arrival. The sound of brass on good sturdy oak; something one could count on, she reflected as she gathered up her things. Before Judy's arrival and Allie's ridiculous investigation, her life had seemed as stable and solid as her door. Now Lavinia felt as if it were constructed of the cheapest veneer, ready to peel away and reveal the shoddy material underneath.

12

Shana sniffed into a tissue as Judy patted her on the shoulder. They'd fled to Shana's sunshine-yellow craft room on the second floor, ostensibly to gather materials for Judy's séance. Luckily, the Vixen crew was occupied in Shana's exercise studio, where Shontae was teaching Caroline the fitness benefits of exotic dancing.

Judy and Shana sat facing each other on a pair of pink-and-yellow floral chintz poufs, near a bay window adorned with matching balloon shades.

With a shuddering sigh, Shana burst into a renewed bout of tears.

"What's really wrong Shana? It can't just be Allie blowing off your party."

"It's just that, it's just that … oh, Judy, I know you think I'm a silly woman puttin' such store in this TV show, and having these ladies as friends."

"Honey, I spent over a decade thinking an old horny acid head was God, so I'm not really into judging."

"See that picture?" Shana stood up, walked to a wall filled with wooden-framed family photos, and touched an old snapshot of a skinny redheaded girl, standing in the battered dirt yard of a ramshackle white and mint-green single-wide trailer.

"We were so poor Judy. Me and Billy, that's my older brother, we had different daddies, but neither of them ever came around. We had this old TV that barely worked. I learned to read using my Mama's movie magazines. I'd look at pictures of stars and think, someday, I'll have a big house and pretty clothes, and be on TV."

Judy remained silent.

"And look." Shana pointed at a picture of herself in tennis whites, posed in front of the Jones Belle Vista sign with her family and the Vixen crew.

"I just wanted it all to be real. Then maybe I could finally be completely… "

"Happy," finished Judy. Shana nodded, sitting back down on her pouf.

"Shana, I don't know if you've noticed, but the women that grew up with all this stuff are not exactly an advertisement for buying happiness."

"Maybe that's why my journey brought me here," said Shana thoughtfully. "You know, if it's my mission to help these ladies in some way?"

Judy laughed. "A *mission*? To save the Bitches of Belle Vista? "

Shana frowned, reaching over to her craft table for up a half-finished scrapbook with pictures of the team set on perky tennis-themed paper, framed in Jones Belle Vista teal ribbon. She sat with the book open on her lap, tracing the outline of the team photo with her finger.

"Maybe they're not happy because they don't believe in themselves or love themselves."

"That's because they aren't very loveable."

"No!" said Shana, jumping up so quickly she dropped the album, sending loose pictures skittering across the floor like playing cards. Ignoring the mess, she began to pace around the little room.

"I know you're not a Christian, Judy, but I believe God loves us all. I part with some folks at church who think God don't love gay people or Muslims or whoever. I've been so blessed, I think if I share a little of that with the girls, well, it could make a difference."

She turned her back to the room, crossing her arms protectively over her chest, and stared out the picture window at the darkened streets below.

Judy struggled awkwardly off her pouf, and studied Shana's picture wall. Why would someone who chronicled every detail of her miserable trailer park childhood, including the funeral of her pet grasshopper, take absolutely no pictures between her junior prom and her wedding? Those missing years were a red flag. Shana was hiding something, not just from the world in general, but also from herself.

"So you say you're blessed, yet you're trying to fill some hole in your life with country club tennis?"

"*And* reality television," replied Shana, defensively. "Ohhh, I mean I don't have a hole in my life. I just need it to be perfect. I mean, *more* perfect, because, of course, it already is."

An uncomfortable silence settled on the room. No doubt about it, Judy thought, Shana was not in harmony with the universe. There could be no going forward until she went back into her past, and restored her karmic balance, much as Judy herself was doing (Judy was mostly restoring her bank balance, but whatever).

"Maybe the spirits will give you some guidance," said Judy, as Shana continued to gaze into the night. "Let me go get my crystals, and you gather up the candles. It's séance time."

Karen wiped angrily at her soaked polo shirt with a bright yellow hand towel embroidered with an intertwined gold S and W. What on earth had persuaded her to give Taylor and Caroline a ride to the barbecue?

Not wanting to go alone, she admitted. Greg had refused to come, claiming he had work to catch up on, but the truth was, an argument had been smoldering between them ever since the day of Taylor's arrest.

She'd arrived home from the police station at 6:15 to find an angry Greg on his third gin and tonic. After getting her text that morning (*Meet me at 4 to make a baby!*) he had left work early, giving his Dad some bogus excuse about a dental appointment. He couldn't believe that his ultra-organized, baby-focused wife had *forgotten* they were supposed to procreate. She could barely believe it herself.

Was there anything Taylor Thomas couldn't screw up? But as much as she wanted to believe otherwise, Karen knew that neither Taylor Thomas, nor Greg's loathsome, overbearing mother was the problem. She leaned her head against the cool glass of the mirror over the sink. She would *not* cry.

"Karen?" Karen barely recognized Taylor's voice outside the door. It sounded strange, almost apologetic.

"Karen, I'm sorry. Honest. It's just Spencer and I had a fight right before I left, and the storm freaked me out; at least it was club soda – no stains. Open the door, please, Karen, I really need you. Practically everyone else has given up on me."

"Really?" said Karen drily. "I can't imagine why." Reluctantly, she opened the powder room door a crack.

"I brought you a present." Taylor stood outside, holding a bright purple stretch top with a plunging neckline by the shoulders. She wiggled it seductively.

"Shana gave me this for you to wear till yours dries. She says it will bring out the violet in your eyes. Like anyone's going to look up at them."

The two women burst into laughter.

By the time Taylor and Karen (shoulders hunched in a failed effort to hide her purple-framed cleavage) entered Shana's capacious formal dining room, séance preparations were in full swing.

"Holy shit Shana, what did you do, rob a Yankee Candle outlet?"

"Oh, Taylor, you know me too well. Granny and I practically bought out the Yankee Candle in Williamsburg on Wednesday," said Shana, who was arranging more than a dozen candles – the conflicting fragrances nearly knocked Karen out of the room – on an enormous white-draped round table. "Actually, I got way more than this, but Judy says only to use white, cream and purple, cause that's what the spirits like."

Shana's gloom had vanished as soon as preparations for the séance got underway.

In the far corner, Rex and Jamal argued in hushed voices over how best to film Shana's foray into the occult.

"I'm the head cameraman, and I'm telling you that shaky, fakey *Ghost Hunters* home video-style shit sucks," Jamal said sulkily. "Those guys are *fucking plumbers*."

"So *that* must explain the high ratings," Rex said sourly. "I'm going to get some more deviled eggs, and the video camera, while you try to remember what the verb *direct* means."

"Negativity can drive good spirits away and attract nasty ones," warned Judy, who was positioning crystals at varying points around the table. "We'll pass these around; get everyone to charge them with positive energy."

"I'm afraid you'll have to count me out Shana," said Karen touching the cross hanging from her neck.

"Oh come on, Karen," said Taylor.

But Judy held up her hand. "We don't want non-believers. Not to mention your aura is pulsing from muddy red to blue. That signifies anger combined with fear of the future; spirits hate a Debbie Downer."

"You *are* always kind of pissed off," Taylor said, impressed.

"Never mind, honey," said Shana, steering Karen back toward the kitchen. "There's a whole group gonna hang downstairs with the kids. Reverend Charnisse thinks Judy's the devil, Wayne and Mountain want to watch a NASCAR race, and Crystal's scared of the dark."

Karen was contemplating whether watching NASCAR with a bunch of sugared-up kids, a Pentecostal preacher and a couple of refugees from a strip joint qualified as martyring herself for her faith, when she walked smack into Sean Flannery.

"Whoa, pretty lady; you almost lost me my fried chicken. *Karen*?" Sean's eyes went straight to her cleavage.

Karen followed his gaze, pointed at her chest and sputtered, "This belongs to Shana; mine is all wet. I mean, this *shirt* is Shana's." She felt a red flush spreading up her neck. Sean just stood there smiling. If possible, he looked more handsome in shorts and a Nationals t-shirt than in his uniform. "I mean, why are *you* here?"

"Whatever happened to "Glad to see you, Sean?" He laughed. "Got to know Shana when she brought over some of this ace fried chicken to Dan Butts and my team of marshals after his wife died. All his "friends" pretended they didn't know him, but she let him cry on her shoulder. Hey, want to grab a plate and go into the sunroom and talk? I can update you on all the courthouse gossip."

From the dining room Judy watched the muddy red in Karen's aura turn bright, clear pink, and the blue shift to green. "Hmmm, romance and change," she mused. "Either that, or she's channeling Lilly Pulitzer."

13

The crowd gathered silently in the dining room, which was pitch black except for candlelight casting flickering shadows on the white tablecloth. A sharp knock sounded on the Joneses' massive double doors, and Shontae and Caroline squealed.

"Babies," scoffed Taylor, who'd fortified herself for any spiritual encounters with a substantial amount of Big Wayne's Southern Comfort.

"Relax, that'll be Lavinia and Bethany, not Marley's ghost," said Judy. "Although I don't know why that's less scary."

A few minutes later, nine participants were seated around the table, passing crystals from hand to hand. It was, even by Judy's sixties California standards, a weird group. Shontae and Caroline giggled over a piece of white cake, while Taylor swayed with her eyes closed, humming an off key version of "Me and Bobby McGee".

Shana sat clasping a crystal devoutly, eyes closed, next to Lavinia, who stared straight at Judy as if fervently hoping looks could kill. (Judy was not worried. She had plans for Vinnie.) As for her granddaughter, well, Bethany reminded Judy a little of herself back in the day, using the old under-the-table grope to keep that handsome boyfriend of hers under control.

Bethany fumbled in her lawn-green patent Kate Spade clutch for a frosted lipstick – so great on camera in the dark – as Enrique whispered to her.

"Don't you think being on camera doing this black magic shit is a bad idea?"

"Honestly, Enrique, it's a party game. What did Thorne do on that little walk, remove your balls? Anyway, my Dad will probably already be elected by the time this show is on TV."

"Well, the press could find out, and he'll never get *reelected* if they think his daughter is a witch."

"Careful, or I'll put a spell on you," she said, laughing as she slid her hand up his leg under the table. Enrique sighed. This handler thing was not going to be easy.

Jamal stood against the far wall by Shana's ornate French provincial china cabinet, obediently wielding a tiny video camera (Judy had sided with Rex on that, less disruptive), while Byron sat next to Shana. Rex had been declared a cynic, and banished.

And then, there was visiting Granny Rose, a compulsive knitter who insisted on having an empty chair next to her and kept mumbling to herself.

Next to Granny, the translucent Captain Bradley, a regular "visitor" visible only to her, leaned toward her and asked, "Why the smelly candles?"

"That hippie lady says spirits like 'em," replied Granny. She and the captain laughed.

"Let us begin," intoned Judy solemnly. "Everyone close their eyes, join hands and take deep, slow, even breaths.

Judy was an expert at conducting séances for cash, despite the fact she had never once conjured a departed one from the great beyond. Like many mediums before her, she'd become adept at figuring out what her living clients wanted to hear and giving them answers on behalf of those who'd passed on. She figured she was doing both parties a favor.

Her goals tonight were clear: give Shana some spiritual guidance, and scare Lavinia into submission. She inhaled deeply, coughing slightly as she got a snootful of Yankee Candle's popular Bahama Breeze, and gave her standard invocation.

"Our beloved spirits, we ask you to commune with us and move among us. Chant with me, please."

"Our beloved spirits, we ask you to commune with us and move among us," the group repeated in the weird zombie voices people used at these things.

A gust of wind blew through the windows, which Judy had opened earlier, blowing out several candles. The participants gasped, and Judy smiled. Stormy weather was much more reliable than the restless dead when it came to producing special effects.

"They are among us," Judy intoned gravely.

"Who's here?" whispered Granny to the captain.

"Oh, she's just fakin'," he replied.

"Is anyone feeling a message from the beyond?" asked Judy.

"I feel Janis Joplin," said Taylor, swaying to a beat only she could hear.

Judy cut her off.

"Is anyone feeling a message that did *not* come in a bottle? Wait – in my mind's eye I see a bird flying through a gap between blue mountains."

"That must be Granny's mama, Great-Grandma Byrd," said Shana in an awed voice, as Judy silently thanked her for labeling all those family photos.

"Is not," mumbled Granny.

"Yes, yes it is," said Judy, cocking her head as if listening. "She wants Shana to find what she's lost."

The candles flickered again and Shana gasped.

"If it's Mama's locket, I fed it to the pigs after she beat me with a wooden spoon," Granny piped up.

"What *Shana* has lost," Judy said, giving Granny the fisheye. She could feel the tension in the room; the belief. Shana seemed entranced.

"What does Great-Grandma say I should do?" she asked, as Jamal zoomed the video camera in on her mesmerized face.

"Oh, of all the bunkem," muttered Lavinia.

Judy had planned on leaving Lavinia until later, but decided she needed to be taken down a peg. The anticipation would keep Shana hooked. "Wait, other spirits have joined us," she said. (Looking at Granny, the captain shook his head no.) She deepened her voice and chanted; "Audacter calumniare semper aliquid haeret."

Lavinia inhaled sharply. The Merrywood School motto. What was Judy playing at? Surely she wouldn't …

"What'd she say?" Bethany whispered to Enrique.

"That's Latin," he whispered back.

"And you're Latino, so it's like your second language. Uh,ohhhh…uhhhh."

Enrique looked over at Bethany nervously. Her hand had turned clammy, she was shaking, and she didn't look so good. In the candle-light, her face shone deathly white, and her eyes were closed.

"Let's get out of here," he said, trying to stand, but Bethany had his hand in an iron death grip. Her eyes flew open, and she looked him up and down with a stranger's gaze.

"Hel*lo* handsome," she said, her voice weirdly deep, throaty and somehow … older. She tickled his palm in a way Enrique did not like at all. Then her head snapped sharply to the right, and she eyed Lavinia with overt hostility.

"You're right to worry, Vinnie. But it isn't old Easy Virtue Simpson you should worry about," said Bethany, her voice harsh and gravelly, like a pack-a-day smoker. "You should worry about me. I *will* find a way to come back."

"Is *she* fakin?" Granny whispered to the Captain.

"Nope," said the captain. "And this new lady scares me." With that, he faded away.

Lavinia stared at Bethany with horror. "Bethany, what on earth…"

A horrible, unearthly laugh erupted from Bethany, who threw her head back as her eyes rolled back in her head, then closed. Then she abruptly straightened up, opened her eyes, batted her lashes and smiled as if nothing had happened.

"This is so much fun," she stage-whispered toward the camera, flipping her hair, her voice back in its natural register. But her smile faltered as she took in the blanched, wide-eyed faces around the table. "What?"

"Oh my God," said Shontae. "This is freakin' me out."

"No shit," agreed Taylor, getting up and turning on the lights. "I don't know about the rest of you, but I need a drink!"

14

Sage watched the YouTube video of a poetry reading by Sarah Lawrence Poet in Residence, Althea Bainbridge, for the third straight time. Sage studied the tall, soft-spoken woman closely. With short red hair, big green eyes and a long white neck draped with a deep purple pashmina, she looked younger than her thirty-seven years. She read her poem "The Empty Space" to a packed crowd.

Sage knew the poem by heart. It was about giving up a baby for adoption. Althea was open about her story in interviews. She'd become pregnant as an undergraduate at Colton College in West Virginia, after an affair with a married literature professor. Althea had only held the child in her arms briefly before handing it over to a waiting nurse in a Morgantown hospital.

The poem "The Empty Space" had touched Sage deeply. She wondered if her birth mother ever thought about her, then wondered if Althea Bainbridge *was* her birth mother. Her heart began to race. It made sense. They both had red hair, and Sage was born in West Virginia in May of 1995. Then there was the poetry connection. Sage called Jasper, and they met on the Promenade in Brooklyn Heights, walking side-by-side on a bright, breezy afternoon. When she shared her suspicions, he stroked his chin silently and nodded.

"I think we're talking road trip," said Jasper, and Sage gave her friend a big hug.

That Friday afternoon, they made the thirty minute train ride from Grand Central Station to Bronxville Station. Jasper was thinking of applying to Sarah Lawrence, so he was a font of information about the legendary liberal arts school.

"The student body is seventy-one percent female and only twenty-nine percent male. That's a great ratio for a guy like me." Jasper smiled sheepishly. "Plus, it's a really good college," he added as an afterthought, as the train pulled into Bronxville station with a lurch and a hiss.

The campus was beautiful, leafy and quiet. Jasper had mapped the route to the Alice Walker Building on his iPhone, which as Siri informed them, was named for distinguished author Alice Walker, Class of 1965.

Professor Bainbridge's office was on the third floor, and she had office hours today from 4 to 6 p.m. Her door was closed. It was 4:45, so Sage figured she was meeting with a student. She and Jasper sat on a bench outside the door. Sage took a deep breath.

"I'm really nervous," she whispered.

"It's exciting. What if you are related to a famous poetess? Pretty cool."

They sat for several minutes in silence, then heard a chair push back. The door opened, and there was Althea Bainbridge, wrapped in a southwestern-looking poncho. Her clear green eyes reminded Sage of the sea glass she'd collected during summers on the coast of Maine. She nodded in their general direction but remained focused on her student, who rambled on as she tried to usher him out.

"I'm just really struggling with the waterfall metaphor. It's beautiful, right? But then it can also be destructive, right? It gives and it takes. Yin and Yang," said the bearded multi-pierced student who stood blocking the doorway.

"What a tool," Jasper whispered to Sage. She kicked him.

Professor Bainbridge placed a hand on the student's back and propelled him into the hallway.

"I look forward to reading it."

Althea looked directly at Sage, who felt her anxiety in her stomach as she walked through the open door into the dark office. Althea closed the door behind her and settled herself behind her oak desk. Two little boys in swim trunks smiled out at Sage from a hand-crafted, macaroni-covered picture frame.

"Are those your sons?" Sage asked as sat in the chair facing the desk. It was still warm from the waterfall guy.

"Yes, Dylan and Thomas." Althea beamed. "Quite a handful." She looked at Sage. "Are you a student here? I don't recognize you. I doubt I would forget such beautiful hair, being a redhead myself."

Sage took another deep breath. "No, I'm still in high school."

"Are you looking at Sarah Lawrence?" Althea seemed amused.

"No, I live in Brooklyn. I want to go a bit farther from home." Sage clenched her right fist. "I came to ask you a question. You'll probably think I'm crazy."

Althea arched one eyebrow.

"I love your poem 'The Empty Space'. I feel a real connection to it. I was born in West Virginia in 1995 and given up for adoption. I love my mothers, but I have been feeling that empty space in my heart."

Sage looked up at Althea, who smiled back warmly at her.

"It's hard, isn't it? Not knowing." Althea ran her fingers through her short red hair. "Have you been able to locate your adoption papers?"

"They were destroyed in a fire," Sage answered. She decided she was just going to say it. "Do you think I might be your biological daughter?"

Althea looked confused for a moment; then she regained her composure, leaned forward and smiled sympathetically at Sage.

"The baby that I gave up for adoption was a boy." Althea spread her fingers out on the desk in front of her. She wore lots of silver rings. Sage heard a whooshing in her ears, like a waterfall.

STATE OF WEST VIRGINIA
OFFICE OF ADOPTION RECORDS
June 23, 2013

Dear Mrs. Jones;

We received your letter regarding adoption records from May, 1995.

By law (WV Code §48 4A 1 et seq.), all proceedings and documents relating to an adoption that took place in West Virginia, or for a birth that occurred in West Virginia are "closed", or sealed by the court that ordered the adoption. Without a court order, we may not unseal these records or provide you with any information regarding a particular adoption.

We also regret to inform you that a 1999 fire destroyed many of the original birth records from the time period you cited. In addition, the lawyer named in your letter, Mr. Jack Shirley, was under investigation at the time of his death for suspected fraud and falsification of adoption records.

West Virginia has a voluntary mutual consent adoption registry, which has a procedure in place to facilitate communication between birth parents and their biological children when both parties have submitted information to the system. You may access this system at www.adoptionrecords.wv.gov. Many birth parents and children have successfully utilized this service.

We wish you all the best in your efforts.

Sincerely,
Jo Feldman
Assistant to the Director
Office of Adoption Records

Shana dreamed she was walking on a college campus, and autumn leaves were falling all around her. She was wearing a plaid skirt and a tight fitting green sweater. Her hair was pulled back into a pony tail and fastened with a tortoise shell clip. She was looking for something; walking in and out of the white-trimmed brick buildings, opening and closing doors. But what was she looking for? Suddenly, the wind blew through the campus, forcefully slamming every door shut. The noise startled Shana, who sat up with a gasp and opened her eyes. There was Lil Wayne, peering into her room, an impish smile on his face.

"Time to get up, Mama!" He giggled before slamming the door and running off down the hall.

Shana brushed Destiny's thin brown hair slowly. She didn't want to hurt her. She brushed it off of her pale face and started a tight French braid. A stray piece of hair wrapped itself around Shana's diamond and emerald engagement ring. She untwisted it and continued to work on her daughter's hair. The ring had been missing for almost a week when she found it in Destiny's "Pretty, Pretty Princess" game.

Shana had wondered at first if the ring could be the "something lost" Judy had hinted at in the séance, but in her heart she knew it wasn't. Shana was missing a living breathing human being, flesh and blood; someone who was going to be much harder to find than the lost ring.

Shana finished braiding Destiny's hair, and hurried her out the door to the Suburban so they wouldn't be late for Miss Sally's Ballet School. Shana had always thought that her daughter would do pageants. When she was a child, Shana had desperately wanted to compete in the Little Miss Spunky Supreme Pageant at the Days Inn in town, but her mother couldn't afford the entrance fee or the fancy costumes. Since joining Belle Vista, Shana had sensed that child pageants would be frowned upon by Allie and others in her new circle of would-be friends, so ballet it was.

Miss Sally's studio was at the top of a long creaky staircase, in an Old Town townhouse discreetly tucked into a mews near Duke Street. The door to the studio was closed, and several mothers and daughters waited on the landing, chatting and laughing. Shana and Destiny had been running late, so Destiny was clutching her breakfast, a bagel with peanut butter, in her right hand as she mounted the stairs. Shana trailed behind with Destiny's dance bag, a pink sack with a ballerina embroidered on it. Seeing the crowd at the top of the stairs, Shana was suddenly grateful for Judy, who had taken Lil Wayne to the pool. This particular group of mothers did not appreciate his energy.

As Shana and Destiny approached the landing, Tracy Logan came into view. She was a tan, sinewy woman who ran ultra marathons, and Botox, fillers and chemical peels did battle with the effects of sun and wind on her face. She wore a tight-fitting orange tank top, matching nylon shorts and lemon-yellow Nike running shoes. She stepped between Destiny and her daughter, Meredith, a chunky, cheerful girl with brown braids.

"*What* is Destiny eating?" she asked Shana tensely, pushing Meredith backwards with her free hand.

"Just a peanut butter bagel."

"Meredith is deathly allergic to peanuts. How dare you bring that in here?" She shot an incriminating look at Destiny, who looked down at her breakfast guiltily. Ever since Lou's death, "allergic" had been a bad word around the Jones household.

"I'm sorry. We didn't know," Shana apologized.

"Get it out of here, before you kill someone." Tracy pushed Meredith back against the wall as the other mothers stared. One of them shook her head.

Shana took the bagel from Destiny. "I'm sorry," she muttered again.

"Destiny will have to wash her hands with warm soap and water for three minutes. I can't have her spreading that stuff all over the barre," Tracy declared, pointing to the restroom door. "Now, Destiny, before you cause a reaction. Wash your face, too."

Shana watched helplessly as Destiny disappeared into the restroom, her little shoulders slumped, her French braid swinging slightly. The door to the studio opened and Miss Sally's lined, smiling face appeared. "Bonjour," she said with flourish. Tracy put her hand on Meredith's back and guided her through the door.

"We had a peanut violation just now," she said, looking angrily over her shoulder at Shana and the bagel. Shana blew the air out of her lungs and let her shoulders sag as she waited for Destiny to finish scrubbing her little hands. She looked down at the peanut butter-smeared offending item in her hand, feeling like she was holding a giant turd.

Sage dreamed she was dancing in a strip club, but thankfully she had clothes on – a tennis skirt and top. Even in her dream, Sage had to laugh. She spun herself around a pole awkwardly. Then the pole turned into a tennis racquet, and the racquet turned into a large boa constrictor. She dropped it and it slithered away into the woods that had somehow sprouted up in the club. Her alarm went off, and she opened her eyes and sat up. "That was weird," she said to herself. She looked at Sylvia, who was coiled up tight. Suddenly, the snake's eyes opened, and it looked as if she were smiling.

On Saturdays, Sage worked the register at The Moon Goddess. She walked to work along the edge of Prospect Park, listening to Incubus on her iPhone. She wore a gauzy white top she'd picked up in a thrift store, an Indian wrap skirt and her favorite brown Tom's.

She was just about to peel off from the park, when something odd caught her eye; a Union soldier with a beard and a rucksack sat on one of the park benches, whittling a small piece of wood. Sage stopped and stared. Galen and Fern believed in ghosts, and certainly the spirit of someone who had experienced the violence of battle might be restless. Then she noticed a woman dressed in a long skirt and bonnet, carrying a bucket … and a Diet Coke. Above her hung a banner reading, "Civil War Reenactment, Saturday, 9 a.m.". Sage laughed at herself.

Her mothers had been sympathetic when she told them about her disappointing visit to Sarah Lawrence. They had emailed the

Department of Records in West Virginia, but, as they'd already known, the records were sealed. Between that, the fire that had consumed the hospital birth records, and Jack Shirley being a literal dead end, Sage's search had come to a grinding halt.

Jasper, however, was not intimidated by either sealed records or dead shyster lawyers. He offered to set up a Facebook page dedicated to finding Sage's birth parents. "You underestimate the power of The Net," he said. "If your Mom and Dad are alive and on this planet, we will find them. Or they will find you."

"I had the strangest dream this morning," Sage told Galen when she arrived at The Moon Goddess. Her mother was taking a tray out of the huge baking oven, and Sage inhaled the warm, homey smells of the bakery. This morning, Galen was baking carrot cake canoe boats, one of Sage's favorites. "I think I might have been a stripper in it. What do you think that means?"

"It means you watch too much junk television. The Kardashians are just awful," Galen said, wiping her hands on her floury apron.

"But they aren't strippers," Sage replied.

"They might as well be." Galen tossed a dish towel over her shoulder and smiled.

Two men walked in, setting the little bell above the front door jingling.

"Hi Patrick," Galen sang out, looking over the counter. "So nice to see you."

Patrick, a New York City Detective, was 6 feet 4, a vegan and a Cross Fit junkie, with toned muscles and close-cropped blonde hair. He was with a slight man in tight pegged jeans and a black t-shirt, who stood right in the center of the Wiccan pentagram painted on the floor. Its five points were illustrated: earth, air, water, fire, spirit. Patrick draped his arm around protectively around his companion's shoulder.

Shoot, thought Sage. Patrick was waaaay too old for her – he might even be thirty – but she'd always thought he was cute. She sighed. Sometimes it seemed as if half the guys in Brooklyn were gay, and the other half rejects from The Jersey Shore.

"This is my husband, Byron." Patrick beamed. Galen came out from behind the counter. She clasped her hands in front of her.

"Finally we get to meet you, what a treat. Welcome to The Moon Goddess. I'm Galen, and this is my daughter, Sage." Galen made a theatrical gesture with her right hand.

"Nice to meet you, Byron," Sage smiled. "Where has Patrick been hiding you?"

"I'm working on a reality show down in Virginia," he said. There was something eerily familiar about the girl. He couldn't put his finger on it.

"I love reality shows," Sage gushed. "What's it about?"

"Ladies' country club tennis. It's called *Queen of the Court*."

"Oh. Sounds kind of boring," said Sage, disappointed.

"That's what I thought, but the first day of filming, a woman dropped dead on court from a bee sting while her congressman husband, who had her medicine, was being busted at a massage parlor. We have strippers, séances and a tennis cat fight, with blood and everything. I think it could be a hit."

"Wow, now I can't wait to see it," said Sage.

"Sage!" admonished Galen, horrified.

"No worries, Galen. We're still in production, and we don't even have a cable contract, so you don't have to worry about our show corrupting Sage just yet."

They all laughed as Galen went back to fill their order.

Byron studied the girl as she stepped out from behind the counter and walked to the coffee bar. Who did she remind him of? He tried not to stare as he and Patrick ate their wheat berry muffins and sipped their coffees. But once breakfast was over, and they headed back to their brownstone, Byron didn't give Sage another thought.

15

"Now Taylor," Karen said. "I spoke with Judge Lanier yesterday, and he wants you to begin your community service right away." The two women were having Diet Cokes together after practice at one of the wrought-iron courtside tables. On Karen's advice, Taylor had pleaded guilty to Driving Under the Influence, and agreed to pay a $2500 fine and perform one hundred hours of community service. To her great distress, her license had been suspended for a year, pending judicial review.

"Judge Lanier can go fuck himself," Taylor said, flicking the straw in her drink with her fingernail."

"You were lucky. You have a lousy record and you blew a .12. You should be spending weekends in jail. Frankly, I'm not sure I did you a favor by getting you out of it."

"I'm kidding, lighten up." Taylor pulled her tennis bag from under the table and began looking through it for her phone. "I'm just really nervous about going to the shelter; I've heard it's full of alcoholics and addicts, and all kinds of dangerous people."

"Oh, the horror," said Karen.

"I'll come with you." It was Shana, fresh from her shower. She plopped herself down in the chair beside Karen. "I couldn't help overhearing. I've been meaning to do some more service projects. I feel so lucky, and there are so many folks hurtin' right now."

"That would be nice. Say thank you, Taylor." Karen looked over at Shana. She'd changed into the exact same blue-and-red color-block Milly sheath Allie had worn to the tennis social a week earlier, and her wavy hair had somehow been slicked into an Allie-like ponytail.

"Hey Shana, did you swipe Allie's dress?" asked Taylor, forgetting the thank you.

"Does Allie have this one too?" said Shana, her eyes wide with feigned surprise. "I'm not surprised, we have such similar taste."

Allie chose that moment to emerge from the tennis shop and head toward the courts for a private lesson. She stopped dead when she saw Shana.

"Hey Allie, come on over here a minute," said Shana with a friendly wave, ignoring the other woman's hostile look. "We're just talking about joining Taylor for her community service at the shelter tomorrow."

To her own surprise, Allie sat down and refrained from making a caustic remark about Shana's copycat dress. Ian had been urging her to do something public spirited for her image and Roy's campaign, and Shana Jones, of all people, had come up with the perfect idea. Allie would lead the entire team in volunteering at the shelter, and turn it into a campaign promotion.

"I have a great idea," said Allie, clapping her hands together. "Why don't we all volunteer as a team?"

Karen eyed her suspiciously. Allie struck her as more of a charity check-writer than an eager hands-on servant of the poor.

"Shana, if this turns into a team event, please let Rex know that cameras aren't allowed inside the shelter," Karen said, looking directly at Allie.

"Oh my goodness, of course," said Shana.

"Well, I've got to head over to my lesson. Shana, please text me the time and address." Allie smiled as she rose to leave. She'd forward that text to Ian and ask him to arrange some publicity.

Taylor, Karen and Caroline stared out the windows of Shana's red Suburban as it pulled into the parking lot of the Millie Meadows Shelter. Built in 2010, it boasted eighty beds and included a clinic, job center and children's center. The red brick two story building was contemporary, yet approachable, with big windows and a row of pink crepe myrtles. It reminded Karen of a Residence Inn.

"Wow," said Taylor. "It's so modern and cheerful. I was expecting something more… "

"Institutional?" asked Karen.

"I was thinking nasty, but yeah, that works."

As they were buzzed into the shelter, Karen noticed a sign by the door. "Residents are required to be clean and sober". She noted, ironically, it said nothing about volunteers.

Allie and Bethany arrived a few minutes later in Allie's Mercedes, Allie chatting on her hands-free phone. "They said we'd be done in two hours, so the press could meet us outside then. My car is in the lot behind the building." Allie hung up on Ian without saying goodbye.

Inside, Taylor checked in with her contact person, Lisa Gibson, a tall African American woman around forty, with short cropped hair and several earrings. Lisa had been a Washington Redskins cheerleader until drug and alcohol problems landed her on the street. She had been sober for seven years and now worked full time at Millie Meadows.

"Lisa Gibson, nice to meet you," she gave Taylor a firm handshake. "And welcome to your friends, too."

"Taylor Thomas, thank you for saving me from picking up trash at the side of the road in one of those horrible orange vests. I'm pretty sure that at least here, I won't see anyone I know."

Lisa held her tongue. Sadly, government cuts being what they were, the shelter depended on donations from the clueless rich. But she made a note to tell Judge Lanier that, if this one got in trouble again, put her on a road crew. She allowed herself one small dig.

"So, is everyone here under a court order? Do I need more forms?"

"Oh, no, the rest of us are just members of the Belle Vista Ladies' Tennis Team," said Caroline. "In fact, here comes our captain and her daughter. We're making it a group project."

A tennis team. That was a new one. Despite her reservations, Lisa extended her hand to the pinched-looking socialite who'd just entered the door with teenager in an inappropriately short skirt and too much makeup.

"Lisa Gibson, welcome."

"Allie Beech. My husband Roy is running for Congress, and he really wants to help the homeless be less dependent on government – get them back to work."

"Yes, well, maybe you should tell him that over half of our residents have jobs, and many have more than one. But they lack affordable housing, not to mention child care and ... well let's get started."

"Hello Ms. Gibson, I'm Shana Jones," said a redhead who reminded Lisa of a country singer. "What a lovely place this is. I'm really excited to help out." Lisa smiled back; maybe Reba McIntyre there would actually prove helpful.

"Follow me," she said, beckoning the others as she walked down the hallway toward the cafeteria and kitchen.

Walking behind Shana, Allie noted with horror that she and Shana were both wearing dark straight Seven for All Mankind jeans, white LaCoste polos and gold Tory Burch flats. That little sneak Byron must have given Shana a guide to Allie's entire wardrobe.

Caroline stopped in front of the community bulletin board outside the kitchen. There was a class on Monday nights about how to prepare for interviews. Every week they had guest speakers. I could do that, she thought to herself. She'd watched every episode of *The Apprentice.*

"Caroline, get over here,' Allie snapped.

"Excuse me," Caroline said to Lisa, who'd been trying to avoid her. As an ex-cheerleader, Lisa knew a bubble-headed blonde when she saw one. "I see here that you have a class on job interviews. I think I might be very inspirational as a guest speaker."

"Are you fucking kidding me?" Taylor laughed. "You haven't had a job in twenty years."

"It's not my fault my ex-husband convinced me to quit my job and stay home with our children, and then left me for a Russian whore!"

Oh brother, thought Lisa. The Real Housewives Help the Homeless. She couldn't wait to tell her husband about this when she got home.

"Maybe I should introduce you to our volunteer chef, he'll be supervising you."

"Do you pay guest speakers? I have some great tips. One really should have a nice spa treatment before interviewing, and I could also discuss cost-effective wardrobe solutions. The security at Nordstrom has gotten very lax."

"I'm pretty sure that all of our guest speakers have been scheduled," Lisa said. "Gus, I need you. *Now*!"

A short man in his late thirties with a neatly trimmed hipster beard and tattoo sleeves on both arms emerged from one of the walk in freezers, wearing a spotless white apron.

"This is our volunteer cook Gus, who is also executive chef at Maison Fraîche."

"Maison Fraîche," said Allie with awe. "It takes three months to get a reservation there."

Lisa touched Gus's shoulder and smiled. "He is remarkable and can create a masterpiece out of anything in the food bank. What's cookin' today?"

"Let's see." Gus smiled brightly and pressed his palms together. "A local fisherman donated his catch of snakehead, so we'll have that baked with lemon, some fresh green beans courtesy of an organic farmer friend of mine, a vinaigrette potato salad, and apple pie for dessert.

"You're feeding them those creepy monster fish that walk?" asked Bethany. "I mean, I know they're poor, but that's harsh."

Gus gave her a curious look. "Snakehead is on the Maison Fraîche sustainable tasting menu, which is $130 per person, plus drinks, tax and tip. My policy is not to cook anything here that I wouldn't serve there."

"If you get that reservation," Bethany said to her mother, "count me out."

"Let's get you ladies situated with aprons and hairnets," said Lisa with a big smile. She loved the idea of society women in hairnets.

Gus put everyone to work setting up the serving station and wiping down the tables in the dining hall, some more competently than others, Lisa noted. At least Shana and Karen knew how to hold sponges.

"I really can't get over this food," Caroline remarked, as delicious smells began to permeate the kitchen. She wondered if it was really tacky to ask for a doggy bag.

Despite several calamities, including Caroline nearly boiling Taylor alive as she drained the green beans, by 5:30, seventy residents had been successfully fed, the tables cleared, and the kitchen more or less cleaned.

As the group made its way out, Shana stopped and lingered by the doorway of the Learning Center, where a dozen children sat in a circle as a staff member read *The Gingerbread Man*. Lisa appeared at her side. "It's a very nice place, really it is, but it makes me sad to see children here."

"Unfortunately, these kids are the lucky ones. We have a long waiting list for families."

"I was very poor growing up, and my husband is an ex-convict, so we know something about hard times; but our children don't, and in that we're truly blessed."

"Do you want to go in?" Lisa asked. "I'm sure Mia over there would love it if you would read to her. Poor kid, she was given up for adoption at birth, then last year her adoptive father died and she and her Mom ended up homeless."

Lisa saw Shana's eyes well with tears.

"Mia, come here, I want to introduce you to someone." A small girl with mismatched clothes and big brown eyes came trotting up. "This is Miss Shana and she's going to read you a story. How about that?"

"Any story I want?" Mia eyed Shana suspiciously.

"Sure," Shana smiled as Mia returned with *The Tale of Despereaux*, a chapter book about a very human mouse. Shana felt its weight in her hand. She looked at Lisa and then back down at Mia.

"Oh this looks good," said Shana. "But it's too long to read today." Mia frowned. "I have an idea. Why don't we read a few pages today, and I can come back later in the week, and we can read some more." Mia smiled and grabbed Shana and dragged her toward the couch. Shana looked over her shoulder at Lisa and beamed. Lisa smiled, then turned and left the learning center. Occasionally, she got a good one.

"Where is Shana?" Taylor looked anxiously around the lot. "She's my ride home."

"She's my ride too, and my feet hurt," griped Caroline. "Maybe I should have worn flats."

"I'm sure she'll be along in a minute, I'm just wondering what those two are up to," Karen replied, eyeing Allie and Bethany as they emerged from the shelter, hair and makeup perfectly retouched. "I would have thought they'd have run like the wind once this was over. Come to think of it, why is Bethany even here?" Karen saw Allie wave enthusiastically, signaling to someone in the parking lot behind them. She turned and saw a white van with "Fox News – Channel 5" on the side pull in.

A spray-tanned reporter rolled down the passenger side window. "Max Mavis, Fox News," he said, his grin showing off some impressive cosmetic dentistry.

Allie hurried past the other women without a word. "Allie Beech, wife of Republican congressional candidate Roy Forrest Beech IV," she said as she stepped forward and extended her right hand to Max. "I'm so glad you could come today. I think it's important to show people the great work that is done here at Millie Meadows by volunteers." Allie flashed her best sympathy smile. "My daughter Bethany and I just cooked and served dinner to hundreds," she continued as Bethany strolled up. Her orange bandage skirt, heels and false eyelashes definitely caught Max's attention.

"I thought we weren't allowed to film here," Taylor said, cocking her head. "They wouldn't let Rex and Jamal come, so why is Fox News allowed to be here?"

"I never thought I would say this to you Taylor, but good point. I am about to go find out." With that, Karen strode over to Allie and Max, who was getting out of the van along with his cameraman. "I thought we agreed that there would be no filming," she said to Allie, ignoring the Fox crew.

"This is not a reality show crew, and we are not inside the shelter," Allie replied with a frosty smile. "We have constitutionally protected freedom of the press in this country." She turned to Max. "My husband is a strong defender of the Constitution, although in most cases, the First Amendment isn't one of his favorites."

Max Mavis smiled past Allie at Bethany. She nodded at him and snapped her gum.

Heads turned as Ian's blue beemer squealed into the lot. He frantically searched the back seat for his navy blazer, jumped out of the car, and in five quick strides, was standing next to Bethany and Allie.

"Ian Thorne, we spoke on the phone. I'm with the Beech Campaign." He shook Max's hand. Ian surveyed the parking lot and his gaze settled on Taylor and Caroline. He needed to keep them off camera and make sure that Bethany did not open her mouth. If only Enrique had not had that Georgetown interview today.

But Max had his own ideas and was already chatting up the ladies (except for Karen, who'd retreated into the shelter to find Shana and lay low until this circus was over) as the cameraman shot background of the shelter.

"So what brings all of you here today?"

"Allie wanted us to come. We pretty much always do what she says. She's the captain of our tennis team," Caroline offered.

Ian's neck tightened. "This story isn't about country club tennis," Ian said, as he stepped in front of Caroline. "It's about Allie Beech and her tireless commitment to the downtrodden."

"No offense, dude, but this segment is *Max Mavis in Your Community*, meaning I get to decide what the story is. Now let's get started," said Max, licking his lips. "I've got a charity pet show to cover in Rockville in an hour."

MAX MAVIS FOX NEWS INTERVIEW

Max faced the camera with a wolfish grin.

Max Mavis: ***"I'm standing outside the Millie Meadows Homeless Shelter with Allie and Bethany Beech, wife and daughter of Republican congressional candidate Roy Beech, and their friends, who just helped feed the families here. Why do you volunteer in your community, Allie?"***

Allie: ***"I've always had great concern for the homeless. My husband, Roy Beech, candidate for Congress in the fourteenth district, shares that concern, as does our daughter."***

Max held out his microphone to Bethany.

Max Mavis: ***"So you felt moved by the suffering of these families?"***

Bethany: ***"Actually, not so much once I realized we were feeding them stuff my mom pays major bucks to eat at Maison Fraîche. You know, this place is pretty nice. If I were homeless, like that's gonna happen, I'd want to be homeless here."***

Ian felt the sweat start to pool between his shoulder blades as he watched helplessly.

Max Mavis: ***"So, how about the rest of you ladies?"***

Caroline: ***"We all came down here today together as members of the Belle Vista Country Club tennis team."***

One of the veins in Ian's forehead started to throb angrily.

Bethany: ***"Just for the record, it's now called Jones Belle Vista, after Big Wayne and Shana Jones. The club was broke and the Joneses took it over."***

Caroline: ***"They made a fortune in strip clubs."***

Bethany: ***"My mom and my grandmother are really pissed off about the whole thing, but I like Shana, she's like a cool reality-show redneck."***

Allie stood paralyzed, unable to speak. Off camera, Ian motioned cut, slicing his hand across his throat.

Max Mavis: ***"So now that you've seen life at a homeless shelter, Mrs. Beech, what do you think your husband should do about poverty if he's elected?"***

Max forced himself to look serious. He was really having too much fun.

Allie: ***"That's a very good question."***

Allie's mind went blank; her talking points erased by a wave of panic.

Allie: ***"Uh, both my husband and I really feel that people are too dependent on government. Everyone needs to take personal responsibility, and not expect hand outs."***

Max Mavis: ***"So, you're actually opposed to programs like those at Millie Meadows? You feel the families here have not taken responsibility for their lives?"***

Allie: ***"I didn't say that."***

Max Mavis: ***"You implied it."***

Taylor: ***"I know what I'd like to see Roy do for the homeless. I think that Medicaid should cover cosmetic procedures. I mean, just because you're poor, you shouldn't have to be ugly. My husband, Spencer, is a noted plastic surgeon, by the way."***

Bethany: ***"I totally agree. I mean, maybe they're poor because they're ugly, you know? Like no one will give them jobs because customers won't want to look at them and stuff?"***

Ian walked over to the exterior brick wall of the shelter and began to quietly pound his forehead against it.

Taylor: ***"One more thing, I think DUI laws are too tough in this state."***

Allie remained frozen in horror.

Caroline: ***"Drunk driving is actually why we're here. Taylor was convicted of a DUI after one of our tennis matches and sentenced to community service."***

Taylor: ***"You stupid bitch. I'm hiding that from my husband, remember? Now it'll be all over the news. Spencer, I'm sorry honey!"***

The cameraman laughed silently. He looked like he might wet his pants.

Max Mavis: ***"This has been Max Mavis live from the Millie Meadows Homeless Shelter, where Allie Beech, wife of congressional candidate Roy Beech, and the Jones Belle Vista Country Club***

tennis team are working to bring government-funded cosmetic surgery and lax drunk driving laws to your community."

"Those were gotcha questions!" said Allie, who unfroze when the camera shut off.

"Yeah, I thought they were pretty good too," said Bethany, smiling flirtatiously at Max. "Hey, Ian, what's that red spot on your forehead? Is it bleeding?"

16

Hector Ortiz was sick of the county jail. The food sucked, it smelled bad and half the guys were crazy. Like now, in the TV room, they were stuck watching Fox News instead of baseball because some guy screamed his head off till they changed the channel. Called himself a neocon, which must be an old white guy word for junkie. Hector sat at a sticky linoleum table, playing solitaire with a forty-three-card deck and cheating to win. He only looked up when wolf whistles alerted him that a hot chick was on TV.

In some ways he was lucky. The watch that bitch had planted on him in Nordstrom turned out to be a knock off, worth less than the $200 needed to charge him with felony theft. Plus, she hadn't shown up to testify in court. The Commonwealth's Attorney had come up with a bunch of outstanding warrants, but, as usual, all the witnesses against him mysteriously changed their minds or disappeared. He smiled. In just two more days, he'd be out. Then he'd make it his business to settle the score with that little bastard Enrique and his puta girlfriend.

He put a hand to his temple. Damn, there was still a scar where she and that nasty little red-haired elf had dumped that rack of purses on him. But the dent in his temple was nothing compared to the dent in his pride. Even in here he'd heard someone mutter "Bolso Boy" when he walked by. His old street name was Hellboy. How the hell was he supposed to scare witnesses (or get women) with a nickname like "Purse Boy"?

An eruption of whistles, cat calls and stomping interrupted his thoughts, and he lifted his eyes to the TV. Suddenly, Hector was out of his chair moving toward the screen. It was her, the rubia loca from the mall.

"Sit your fat ass down, Purse Boy, so we can see," someone yelled. Normally Hector would deal with that, but he was focused. He got up close just in time to hear some bitch say "Belle Vista Country Club." Oh man, this was gonna be sweet.

Bethany had to write a poem for a summer English assignment, but every time she sat down with her laptop she blanked out or ended up on Bluefly.com. "Roses are red, violets are blue, this is a stupid assignment that I don't want to do," she muttered to herself as she curled up on a chaise in the Beech's sunroom. There were millions of dumb poems out there in cyberspace; she didn't need to write one of her own.

She found a website called Poetry Slam and started skimming poems. She realized that she couldn't hand in a really sophisticated poem, because her teacher would know she hadn't written it. There was a link called High School Poetry; that would be better. That led her to the Saint Ann's literary magazine and a poem called "Searching" by Sage Silverfox Shapiro. "What a weird name," Bethany muttered.

But she actually liked the poem, and she thought that she understood it, which was a good thing in case she was asked to explain it. It was about missing something in your life and looking for it. Possibly this Silverfox chick had lost her dog or something. She copied the poem into her documents folder and changed the title to "Looking" by Bethany Beech.

She was about the exit the website when she noticed a link to a Facebook page. Bethany was addicted to Facebook and was kind of curious about what a girl named Silverfox looked like. Up popped Sage's adoption page.

The girl was pretty, with long red hair and green eyes, although Bethany thought she could use a little makeup. She read a few of Silverfox's postings. So that's what she was looking for, Bethany mused. Not shoes or a dog, but her parents. Bethany remembered wishing she were adopted when she was little and Allie would yell at her; she'd never considered how weird it would be not to know anything about your real parents. She was Allie and Roy's girl all the way, with more than a little Lavinia thrown in.

This Sage girl lived in Brooklyn, which was so cool, but had been born in West Virginia and was seventeen, same as Bethany. Her mother had put her up for adoption, and the records had been destroyed in a fire. Bethany stared at the face on the screen for over a minute. This girl looked really, really familiar. This girl looked just like *Shana Jones*.

It made sense. The Joneses were from West Virginia. The image of a teenaged pregnant Shana walking down a dusty dirt road popped into Bethany's head, as vivid as a crime reenactment on TV. If Shana was Sage Silverfox Shapiro's biological mother, that was some good scoop. Bethany chewed the inside of her cheek as she pondered what to do with this potential bombshell. Then her iPhone buzzed. Enrique!

"Hey baby," she answered, getting up from her chair and going out to the back patio in case her mother was lurking around. "Meet you at Starbucks on M Street? Awesome. Be there in thirty."

Bethany walked straight out the side gate and toward her waiting Audi, her single-minded focus on Georgetown and Enrique banishing all thoughts of the girl on her computer screen, the one whose poem she had plagiarized, the one who looked like Shana Jones. Nothing held Bethany's interest for long – except Bethany.

Allie entered the sunroom and shook her head, the door to the patio was open, allowing air conditioning out and mosquitoes in, and now she heard the sound of Bethany's car pulling away. And there was her daughter's new MacBook Pro, open on the glass coffee table.

Allie cringed. She was afraid of what she might see on Bethany's Facebook page, and after the Fox News debacle, it was particularly terrifying. Roy did not need any more bad publicity. Still, she sat down on the chaise and forced herself to look. Opportunities to spy on her secretive daughter didn't present themselves that often.

The image on the screen didn't seem scandalous; no red party cups, or bongs, or clothes falling off. Just a plain headshot, and not of Bethany.

She shifted the laptop out of the sun's glare so she could see more clearly. Was that Shana as a teenager? It was obviously too young to be Shana now, but the resemblance was unmistakable. Allie pulled up a chair and read the postings on Sage Silverfox Shapiro's adoption page. She exhaled, then stood up, walked into the kitchen, opened her refrigerator and poured herself a glass of wine, even though it was only 4:15. She took a substantial sip and wondered what she should do. Then her eye lighted on her bulletin board and the invitation to Belle Vista's annual Founder's Day Celebration.

She returned to the sunroom, sat down at the computer and created a new email account under the first pseudonym that came to mind. Then, using her new false identity, she emailed Sage Silverfox Shapiro.

Sage stared at her computer screen for a long time. Someone named Pippa had seen her adoption page and emailed her, attaching a picture of a woman named Shana Jones. Shana was from West Virginia, Pippa informed her, and now lived near Washington with her husband and two children. In the picture, Shana wore a tight, low-cut white tennis dress and was holding a racquet, waves of red hair curling around her shoulders. It appeared to be the same shade as Sage's, and her eyes looked very green, although Sage knew you could doctor photos really easily. The woman wore a lot of makeup and had what looked like fake breasts. Sage looked down at her own unremarkable chest. She couldn't imagine having big boobs or dressing like that, but something stirred within Sage when she looked at Shana Jones. "Are you my mother?" she asked the picture.

"Mom," Sage called into the dark living room where Fern was meditating. "Mom, come here quick!"

"This better be good, darling. I was in a completely calm and peaceful state." Fern groaned as she got to her feet, walked to the kitchen, stood behind Sage and waited for her eyes to adjust to the light.

"Look at this. Someone named Pippa in Virginia sent it to me." She gestured towards the picture on the screen.

Fern squinted and reached for her reading glasses on the kitchen counter. "Pippa? Isn't that Kate Middleton's sister's name?"

Sage laughed. "I didn't realize that you knew who Pippa Middleton was."

"I know it all, my dear. The Kardashians, *Swamp People*, you name it." Fern patted Sage on the back and moved closer to the screen.

"Do you think she looks like me?" Sage asked. "Her name is Shana Jones."

Fern was silent for a long time. The woman was an older version of her daughter, if you took away all the makeup and the fake boobs.

"She does look an awful lot like you," Fern admitted, then kissed the top of Sage's head. "What does this Pippa say?"

"She says that Shana is married, with two children. She doesn't know if her husband would know if she had given a child up for adoption, and he used to be in a motorcycle gang, so we should be cautious. She also attached an electronic invite to a party in a few weeks at a country club called Jones Belle Vista. She said I could come and have a look at Shana and see if something clicks. Then we could decide what to do. What do you think?" Shana turned to Fern anxiously.

Fern wrinkled her brow. "I don't know. I suppose we could drive down to Virginia. I know how important this is to you."

"You know how much I love you guys. I wouldn't trade you for anyone." Sage hugged her mother. "It's just something I need to know.

"Let's talk to Galen when she gets home. When is this party anyway?" Fern turned back to the computer. The smell of patchouli oil rose from her damp skin and settled around Sage like a blanket.

"I don't like this Pippa person," Galen said, her arms crossed protectively over her ample bosom, as the little family gathered around Sage's laptop in the kitchen. "She's not straightforward at all.

What's her motivation anyway? And sending an invitation to that ridiculous country club party. Plus, this man from a motorcycle gang sounds dangerous."

"Pippa just saw my Facebook page and thought I looked like someone she knows named Shana Jones, that's all. She's trying to be helpful."

Sage sighed. Fern was one thing, but convincing Galen was another matter.

"We're just thinking this through," Fern said in a conciliatory tone. "We agree that Shana Jones looks like you, but we don't want you to get hurt and we really question Pippa. She didn't give you any contact information, just an invite to a party where she says this Shana may be."

"Did you get a look at that clubhouse?" snorted Galen. "It's probably stuffed to the gills with rich, white Republicans. It looks like a freaking plantation."

"Hey," Sage said excitedly, "let's look it up online." She Googled Jones Belle Vista Country Club and clicked on the link. "Oh my Goddess! Check this out. The clubhouse is built on the site of Belle Vista Plantation. You were right Mom! The house was burned to the ground by federal troops during the Civil War."

"Bad karma for sure," Galen muttered as she walked over to the stove and checked a pot of boiling noodles. She was making noodle kuchen for dinner.

"Here's their Vision Statement," Sage clapped her hands excitedly. "The Jones Belle Vista Country Club strives to be a lifelong haven for our exclusive membership. In our superb setting, one can relax and enjoy recreational and social activities with people who share similar values and traditions."

Fern let out a snort. "How deeelightful," she said in a fake English accent. "How much is the membership?"

"One hundred thousand dollars for the initiation fee, and then $900 a month after that."

Galen whistled. "That's high cotton, as they used to say on the plantation." She wiped her hands on her Moon Goddess apron.

"Very funny," Sage said, still focused on the website. "Do you think that Shana Jones owns this Jones Belle Vista club?" Sage scanned the webpage for a tab on ownership, but couldn't find one.

"Plantations, country clubs, six-figure memberships… Why don't we come back to planet Earth, or rather planet Brooklyn? What do you want to drink with dinner?" Fern asked.

"Soy milk," Sage replied. "But can we go to the plantation … I mean club? I just want to see Shana Jones, maybe ask a few questions. Please?" Sage gave them a wide-eyed plea.

"We'll talk about it tomorrow. I'm still getting used to the idea." Galen dumped the steaming noodles in a colander.

"What on earth would we wear?" Fern said with a laugh, glancing over her daughter's shoulder at the country club on the hill.

17

Shana's hands trembled as she booted up the computer in the luxe Jones Belle Vista ladies locker room, which featured a floor of handcrafted Italian tile and mahogany-faced lockers with oval brass nameplates. The top of the line Hewlett Packard was ostensibly for women golfers to enter their scores, but the club had Wi-Fi. She chewed her left thumbnail, obliterating the tiny flower embellished on it (just like Serena Williams), as she accessed the West Virginia adoption website.

She scrolled through the new postings. Nothing. Her hands wavered over the keyboard. It would be simple to post a notice of her own, but the idea terrified Shana. Shana's family had never had a computer until she'd bought one for her Mama a couple of years ago. Lurleen had promptly met a jobless (and, as it turned out, married) Vermont man online who relocated and moved in with her. Three months later, he moved back out while Lurleen was working her waitress shift, taking everything valuable with him, including the laptop. To Shana, the Internet was the realm of scam artists and the Craig's List Killer and a posting was an invitation for them to come right through the screen and invade her home.

Shana sighed. If only her letters to West Virginia had gotten results.

She was so sure after the séance that she'd be able to unlock the doors she'd closed on her past, but they'd remained slammed, locked and bolted. She had to wonder, was this God's way of telling her that she wasn't meant to open them?

Shana's thoughts were interrupted by a literal door flying open and a visibly tense Allie striding into the locker room. Shana jumped away from the computer as if she'd been scalded.

"Oh," said Allie looking down at Shana. "I assumed, given this team's penchant for late arrivals, I would be the first one here."

"Good morning, Allie," said Shana, forcing a smile and turning so she blocked Allie's view of the computer screen. "I wanted to make sure things were set up all nice before the league officials get here. I had Maria do some special pastries..."

"*Pastries*!" Allie exclaimed. "If those old busybodies want to micro-manage our match they can provide their own breakfast. Besides, nobody here eats pastries except Caroline, and she only does it in secret."

Without another glance at the flustered Shana, she headed into a stall.

Relief washed through Shana as she turned, exited the website, and turned off the computer. For once, Allie's tendency to ignore her had been a good thing.

Shana felt like running away, but decided it would be rude not to wait for Allie. She stood up and twirled and bounced in front of the mirror making sure everything was in place and likely to stay that way on court.

Since the league rules committee had banned the Jones Belle Vista uniforms for this match – she kind of felt guilty about that, she should have worn extra boob tape at River's Edge – she'd bought a whole new outfit from Venus Williams' EleVen line for the rematch (Byron had told her flat out to stop dressing like Allie. Instead, he was helping her modify her clothes and makeup to be more country club without being, as he phrased it, a Beech Bitch Clone).

She'd never forgotten her first tournament at age twelve; her hand-me-down tennis skirt, an old, yellowing pleated thing donated by a tournament organizer, kept slipping down and threatening to fall off. Her ears still burned when she recalled how the other girls laughed, until she beat the pants off them and bought herself a brand new skirt with her fifty-dollar gift certificate to the Briarwood pro shop. That incident had taught Shana a few valuable lessons not included in Pastor John's weekly sermons; namely that that people treat you better when you win, especially if you win in new clothes.

As she absentmindedly adjusted her skirt she heard a flush and a horrible gurgling, as if the Loch Ness monster had emerged from a toilet and swallowed Allie whole. She allowed herself a small, un-Christian smile at that mental picture.

Allie emerged looking flustered.

"Geez, Allie, what was that? Sounded like..."

"Shana," said Allie sharply. "We do not discuss bathroom noises." All the same, Allie thought, after the match it might be wise to have the maintenance staff check it out.

Without another glance at Shana she strode out of the locker room, nearly slamming the door in her teammate's face.

Clare Buxton parked her battered Toyota Celica in a visitor's spot and looked up at the behemoth before her. What on earth was it supposed to be? Georgian? Victorian? Newport in the age of the robber barons? Clare shook her head. She did kind of like the kitschy Vegas-style Jones Belle Vista sign, though.

But Clare wasn't here to critique architecture; she was here to dig up dirt on Pippa Edgemoor. The Internet had turned up nothing, not that Clare exactly expected to see her pop up on Facebook.

Pippa had left Belle Vista on December 26th, 1972, supposedly to drive to Palm Springs as she did every year. She'd been spotted partying it up in Las Vegas on New Year's, spreading cash all over town. From her rooftop suite at the MGM Grande, she'd written her lawyers informing them that her plans had changed; she'd be traveling abroad for the foreseeable future, and they should continue to manage her investments and property in her absence. She never arrived in Palm Springs.

There had been no activity involving Pippa's social security number since then. She'd never set up a checking account, taken out a credit card, filed for a marriage license or bought a home, at least not in her own name.

In most cases, this was a sure tipoff that the subject was dead, but there had been some notable exceptions. Like Katherine Ferrand Dyer, who disappeared in Colorado in 1954 and was presumed murdered, but instead lived to a ripe old age under an assumed name in Australia.

And Pippa was – or had been – rich. Rich enough to disappear for as long as she chose. She hadn't tapped her trust, but people like that were lousy with offshore accounts that could provide a secret income stream for a lifetime.

Speaking of income streams, there was Allie Beech, all in white like a vestal virgin. This was a good case in that Clare hadn't yet found any conclusive evidence that Pippa was either alive or dead, which meant more billable hours. However, Clare knew that if she didn't turn up some kind of lead soon, she'd be out of a job. Allie was not a patient person.

"Oh good lord, is that the best you could do?" said Allie as she looked Clare up and down.

Clare had worn a khaki skirt and off-brand lavender polo, as well as her sensible Clarks. (Detectives always had achy feet.) She carried a beat up L.L. Bean boat tote stuffed with papers and a reporter's notebook.

"If you want me to pick up something spiffier, I'll hit the golf shop and charge it to you," replied Clare.

"Oh, never mind," said Allie. "Walk with me." They headed through the parking lot toward the back of the clubhouse. "As I informed you, today is not only the River's Edge rematch – which cannot be interrupted for ANYTHING – it is also Senior Social day. The senior ladies will be playing bridge, then having a light luncheon in the Jardine Room. Until then, you may do research in the library, which includes photograph albums, scrapbooks and old newsletters. Here's a list of the women who knew Pippa. Do you remember your cover story?"

Clare sighed. Why did her clients always act as if they were extras in a spy movie?

"I'm doing research for a history of Belle Vista, which will include Pippa's disappearance, and her legacy as the last of the founding Edgemoors," she recited obediently, adding, "You realize if your mother comes to this lunch she'll blow my cover?"

"Mother will be watching my match. She skips the luncheons if Genie Walters is attending. Genie is a cat feeder."

Clare decided not to ask what that meant.

"I'm still not exactly clear on why you need to go back so far," Allie continued. "Clearly, since Pippa has been in touch with Mother in the past decade, all this ancient history is hardly relevant."

Clare contemplated telling Allie that her mother was a big fat liar, but decided that would not keep the checks coming.

"People rarely change," she explained instead as they climbed the wrought iron outdoor staircase to the main level. "The more I learn about who Pippa was, the closer I'll get to finding out where she might be now, dead or alive. With a significant trust at stake and with evidence from two sources – I really need to talk to that Judy – that she may be alive, we're going to have to come up with some pretty strong proof to the contrary to have her declared deceased."

Allie grimaced. "Strong proof" sounded like code for "more billable hours". "Just how strong will this proof need to be?" she griped. "It sounds as if you should be digging for a body, not dirt from fifty years ago."

A half dozen tennis league officials and a smattering of Vixen freelancers had descended on the refreshment table by the time Allie arrived courtside. Because of the "situation," as it was known in club tennis circles, the DCTLA had called out the Stasi of country club tennis: The Rules Committee.

Like Lavinia, most were waspy women of upright bearing in their sixties and beyond, who cared deeply about the game of tennis; or to be more specific, about the rules that governed the game. League President Currituck "Currie" Holmes firmly believed the nation's moral deterioration could clearly be seen on the courts. Clubs were allowing players to wear colors and collarless shirts, to converse and laugh during play and take water and bathroom breaks when needed, rather than at authorized times. "As tennis has become more 'fun'," she lamented to Lavinia, "it has begun to attract the wrong type of people."

"Good morning Currie," said Allie, air kissing her on one cheek. "So grateful to you for doing this."

"As I was telling your mother, Allison, I really don't approve of the cameras and so on, but I hear this is what you agreed to in order to pay your bills for…this," she waived her hand dismissively at the new clubhouse. Currie Holmes had personally blocked the renovation of Dominion Golf for nearly a quarter century. Legend had it that the stained red-plaid carpet in the club grill had been selected by Mamie Eisenhower.

"Oh, don't worry, they've learned to be quite discreet," replied Allie. "We'll barely know they're here."

At that moment the crew began blasting the Billy Paul soul classic "Me & Mrs. Jones" on their sound system and cheering as Shana walked toward the courts smiling and waving.

"Yes, I can see that," said Currie Holmes. "Perfectly discreet."

Clare nestled into a high-backed, leather wing chair. The beautiful library, with its mahogany bookshelves, brass colonial chandelier, pale Williamsburg blue paint and oriental carpets was completely empty. She opened the club scrapbook from 1962, when Pippa, Judy and Lavinia were seniors in high school. As she opened the book, a small gray cat appeared as if out of nowhere, jumped up and settled in on the chair's back.

"Well, hello there," said Clare, reaching back to scratch the cat between the ears. She was rewarded with a deep purr. "Are you as curious about Pippa as I am? Better be careful, you know the old saying." She chuckled, and turned to a page titled "Christmas Cotillion".

There, on the Cotillion Court, were the three of them. Lavinia, the queen, posed in the center in a pale gown with a sweetheart neckline, while on her left Judy grinned mischievously in an off-the-shoulder dress and dangling earrings that looked more London mod than country club dance. The camera had caught Pippa Edgemoor, a handsome, raven-haired beauty in a black sheath and white fur stole, glaring daggers at Lavinia. Hmmm.

Clare readjusted the scrapbook on her lap and a small spiral-bound book fell out of the back. She opened it to the first page, which was titled "JS" – underneath someone had written in girlish script:

"J.S. cheers "win" on the Jardine field but behind the bleachers says "I yield, yield, yield!'"

Clare chuckled. Clearly she'd unearthed a kind of 1960s slam book concealed among the club's memorabilia of cotillions, parent-child tennis championships and golf tournaments. So much for the "sweet" Merrywood girls.

Underneath that first evil little rhyme the writer had added:

It says 'For a good time call J.S.!' on the Jardine boys' locker room wall! -anonimouse

Then, in bold script:

Taffy, you moron, you don't have to sign "anonymous", you just don't sign AT ALL, and I'd rather be a good time than a frigid little bitch.

The last word was scratched out, but the signature wasn't – a big, bold

JUDY SIMPSON

Clare laughed out loud. She liked this Judy, even if her Pippa-sighting story was bullshit. Taffy would be Taffy Layton, now Dandridge, one of the women on Allie's list. She read on.

J.S. – You know we have RULES, no names! L.E.

Clare suspected that was Lavinia Winter, nee Endicott, apparently a stickler for rules even at sixteen.

The entire next page was taken up by a message in gothic-looking calligraphy – clearly the writer had been a talented artist. Not to mention a little disturbed.

Here's a rule for you, L.E.,
When you take something I want,
Like the Cotillion Crown,
Then I take something you want.
And I'll wait till it's something you really want.
Because I'm patient.

Even though it had been written more than a half-century ago by a seventeen-year-old girl who, if she were still alive, would be nearly seventy, Pippa Edgemoor's threat gave Clare chills.

The Jones Belle Vista team had been warming up for ten minutes, waiting for their River's Edge rivals to arrive. Allie had just marched into the tennis shop in a fury; two feral cats, a tabby and a black male with one white sock, were enjoying enthusiastic conjugal relations in the bushes adjacent to court one. Although there were no specific injunctions against noisy cat sex in the DCTLA rulebook, Currie Holmes demanded they be removed.

"I can't believe you got me up so early," whined Taylor over the yowling as she traded baseline strokes with Karen and Caroline.

"Ditto," huffed Caroline.

"Oh, good grief," said Karen, sailing a forehand long in her frustration. "Whatever happened to 'Thank you for the ride'? If it weren't for me, you two would have to take the bus."

"Car service," corrected Taylor, sliding a spare ball out of her tiny white ball shorts and feeding it back to Karen. "What's with the 'ditto' and 'good grief'? Are we filming an after-school special?"

"Not in those shorts," retorted Karen, coming to the net and angling off a volley. "Aren't they supposed to go *under* a skirt?"

Elena Walinsky strode on the court and took the spot next to Taylor.

"Not everyone wants to be bombing with the F on television, Mrs. Doctor," she said, returning a deep, hard backhand without missing a beat, sending Caroline stumbling backward.

"I'm warmed up enough," huffed Caroline. Glaring at Elena, she grabbed a towel and headed off court toward Shana and Allie.

"Why don't you go warm up with Elena and Taylor," Allie suggested to Shana in a tight voice, as she watched Lauren Lippert emerge from the parking lot, wheeling the ever-present F. Brand.

"Oh, that wouldn't be fair to you Allie," said Shana. "I kinda thought since we never named a co-captain after Lou died that I would help you out with the score books…"

"We don't need a co-captain," said Allie coldly.

"But you were co-captain."

"That was different. Lou and I were very close. We were both more like *captains*, really … are you *filming* this?" Allie turned on a freelancer whose camera was pointed in their direction, but before she could continue, Shana let out a happy, ear-splitting shriek.

"Papa Bear!" she shouted as she saw Big Wayne lumber toward the courtside tables. She jumped up and ran to him, throwing her arms around his neck.

"*Really*," sniffed Currie Holmes as she bit off a tiny piece of croissant. She made a mental note to address inappropriate courtside displays of affection in the next tennis league newsletter.

"Did you come to cheer me on?" Shana asked after she untangled herself from Big Wayne, who was dressed in enormous madras plaid Bermuda shorts and a rhino-sized bright orange LaCoste polo, both birthday gifts from Shana.

"Uhhhh," said Wayne awkwardly. "Sure honey. But first I gotta have a little man-to-man talk with F. Brand," he said, nodding at the blanket swathed figure Lauren was rolling up to the pastry table. Jamal had nicknamed F. Brand "Mr. Burns," and the resemblance to the ancient Simpsons' villain was eerie. "Then there's some problems with the golf course restoration, and the county inspectors found substandard electrical work in the ballroom, and I gotta go over the tennis shop books with Dick."

Shana pecked Wayne on the cheek. "You poor thing, I think you work harder now than when you were managing our…" Shana almost blurted out gentlemen's clubs, but then realized that both the camera AND Currie Holmes were following every word. "…businesses," she finished lamely.

Big Wayne sighed. "You got that right, buttercup. Now you go have some fun with your friends."

Shana beamed as Big Wayne walked away. How could she ever feel blue or insecure with a loving husband like that? He was her rock. And as long as she had him, nothing could ever truly go wrong.

18

"Captains, please assemble the players for a review of the rules," Currie Holmes announced over the PA system. The courts had been set up as if the River's Edge/Jones Belle Vista rematch were the US Open, with elderly lineswomen in elevated chairs on each court.

As the players gathered, a late River's Edge arrival jogged up to the official's table. "Sorry I'm a bit late, but I ran here from home," said Tracy Logan, who appeared barely out of breath although she lived at least twelve miles away. She sat down and shrugged a bright pink Nike tennis bag, off her tanned, muscular shoulders and pulled out a pair of court shoes. "Hello, Shana," she said without smiling.

"Uh, hi, Tracy," replied Shana, looking a bit queasy. "I need to warn you, there's almond croissants on the pastry table."

Tracy glared as she slipped out of her lime green and white ECCO Biom running shoes and stuffed them in her pack.

"It's my daughter who is allergic, and who is still traumatized, thank you so much for asking. Besides, almonds are *tree nuts*; peanuts are *legumes*. Everyone knows that."

"What was that about?" whispered Karen to Taylor.

"Beats me," she replied. "But Tracy's a huge fucking bitch. She quit tennis for running and Cross Fit because they don't require social skills."

Karen wondered what kind of woman had fewer social skills than Taylor. It was a frightening thought.

Caroline sidled over to the two. "You see those running shoes," she said in her extremely audible stage whisper. Tracy shot her a look. "Himalayan Yak leather."

"Shhh," said Karen, adding, "Gross. How do you know? Oh, no, please say it isn't so."

"Well, I *was* going to start running to lose weight, and I need the absolute best shoes because of my knees, so I went online to Zappos…"

Karen buried her face in her hands, causing Taylor to emit a little snorting laugh.

"Hey Caroline, looks like you made Karen want to 'yak'!"

"Quiet, everyone, please." said Allie, noting Currie's disapproving look. Maybe it was time – once the club was back in the appropriate hands – to reevaluate whether Taylor and Caroline really had a serious commitment to tennis. Of course, if Belle Vista won this match, and cemented its position at first place in the league, she'd be more inclined to keep the current roster. With certain notable exceptions, she thought, watching Shana nervously twirl a titian curl around one of her flower-embellished nails.

"Allison, I asked if you had any changes to your roster," said Currie Holmes impatiently.

"My apologies. No, our roster is as submitted."

"And you, Lauren?"

"We have Tracy Logan for Yasmine Shah and Lila Chang for Riva Lowenstein."

Lila Chang. It was all Allie could do to keep from gasping. That witch Lauren.

Lila was a six-foot two-inch blonde who'd played number one singles at Pepperdine, where she'd met her future husband, five-foot-five-inch tech genius Mike Chang. At the age of nineteen, Mike had developed "Berzerkiller," an addictive ultra-violent video game that became a lucrative worldwide sensation. Rumor had it he'd created a special tennis version for Lila's Wii where her opponent's head exploded in a rain of scarlet spatter whenever she hit a winner.

"Now," said Currie, eyeing the players like Patton reviewing the troops, "I want to go over the rules."

As Currie droned on about penalties for cursing, cell phone rings and unauthorized water breaks, Shana looked over at Big Wayne, who squatted awkwardly near F. Brand Lippert's wheelchair. She knew he must be saying something kind, because F. Brand was smiling.

"What do you mean you're not involved with Capitol Capital Investments?" said Big Wayne, a knot twisting in his stomach.

"Pay attention, young man," said Lippert with a rictus grin. "I said I am *no longer* involved with Walinsky's fund. Got out six months ago with a substantial profit. As did big blondie's little husband," he poked a bony finger in the direction of Lila Chang.

"But your name is on the list of investors!"

Lippert emitted a dry cackle.

"Ah yes, well I have a feeling that our mutual acquaintance Jack Walinsky may be playing a bit fast and loose with his promotional materials."

F. Brand Lippert fixed his reptilian stare on the crouching, ungainly Big Wayne with a look that wavered between pity and amusement. "You know, Jack got a dog a while back, and he asked me what to name him." He gave Wayne a chilling, thin-lipped smile.

"I said he should name the pup 'Ponzi'."

Lippert's cackle ended with a racking cough that nearly wrenched him out of his wheelchair.

Clare was headed toward the Jardine room when she realized she'd left her reading glasses in the library. She turned back just in time to see Judy Simpson slinking into the library and closing the door behind her. Clare was ex-FBI, and it wasn't difficult for her to open the door slightly without alerting Judy.

She observed Judy pull a dusty tome on the Civil War from a shelf, open it, remove a plain white envelope from between its pages and check the contents. Clare kept the door open long enough to confirm that the envelope held cash, then silently closed it and slipped away.

"Shana, get your ass out on the court before we forfeit!" The locker room door banged open and Taylor entered, followed by

Caroline and Karen. "Allie is going to shit a brick if you don't get out there!"

"What are you trying to do, get your cursing out of your system?" said Karen irritably to Taylor.

"Exactly!" Taylor replied. "That stupid old bitch made me buy a skirt at the pro shop to wear over my ball shorts, so I'm in a cursing mood, and I don't want to lose points. Come *on*, Shana, it's Tracy and Lauren, not a firing squad."

Shana was sitting on a bench, head in her hands, her face deathly pale.

"It's just that Tracy got Destiny kicked out of ballet," she said miserably.

Caroline inhaled sharply. "Not Miss Sally's."

Shana nodded.

"Miss Sally's is a must for all little girls who hope to take Cotillion and later have a debut," Caroline explained to Karen and Taylor, who were unfamiliar with the cutthroat parenting world where the right preschool, playgroup and dance class determined a child's future. "Maggie and Bethany took it, all the girls do."

She didn't add that Maggie had refused Cotillion, demanding to play ice hockey instead.

"What on earth did Destiny *do*?"

"Not Destiny, me! I brought her a peanut butter bagel, and Tracy's daughter is allergic."

Caroline frowned, her arched eyebrows nearly meeting as her forehead wrinkled in puzzlement (she was behind on Botox injections because her medspa wouldn't run a tab).

"You never get kicked out for a first time peanut offense. You just have to sign the 'No Nuts' pledge."

"That's the one Allie's husband signed when he married her," interjected Taylor with a laugh.

"Shhhhhh," admonished Karen.

"Tracy told Miss Sally that little Meredith – that's her daughter – has anxiety, and that even looking at Destiny would give her an asthma attack," said Shana, hanging her head.

"What a load of crap," scoffed Taylor. She put her hand on Shana's shoulder. "Shana, I've been sober for…" she checked her white ceramic Chanel watch "…about three hours and twenty minutes. If you don't come out on that court with me, well, I could fall right back off the wagon."

"Does Destiny even like ballet?" Karen asked.

Shana shook her head.

"No, she'd rather take art."

"Then let her take art. It's the twenty-first century, Shana. Dancing class and debutante balls are ludicrous anachronisms."

Karen was met with trio of blank stares.

"They're old fashioned and silly," she explained, "like beauty pageants."

Shana looked as if she'd been slapped.

Caroline sat down next to Shana and put her arm around her. "Maggie is never going to be a debutante either," she said sadly. "Maybe Karen is right and our girls don't need all this old anchor cronyism. But that is not the point. The point is that Tracy pushed you and Destiny around because she thinks she's better than you. You need to show her she's wrong."

Shana stood up, hugged Caroline tightly, and then picked up her racquet.

"Let's go. Someone needs us to teach her a West Virginia lesson."

The lovely pale yellow Jardine room resembled a sunlit field of dandelions nodding in the breeze as dozens of silver and white heads on slender, bejeweled necks dipped toward plates of chicken salad on white toast, glasses of sweet tea and double-shot highballs.

Clare slid into a chair at a large round table for six. The five older women already seated smiled tight smiles in her direction.

"Taffy Dandridge," said the woman immediately on her left, her white hair coiffed in a version of the Lavinia Winter power helmet. Taffy wore a bright pink woven Chanel suit shot through with gold threads and complemented with the requisite gold buttons.

"This is Martha Hastings, Genie Walters, Kat Moreland and Georgianna Davis," she said, going around the table clockwise as Clare nodded in greeting. "Clare Buxton is putting together a history of Belle Vista under Allie's supervision and we're to give her some help on the swinging sixties and so on."

The women giggled.

"And of course, we know it all because we've all been members since childhood and we all went to The Merrywood School together." Taffy pulled a square silver pendant with a tree embossed on it from the neckline of her jacket. Immediately, all the other women did the same.

"Could I see one of those?" said Clare curiously.

"Oh no," said Georgianna, shaking her head. The entire group emitted another tinny giggle, and Clare couldn't escape the idea that she'd been captured by some weird preppy cult.

"We can't take them off," Georgianna continued. "The chains were soldered on when the headmistress presented them. Each has our initials and graduation date. One wears it for life."

"Not to be grim," added Kate, "But also in death. A Merrywood girl is buried wearing her pendant."

Clare made a note, careful not to look too excited. This could definitely be helpful in identifying Pippa – if she could find her, that is.

Georgianna reached for the whiskey sour in front of her. "I hope you're not looking for anything too naughty. That was quite the time, you know."

More giggles.

"Oh no, nothing like that," Clare assured her, looking around for a waitress. She was going to need a drink herself to keep up this charade.

"I'll have a vodka martini and the rib eye, rare." Clare rattled off Allie's club number to the server as her companions looked on with disapproval. A rib eye at lunch!

"So, to my mind, the biggest event of the 60s and 70s had to be Phillippa Edgemoor's disappearance, correct?" asked Clare.

"That, and hosting the Ryder Cup in 1968," said Georgianna, a platinum blonde with shocking pink lips in a turquoise sheath.

"It was the Bellham Cup," corrected Martha Hastings, whose unnaturally black Cleopatra bob contrasted starkly with her bright yellow Dana Buchman summer suit.

"Oh, absolutely, how could I forget?" Georgianna exclaimed. "It was a pro-am and that handsome George Hamilton played."

Clare cleared her throat. "Uh, back to Phillipa…I've read all the clippings from 1972, but I'd like to know what you all, as her friends, thought might have happened."

A look went around the table. It was subtle, but it confirmed what Clare already knew. Pippa Edgemoor had never had any friends.

"Well it was very odd, her leaving like that," said the woman introduced as Kat. Her hair was white and sensibly short, she wore little makeup and a tailored navy shirtdress. "Pippa was always, um, a bit erratic. But she wasn't like Judy."

"Judy Simpson," said Taffy helpfully. "A dear friend who ran off right before high school graduation in 1963. Free spirit type, we'd always hear she'd been spotted at a concert or protest," Taffy continued. "You know, girls, we must include Judy in these lunches now that she's back." The group smiled and nodded.

When hell freezes over, thought Clare as her badly-needed martini arrived.

"Anyway," Kat continued, warming to her tale. "One expected Judy to leave; she told everyone she couldn't wait to escape and even painted a rather rude goodbye message on the school wall. Pippa, on the other hand, valued her place in Belle Vista society and her heritage."

"The Edgemoors, and their cats, have lived on this piece of land since Virginia was a colony," said Genie, a morose looking spinster in unseasonable burgundy boucle.

"Now, some of us believe they've quite overrun the club," said Kat.

"The Edgemoors?" asked Clare, confused.

"The *cats*," replied Kat.

Genie shot Kat a hostile look. "I believe Ms. Buxton is interested in Pippa, not our *beloved, historic* cats. Perhaps we should tell her about the Edgemoor curse?"

"Anytime an Edgemoor abandons Belle Vista permanently, something tragic happens," said Taffy, in between bites of chicken salad. "Phillipa's grandfather moved to New York and was hit by a falling stockbroker when Wall Street crashed. *His* grandfather was eaten by wolves in the Yukon during the gold rush."

"Bears," countered Kat.

"Polar?" asked Taffy.

"Grizzly," said Kat with certainty.

"Just like *Grizzly Man*. So gruesome," exclaimed Taffy gleefully, sipping her drink.

Clare took a swig of her martini. It was going to be a long lunch.

"And then there was Pippa's aunt," Taffy continued.

"Oh yes, that was tragic," said Georgianna with the hungry look of one who feeds on tales of others' woes. "Eloped with a Hindu student she met at university, a terrible scandal. At their wedding in New Delhi, an elephant threw them off and trampled her."

"It was *exactly* like that movie with Elizabeth Taylor," said Taffy.

"No, in *Elephant Walk*, Elizabeth Taylor *escapes* the elephant stampede," corrected Kat.

Oh, for Pete's sake, thought Clare.

"So the point here, if there is one, is that it was unexpected and out of character for Pippa to leave suddenly and permanently?"

"Absolutely," said Martha. "Curse or no, she had no reason to leave. She was the queen of the social scene, she'd just renovated the Edgemoor estate, and there were rumors that after years of, shall we say, playing the field, she had finally settled on the man she wished to marry."

"Do you know his name," asked Clare, jotting a few notes on her pad. "Did *he* wish to marry *her*?"

There was an uncomfortable silence.

"Frankly," said Georgianna, "his wishes hardly mattered. Phillipa Edgemoor always got her way."

The top three teams from each club faced off on the "show courts" near the clubhouse. Lines four and five were exiled to courts fourteen and fifteen near the ninth fairway, where the Donaldson twins, Kendall Pedersen and Hayes Grant dealt with the racket from golf course renovations. The Edgemoor cats also regarded the back courts as giant litter boxes. Allie, however, felt they were good enough for players unable or unwilling to pay for the many lessons and clinics needed to successfully play a top line.

Caroline and Karen miraculously dispatched their River's Edge rivals in less than an hour, and Karen felt upbeat about the overall match outcome until she decided to retrieve a pair of flip flops from her car. Out in the parking lot, a handful of River's Edge players were dancing around a tailgate spread featuring a margarita machine as "Joy to the World" blared from the sound system of a dark blue Lexus SUV. Jamal, beside himself with glee, was filming the whole thing.

She returned to find Caroline at a courtside table watching Allie and Elena. "I think our lower courts tanked," she said.

"How did you find out?" asked Caroline, running her finger through the whipped cream on a mini key lime pie she'd snagged from the luncheon buffet.

"The River's Edge winners are filming a *Girls Gone Wild* victory video in our parking lot," she said with disgust. "It's only a matter of time until the wet t-shirt contest. I hope Shana and Taylor and Allie and Elena come through."

Caroline nodded, although secretly she was torn. Watching Lila Chang pound Elena into submission would be extremely rewarding.

Allie and Elena had lost the first set in a tiebreaker. Now the second set was in a tiebreaker as well, and neither player was competing for the supportive partner award.

"You played on the tour, and you're letting yourself get beaten by an amateur who's ten years older than you," snarled Allie to Elena as they conferenced before the tiebreaker.

"This might be truth," said Elena icily. "If Asian woman and I were playing singles, we would see. But sadly we are being stuck with inferior partners. Some more inferior than others. I am thinking this

Kristen is being much younger than you and having better forehand, no?"

"How many times do I have to tell you Lila Chang is NOT Asian?" whispered Allie. "And Kristen was only two years behind me in high school."

"Really?" said Elena, with exaggerated surprised. "After match you should ask her what face cream she is using and buy some."

"Time!" called Currie Holmes.

On court two Shana was breathing hard. She and Taylor had taken the first set 6-4, partly because she was so fueled by rage at Tracy Logan. But the second set wasn't going well; they were down 5-0 and after this changeover, Taylor would have to serve just to keep them in the set.

Shana was not one to blame her partner, but Taylor had no energy. Shana found herself harboring a very un-Christian hope that Taylor had vodka hidden in her water bottle. Sober, Taylor really sucked. She took a discreet sip out of Taylor's bottle as they passed under the awning while changing sides. Nothing but water. "Damn," mumbled Shana to herself.

"I suck sober," whispered Taylor. On top of everything else, the sun was now in their eyes.

"How 'bout this," whispered Shana. "There's bound to be tons of alcohol and chemicals stored in your brain. Just see if you can use them." Shana had no idea if this were true. Her high school science teacher had been a Creationist, so her grasp of biology was tentative at best. She could, however, name all the animals saved from The Flood in alphabetical order.

"Okay, I'll try and get in touch with my inner drunk," sighed Taylor. "Here goes nothing."

Miraculously, Taylor managed to resurrect her game and take the second set to 5-3, but it was too little too late, and they lost the final game and the set after three deuces.

"We're gonna do great in the third," said Shana as they walked off court.

"I don't know if they'll even make you play a third," said Karen glumly as they sat down for a brief break. "If Allie and Elena lose this tiebreaker, it's over; we've lost. It's been really long and close, but now it's 15-14 River's Edge. "

Shana sat down between Caroline and Karen, but Taylor noticed that Mike Chang had arrived – he had a lot of free time, like most multi-millionaires – and was seated at a table directly in front of court one, playing with his iPad.

"'Scuse me while I go say hello to someone," she said.

Taylor kissed a flustered Mike on the cheek, plopped down next to him, put a hand on his thigh and whispered conspiratorially in his ear. On Court one Lila looked over, and the ball she'd tossed in the air to serve dropped right on her head. She double faulted to tie up the game, then blasted a return over the fence and, finally, hit an easy winner into the net, handing Allie and Elena the second set. The Jones Belle Vista audience erupted in applause; the match was still up for grabs.

Taylor sauntered back to her team table as Lila Chang stormed off court toward her husband.

"Wow," said Caroline to Taylor, "Lila sure looks jealous. I didn't even know you knew Mike Chang."

"Never seen him before in my life," said Taylor, smiling.

Lunch in the Jardine Room was winding down, and Clare gloomily stuffed the remains of her rib eye in a Styrofoam takeout container. She'd hit a brick wall when she'd tried to get the ladies to gossip about Pippa's relationship with Lavinia, who still wielded considerable power among the club's seniors.

The ladies got up to go and said their goodbyes to Clare, who nodded and thanked them. But as Taffy started to leave, Clare spoke.

"Mrs. Dandridge, I wonder if you could stay a few minutes longer. I want to show you something puzzling I found in the library." She pulled the slam book out of her tote bag.

Taffy looked behind her to make sure her companions had left, then made a lunge for the little notebook.

"Give that to me!"

"Oh, 'fraid not," said Clare. "You seemed to have a lot to say back in the day about your friends. Of course, I could be persuaded."

"What do you want to know," Taffy whispered, narrowing her eyes.

"Lavinia and Pippa. Their enduring friendship. Why Lavinia is the only person Pippa ever contacts."

"All right," said Taffy, sitting back down and lowering her voice. "That is a complete crock. Pippa wouldn't write Lavinia if she were the last person on earth. Lavinia and Pippa hated, hated, hated each other. They competed for everything. Pippa didn't like to lose. She dropped tennis because Vinnie could beat her. When Vinnie won the Cotillion Crown – well, many of us thought she would end up like Betty Greig."

Clare raised her eyebrows.

"In sixth grade Betty beat Pippa in the camp swimming competition. Then, one night, Betty Grieg snuck out of her cabin and drowned."

Clare gave her a confused look.

"Pippa was my bunkmate. I woke up and saw her sneaking in late that night, *soaking wet*. It was right out of *The Bad Seed* with Patty McCormack. And it's not just Betty. When Pippa had a grudge, accidents happened. Maybe you want to ask around about the fiancé who jilted her, or her slutty stepmother."

Clare sighed. This old lady had some wild imagination. Before she knew it Taffy would be claiming Pippa was a vampire, "Just like in *Twilight*!"

"Okay, let's assume that Lavinia did not suspect Pippa of being a murderous psychopath," said Clare sarcastically. "She left ten years after that Cotillion thing. Isn't it possible she and Lavinia patched things up?"

Taffy gave her a pitying stare.

"For a historical researcher, if that is indeed what you are, you are no Ken Burns. You certainly don't seem to have a sense of Pippa at all. Do you have any idea who she planned on marrying? *Do* you? Prescott *Winter*, Lavinia's husband!"

With that she snatched the slam book out of Clare's hands and fled the room.

Byron hurried over to the Belle Vista ladies' table with his stylist emergency kit, accompanied by his assistant, Shelli, a twenty-something with blue hair, combat boots and multiple tattoos.

"It's touch up time," he trilled just as Currie Holmes stalked by, followed by Lauren Lippert, who was complaining that light reflecting off the Vixen camera lenses was interfering with her shots.

Currie stopped near the table and eyed Byron and Shelli disapprovingly.

"There will be ten more minutes to this break, then the third set will commence. Immediately. Anyone not on court will forfeit."

With that, she turned and walked toward the tennis center.

"Baba Yaga is needing new glasses," sniffed Elena as she arrived at the table, pointing toward the retreating Currie. "Line calls all going to other team." Only Karen got the reference to the Russian fairytale witch with chicken legs, but the others understood and appreciated Elena's disdain.

As Byron powdered faces and relined lips, Shana looked at her watch. "I need to use the ladies, but I don't fancy going in the tennis locker room with Currie and Tracy and them. Anyone else want to run up to the main clubhouse?"

"I'll stay here," said Taylor. "Without alcohol my whole system is shutting down. I don't even need to pee."

"Oh for God's sake," said Allie. "We are ALL going to use the restroom right now, the one in the tennis locker room, so we're back on court ON TIME. Enough make up! Up! Now!"

Shana, Taylor and even Elena jumped up and followed Allie obediently.

"She reminds me of my Dad," said Shelli to Byron. "He's a prison guard."

All the stalls were occupied, so Shana fixed her hair in the mirror while the other three sat on benches. They heard a flush (although Shana, per Allie's instructions, was trying not to listen), followed by the glugging and burbling Shana had heard earlier.

"Hey, Allie," said Shana. "There's that noise...."

But she never got to finish her sentence. Five loud gushes, one after another, erupted in the stalls, followed by screams and rattling as the horrified occupants fumbled with locks. Tracy Logan, the runner, escaped first. Covered with brown, reeking sludge, she bolted from the locker room as if she were heading for the finish line at the Olympics.

The Belle Vista ladies jumped up on the benches as the remaining three River's Edge players and Currie Holmes emerged covered in sewage, which continued to flow from the toilets.

"Oh, dear, there must be a plumbing issue," said Allie lamely.

"*Plumbing issue*? You *think*? I'll fucking get you for this, Allie Beech. You and your stupid whore teammate," Lauren screeched as she stripped off her reeking tennis wear and bolted naked for the showers, followed by a gagging Lila and sobbing Kristen.

"That's deplorable language, Lauren," said Currie, who walked at her own measured pace from the stall area toward the showers. Even raw sewage was not going push Currie Holmes around. She turned briefly toward the Belle Vista team members, looking as dignified as she could with shit dripping from her hair.

"Due to unacceptable facility conditions, Jones Belle Vista forfeits this match and the *entire* season."

19

Maria and Consuela were clearing the remains of salmon salad from the team's usual long terrace table after a much subdued version of the end of season luncheon.

"As you all know, we have forfeited the entire season due to our...facility issues. A sad and unprecedented event in Belle Vista history," Allie solemnly intoned.

"It's not as if Lincoln was just shot," Karen muttered under her breath.

"To wrap things up," said Allie, checking her Tag Heuer, "we are now in last place in our league for the first, and I hope, last time ever. We will not speak of it again. Next on the agenda is, of course, Founder's Day, where I hope to recapture some of the respect of our community."

Founder's Day, held on the final Saturday of July, was the biggest social event on the club's calendar. To the dismay of Belle Vista's golfers, it was a tennis-centric celebration that culminated in the highly competitive ladies' singles championship – the Edgemoor Cup.

"I expect team members to sign up for the round robins and ladies' doubles," said Allie, who pointedly left out ladies' singles. She was frankly hoping Elena would be out of town. Now that Lou was out of the running, she planned to take home the Edgemoor Cup herself. "Also, there are still shifts available supervising children's activities."

Shana raised her hand timidly. "I didn't even know there had been a Founder's Day committee meeting. Don't we need to plan the food and entertainment? Wayne and I know this great Randy Travis cover band and we could have a new trophy designed for the ladies' championship, something honoring Lou."

Allie glared at Shana. The woman was more annoying than ever. Her plain white Ralph Lauren tennis dress looked eerily familiar, especially when paired with neutral lipstick and smooth, straight hair pulled back in a neat pony tail. As if you could hide trailer trash breeding under a thin veneer of designer clothing and cosmetics.

"Planning meetings began last January, long before you and Wayne arrived," said Allie dismissively. "As for a new trophy, well, I don't suppose you can be expected to appreciate the significance of the Edgemoor Cup, but suffice it to say, everyone else does. If you wish to be useful, make sure we have properly flushing toilets." She looked long and hard at Shana. "I assume your husband is working on that?"

Shana felt the color rise in her face. She didn't want to snap at Allie, even though for once the cameras were absent (Jamal had flatly refused to film one more moment of women eating salmon). But she wouldn't stand by and let her imply that Big Wayne wasn't doing his job.

"You know, Allie, this club had a ton of problems before we got here and Wayne is not going to be able to wave a magic wand and fix them all overnight," she said.

Allie was not accustomed to anyone, except her own children of course, talking back.

"That is the *entire* reason you are here, Shana," Allie said, closing her notebook and rising from the table. "I hope you know that."

An uncomfortable silence enveloped the group as Allie retreated from the terrace.

"Allie always gets a bug up her ass around Founder's Day," Taylor said finally. "I mean, a bigger bug than usual. What do you say the rest of us go hit some more balls?"

"Sorry, am having massage, then waiting for husband to call from Croatia," said Elena, rising and pulling her bag on her shoulder. "Three weeks now he is on business trip, so we are needing daily phone sex."

"What, exactly, qualifies as too much information for Uziwhatevers?" said Taylor.

Elena looked offended. "I am *Russian* raised in Uzbekistan. Father was Minister of Oppression of Religion in Soviet Union days." She turned her back on the group and stalked away.

"Next thing, I'll be expected to tell one type of Asian from another," said Taylor. "Karen?"

"Not today," said Karen, forcing herself to ignore Taylor's latest foray into political incorrectness. She'd agreed to give Sean's two nieces a tennis lesson – on the public courts near his townhouse, not at Belle Vista. Not that she was sneaking around. After all, she wasn't doing anything *wrong*.

"I need to grocery shop," said Caroline, inexplicably ducking under the table. Ah ha! That Elena thought she was so clever, but Caroline had managed to flip a credit card out of Elena's wallet and drop it to the floor. She could tell by feel it was a MasterCard – jackpot! "Grocery shopping always makes me so tired, I think I'll treat myself to a mani-pedi after," she said, popping back up and slipping the card into her bag.

"Shana?" asked Taylor almost timidly.

Shana sighed. She'd already had a lesson with Justin *and* team practice, plus she'd planned to sneak off to the public library and go through the adoption website postings. But Taylor was trying so hard to stay sober, and Shana had yet to make good on her vow to help her teammates. She could feel the Lord putting Taylor's sobriety in her hands, at least for the next hour.

"That sounds great," she said with false cheeriness. "Let's hit the courts."

After more than an hour of singles, Shana was wiped out. She walked to the awning-shaded bench beside the court, filled her water bottle from the ornate brass water fountain and took a long drink. She smiled as she saw Smokey Joe, a battered old gray Tom, and Janie, a much younger tabby, grooming each other on the lawn nearby. Even the cats here had trophy wives. She checked her watch.

"My goodness, it's almost four o'clock. I need to pick up Destiny from art and Lil Wayne from computer camp, get myself showered up and think about dinner."

Taylor's face fell as she sat down on the bench and crossed her long caramel colored legs. Shana thought she looked like a sunflower, her lovely golden head drooping over her slender body.

"I guess I'll go to the gym for a while, and then maybe out to Neiman's to see the new fall clothes, plus I've got twenty hours of *The Real Housewives* on DVR, although it's kind of hard to watch without wine, especially New Jersey."

"Isn't Spencer gonna be home soon?"

"Spencer is hardly ever home – people talk about doctor's hours, but he does a lot of other stuff too, like nonprofit work."

"Like with burned children and poor patients?" Shanna asked. She certainly understood that; Wayne spent a lot of hours teaching reading at the detention center.

"Not exactly – he's president of the Plastic Surgeon's Defense Fund. You know that doctor Harbagian whose patient died after liposuction? Spencer raised the money for the lawyer that got him off."

To Shana's surprise, Taylor started to tear up. "I didn't mind so much when I was drinking, but now I'm kind of lonely." She laughed. "I guess I'm bad company when I'm sober, even for myself"

Shana got up and pulled Taylor up with her. "Taylor Thomas, you are coming home with me for a nice family dinner. I'm going to teach you to cook something that will put some meat on that skinny, overworked doctor husband of yours. I'll bet he's lonely too, but he just doesn't know how to change things up."

Big Wayne sat in the farthest recesses of the least used bar at Belle Vista, a dimly lit nook hidden behind the "cigar room" that only the most dedicated drinkers ever located. He was alone except for Jorge, a tall, morose Peruvian who spent most of his time polishing bar equipment and dusting liquor bottles in silence.

"Hit me up again, Georgie," said Wayne, extending his highball glass toward Jorge, who poured him his third Wild Turkey straight up.

"That's a pretty mean before dinner drink," said Judy, who'd entered silently and slipped onto the barstool next to Big Wayne. "Jorge, el habitual por favor." He nodded and mixed her a Cuba Libre.

"Don't he mind you callin' him whore whatever?" whispered Wayne to Judy.

"That's how you say his name in Spanish. Hor-hay," said Judy smiling.

"Just one more thing a big, dumb redneck don't know," said Wayne glumly. He picked up his glass and slammed back his drink in one big gulp.

"Hey, you're talking bad about one of my favorite people," said Judy, taking a sip of her drink. "And you found my private bar. To make it up to me, you have to tell me what's wrong."

To Judy's surprise (and probably Jorge's as well, although the bartender remained stoic), Big Wayne put his head in his hands and began to sob.

"I've ruined things for everyone; me, Shana, the kids – even you Judy. I'm goin' broke."

Judy practiced the one useful thing she'd learned (other than beekeeping and various Eastern sexual techniques) in the Universal Family of Truth. She sat completely still, listened and waited.

"I sold my gentlemen's clubs and invested in Jack Walinsky's Capitol Capital Fund. Not only am I not earning interest, my principal is gone, and Jack is in Eastern Europe somewhere and can't be reached," Wayne shook his head. "Hit me up again, Georhay."

"Whoa," said Judy, holding her hand over Wayne's glass. "Slow down. Wayne, you still have your car washes and other businesses, right?"

Wayne laughed bitterly, hiccupping at the end. "Oh, that's enough for us to live on but not enough to run this club. I signed a contract and own fifty-one percent of Jones Belle Vista. The damn thing's a money pit. Contractors put in corrugated plastic instead of PVC waste pipes, so we got that sewage backup and now the electric's not right. The pro shops buy all this expensive inventory and keep it till it gets dusty because no one knows how to sell it, and the members are pilfering the club blind."

Silently, Jorge walked over and patted Big Wayne on the shoulder.

"Why don't you sell?" asked Judy.

Big Wayne guffawed. "This ain't the economy to sell a country club losing more than two million a year. Apparently, there was only one fool big enough to buy this one, and he's sittin' here next to you and Horgie." He reached into a bowl of pretzels, stuffed a handful in his mouth and munched morosely.

"I even called Donald Trump," Wayne continued through a mouthful of crumbs. "But he says he's got enough clubs, plus tennis ladies cause him more problems than all his wives put together, so no thank you."

"How do I tell my Shana? She's got used to this lifestyle. The kids have tennis and swim and golf lessons, and art and computer camp, and next year she wants them in Belle Vista Country Day so they can get into Jardine Academy for high school. That's twenty-five thousand a year each. Plus Shana's got her reality show, and tennis lessons, and her designer clothes and exercise classes. Why does hot yoga hafta cost more than regular yoga?" moaned Wayne.

"La calefaccion?" suggested Jorge.

Wayne put his head back in his huge, calloused hands. "We're going to go back to havin' nothin' and to bein' nothin'."

"Wayne, that is not going to happen," said Judy, sliding off her barstool. "You're a man of faith, and you need to call on that faith now. I believe the universe has a way of making things right for good people. This is all going to work out fine. Jorge, make our friend here a pot of strong coffee." She patted Wayne on the back. "I'm going to visit the little girls' room, then we're going to sober you up and I'm going to drive you home."

Judy walked around the corner and into the ladies lounge, pulled out her cell phone and dialed.

"Hello Vinnie, it's Judy. We need to talk."

"You're kidding me, right?" said Taylor wrinkling her nose as she stared at the pinkish mound of ground beef topped with two gelatinous raw eggs, chopped onion and fluffy white bread crumbs.

"Uh uh," said Shana. "You just squirt in some ketchup, like this, some Worcestershire sauce (she pronounced it wortchestersheer), like that, then go like this." She began to knead the ingredients. "C'mon, you try." Shana pushed the bowl toward Taylor.

"My French manicure!"

"Don't worry; you just pick the meat right out of your nails."

"Gross." Taylor gingerly patted the meatloaf mixture.

"Get your hands into it, work out some anger."

"Hey, this isn't too bad. I'm just pretending that it's Lauren Lippert's brain," said Taylor, enthusiastically digging into the raw meatloaf.

Shana giggled. "*That's* gross. Now we just form it into a nice little loaf on the baking sheet, squirt some more ketchup on top, and put it in the oven for forty-five minutes at three fifty."

When they sat down to dinner, Shana was touched by how pleased Taylor was with her role in the simple dinner, which included mashed potatoes and reheated green beans. It was too bad Big Wayne had come home with a stomach bug and had to go to bed, but Judy and the kids, after a few hints, raved about the meal. After cleanup, Destiny ran off to spend the night with a neighbor, and Judy and Lil Wayne retreated to the basement.

"Lil Wayne," said Judy when they were downstairs, "I need your help with a top secret computer project. Think you can do it?"

"I'm in the class with the sixth graders," Lil Wayne said proudly. "I did a PowerPoint on Bethany."

"One can only imagine what a hit that was with eleven-year-old boys," chuckled Judy. "Now this is strictly between us, okay? And you'll even get to learn some French."

Upstairs, Taylor and Shanna curled up on the huge red ultra suede sectional in the family room with cups of Constant Comment tea, and Taylor picked up the remote and turned on the TV. "Oh, man, a *RuPaul's Drag Race* marathon. This should keep me busy till Spencer picks me up – I hope you don't mind it won't be till after ten?"

"I am really enjoying spending some girlfriend time with you, Taylor."

"Me too. And I loved having dinner with the kids. You know, I'm kind of hoping that once I'm through this sobriety program, Spencer and I will finally have a family. I'm thirty-seven, it's not too late. "

Shana had wondered whether Taylor couldn't have children or just didn't want them. Taylor talked a lot, but not about things like that.

But for the next three hours, as RuPaul transformed one hopeful drag queen after another, Shana got an earful. The Thomases had been married for ten years, and from what Taylor said, Spencer didn't show much interest in his amazingly beautiful wife. Especially in the bedroom. Taylor was not shy about details, and Shana doubled checked more than once to make sure the door to the basement was closed. Lil Wayne had some serious radar when it came to eavesdropping on conversations about sex.

"You know, a lot of people think because Spencer's a plastic surgeon, I'm all reconstructed," said Taylor, training her wide hazel eyes on Shana. "But other than a little Botox and some fillers in my laugh lines, this is all me, even the boobs. Not many people around here can say that."

"I sure can't," admitted Shana, whose implants had been a business decision back in her "bookkeeping" days at the Do It All Night.

"Sometimes I've wondered if Spencer's seeing another woman, but when we go out, he's not the kind of guy who stares at women or flirts. I mean, shit, he's more likely to admire some guy's tie than his wife. It must just be me," she sighed. "Well, I'm not the only one with man trouble. Karen and Greg are on the outs over trying to get preggers, and Caroline got dumped by that scumbag Jack and can't stop spending cash she doesn't have anymore."

Taylor prattled nonstop until Spencer picked her up. He pecked his wife politely on the cheek as she met him at the door, and Shana couldn't help but compare that to the big warm bear hug Wayne always gave her.

After they left and she finally got Lil Wayne off to bed, Shana grabbed a box of Oreos and a glass of milk, curled back up on the sofa and tuned to *Sleepless in Seattle* on Lifetime. It was so cute how Meg

Ryan and Tom Hanks got together. If only her friends' lives could be more like romantic comedies.

Shana pulled apart another Oreo and began to lick the sugary white icing while she thought. Why couldn't they be? She grabbed her pink "idea" notebook off the coffee table and wrote "Taylor" at the top of one page, "Karen" on another and finally "Caroline". Shana was ready to make good on her vow to help her friends, and write a script that would solve all of their problems! Even better, she'd make sure their happy endings were captured on film, just like Meg's and Tom's and RuPaul's.

20

Maria Delgado eyed the buffet and the cooking stations set up on long tables surrounding the pool. The Prestons were customers at Cancun, the little mall restaurant where she worked, and they'd hired her to cater their fiftieth anniversary party. Everything looked beautiful; the paella, tacos mariscos and flautas were done to perfection, and the staff was at their professional best in their white chef coats and hats. Except, Maria noted with despair, Caroline Walinsky, who was stuffing a flauta into her mouth.

"I don't know if this is such a good idea, Miss Shana," Maria had said when Shana called last week to ask her this special favor. "All these years I wait on Miss Caroline, I don't know if she can take orders from me. Besides, I can't afford another helper."

But Shana had offered to reimburse her for Caroline's wages. Maria had hoped her clients would veto Shana's other request – a small Vixen crew filming Caroline as she worked – but the Prestons were absurdly excited about their anniversary party being on TV.

Shana said she hoped to give Caroline the self- esteem she needed to look for a real job. But Maria privately thought that Caroline had plenty of self-esteem. What she lacked was self-control. Not to mention common sense and anything remotely resembling a work ethic.

"Miss Caroline," said Maria as sweetly as she could manage. "We are bit short of flautas, so we should save them for the guests."

"Well, you ought to plan better," said Caroline. "I didn't get a chance to eat lunch, and I'm sure you don't want me fainting dead away when the guests arrive."

Maria counted to ten silently. It was all she could do not to throw Caroline Walinsky into the pool, provided she could lift her after all those flautas.

"Now remember, Miss Caroline," she said with exaggerated patience, "it is your job to greet the guests politely and answer any questions they have about the food. You read the descriptions of the dishes I gave you, right?"

"Of course," said Caroline huffily, as she straightened her "Chef Caroline" nametag. "Maria, you have nothing to worry about. Shana explained to me that you really need someone who can relate to your clients. I know how hard that must be for you," she added with a condescending look that made Maria fume. "And it's not as if I'll be serving or cleaning up. After all, I'm Chef Caroline!"

"Oh brother," said Consuela under her breath as she walked by carrying a tray of mini empanadas.

With great trepidation, Maria left "Chef Caroline" in charge of the buffet and went to check the bar and the dessert stations.

Caroline stood by her table with a smile that she'd copied from the woman who sold cupcake pans on QVC. Now *that* would be a great job. And maybe this was good practice, even if it was a little humiliating. She'd never have agreed, but Shana had said she'd had a vision that Caroline's future would involve food. So of course she couldn't say no, because Shana had foretold it, which meant it was like it had already happened. Or something.

Still, that Maria certainly was bossy. Read descriptions of the dishes! It wasn't Caroline's fault she'd accidentally dropped them in her tub while taking a bath; a real business woman multitasks, she'd learned that on *Celebrity Apprentice*. Besides, how hard could describing food be?

A couple in their seventies, in shapeless linen shorts and matching blue polo shirts, advanced on the buffet.

"Hi, I'm Chef Caroline," Caroline greeted them.

"What's this pallella business," said the husband, a crabby retired insurance salesman who longed for the days when a barbecue meant steaks on the grill.

"Pah-yay-ya," corrected Caroline self-importantly. "It's made in a very special copper pan from Spain that normally retails for one hundred seventy-nine dollars or more, but this week is available for just ninety-nine. If you order by midnight, you'll get a free olive pitter!"

"Are you selling pans?" asked the salesman's wife, confused.

"Of course not! You buy them from QVC. Also Sur la Table, but then you don't get the free olive pitter," Caroline explained.

"So how is this made?" the wife persisted.

Caroline tried to keep smiling, but was getting a bit exasperated. She tried speaking *very slowly*.

"Like. I. Said. In a *special copper pan. From Spain*."

The couple drifted off toward the flautas without trying the paella. Caroline frowned. She would have to improve her sales technique.

"Excuse me, Chef Caroline," said a petite, bespectacled woman in her fifties wearing an extremely regrettable pair of orange flowered Capri pants. "Is this sausage paella or does it contain shellfish?"

"Sausage," said Caroline, figuring she had a fifty/fifty chance of being right.

The woman, who was named Verna and taught literature at a local community college, proceeded to heap her plate with paella and move on. Caroline beamed and adjusted the toque balanced precariously on her teased hair. She knew she'd be good at this!

Taylor reached over and slipped her hand into Spencer's as the house lights dimmed. This had been so sweet of Shana, treating them to a romantic night out after she'd told her how much they enjoyed musical theater. It was opening night for the Tony-award winning play *Life is a Drag* at the Kennedy Center and they had amazing orchestra seats. Afterward, a room at the Ritz-Carlton and room service complete with champagne and caviar.

"Doesn't this remind you of when we saw *Phantom*?" whispered Taylor, slipping her hand onto Spencer's thigh. That had been the first night they'd ever made love. Well, the first night Spencer had ever made love. Taylor's virginity had been left in a Richmond stadium parking lot after her high school boyfriend won states in lacrosse. She'd been all set to fake innocence, but poor Spencer had been so awkward she'd had to abandon that plan and take the lead.

Spencer smiled, patted her hand gently and put it back on the armrest, then pointed to her Playbill. "You should read up on the play before they dim the lights. It's gotten fabulous reviews."

The John F. Kennedy Center Presents:

Life is a Drag
By Andrew James and Melvin Williams

Set in 1963 in the small town of Sugar Creek, Kansas, Life is a Drag chronicles the unlikely romance of Norman George, a 40-something "confirmed bachelor," and Betty Bombazine, the new secretary at his candy company, Amazing Confections. Family, friends and Norman himself are delighted when he falls for the curvaceous, vivacious Betty, a newcomer to Sweet Creek. Secretly, they'd all feared Norman might be "different".

What Norman and the rest don't know is that Betty and her bevy of beautiful friends, who now work at the chocolate factory, are New York City drag performers. They're on the run from the law in an era when being gay, or dressing in drag, could mean a stint in jail or a mental hospital.

When the Feds track down Betty and her companions, the good citizens of Sweet Creek must make a choice; fall in line with conventional morality, or protect the "girls" who give new meaning to the town and company motto "We'll Make Your Life Sweeter".

As the first act began, Taylor surreptitiously observed her handsome husband with newly sober eyes as Betty and the chorus of "Candy Queens" sang the opening number "Amazing Confections".

Spencer sat with perfect posture, eyes glued to the stage, silently lip-synching the lyrics Betty Bombazine belted out:

"Oh, I'm an amazing conFECtion, my hair and my clothes are perFECtion."

Spencer's hair was *perfectly* blow-dried and gelled. In fact, Spencer had taken so long with the blow dryer, her own hair was still damp. At forty, he still had the looks of a Ralph Lauren model, just tanned enough, blue eyes with the *perfect* bit of crinkle. And he looked so *perfectly* smart in his textured grey Lanvin two-button suit, white Givenchy dress shirt and Ralph Lauren Black Label grey-and-black striped tie. He'd given her the designer rundown as they dressed.

"We love our lace and our satin, our pearls, heels and furs," sang the Candy Queens.

"Our equipment is 'his' but our style is pure 'hers'."

Taylor frowned. Most of her friends' husbands were hopeless at buying clothes, but Spencer loved keeping up with trends. She started to feel a little queasy. A line of cold sweat formed on the back of her elegant neck. Tonight, when she'd tried to pick out a tie for him, he'd just laughed and rejected her selection as "very last season". Then, when she tied it for him, he'd retied it, complaining her "half Windsor" was sloppy; he preferred a "dimpled four-in-hand". Spencer was singing aloud now, his whitened teeth gleaming in the dark theater as he half-whispered the lyrics.

"We're amazing conFECTions, sweet but with GUTS;
Each one, soft and creamy, a creation so dreamy, but take a bite and you'll find we've got … NUTS!"

"Oh my God!" shrieked Taylor, jumping up and throwing her Playbill on Spencer's lap with an audible thwap. "You're *gay*!"

"Shhhh," hushed Spencer, grabbing her arm and trying to pull her back into her seat. Taylor teetered on her Louboutin platforms, but after a decade of competitive tennis she had the musculature of a professional arm wrestler. She regained her balance and shook him off like a mastiff flipping a Chihuahua off its neck.

"Don't you shush me, Mr. Dimpled Four in Hand!" Taylor yelled, oblivious to the shocked murmurs around her. "It all makes sense now; I was always just too drunk to put it together! You never leave dirty underwear and socks on the floor, or make me watch Monday night football!"

Behind them, a middle-aged couple visiting from Milwaukee broke into laughter. "I didn't know this show had audience participation," Jeannie Murphy whispered to her husband.

"Like the murder mystery nights at the dinner theater at home," said her husband Bob with relief. He'd been a little worried about telling the guys at the plant he'd seen a gay show, but now he could talk about the good looking gal who practically fell in his lap.

"Don't be ridiculous," whispered Spencer. Or he tried to whisper. They audience had gone scary quiet trying to hear them. There wasn't even the comforting crinkle of a cough drop being unwrapped. Spencer's voice rose in panic. "I'm a husband, and a doctor and I was raised Mormon!"

The entire audience roared with laughter.

On stage, the actor playing Betty whispered to the baffled chorus, "I think we've got to run with this, at least until security takes them. Hell, they're getting more laughs than we are. Everybody here's done improv, right? Let's roll!"

"Oh he's an amazing conFECTion," belted out Betty, motioning to the orchestra to follow.

"Puts his socks away without diRECTion!" replied the Candy Queens.

A spotlight swung and highlighted Taylor and Spencer.

"Oh for craps' sake," said Spencer, trying to duck out of the light.

"You lectured me on the difference between crème brûlée and crème caramel at dinner!" Taylor wailed, oblivious to the spotlight. "You said the floral arrangement was overwrought! Straight guys do not call floral arrangements overwrought! They don't even call them floral arrangements! They call them fucking *flowers*, and that's if they don't think they're a fancy salad and eat them by mistake!"

"He thinks too much about the flowers," sang Betty.

"He can go on and on for hours and hours, and yet we hear him say," echoed the chorus.

"He could not possibly be gay!" sang Betty.

"A Mormon doctor can't be gay!" the chorus sang lustily.

When security arrived, Taylor was battering Spencer about the head with the bejeweled snakeskin patterned Judith Leiber clutch he'd selected to match her raw silk cranberry Nicole Miller evening dress. After a minor scuffle (Taylor did not take kindly to having her beat down of Spencer interrupted) the guards marched them down the aisle and out of the theater to a reprise of "Amazing Confections". As they exited, the audience leapt to its collective feet and erupted in wild applause.

Karen found the invitation wrapped around the handle of her tennis racquet. "Tonight is for romance. Meet me at the Ritz Carlton at eight. Suite Five Twenty Four." No signature. Just a heart.

Sean must have slipped it around her racquet this morning when they'd stopped for coffee after another lesson with his nieces. She knew they had developed feelings for each other, but she didn't think…

She was going to have to call him. Tell him it wasn't ever going to happen, that even their friendship would have to end, because she wasn't the kind of woman who did things like this. Even if her husband was out of town on business and ignoring all her calls because she'd refused to have dinner with his overbearing parents last week. Even if Sean was the kindest, funniest, sexiest…

"Stop!" Karen yelled at herself, leaning on the horn so that it bleated. The driver of the Peapod delivery van in front of her stuck his hand out the window and flipped her off.

That decided it. She was in no frame of mind to call Sean. Not yet. She'd have to calm down first. Maybe have a decaf at Starbucks. Just walk around a little and think. Nowhere in particular. She turned into the mall parking lot and slipped into a parking space right outside the entrance to Victoria's Secret.

Caroline was happily chatting away to a couple visiting from Florida. She was getting much better at her paella spiel, throwing in lingo memorized from *Top Chef*, including braising, roux and sous vide, when a commotion poolside interrupted her patter.

"Someone get Benadryl," she heard a man yell, and peering over her audience saw Verna clutching her throat, her face covered in huge orange welts that matched her hideous pants.

An angry Maria strode up and poked her index finger at Caroline's nametag.

"Did you not tell that woman that this is paella with shell-fish? She is allergic!" Maria yelled, heedless of the Vixen cameras and Caroline's live audience.

Allergic. There were not many things that could get Caroline moving, but ever since Lou's death, the word *allergic* worked on her like an electric cattle prod.

"Out of my way," she hollered, pushing Maria aside and pulling an Epipen out of her pocket; she now carried one at all times. She bolted through the crowd to the poolside chaise where Verna sat, feet up, having just taken a long gulp of Benadryl.

"Don't worry, I'll save you," Caroline shrieked, pushing her down and straddling her, the white chef's toque flopping precariously to one side.

"Please, stop," gasped Verna her eyes rounding with horror at the Sweeney Todd vision of mad Chef Caroline poised above her, injector pen in hand. "Took Benadryl … will be fine."

"No offense," said Caroline, holding Verna down with one hand while she raised the Epipen in the air. "But I've already allergy killed one person this year. Two would really make me look bad." And with that she jabbed the injector right into Verna's orange-flowered thigh.

Karen walked tentatively down the fifth floor hallway of the Ritz Carlton, trying not to trip. Even though she was Catholic, she wasn't used to wearing a full-length nun's habit.

An extreme disguise perhaps, but she purchased it at a costume store figuring as long as she was going to hell, she might as well go all in. Underneath the flowing robe, her new silk cami from Victoria's Secret swished tantalizingly against her skin. Karen hated to admit it, but this whole cloak-and-dagger thing was a turn on. She had never done anything remotely like this in her entire life. But why shouldn't she? It seemed as if everyone else did.

She felt a niggling, uncomfortable tentacle of guilt weave its way into her adrenaline charged, lust-addled brain. She'd never wanted to be like everyone else. That was the point of studying instead of partying, the stint as a prosecutor, the time off to start a family. She'd always believed in doing *the right thing*. Not the exciting thing. Not the easy thing. The right thing.

Slowly, she slid the key card into the door lock, pushed the handle down and opened the door. The suite was pitch black, and she felt a moment of fear as the door clicked shut behind her (too many criminal prosecutions). Then a pair of strong arms slid around her, and a deep masculine voice whispered, "Karen" into her ear.

Her stomach clenched. She couldn't go through with it.

"Sean, I'm so sorry. I can't do this. I really, REALLY want to, but I can't. It's wrong."

The overhead light switched on, nearly blinding her. There, stark naked, with a steadily deflating erection and an angry, puzzled expression, stood Greg. Her husband.

"Who the fuck is Sean?"

21

Edgar Chastain leaned back in the incongruous modern leather swivel chair that provided something called "lumbar support" to his aching ninety-year-old back. He loathed the way it looked behind his venerable mahogany partners' desk, but fortunately, he instead faced Lavinia Winter and Judy Simpson seated in a pair of regal old oxblood leather and mahogany library chairs. Both were quite attractive for their age, although what on earth was the Simpson woman wearing? It looked to be some kind of caftan topped with scarves, and her hair was wild. Edgar admired Lavinia's tasteful navy Hermes scarf and motionless silver bob, and wondered if she'd be interested in accompanying him to the club's Big Band Night.

"Edgar? Are you listening," said Lavinia. "I said this came in the mail recently. Needless to say I was quite, uh…"

"Distraught," filled in Judy cheerily. "I was there when she got it, and she was *completely distraught.*"

Lavinia pushed the papers, an official-looking document and letter, both in French toward Edgar, who picked them up and perused them. He still had a decent command of written French, and his stint in the OSS during the war had left him with a lifelong suspicion of foreign documents, especially when they popped up at convenient times.

"Seems to me young Allison was just asking about the Edgemoor Trust, and, voila, here is her lovely mother producing documentation – from a small island in Polynesia it appears – that Pippa Edgemoor is dead. A man who didn't know you well, Lavinia, might find that suspicious."

Edgar had to hand it to the two ladies: their expressions did not waiver. He would have to remember never to play poker with these two.

"Well, actually, Edgar, it's not suspicious at all. Allison's inquiries into Phillipa's whereabouts – you know she was just looking after the club's interest, so civic minded – got me thinking about Pippa. You know, she and Judy and I were classmates."

"I remember you all on Cotillion Court," said Edgar fondly, laying the papers down and steepling his fingers.

"Yes," continued Lavinia. "So earlier this summer, I wrote Pippa at the last address I had for her, in Bora Bora, to let her know Judy had returned. I certainly didn't anticipate…"

"The tragic news," interjected Judy. Lavinia gave her an evil look, then recomposed her face.

"In reply, I received this letter from Monsieur Grenouille, who informed me sadly that Phillipa had died two years ago while sailing between Polynesian islands. Well, you can read French. Knocked on the head by an errant boom then buried at sea, poor dear."

"Yes," said Chastain. "And I see that shortly after her companions reported her death and dropped off her personal effects, their boat sank with all on board. So confirming her death would be…"

"Difficult," chimed in Judy. "Especially since a typhoon swept through last year – lots of records destroyed. We're very lucky to have this death certificate." Judy pointed to a document on the desk with "Certificat de Décès" printed at the top in ornate black lettering.

"Indeed," said Edgar, narrowing his eyes at Judy.

"Well, Edgar, if you have any doubts, Mr. Grenouille sent me this," said Lavinia. She shook a small brown envelope and a tiny rectangular charm embossed with a tree on a broken silver chain spilled out on the desk. Edgar Chastain picked it up carefully and placed it in his palm. The reverse side was engraved "P.S.E. – June 8, 1963". "It's her Merrywood medallion. They have no clasp and we wear them for life."

"Phillipa Spencer Edgemoor" he said. She'd been an alarming girl, very demanding. He'd breathed a private sigh of relief when she'd vanished.

Lavinia, Allison, Judy. They had nothing to gain from Pippa's death. And Chastain, Peregrine and Spencer would continue to manage the trust for Belle Vista. So there was no question of even the appearance of impropriety.

"Lavinia, if you could just make a brief statement attesting to all this, we will have it notarized and I will take these documents over to Judge Peregrine and have Phillipa declared deceased. I trust you ladies will arrange a proper memorial service at Belle Vista?"

As the women got up to leave, Edgar Chastain decided he'd have just a bit of fun.

"I suppose I should at least attempt to contact M. Grenouille?" he said, pretending to carefully review the letter one more time.

This time, he had the satisfaction of seeing a touch of panic seep through Judy's calm façade.

"No phones or Internet on that little island," said Judy quickly, shaking her head.

But Lavinia remained unflappable. How he admired her WASP sangfroid.

"If you read his letter, Edgar, M. Grenouille states that he has *officially closed* her file. Well, you know the French. Quand c'est fini, c'est fini."

"Mais bien sûr," said Edgar, giving her his most charming smile. "Au revoir, mes belles dames."

Edgar decided he'd spend this afternoon remembering Paris after the war with a nice bottle of Chateau Margeaux, charged to the Edgemoor Trust.

Clare Buxton picked up her cell phone when Allie's number flashed across the screen.

"Mrs. Beech, I'm glad you called."

Not when you hear what I have to say, thought Allie as she slid her feet into the bubbling hot water of the nail salon foot spa. She only hoped the "nail technicians" would keep their Vietnamese yammering to a minimum ("This one rich, but very cheap. Also has bunions," Allie's pedicurist informed her co-workers).

"Yes, well, I just called to say that Pippa has been located, deceased, without your assistance. My mother, who barely knows how to turn on a computer, found her. Needless to say your final bill will not be paid."

Clare sighed.

"Mrs. Beech, I've unearthed some pretty interesting stuff, I think you might want to…"

"You are a charlatan and you are not gouging me for one more cent. If I thought it was worth the bother, I'd have your license revoked." With that, Allie hung up and concentrated on selecting a color for her toes.

Clare stared at the framed photo of the J. Edgar Hoover building that hung crookedly on her office wall. Too bad about that final check, but Clare was thrifty, and she had no intention of taking another case until she found out the truth, the real truth, about Pippa Edgemoor.

"Oh sh…ugar," hollered Shana as a jar of Granny's homemade bread and butter pickles dropped on her foot and shattered, soaking her sneakers and freshly mopped floor in vinegary pee-yellow juice. Underneath a few limp pickle slices her toe hurt like hell. She burst into tears.

"Honey, you okay?" asked Big Wayne, who'd rumbled out of the garage and instantly taken her in his arms. (And tracked dirt through the pickle juice, Shana noticed with annoyance.) She wriggled out of his embrace.

"I'm fine," she said. "Just havin' a bad day. Lord, Granny's pickles smell as nasty as they taste!"

"Shouldn't you be getting ready for the memorial?" Wayne asked. Pippa Edgemoor's service wasn't for another two hours, but that was cutting it close for Shana, who took hair and makeup very seriously. In fact, since Vixen was filming the memorial (it was at the club, not a church; Wayne would never understand these people) he'd expected Byron to come do the honors. Although … he'd told Rex yesterday that he'd written his last check to Vixen.

The Belle Vista board had offered to buy back his share of the club with the Edgemoor inheritance money, so Wayne was not going bankrupt, thank the Lord. But the damage to their family finances was worse than Wayne had originally thought, and they might have to sell the house after all. As for paying that one hundred thousand dollar initiation fee to remain members of the club, well, pigs were more likely to fly out of Wayne's butt.

He knew he should tell Shana, but she looked so down. The agreement wouldn't be official until after Founder's Day. Wouldn't it be kinder to let her have one last big moment at Jones Belle Vista, going to the party and playing in the Founder's Day tournament?

"Wayne, are you listening?" said Shana in a tight, angry voice. "I said keep Hello Kitty out of that mess."

Wayne picked up Destiny's fluffy white kitten, which had wandered into the kitchen, and for lack of a better idea set her on the counter. Shana knelt down and pulled a dustpan out from under the island sink and began to sweep up pieces of broken glass and pickle.

"Great idea, Wayne, now she can track stuff on the counter. Just bring me the trash can so I can dump this, please," she snapped. "I just don't see why we should go to that service," Shana continued, her tone still sharp. "We didn't even know Miz Edgemoor. We don't belong."

Wayne frowned as he used his thumb and index finger to gingerly pick up a jagged piece of glass with the partial label 'ill pickles' (he thought that described Granny's bread-and-butters pretty good) and tossed it in the trash. This wasn't like Shana. They went to funerals at church all the time where they didn't know the departed to comfort the bereaved.

"Don't you want to join with your friends in prayer?" suggested Wayne encouragingly, hoping to see his familiar Shana smile out of that glum, tearstained face.

"Owww. Dammit," shrieked Shana bursting into tears again as a thin line of red appeared on her palm. She jumped up and ran out of the kitchen and up the stairs.

No, now was definitely *not* the time to tell her that Jones Belle Vista and *Queen of the Court* were headed for the dustbin, along with Granny's awful pickles.

Shana pulled a long splinter of glass out of her palm with a pair of tweezers and, wincing, tossed it in the sink. Then she washed out her cut with peroxide, squeezed some Neosporin on it and placed a bandage over it. Granny used her pickle juice as an antiseptic, but all those home remedies were nothing but poor people pretending that the only thing they could afford was good enough, she thought bitterly as she turned brass faucet handle and rinsed a trail of pinkish blood down the drain.

She felt bad about being so short with Wayne, but she just couldn't tell him the truth. She couldn't go to Pippa Edgemoor's service with her friends because she didn't have any. Not anymore. What had made her think that Shana Lee Jones, an ex-stripper from a trailer park, could be friends with a bunch of rich country club women? Trying to dress and act like Allie had just made matters worse; Shana was no more convincing than one of RuPaul's less successful drag queens. No wonder her teammates were so ready to believe the worst. They looked at her and they saw what they expected to see – trash.

Karen, Taylor and even Caroline had accused her of setting them up to spice up her reality show. As Karen had put it, "We'll all look like idiots, and you, the star, will seem smart and together by comparison!" Karen's phone tirade had been as long and angry as any closing argument Shana had ever heard on *Law & Order*. At the end even Shana would have believed she was guilty. Except she knew wasn't.

"All this time, we thought Allie was the villain, pushing you around," Karen said. "Well, she may be a little uptight and bitchy, but let me tell you I prefer that to your fake 'Hi, ya'll, I'm just a little ol' gal from the hills, and I want to be your friend' fakiness."

Even Maria and Byron had turned against her – Byron refused to listen to her plea that she hadn't known Spencer Thomas was gay. "You sent them to *Life is a Drag*, Shana, am I supposed to believe that was a coincidence?"

But it was just that, a horrible, horrible coincidence. She'd tried to get tickets to *The Best Little Whorehouse in Texas* at the Signature, but it was sold out.

Shana wasn't surprised when Taylor and Caroline screamed at her and had hysterics. But Karen made her angry. She always acted so holier than thou, but she didn't cotton to the concept of forgiveness, not one bit. After all, *Shana* had not been the one prepared to commit adultery while dressed as a nun. *Shana* had not been the one who chased her husband through the lobby of the Ritz Carlton dressed in sexy underwear screaming, "Come back!" like he was Lassie. (Unfortunately, several bystanders had posted this on YouTube.)

When Shana had sent those romantic notes to Karen and Greg, she had assumed, naturally, that they would think they were from each other. She had no idea Karen had even talked to Sean at her party, let alone seen him after.

"Even if I did believe you, and I'd like to make it clear I don't," Karen had said, "The point is you had no business interfering in my marriage. Don't you have your own problems to solve?"

That hit home. Shana knew Karen might be wrong about everything else, but she was right about that. Shana needed to tell Big Wayne about her secret and her search. But what if…

Shana stripped off her pickle-soaked cleaning clothes, stepped into the mammoth, roman-tiled shower, turning all six jets on high, and letting the hot water pulse against her skin as she sobbed. She couldn't bear the thought of seeing Big Wayne's face when he learned she'd lied to him for so long. If he left her, her already bruised heart would truly break. Just like that damn lousy jar of pickles.

The mourners gathered in the Howland Room, informally known as the funeral parlor. The interior designers had realized, that with half of Belle Vista's membership over sixty, the new clubhouse would need a dignified place to honor members who were going inactive in the truest sense of the word. The result was a dimly lit rectangular box with heavy gold velvet tasseled draperies and wallpaper embossed with tiny gold Napoleonic bees. It was a twenty-first century re-creation of a 1938 imitation of a gloomy Federal drawing room.

"This place gives me the freaking willies," whispered Taylor to Caroline. They'd shared a cab since Karen steadfastly refused to come, knowing her mother-in-law Georgianna would be there. Greg had moved back in with his parents and asked for a separation.

"Your breath smells like wine mouthwash," replied Caroline. "And it's only 11 a.m."

"That's why I bothered with mouthwash," said Taylor swaying precariously in her sky-high black Jimmy Choos. On the other side of the room she could see Spencer trying to catch her eye as he showed his ancient mother, Gwyneth, to a seat. Like Greg, Spencer was back home; Taylor had thrown him out after falling off the wagon with a resounding thud.

"If Shana keeps planning romantic evenings, every man in this club is going to end up living with his mother," Taylor said a bit too loudly.

"Shhhhh," said Caroline.

"God, this place is so stuffy," Taylor continued. She teetered over to one of the large windows and wrenched it open as the matrons in the room murmured in disapproval. Fresh air was not a noted feature of the Howland Room.

It was a small gathering of no more than fifty people, including members of the board and a coterie of Pippa's Merrywood classmates; still, not a bad turnout for someone no one had seen for forty years. Of course, in Pippa Edgemoor's case it was vast wealth, not absence, which had made hearts grow fonder. Jamal stood discreetly in a corner with a small camera. Unnoticed by the assembled guests, the old tomcat Smokey Joe slunk in and curled up behind the tasseled drapery nearest the exit.

Pippa's old school chums perched on the straight-backed chairs in the first row like a murder of crows in vintage black suits. Judy Simpson, swathed in deep purple scarves, sat alone. All heads turned as Lavinia Winter entered on the arm of Roy Beech, followed by Allie, head held high, in her black Chanel funeral suit. Behind them came the Reverend Tim Channing.

"Look at them, swanning in like the Royal Family," Taffy Dandridge whispered to Martha Hastings. "They're not Edgemoors!"

"Is Allie Beech in charge of every funeral these days?" groused Genie Walters. "She's getting to be a real bossy pants, just like Lavinia."

Reverend Channing went through his Episcopal paces fairly quickly, but the "Merrywood girls" noted with disapproval that Allie, who had never known Pippa, read the Gospel. Then, it was their turn.

Pippa's old schoolmates had gathered yesterday to discuss an appropriate eulogy. It was a difficult task because all of them had loathed and feared Pippa to varying degrees. "One does not wish to speak ill of the dead, however, neither does one want to perjure oneself before the Lord," Kat had said. In the end, they'd decided to simply stand together and recite the Merrywood Creed.

"If Miss Edgemoor's friends would please come forward to deliver the eulogy," said Rev. Channing.

As Lavinia, Judy, Georgianna, Genie, Taffy, Kat and Martha gathered around the podium, Clare Buxton, dressed in her usual dingy suit, slipped into a seat at the rear. All the women held candles, except for Lavinia, who clutched a small silver jewelry casket. Clare noted that Lavinia's hands were shaking rather badly.

"Today we lay to rest our dear departed friend and Merrywood classmate, Phillippa Edgemoor," said Taffy. Outside, thunder rumbled in the distance.

"Shit," mumbled Taylor. "It was totally sunny earlier – this dress is silk."

"Phillippa died tragically at sea, which wasn't a surprise, considering the Edgemoor curse. Her corpse was probably devoured by hungry sharks, like *Jaws*... " Taffy continued until Kat interrupted.

"Taffy, the creed!"

"Too bad," Caroline whispered to Taylor. "The shark stuff was interesting for a change."

"Ah, yes. Well, in honor of Phillippa, ladies, please place your hands on your medallions." The ladies slipped their hands inside their necklines. Then Taffy recited:

"We students of Merrywood promise to always follow a path of virtue. We seek knowledge rather than riches. We esteem truth above all. And we will remain forever bonded and loyal to all who wear the Merrywood medallion to the end of our days and beyond."

"To the end of our days and beyond," echoed the others.

"May Phillipa Edgemoor, whose Merrywood medallion was entrusted to us, rest in peace," concluded Lavinia in a tremulous voice.

Thunder shook the darkened sky outside as a gust of wind whipped through the open window, scattering the Reverend's notes like autumn leaves, extinguishing each and every Merrywood candle. With an anguished howl, Smokey Joe fled the room.

22

Allie crushed forehands again and again as the ball machine spit out worn yellow tennis balls in her direction. Out of the corner of her eye, she saw Shana Jones and her hideous little brats heading toward the junior hard courts. They should already be gone, but her mother and that withered old lawyer Chastain had insisted that the Edgemoor trust money and the club buyback remain secret until the board finalized the deal with Wayne Jones. That would not be until *after* Founder's Day. Shana herself was not to be told. But surely Shana could feel the permafrost that had descended every time she set one of her tacky little floral-pedicured toes on club grounds.

Allie smiled as she whacked yet another ball deep into the opposite court. The beauty of the entire situation was that she had not lifted a finger to turn her team members against Shana. The little redneck meddler had managed that all by herself. Of course, they'd still ended the season in disgrace with a forfeit that plunged them into last place. But next year would be different.

Allie was seriously reconsidering the little Founder's Day surprise she'd planned for Shana after finding that Facebook page. Really, why should she bother? Shana was beneath her notice and would soon be gone. Forever. When she got home she would just send an email saying she'd made a terrible mistake.

Allie walked into the Beech house to find a grim Ian and Roy huddled in Roy's office over Ian's laptop. Roy motioned her in and Ian turned the laptop in her direction. It was a clip of a Fox morning show, where a thirty-something blonde in an extremely tight royal-blue suit was interviewing a grown version of Opie from *The Andy Griffith Show*.

"What on earth?" said Allie.

But Ian shushed her and said, "Just listen."

"I'm Kelley Morgan, and I'm here with an exclusive from Billy Johnson, director of the American Family Values Council, who has just jumped into the race for the fourteenth Virginia Congressional District." Kelley flashed the audience a pageant-winning smile.

"Billy, there already is another Republican candidate, Roy Beech, running to fill Dan Butts' seat. Why would you challenge him?" queried the newscaster, who abandoned her cheery smile for a serious frown, demonstrating her complete mastery of two entirely different facial expressions.

"I've come to feel that Roy Beech is what we call a RINO; Republican In Name Only," said geeky Billy in a disapproving schoolmaster tone.

"Of all the..." Allie interrupted, only to be rudely shushed by Ian again.

Kelley Morgan went for the Fox Expression Trifecta, communicating shock with doll-wide eyes and a slightly gaping mouth.

"Why would you say that?"

"As an Evangelical Christian and Tea Party member, I am a family values candidate. Roy Beech talks family values, but earlier this year he accepted a rather large campaign donation from a Mr. Wayne Jones, former owner of Big Wayne's, a chain of strip clubs."

The blonde made the doll face again. "But isn't it possible that Mr. Beech was unaware of exactly how Mr. Jones made his money?"

"Not likely," said Billy Johnson, a smug grin on his face. "His wife is a close personal friend and tennis partner of Mr. Jones' wife, an ex-stripper. They are partners on a team at the exclusive Jones Belle Vista Country Club, where the Joneses own a majority interest."

"Oh my," said Kelley, sadly shaking her head. "Sounds like Wayne Jones might be trying to buy influence, doesn't it?"

"That's for the voters to judge. But I can tell them that I represent the regular guy and you won't find me at any country club, and I won't be funding my campaign with money pulled out of the sweaty g-strings of half-naked women," said Billy, crossing his arms over his chest and jutting his jaw.

"And there you have it," said Ian, closing the computer and shaking his head far more sadly than Kelley Morgan.

"Well, that man is obviously a charlatan and a liar," said Allie indignantly, hands on hips. She certainly had no intention of calling off Sage Shapiro now. Shana had clearly NOT suffered enough.

Ian and Roy looked up at her, clinging to the vain hope that she had some tidbit of career-ending dirt on the unctuous Billy Johnson.

"I am *not* Shana Jones' close friend or her tennis partner."

With that, Ian put his head down on the laptop and moaned in utter defeat.

Karen, Taylor and Caroline sat jammed together on the tiny settee in Karen's townhouse, squabbling over what to watch on her tiny television set. They'd vetoed Karen's picks of CNN and *Masterpiece Theatre*, and Caroline's bid for QVC. They'd finally settled on Taylor's suggestion; a Dateline ID marathon featuring wives who'd murdered their husbands. Karen found Taylor's cheers every time a husband dropped dead more than a little disturbing.

"I don't know why we even bother," complained Taylor. "This is like a freaking mouse television."

"It's a television for people who don't really watch television," explained Karen.

"Look," said Taylor, "if you're going to be a snob about TV, just don't have one. It's not like it doesn't count just because the people on it are, like, the size of ants. I can't believe you don't have any wine."

"You've got to go back to court in two weeks – you're lucky they didn't charge you with assaulting an officer that night at the theater. You haven't been going to AA…"

"Hey," said Taylor. "AA is secret, how do you know I'm not going?"

Karen sighed. "You told me last time you were drunk."

"Oh."

"I think we should all go to Founder's Day tomorrow," Caroline blurted, apropos of nothing.

The other two looked at her as if she were insane.

"Look, Caroline," said Karen, turning toward her. "I can see why you'd want to go and take your kids. It's a family event. But Taylor and I don't want to run into our estranged husbands."

"Not to mention that bitch Shana Jones," Taylor added, taking a gulp of her Diet Coke and trying to pretend it was scotch.

Caroline started to sniffle.

"First of all, Karen, it's only Taylor's husband who's strange. Greg's just pissed because he thinks you were boffing Sean! You know, if we don't play, Allie says she won't let us be on the team next season."

"Oh, who cares," said Karen standing up. "I plan on going back to work."

"And I plan on going back to getting drunk," said Taylor.

"Well, that never stopped you from playing before!"

Taylor narrowed her eyes and looked hard at Caroline. "Caroline Walinsky, I've known you for a really long time. What has Allie got on you?"

"Nothi...noth...ohhhhh it's the Waaaalllll!" she wailed. "They're going to post me on the Wall of Shame TOMORROW," said Caroline, referring to the infamous public list of suspended members. "My kids won't be allowed to go to the party, let alone play in anything. Allie says if I get you two to play, she'll make sure my name doesn't go up until after, and maybe not at all."

Caroline burst into tears.

"But I thought Jack paid your membership as part of your divorce agreement," said Karen.

"But he hasn't," she sobbed. "Not only that, the house is going into foreclosure, and I can't get a hold of Jack to find out why he didn't pay the mortgage. Elena says he's still in Crow Nation or some other weird place. I didn't even realize Jack knew any Indians! That bitch Elena refuses to help. I sat outside their apartment for an hour yesterday hammering on the door and yelling, but I just pissed off their shitzu."

Karen looked at Caroline in amazement. "You might lose your home, and you're worried about some stupid notice on the Belle Vista wall?"

Taylor and Caroline exchanged a look. For an Ivy League grad, Karen could be really thick sometimes.

"You don't understand, Karen," Taylor explained. "Around here, it's easier to come back from living in a cardboard box than being on The Wall. It'll kill Caroline's chances of a decent remarriage faster than her expanding waistline."

"I'll have you know I've lost nearly a pound since Allie called," said Caroline indignantly. "Stress can be very aerobic."

Karen stood up and started to pace in front of the TV.

"Hey, easy, I can't see any of the little ant people, and I think Arkansas Annie is about to get her cheating husband between the eyes with an axe," said Taylor.

Karen ignored her. "Well, if we go tomorrow, I can corner Elena and tell her that her sneaky husband could land in jail if he doesn't pay Caroline's mortgage. We don't want you homeless, Caroline, so call Allie and tell her we will all go to Founder's Day and participate in her little charade."

"We will?" questioned Taylor, her eyes still glued to the TV. "Can I bring my axe?"

The Prius was packed and ready to go by noon on Friday. It had taken two weeks of solid begging and nagging, but Galen had finally come around and agreed they should all go to this Founder's Day party and put the issue of Shana Jones to rest. She'd arranged for them to stay at an inexpensive hostel for three nights. That way, after Saturday's party, they could spend Sunday touring the city and Monday lobbying Congressional representatives on issues ranging from marriage equality to fracking. St. Ann's had agreed to give Sage extra credit next fall for the experience.

Sage squeezed herself into the back seat while Galen took the steering wheel and Fern brought Google Maps up on her phone. Sage was nervous and keyed up. She looked at the two women in front of her and felt gratitude and affection. They had arranged for their good friend Kiah to manage The Moon Goddess and take care of the pets. Fern was actually intrigued by the idea of a Founders Day Picnic.

"I'm excited. I've never been to a country club." Fern smiled over her shoulder at Sage.

"Well, I waitressed at one during the summer as a teenager and haven't been longing to repeat the experience," replied Galen.

"No one's going to make you bus tables, Mom," said Sage with a laugh. "Did you remember the invitation Pippa emailed? She said we would need to show it to get in."

"That Pippa," said Galen. "Always thinking." And off they went.

Big Wayne tightened the belt on his plaid plus-fours and headed to the garage to toss his clubs in the back of the Ford 150. The last thing he felt like doing was going to Founder's Day, even though he was damn proud that he'd figured out a way to make Allie Beech's ridiculous party turn a profit. Turns out social members and folks from other clubs were willing to pay to come. F. Brand Lippert even paid for the acrobats and fireworks, and all he wanted in exchange was some sponsorship signage.

The board had been reluctant at first, but when Wayne had showed them the figures, including the hit the club would take if they did it the usual way, they went for it big time. Board President Bob Dandridge had even patted him on the shoulder and said, "We're sorry to see you go, Wayne, this club has never been so well run as during the past few months." Wayne had only made two requests; that the club resale not be announced until after Founder's Day, and that half the profits go to reduce Belle Vista's debts, the other half to staff bonuses.

Wayne had even helped Rex Range find other funding for Vixen so Shana's show could film the party for their big finale. He'd brokered a deal with one of his old biker buddies who'd decided that being a cable exec paid better than busting up bars. He was launching a channel he hoped would be the "Redneck Bravo" and thought Shana's show would bring in female viewers, who'd polled pretty negative on *American Deer Skinners* and *Pimp My Tractor*.

Wayne knew he wasn't much of an actor, but he was gonna put on a big ol' act for Shanna and pretend to enjoy the hell out of Founder's Day. Then, when they got home and got the kids to bed, he would tell her the truth; that their days as members of the country club set were over.

Shana sat in front of her vanity trying to glue her left false eyelash into place, but it kept slipping. She was glad she'd sent Judy on ahead with the kids; it was going to be hard enough putting on a show for Wayne, acting all excited about the party. She'd thought about pretending she had "women's troubles" and staying home, but poor Wayne, he'd put in so many hours getting Founder's Day together, figuring out how to pay for every silly thing Allie wanted. He kept going on and on about how he wanted to see her play in the Ladies' Singles Tournament, how after all those lessons she must be real good. Well, Wayne had worked damn hard to pay for those lessons, so Shana was going to make him proud.

She finally got her eyelash into place, then looked herself over. She had on her Jones Belle Vista uniform; the one Allie said was "showy" and "vulgar". Her hair was sprayed and teased into the style Taylor had called her "Opry-do" and she'd done her makeup the way she liked; not the sophisticated Allie Beech country club look, but the Dolly look. She was Shana Lee Jones, straight out of a trailer in Moneton, West Virginia, and she was going to hit that tennis court and kick the spoiled, skinny ass of every one of those snotty bitches.

23

Taylor stood in the driveway of her oversized townhome in Serenity Knolls, waiting for her ride to Founder's Day. It wasn't like Karen to be late. Taylor was tempted to open the garage and release her beloved BMW, but if she got caught driving on a suspended license she could lose it permanently.

A yellow VW Beetle rounded the corner and headed toward her. Taylor frowned. The little car looked vaguely familiar…

"Hey Taylor, Karen's running late so I said I'd pick you up. Hop in," called Byron from the driver's seat. Beside him sat a ruggedly handsome blond man. Taylor gave him her best sorority girl smile and slipped in behind Byron.

"What was that sloshing sound?" asked Byron.

"Water bottle," replied Taylor, shoving her box of Chardonnay farther down in her bag. "Who's your friend?"

"Tay, I'd like you to meet my husband, Patrick."

"Dammit," said Taylor, smacking Patrick in the back of the head.

"Owww. What was that for?" Patrick asked. "You know it's not smart to go around hitting cops; from what I hear you're making a habit of it."

"*That* was for being handsome and gay," said Taylor. Then she gave the back of Patrick's head another sharp smack. "*That* is for being a cop."

"You meet the nicest people in your business," said Patrick to Byron with a grimace.

The little car slowed to a stop as it rounded the corner, and before Taylor could take in what was happening, Spencer slid into the seat beside her and closed the door.

"Let me out," yelled Taylor, but exiting a tiny two-door car with a rather large cop in the front passenger seat proved impossible.

An elderly man walking his equally elderly golden retriever down the street looked over just in time to see his crazy neighbor (she'd come over last week at 4 a.m. wanting to borrow a cup of vodka) swatting the other occupants of the VW as it drove away. He wondered briefly if they were kidnapping her. If so, he wished them luck. They were going to need it.

Caroline came hurtling out of her glass and cedar California modern hilltop home (the only one of its kind in staunchly colonial Belle Vista, it was universally loathed by the neighbors) down her driveway toward Karen's waiting Jetta. She tossed an expensive-looking quilted gold tennis bag into the back, and literally bounced into the front seat.

"New bag?" queried Karen, noting that Caroline's front yard was a tangled mess of weeds and knee-high grass, her roof seemed to be missing several shingles and a gutter filled with leaves and twigs hung precariously from the eaves. QVC obviously had yet to market home and lawn care services.

"Ooooh, Karen!" exclaimed Caroline, shaking her hands in the air. "You will never guess what happened?"

Karen hated guessing games, and given the recent trajectory of Caroline's life, any guess was likely to involve the words "repossession" "eviction" or "public humiliation". She kept her lips resolutely sealed and put the Jetta into gear.

"I got a job! A real job! I'm going to make enough money to pay my mortgage!"

Karen slammed the Jetta back into neutral. "You *what?*"

"Well, you remember how when I was Chef Caroline I jabbed that woman at the party? Guess what? Vixen wasn't the only one filming it. Some guy got it on his cell phone and it went viral, not just the part where I stab the lady with the needle, but my whole 'Chef Caroline' routine. It's been viewed two hundred thousand times!"

Karen put her hand on Caroline's arm. "Oh my God, I am so sorry. How embarrassing."

"Yeah," said Caroline with a broad grin. "I'm being embarrassed all the way to the bank. Cucina Barcelona called me and Maria. They want us to go on QVC together and sell their pans."

"Come again?" said Karen.

"The sales pitch is 'So easy, Chef Caroline can use it' – it's funny because I can't cook – and 'So authentic, Chef Maria insists on it.' I'm going to be on QVC. They think I can sell the olive pitter too – although I almost cut the end of my finger off using it." Caroline showed Karen her index finger, which was wrapped in a bloody tissue.

"Uh, that's great," said Karen. She was getting that weird through the rabbit hole feeling she'd had all too often since she'd entered the world of Belle Vista. "I'm happy for you Caroline, I really am. But I'm still going to talk to Elena. Jack owes you that support, and just in case your, uh, new career doesn't work out, I want to make sure you get it."

Karen put the car in drive and headed toward the club. She couldn't help feeling a little resentful. Caroline could be an irresponsible idiot for basically her entire life and have it all come up roses, but she, Karen, makes *one* mistake – okay, a pretty freaking huge one – and her life is literally ruined. She hit the gas and ground the gears.

"Karen, what's gotten into you?" giggled Caroline. "You're almost going the speed limit, or maybe even a little over. Uh oh."

Behind the Jetta a blue siren flashed and wailed on top of a black Jeep Cherokee.

"I can't believe an unmarked car would bother to pull me over for going twenty-six in a twenty-five mile zone," groused Karen, who had always hated hearing people complain when they broke the law just a little. "You're on one side of the line or the other," had been one of her favorite courtroom lines. "Oh, shut up, you sanctimonious bitch," she mumbled to herself as she pulled over.

The Jeep pulled up behind her, and Sean Flannery got out and sauntered over to the driver's side window.

"Why haven't you returned any of my calls?" he said, leaning in toward Karen.

"You're using government property to inappropriately conduct an illegal traffic stop," replied Karen, her face flushing. Her hands shook as she gripped the wheel.

"Actually, the FBI asked me to help them locate Caroline. They want to ask her a few questions about her ex-husband." He reached over Karen and handed Caroline his cell phone. "Here, take this. Just press redial, you'll be put straight through to Agent Jim Watson on a secure line. You can make the call in my Jeep so you have some privacy. I'll sit and keep Karen company."

"Maybe the FBI can force Jack to leave that Indian reservation and come back and pay his bills!" said Caroline, getting out of the Jetta and heading toward the jeep, Sean's phone in hand. Sean took her place in the front passenger seat.

"Did the FBI really call you?" asked Karen accusingly.

"No, I called and offered to contact Caroline when I saw Jack Walinsky on a fugitive list. But the stop is legit. I follow the rules, just like you, Karen," he said.

"But I didn't follow the rules at all," said Karen, putting her head down on the top of the steering wheel and starting to cry. "I wanted to sleep with you. I almost did, even though it wasn't really you."

"Yeah, I know," said Sean. "But the point is, you were willing to sleep with me because you are in love with me. And I'm in love with you, even after seeing a YouTube video of you chasing another guy through a hotel lobby in your underwear."

Karen turned to Sean, her eyes glassy with tears. "That's not some other guy, it's *my husband*."

"Not if you agree to divorce him. Look, Karen, I'm as Catholic as you are, but I don't believe God intended us to live in complete misery for the rest of our lives just because you and Greg made a mistake. You have a chance to be happy. With me."

In the Jeep, Caroline was winding down her rant about Jack and Elena as a confused Agent Watson listened on the other end. "...and another thing, do you think it's fair that their shitzu is eating gourmet dog food when I can't even afford Thai takeout? What's that? You want to speak to agent Flannery?" Caroline peered through the

Jeep's windshield and into the Jetta. "I'm sorry, but he's busy making out with my friend Karen. I'll have him call you when he's finished."

Bethany and Enrique walked up to the clubhouse looking like the very picture of Successful Young Republicans; Bethany in a crisp, hot pink Shoshana sundress and gold Kate Spade sandals, and Enrique in an aqua Vineyard Vines polo, khaki shorts and docksiders. "I can't believe you're making me skip Day-Glo for this lame party," complained Bethany. She *loved* the semi-annual outdoor pop-music drunkfest, where concertgoers were sprayed with Day-Glo body paint. Bethany knew she looked good wet, and even better wet and glowing.

"Remember what Ian said, your Dad has invited the press here to show his Belle Vista membership in a positive light. You know, not your typical country club, staff kids playing with members' kids, stuff like that," said Enrique, pausing to pop his collar. It was a Founder's Day tradition for staff and their families to play in the various tournaments, although socializing with members was strongly discouraged.

"Bullshit Enrique, this IS a typical country club; in fact it may be the clubbiest country club in the whole fucking country!" She turned and grabbed him by his popped collar. "I think Georgetown is changing you, and classes haven't even started. You'd rather hang out here with my parents than see me all wet and covered in paint."

Enrique sighed. "I'm just trying to help your Dad," he said, planting a chaste kiss on her cheek in case Roy and his press contingent were already on site.

Bethany narrowed her eyes. Something was wrong, she could feel it.

Nearby, a grounds crew continued work on the golf course, despite the festivities. Hector Ortiz, dressed in a green jumpsuit with the name "Dave" embroidered over the left shirt pocket, viciously applied garden shears to an unfortunate boxwood as he watched Enrique kiss Bethany.

The heat and humidity of the past few weeks had vanished, and fluffy white clouds floated in a perfect blue sky that seemed special-ordered for Belle Vista's celebration. The club looked magnificent: gardens lush and hedges perfectly trimmed, red, white and blue bunting crisp, and balloons waving festively in the mild summer breeze. And the crowd! Allie couldn't recall a crowd this size for Founder's Day since she was a little girl. Yet she was not happy. Not at all.

Allie had just watched the unlikely team of social member Shontae Briggs and kitchen staffer Consuela Guzman win the Ladies' Doubles title while that Rex Range and his team of vultures captured the whole mortifying spectacle on film. Worse, F. Brand Lippert and that hideous bitch Lauren were laughing on the sidelines. Allie had railed against the idea of paying guests at the last committee meeting, but the board had overwhelming backed Wayne Jones' tacky money-grubbing scheme, even though Wayne was officially out.

Now, to top it off, that unctuous little bastard Ian had Roy posing with Shontae and Consuela as newspaper photographers snapped away and Vixen's cameras rolled. Apparently Ian thought tennis-playing minorities were an important voting bloc. He'd tried to corral her for the photos, but she'd fled to the ladies' room where she was now trapped, standing on a toilet seat just in case Ian sent anyone to look for her.

Allie heard the ladies' room door open and peeked through the door. Bethany.

"No, Ian, I don't see her in here," Bethany said, speaking into her iPhone, after a quick check under the stall doors. "Well you didn't really think she'd go for that whole 'We are the world, we are Belle Vista' line of shit you're selling, did you?" Bethany paused in front of the large, gold-framed vanity mirror to reapply her candy pink lip gloss. She smacked her lips together, then licked them in a way that Allie did not approve of at all.

"Okay, I'll do the Gazette interview with Enrique, about him being a poor kid working his way up and how my parents have been so supportive blah, blah blah. But trust me, it's better if my mother doesn't find out the truth until she reads it in the papers tomorrow; she's, like, totally capable of making a huge scene."

With that, Bethany turned and walked out.

Allie was about to step down and pursue her. How dare she lie about something as important as dating a Spanish royal? But at that moment, Taylor, Karen and Caroline walked in.

Taylor checked under the stall doors.

"All clear. Don't want anyone who isn't us spreading gossip."

The trio arranged themselves in the gold brocade-upholstered chairs in the lounge area. Clearly, they were going to have some kind of girl talk, and Allie was stuck for the duration. Unless, of course, she felt like explaining why she was hiding in a toilet stall.

"So," Taylor began, "after I stopped hitting him, Spencer explained to me about how he couldn't face his sexual orientation because his family is so anti-gay. He said the sweetest thing; that he thought if he married the most beautiful woman he'd ever met – that's me – it might turn him straight."

"I don't think that works," said Caroline dubiously.

"Of course it doesn't work, you twit! The point is, he really does love me, just not in a way that produces quality orgasms."

"So you're not going to hunt him down with an axe for lying to you?" said Karen.

"Well, it doesn't count as lying to me, because he was also lying to himself, so he thought he was telling the truth," said Taylor, rummaging through her tennis bag. "Karen, did you take my pills again?"

"Yes," said Karen. "Flushed them."

Taylor gave Karen an exasperated look, then continued.

"Spence and I still have so much in common," she said through her wad of gum. "We are totally vain people who value external appearance over internal qualities, we hate yard work, love musicals and both agree that Marc Jacobs is overrated. We're getting divorced, of course, but we're thinking of staying roommates, at least till I get sober and he figures out how to be gay. Apparently all these years of being a fake hetero have really messed him up. He's hoping they have a class online or something."

"This is so wonderful," exclaimed Caroline, reaching out to hold each of her friends' hands. "Taylor's starting a new, sober life..."

"Tomorrow," interjected Taylor, holding up a finger.

"...Karen, you've found your true love," continued Caroline, "and I'm going to sell pans, and maybe even olive pitters, on TV! And you know what? We owe it all to Shana Jones."

"That bitch!" said Taylor, pulling back her hand as if she'd been burned. In her bathroom cubicle, Allie smiled.

"No, she's right, Taylor," said Karen seriously. "Shana may have been misguided in the *way* she tried to help us, but in the long run she succeeded. Because of Shana, we had to take a hard look at our lives, and we're getting a chance to change them. I think we each owe her an apology. Especially me. I said some really awful things to her."

Taylor stood up and admired herself in the mirror.

"You know, I think you're right." She pointed at the mirror. "Thanks to Shana, I'm getting these hot goods back on the shelf before they expire."

"That is a really disgusting, anti-feminist metaphor," said Karen. "So, I think we all agree that we've treated Shana shabbily and need to apologize. Has anyone seen her?"

The other women shook their heads.

"You know, I'm not blaming anyone but myself for how I treated her, but I have to say that Allie encouraged all of us to be petty and unfriendly to Shana from the beginning," said Karen.

"Allie's pathetic," said Taylor. "She bullies everyone and acts as if being the queen of tennis really means something. She showed up at my community service, but only to use it for her husband's campaign."

"And she put Elena on our team, even though she knew how much it upset me," echoed Caroline.

"Let's get out of here, see if we can find Shana and beg her humble forgiveness," said Taylor, giving herself a final once over in the mirror. "Then let's all warm up for the singles tournament. I hope one of us kicks Allie's nasty old ass."

"Frankly," said Karen. "I hope it's Shana."

And with that they got up and left, leaving Allie quaking with fury on top of her toilet.

24

The Prius with New York plates turned onto Country Club Lane and stopped in front of the security gate. The elderly guard looked up from his newspaper and waived them through before a smiling Sage could even show him her prized invitation. He was two beers past caring if they were guests or gate crashers.

The Shapiros proceeded slowly, following a long line of cars snaking up the leafy drive to the clubhouse.

"This is so nice," Sage said with awe when they finally arrived at the imposing building surrounded by pools, courts and the emerald-green golf course. The parking lot was packed and they had to circle it a few times before they found a spot. There were young families with children in bathing suits, gray-haired men and women in Bermudas and polos pulling golf carts, and scores of tennis players in head-to-toe white. Festive bunting hung from the clubhouse and the Jones Belle Vista sign flashed a garish welcome.

They got out of the car and stretched. Galen looked around suspiciously, while Fern merely looked overwhelmed.

"Wow," said Sage.

"Wow indeed," said Galen. "Perhaps Pippa should have mentioned that hundreds of people would be at this little shindig."

"What are we supposed to do now?" Fern asked.

"Since Pippa declined to meet us, I suppose we're meant to slink around like secret agents and spy on Mrs. Jones. If we can find her, that is," said Galen. "I told you two this was a crazy idea."

"Well, thank Goddess red hair is pretty easy to spot," said Sage, her enthusiasm undimmed.

To their collective surprise, a calico cat, undaunted by the crowds, strolled up and arched against Sage's legs.

"Well, hello there," said Sage, reaching down to scratch the cat between its ears. "Do *you* know Shana Jones? How about Pippa Edgemoor?"

The cat blinked up at Sage, then strolled toward the clubhouse entrance.

Sage laughed.

"I guess maybe we'd better follow her."

Bethany sat at a table on the edge of the tennis courts waiting for Enrique, who was supposed to be getting her iced tea, preferably loaded with gin. Yet there he was, disappearing with that Ian. The reporters trailing her Dad were long gone, so what was up with that? She got up and followed them.

This was weird. They walked past the snack bar, past the men's locker room and into the staff stairwell, which was used by workers to get to the second floor grille kitchen. The idiots never even turned around and looked behind them. Bethany was about to push open the door when she heard their voices right behind it. They were, like, hiding in the stairway talking. Who did that?

Someone who had something to hide. Bethany put her ear to the door.

"Come on, Ian, she's done everything perfectly all day. Can't she just have a little fun?"

"No frigging way. A picture of her shitfaced and covered in Day-glo paint in the paper tomorrow will undo all the work we've done today. Remember, Enrique, I'm paying you to watch this girl and keep her under control, not to make her happy."

"Holy shit!" said Taylor as she saw Shana strut onto the tennis court terrace.

"Oh my God," wailed Byron, who stood at her side, emergency makeup kit in hand. "It's like one of those Harry Potter spells that undoes magic. She's reversed all my work and gone full metal redneck."

To accent her ultra-tight white and teal Jones Belle Vista uniform, Shana had added a pair of sky-high teal platform sandals and her #1 Mama necklace. One of Destiny's tiaras from "Pretty, Pretty Princess" sat precariously atop her teased-up hair. (Even Big Wayne thought the plastic tiara was over the top, but he knew when not to mess with Shana, Queen of the Court.)

"Here, love, let's go into the tennis shop dressing room and, uh, get you ready for the tournament," said Byron, fussing around her.

"All I got to do is change my shoes," said Shana, glaring at Byron and plopping herself down on a bench. "Tell Jamal to come mic me up, y'all aren't going to want to miss any of my commentary."

"Now, Shana, I've called you ten times and left apologies on your voicemail, so don't go all reality show bitch on me," said Byron. "The girls," he gestured over at Taylor, Karen and Caroline, who hovered nearby, "also want to apologize."

"And Allie?"

"Uh, not so much."

"I don't know Byron. I've tried to be friends with all y'all, I've opened my heart and my home, yet when I made mistakes and tried to say I was sorry, not one of you would take the time to listen."

"That's absolutely true – couldn't we just wipe a tiny bit of that bronzer off," he said, lifting a tissue tentatively toward Shana's gilded cheek.

"Don't you touch ONE THING on me," snapped Shana, slapping his hand away. "I like me the way I am, and it's too damn bad if no one else does!"

"I like you the way you are Shana," said Caroline, who'd crept up behind Byron. "You've saved my home and my whole life."

"Personally," said Taylor, who now stood beside Caroline, "I think you look like White Trash Barbie. But that's okay. You were there for me when I needed you, Shana. And it was kind of unfair for me to expect you to know my husband was gay when I didn't."

Finally, Karen walked up and sat down on the bench next to Shana.

"I was a complete bitch to you Shana, because I couldn't face my own problems so I blamed them on you," said Karen taking Shana's hand in hers. "I am so ashamed."

Shana tried as hard as she could to make her hard-ass West Virginia face and failed utterly. She burst into tears, and all of a sudden, all four women were hugging and crying. Jamal, camera in hand, moved in to shoot the reunion, trying unsuccessfully to wave his stylist out of the frame.

"No way!" said Byron, reaching as far around as he could to try and hug them all at once.

Bethany was the first person to admit she was not exactly a reservoir of deep emotion, but when she heard Ian say the words "I'm paying you" to Enrique, she felt an ache start in her chest and work its way up to her throat, where it lodged like a Nacho Cheese Dorito that had gone down the wrong way. Hot, unfamiliar tears formed in the corners of her eyes.

She took a deep, shaking breath and walked purposefully away from the door. She thought about getting in her little convertible and driving straight to the mall, but something told her that this was the kind of heartache that retail therapy couldn't cure.

Instead, she decided to head back to her table and pretend nothing was different, at least until she got Enrique alone. First, she'd stop off in the main floor ladies room to fix her makeup; she wasn't going to be one of those drippy girls who advertised her heartbreak with slimy black mascara snail trails on her cheeks. As she turned into the main lobby, she stopped short. Standing at the welcome desk flanked by two dumpy looking old hippies was that red-haired poet girl from the Internet. Rosemary? Parsley? What the hell was she doing here? Her Facebook page said she was from *Brooklyn*.

Bethany backed around the corner quickly, but not before she saw a couple of tall, fit guys in dark suits that were clearly not here for tennis. They strode through the lobby, their heads doing that side-to-side pivot thing cops did when they checked out a room. They headed straight toward the welcome desk.

"Shit!" said Bethany out loud. She hadn't realized plagiarism was an *actual crime*. She walked quickly to the elevator, stepped in, pulled out her phone and began texting. She barely noticed when a sweaty groundskeeper stepped in beside her, pushed "close door" in the face of a trio of angry senior golfers, and hit the button for the sub basement.

"If you're texting Enrique, you'd better tell him to meet you in the basement utility room. Now," said Hector Ortiz, pointing his gardening shears straight at Bethany's throat.

From her position on court (she'd just presented the Senior Women's Singles trophy to her mother) Allie could see some commotion off to the side involving her team and that wretched Shana Jones, who'd paraded in looking like the tart she was. Thank God those reporters Ian had invited were finally gone. Well, this represented the end of this type of scandalous behavior at Belle Vista.

"Allison, we must announce the beginning of the competition for the Edgemoor Cup," said Currie Holmes, who stood at her side. "Please hand me the microphone."

"Fine," said Allie curtly, handing the microphone to Currie and walking off court to get a Vitamin Water Zero and her racquet.

A suspicious person might think that Allie had stacked the ladies championship in her favor, since all the toughest players were in the other bracket – Shana's bracket. Of course, everyone was gossiping about how the trophy was sure to be Elena's in the end. "Poor Allie," she'd heard Taffy Dandridge remark to her mother earlier (she'd heard many things while stuck in that cursed bathroom waiting for an opportunity to sneak out.) "First there was Lou, and now this Slavic giant. But maybe this will end like *Rocky IV*, with an American victory."

"Taffy, Judy was right about you. You're an idiot," Lavinia had replied. "Of course Allison has no chance against Elena. Every single one of her shots is inferior. Frankly, I don't even think she could beat Shana Jones." Then Lavinia had sighed. "It's looking as if no one in our family will ever hold that trophy again."

Enrique opened the door to the boiler room slowly. It was dark and smelled vaguely of motor oil, but then again, it wouldn't be the first time Bethany picked a weird place for a romantic tryst. Just as well they were someplace no one would hear them; he planned to come clean about his work for Ian. He just couldn't deal with the lying anymore.

"Hey, babe, you in here?" The door slammed shut behind Enrique, and he heard a lock turn. "You don't have to lock me in," he said laughing.

"Oh, I think I do," replied a familiar voice that made Enrique's stomach clench with dread. The light switched on, and he stood face-to-face with Hector Ortiz, who had dropped his gardening shears but now held a gun. Bethany stood in front of him, looking nowhere near as terrified as Enrique felt.

"Don't worry, babe, I won't let him hurt you," said Enrique, although frankly he wasn't sure how he could make good on that, since Hector had what appeared to be a semi-automatic and Enrique was holding an iced tea.

"You shut up, you fucking traitor asshole," said Bethany. "What, is saving my life on your to-do list for Ian?"

"Uh, honey, don't you think your anger is a little misplaced? Hector here is the one who has you trapped in a boiler room at gunpoint." Enrique was trying to hide the fact that his hands were shaking, but the damned iced tea was splattering everywhere.

"Oh, fuck him, who cares about him?" said Bethany.

Bethany's piercing tone woke Old Smokey Joe, the king of the Belle Vista feral cat colony, who'd been sleeping off a lunch of pilfered shrimp on a utility shelf just above Hector's head. He stretched silently and watched the drama with disinterest, hoping he wouldn't have to move.

"Hey..." warned Hector. He was kind of enjoying watching the bitch take some hide off of Enrique, but wasn't going to put up with any disrespect.

Bethany turned on Hector. "You touch me and you're screwed, asshole. Don't you read the papers? You can't get away with killing rich white people in this state, especially if they have political connections."

Hector turned to Enrique. "I can't believe you go out with a bitch who spouts this racist crap. I'll bet she thinks all Hispanics are, like, crazy criminals."

"Uh, Hector, you're not helping to break the stereotype here. Why don't you put down the gun, let her go and you and I will talk."

Up on the shelf, Smokey Joe caught a whiff of something tantalizing coming from the human nearest him. He breathed deeply, his nostrils flaring. Catmint. The scent began to overwhelm his senses.

"Right, and she'll call security the minute she closes that door," Hector continued. It was hot in the boiler room, he was sweating profusely, and his frigging overalls smelled like pot pourri from those plants he'd been hiding in. It was hard to be convincingly threatening when you smelled like a ladies' gift shop.

"If you teach Enrique a lesson, you'll just be saving me the trouble. He's a liar and a sneak," said Bethany.

"Trouble in paradise?" sneered Hector

"Just that I don't deserve her. She's right, I lied to her. I was only doing the same stuff I'd be doing anyway, looking out for her. But I was taking money for it, and that's wrong, because I love her," said Enrique, prattling nervously as he continued to shake. This might be his last chance to tell Bethany how he felt. Anyway, it seemed to be distracting Hector. "Bethany, I'm begging you to forgive me."

"Hey, dude, don't you think it would be smarter to beg the guy *with the gun* for forgiveness?" said Hector.

"Really?" said Bethany, ignoring Hector. She put her hands on her hips and faced Enrique. "I want to believe you Enrique, I really do. But there's a problem, because you are a LIAR!"

"Babe, I'm telling you the truth!"

"Hey," said Hector, annoyed. "I've got a *fucking gun* here. Anybody can start paying me attention any time now!"

"Oh shut up, you moron," said Bethany. "Can't you see we're having an important private conversation here? By the way, you smell like my grandmother."

At that moment, a terrifying howl pierced the air. The irresistible catmint smell that clung to Hector's cap and jumpsuit had slowly, surely driven Smokey Joe insane. He had, had, had to roll in it! NOW! The tough old cat landed on Hector's shoulders, sinking his claws into the exposed, sunburned back of his neck. Hector screamed, twisting and flailing in an attempt to shake Joe off. With another furious yowl, Joe dug his claws deeper into Hector's skin, and bit him hard for good measure.

"Help, I'm being stabbed!" Hector screamed as fell and tried to grab the ball of furry fury on his back.

The gun dropped to the floor with a clatter and fired, gouging a hole in a can of paint used to delineate the numerous Belle Vista "no parking" zones. A spray of neon yellow spurted from the can and coated the writhing Hector, as Enrique and Bethany bolted out the door.

Smokey Joe sprang deftly out of the path of danger and disappeared into the boiler room shadows, leaving only a trail of faint yellow footprints behind.

Back in the elevator Enrique took Bethany in his arms. "Let's get security to take care of Hector, then find Ian and tell him the deal is off."

"We can't call security, or 911. There are cops upstairs looking for me," said Bethany.

"Oh my God, I suck as handler," said Enrique slumping against the elevator wall. "What did you do?"

"Plagiarism. I took this girl's poem off the Internet, and now she's come all the way from Brooklyn and brought cops to get me."

Enrique laughed with relief. "God, Bethany, I know you're the center of your own little drama production in here," he pointed to her head. "But people don't get arrested for plagiarism."

Bethany smiled, leaned over and planted a kiss on Enrique's mouth.

"That's for being so smart."

Then she kissed him again.

"And that's for trying to save me from Hector, even though he had a gun and you only had an iced tea," she said.

"A diet iced tea," corrected Enrique kissing her back.

"Damn," said Bethany, laughing. "We really were lucky that cat stepped up."

25

Currie Holmes stood alongside the official's chair on court one, thoroughly enjoying her role. It was so much more satisfying to punish her rivals by calling double faults on them than to actually play. In competitive tennis, anything could happen; but as an official, Currie always won.

"And now, I'd like to introduce our honorary tournament chairperson, ten-time Edgemoor Cup champion, Lavinia Winter," said Currie.

"That's eleven-time Edgemoor Cup champion," corrected Lavinia. "And this year, I'm hoping we will make this a family affair and finally put my daughter's name on that cup," she added unconvincingly.

On the sidelines Allie gritted her teeth. Her mother made that same comment every year.

"Then let's get on with it. For our first two matches, we have Allie Beech versus Karen Davis on court one and Caroline Walinsky versus Shana Jones on court two."

Beaming, Caroline walked up to the mike, which Currie surrendered after a subtle tug of war. Players did not address the audience. Currie could see that producer fellow chuckling on the sidelines.

"Hi everybody, I'm Caroline Walinsky!"

"We all know who you are," shouted a golfer who'd clearly been at the Pimm's Cup table a few too many times. "I get YouTube on my iPhone."

"Nice to meet a fan. Anyway, I forfeit to Shana Jones. Go Shana! Oh, and one more thing," Caroline pulled a wadded up chef's toque from the back of her skirt and slapped it on her head where it flopped limply to one side.

"The only thing missing from this great celebration is great paella. But no worries, you can make one at home in your own Cucina

Barcelona paella pan. So easy Chef Caroline can use it! Watch for me on QVC!"

And with that she handed the microphone back to a flummoxed Currie.

"Well, unprecedented. In view of the forfeit, Shana Jones will play Taylor Thomas in the first round."

Taylor waved from the sidelines where she was now seated on the tipsy golfer's, lap sucking the last of his Pimm's Cup out of a straw.

"Forfeit," she shouted merrily. "Go Shana!"

Standing next to a smiling Karen, Allie felt her face flush. This was *not* what Caroline had promised. She wished she could take a fat, red Sharpie and put her name on the Wall of Shame right now. Well, she'd take care of it Monday, not to mention placing a call to Judge Lanier about Taylor's drunken behavior. Let her shout "Go Shana" from behind bars.

"Very well," said Currie, who for once in her life wished she could put down the microphone and leave. "Elena Walinsky versus Shana Jones and Allison Beech versus Karen Davis, and both matches are now semi-finals. Any further forfeits?"

Elena strode on to the court, head held high, wearing a skin-tight white lace tennis dress, her leopard print sports bra and ball shorts clearly visible underneath. "You ever hear of Stalingrad? My grandfather fight Nazis with nothing but turnips and slingshot. Russians do not forfeit. Go Elena!"

She broke into mad applause for herself as the crowd looked on in stunned silence.

"Indeed," said Currie. "Five minutes of warm up, then the matches begin."

"I haven't seen you practicing much," said Allie to Karen as they walked toward court two. "Then again, they don't have courts at the Ritz Carlton."

Karen caught sight of Sean in the crowd, and he winked. She felt a girlish smile slide on to her face.

"I'm sorry, Allie," she replied. "Did you say something?"

"You know Greg is divorcing you, right? Despite your silly Catholic scruples, which obviously are situational. Cecily Roberts, the Belle Vista girl Greg dated before he met you, is with the Davises right now at their ranch in Montana."

Allie put her tennis bag down on the bench with a thump and pulled out her racquet. "You've shamed them so much they couldn't even come to Founder's Day."

"Actually, Allie, I talked to Greg earlier. He's having a great time in Montana and I couldn't be happier for him," Karen put her bag down next to Allie's and pulled out her old Wilson Hyper Hammer, then stripped off her Sacred Heart Tennis Team t-shirt. Underneath, she wore the Jones Belle Vista uniform. "Spin for the serve?"

Allie's jaw clenched painfully. She walked stiffly to her side of the net and spun her Babolat. "Up." The handle landed stripes down.

"My serve," said Karen, grinning. She felt kind of naked in her skimpy tennis dress, but she saw Shana give her a beaming smile from the next court.

"You know, once you're divorced your membership here ends immediately," said Allie before turning and walking to the baseline on her side of the court.

"If I hadn't already agreed to the divorce, that would convince me," said Karen. "Let's warm up."

Sean was enjoying watching Karen play. He'd been hesitant to come to the club, but after Karen found out Greg was half a continent away, he agreed, but just till the tennis matches were over. Then he and Karen were going to go somewhere quiet and have dinner and a long talk.

A commotion on the side of the court caught his eye. A gorgeous young blonde in a hot pink sundress was dragging an ancient looking security guard toward the clubhouse.

"I'm telling you, he's in the basement, you have to come now!"

"I'm still eating my lunch," said the guard plaintively. To prove his point he waived a half-eaten tuna sandwich in the air. "Just call the police."

"We did that. They thought it was a crank call."

Sean walked over at the same time as a tall, well-built guy in his early thirties. They instantly recognized each other as law enforcement.

"Sean Flannery, U.S. Marshals," said Sean, sticking out his hand.

"Patrick O'Malley, NYPD," replied Patrick, giving him a firm handshake. Then they both burst out laughing. "This must be a belated St. Patrick's Day celebration."

Bethany rolled her eyes. "So do you two want to sing a few choruses of Danny Boy, or would you like to catch a dangerous criminal gang member instead? He's in the boiler room being attacked by a feral cat and he's covered in bright yellow paint."

Sean and Patrick both looked at Bethany, then burst out laughing again.

"And she wonders why the police thought this was a crank call," said Sean.

Then Enrique jogged up, breathing hard. "Sorry, babe, no luck with front desk security either."

"Is she for real?" said Patrick to Enrique, who seemed more legit than Bethany.

"Yeah," said Enrique. "It's Hector Ortiz of the Latin Locos. He had us at gunpoint and..."

At the word gun all laughter evaporated.

"Let's go," said Sean to Patrick. "You," he pointed at Enrique, "show us how to get to that boiler room."

The three took off, leaving Bethany standing with her hands on her hips. Sexists. Clearly everyone had forgotten that she, Bethany, had taken Hector down before. She sighed, deciding she'd rather watch her mother play tennis than go back to that smelly basement anyway. Especially if she could score a real drink from the bartender, who seemed to be very flexible about checking IDs.

Shana fought hard against Elena, but after twenty-five minutes she'd lost 6-2, 6-1. Off to the side, far from the tables and the bar, two women dressed like aging hippies and a red-haired girl were watching her intently.

Elena smiled down at Shana as they shook hands at the net.

"Congratulations, Mrs. Jones."

Shana frowned. "But I lost."

"Yes, but you are taking three games from me, and all while wearing plastic crown stuck in hair and having to hit backhand around enormous false breasts. You are excellent amateur player, especially for someone who looks like prostitute."

"Uh, thank you, I think. You want to sit down and watch the rest of the match between Karen and Allie?"

Elena looked over at the next court where Allie and Karen were blasting crosscourt backhands at each other. She shrugged.

"Not really. It matters little who wins. I think I will go get massage before next match."

Over in the corner, Sage turned to her mothers.

"Did you see who's over by the camera crew? It's Byron, from The Moon Goddess. Shana Jones must be in the reality show he's working on. Is that karma or what? We should go say hi!"

"I don't think so," said Galen, putting a restraining hand on Sage's shoulder. "He'd ask, quite naturally, why we're here, and we certainly don't want to ambush Mrs. Jones on film. Let's just avoid him until we've spoken to her."

"Do you think we should go talk to her now?"

"I don't see how we can be discreet with this huge crowd and the cameras," said Galen. "Why don't we wait awhile? Surely things are bound to calm down."

Galen had never claimed predictive abilities, and today was no exception.

As Shana and Elena walked toward the sidelines, two men in dark suits approached the court. They opened the gate and walked right in. They didn't seem to care that their shoes were not tennis specific. In her official chair on high, Currie held up her hand.

"What do you think you're doing? We are in the middle of a championship match. Please leave the court immediately," she said with authority.

The men ignored her and approached Elena.

"Elena Maria Dragunova?" asked the taller of the two. "I'm Officer Joe Carter with U.S. Immigration and Customs Enforcement and this is Peter Babcock, Federal Bureau of Investigation."

Rex and two freelance cameramen who'd been filming the matches (Jamal had followed Sean and Patrick to film Hector's arrest) with a mix of boredom and disdain began circling Elena and the officers like sharks who'd just scented blood.

Elena dropped her racquet on the court.

"My name is Elena Walinsky! Now get out of my way."

Instead of moving, Officer Carter pulled out a pair of handcuffs.

"Your name is Dragunova. You are legally married to your former tennis coach, Yuri Dragunov, a Russian national. Your marriage to Jack Walinsky is invalid and you are in this country illegally."

Currie, who had abandoned her chair and Karen and Allie's match, walked toward the officers in a state of shock. She wasn't sure what specific rule this violated, but she knew it was a violation.

Allie and Karen stopped play and watched, stunned, from the far court (Karen had no intention of intervening on Elena's behalf. She had to draw the line somewhere.) The crowd, which had been silent, began to whisper and stir.

"That is false! An American lie! I am legally married to Jack Walinsky! See, I am wearing *very* large diamond ring!" Elena spat at them, showing them the back of her left hand. She began to bounce on her toes, as if preparing for a net volley.

The officers were not deterred, but they moved toward her cautiously, like one might approach a rabid raccoon. Officer Carter held his handcuffs in front of his body while Babcock circled around the frenzied tennis player.

"Back off, or I will be forced to contact my friend Putin and he will retaliate! Do you know how it feels to be slowly poisoned to death with radioactive materials?"

She picked up her racquet and began prancing about like a boxer in the ring. Suddenly, she caught sight of a pair of wide blue eyes in the crowd, sparkling with delight. Caroline.

"You, first fat wife! It was you who called goon squad! How would you like acid in face like Bolshoi Ballet director? Good luck getting new husband then."

Elena's focus on Caroline caused her to temporarily lose sight of Babcock. He was directly behind her now, and as Carter moved towards her, Babcock wrapped his arms around her and grabbed her wrists while Carter snapped the cuffs on. Elena's head whipped around and she bared her even white teeth, an anniversary gift from her absent husband.

The crowd turned in unison and looked at Caroline, who'd been caught in the act of devouring a plate of fries.

"It wasn't me," she exclaimed loudly. Though she wished it had been.

As the second, apparently not legal, Mrs. Jack Walinsky was led away from the party in handcuffs, she shouted, "Someone please call my true husband, Jack Walinsky! Call him this instant! He will not tolerate this for one moment!"

Watching her retreating back, Caroline broke into a huge smile.

Shana looked on as Rex and his crew followed Elena toward the exit, walking right by her as if she didn't exist.

Despite making up with her teammates, Shana felt deflated. She'd been in a defiant mood when she'd dressed and put on her makeup this morning, but the sidelong glances and snickers she'd gotten from the well-groomed crowd reminded her a little too much of the Briarwood. This was their club, no matter whose name was on the sign. Shana decided what she really needed was to curl up in her own bed with a wine cooler and some Lifetime television. It looked as if Karen might lose, and now that Elena was gone, that would make Allie the Edgemoor Cup winner. Shana did not want to see that captured on film.

She decided to tell Rex she wasn't feeling well and had to leave. Not that he appeared to care; *Queen of the Court* seemed to have multiple stars now, all more appealing than some jumped up redneck girl from the sticks.

As she got up to leave, Lil Wayne came rushing out of the crowd. "Mama, they're dragging a yellow man out of the basement in handcuffs and Jamal is making a movie of it. Come see!"

Shana patted him on the head. What an imagination. "Honey, go upstairs and get Judy, I think she's havin' some lemonade on the terrace. I'm gonna need her to keep an eye on you because I'm heading home. Mama's tired out."

"But Mama, there's gonna be fireworks and ice cream and circus people!"

Shana gave him a big hug. "You can tell me all about it when you get home."

"Are you leaving because you lost?" asked Lil Wayne, pulling back and giving her a very shrewd look for a six year old. "You always tell me to be a good sport."

Shana sighed. Lil Wayne's words hit a bit too close to the truth. This would have to be the day those moral lessons she'd hammered into him came back and bit her in the butt.

Lavinia, freshly showered and in a crisp, lemon-yellow shirtdress, watched with pleasure from the grille terrace as her daughter sent another winner down the line past Karen Davis. Allie's decades of lessons and dedication finally seemed to be paying off. She'd even managed to hit that annoying adulterous lawyer twice with very respectable overheads.

Lavinia checked her watch. Nearly five o'clock. Well, there was still plenty of time for the final match before the evening festivities; fireworks were not until nine. She did not approve of all the needless frivolity: face painting, live music, acrobats and so on. But she had to admit that attendance at the event, which had dwindled over the years, was impressive. Even dedicated golfers were watching the ladies' tennis tournament. (She ignored the fact that having a competitor arrested on camera might be part of the draw.)

Bob Dandridge from the Board had stopped by her table a few minutes earlier and told her the event was actually in the black for the first time ever. He'd seemed to attribute it to that awful Wayne Jones, but Lavinia had set him straight. *Her daughter* was chairperson.

"Well Allison ordered the food and entertainment, but Mr. Jones is the one who figured out how to pay for it without forgoing toilet paper or electricity for a month," Bob had said with a very condescending smile. Well, in any case, those horrid Joneses were gone after today. Lavinia, who had a gift for pretending things had never happened, decided to start forgetting them immediately.

That might have worked if Judy Simpson, wearing some horrendous orange and purple flowing thing and Birkenstocks, hadn't plopped herself down in the adjacent chair, after unceremoniously dumping Lavinia's vintage tan-and-white Longchamp bag onto the ground.

"Really," said Lavinia, bending down to pick up the bag, dust it off and place it on the table.

"Well, it's standing room only up here and my dogs are barking," said Judy, putting her feet up on the edge of Lavinia's chair. "Anyway, saving seats is so high school."

"I wasn't saving seats, I just needed a place for my bag," retorted Lavinia testily, edging as far away from Judy's purple-painted toenails as possible.

"Nice," said Judy. "Anyway, I just came to say goodbye. Since this is the Jones's last day, I probably won't see you again."

"From your lips to God's ears," said Lavinia, not bothering to put on an act. "I hope you'll keep your word and not come back for more favors."

"*Favors!* Vinnie, only you could pretend to have the moral high ground here."

As Lavinia opened her mouth to reply, Smokey Joe, who'd wound his way up the service stairway and slunk through the crowd, sprang weightlessly onto the table and delicately picked up the remains of Lavinia's cream cheese and watercress sandwich.

"Dear God," she said, standing up so quickly she knocked over her iced tea.

"These pests are unclean, they have to..."

Judy stroked Smokey Joe with one hand and held up the other, palm facing Lavinia.

"Remember, the cats are part of the deal. Shana and Wayne and I go, but Smokey and his buddies stay," said Judy. "Pippa would have wanted it that way," she added with a wicked grin.

Lavinia looked on in fury as Smokey Joe, having finished his sandwich, walked across her white leather bag and leapt to the ground, leaving a trail of bright yellow footprints like an artist's signature.

"Oh, I like that pattern so much better. Now your bag matches your dress," said Judy as she got up, gave Lavinia a little wave, and followed Smokey Joe towards the stairs.

She caught Lil Wayne in her arms just as he emerged from the stairway.

"Judy, Mama's going home right now and wants you to watch me," he said, hugging her tight. "Destiny's still at her pool party; we're 'sposed to get her later."

"Hmmm," said Judy. She knew Big Wayne had fled to Jorge's back bar after Shana's match, not wanting to bring her down. He'd be crushed if she left early after he'd worked so hard to make her final day at the club special.

"Let's go catch your mama before she leaves, I've got something to tell her."

26

Shana was on her way to the parking lot when Judy caught up with her. She was pondering Rex's reaction to her leaving.

"Well, we have some lovely footage of you in your uniform and tiara, so no pressure," Rex had said. "Byron, see if Jamal is done filming that painted prisoner. We need to get Bethany's interview before she has another spiked Shirley Temple. I think that girl will be ratings dynamite with the eighteen to twenty-six demographic."

Byron had shrugged an apology in Shana's direction and scurried off.

Shana had secretly hoped there'd be more of a fuss when she left, but no one seemed to care.

Karen was with Sean, Taylor was with, well, quite a few people, and Caroline was busy selling pans. She decided against telling Big Wayne she was headed home. She'd seen him on the terrace watching her match with some of the board members. He'd worked hard on Founder's Day and she didn't want him to miss it. A white balloon, one of hundreds in red, white and blue that flew jauntily from the clubhouse fence and light posts, had broken free. Now, partially deflated, it drooped pathetically at the parking lot entrance. Shana thought she knew how it felt.

"Hey, hey Mrs. Jones, Wait up." It was Judy, trailing after Lil Wayne and panting in the heat.

"Shana, you can't leave yet, you have to talk to Wayne," she huffed as she caught up. Lil Wayne grabbed Shana's hand and started to dance around chanting, "Stay, Mama, stay!"

"Now, Judy, no need for Wayne to miss his big night just because I'm tired," she said, pulling her hand away from her son. She was hot, irritated and just wanted out of there.

"Shana, Wayne put his heart into this event for you. I know you don't feel like it, but he's up in the back bar with Jorge, and you really should go see him," Judy insisted.

Shana's bad mood got the best of her; she did not feel like being talked out of her sulk by Judy, Wayne or anybody.

"Why don't you just watch the kids like you get paid for and never mind about me and my husband," she snapped.

Judy said nothing, but that was rebuke enough. Shana watched as she took Lil Wayne's hand and led him away, his eyes wide and mouth hanging open. He'd never heard his mama talk like that to anyone, much less their beloved Judy.

A champagne-colored blonde emerging from a champagne-colored Lexus nodded approvingly at Shana. "It's sad, but you really have to speak firmly to the help if you expect them to respect you," she said. Shana felt sick. She'd let all this country club and television business turn her into the kind of person she hated. She sounded just like Allie. Well, like Allie if she'd grown up in West Virginia and dropped out of high school.

Shana turned around and hurried back toward the club. First, she'd find Big Wayne, and then she'd humble herself before Judy like the good Lord said, apologize and beg her not to leave the family.

As she rushed toward the stairway that led to the back bar, she just missed Sage and her mothers. They had exited through the main front entrance hoping to catch Shana in the parking lot.

Sage scanned the crowded lot looking for Shana's bright red hair, but saw nothing.

"Do you think she left? Did we miss her?" she asked tremulously.

Galen sighed. She was anxious to get out of this hellhole of elitism and sink into a warm bath. But she knew how important this was to Sage.

"Let's go back in and look around," she said. "And if we don't find her, I'm asking for Pippa, whether she likes it or not."

Shana found Big Wayne just where Judy said he would be, in the deserted second floor bar with Jorge. He had a stack of papers on the bar in front of him.

"Hey hon, I thought the ladies avoided this place," he said, putting one arm over the papers on the bar. "I watched your match from the balcony. You played real good. Plus, nobody arrested you after; boy, Rex musta had a field day with Elena gettin' hauled away, and that guy in the basement too."

"Wayne" said Shana, starting to sniffle. "I lost my temper with Judy. I was real mean and snotty like. I treated her just like the ladies at the Briarwood used to treat my mama. I'm so ashamed."

"Why hon," said Wayne, "that don't sound like you. But you have been in a real bad mood lately. I kinda hoped seeing all your friends and having this big party would cheer you up."

"Actually, the girls were real sweet to me today. But seeing that Allie with all her airs, and how she fixed it so I'd play Elena first and lose. Well, she's so petty and mean, and the worst part is she's turned me all petty and mean too."

"Sweetie, you just made a mistake. Go find Judy and explain, she'll understand. Then we can watch the fireworks. You love fireworks, baby."

"Oh Wayne, I just want to go home," Shana wailed. "We can come back another day."

"I think the time has come to tell her the truth, Mr. Wayne," said Jorge in Spanish. He'd been tutoring Big Wayne over beers for a month now. As it turned out, the former biker had a real knack for languages. Other than English, that is.

"You're right, Jorge, how about a shot of tequila first," Wayne replied in Spanish, causing Shana's eyes to widen.

"Why, Wayne, you've learned Spanish! I had no idea. And just when I thought I knew everything about you."

That did it. Wayne decided that he couldn't even wait for the tequila shot.

"No honey, you don't. The reason I want you to stay for the party is that this is our last night at Jones Belle Vista. Belle Vista, that is, as of tomorrow. I told you I sold all our Big Wayne's gentlemen's clubs, but what I didn't tell you is I invested all that money, plus most of our savings, with Jack Walinsky."

Shana blinked, not quite understanding.

"I'm sure Jack is doing a good job with our money," said Shana unconvincingly. Honest businessmen did not have wives who got arrested during tennis tournaments.

"Honey, the FBI called me. Jack's on the run. He ripped off a bunch of investors, including me. I lost all that money. We had to sell Jones Belle Vista back," He pointed at the papers in front of him. "We can't even afford to be members. This is my last memo to the club about the finances and repairs and all, because as of tomorrow we can't even walk on these grounds. And that's not all. I had to quit paying Rex – he's got a company making the show, and you may not be uh, like, the star anymore. I'm not even sure we can keep the house," said Wayne.

He got up off his bar stool and got on his knees before Shana, just like he had on the night he proposed on the stage at Big Wayne's.

"I wouldn't blame you if you up and left me. That money was as much yours as mine, and I just plowed ahead like some dumb ox without even asking you. I don't deserve you."

Shana put a hand on each of Big Wayne's shoulders.

"Wayne, I'm the one who should apologize to you. I pushed you to buy this club and to pay for me to be on TV. And why? Just so I could act like I'm some fancy-pants country club snob like Allie Beech? Wayne, I made a fool of myself, of all of us. I put you in a spot where you felt like we had to keep up with these people. I am so sorry," she said, getting down on her knees to face him.

"I would love you just as much in a trailer in West Virginia," she added, giving him a kiss.

"Well, it won't come to that, honey. But we might have to make do with a townhouse and public schools. And public tennis courts," Wayne said, relief in his voice.

"That's just fine," said Shana, standing up and pulling Wayne up by the hand. "As for tennis, I think I'm done for a while. Come on Wayne, let's find Judy and the kids and go home."

Allie finally finished off a distracted Karen, who kept scanning the crowd for Sean, 7-5, 7-5.

She shook her opponent's hand and insincerely complimented Karen's game, all the while thinking how clever she'd been to look into Elena's background, then call immigration. She was a far better investigator than that fraud Clare Buxton.

Allie strolled over to the official's chair and shook Currie's hand as well. "It's a pity I won't get to test my skills against Elena, but I suppose I am the winner of this year's Edgemoor Cup."

"Not so fast, Mrs. Beech. There are rules for this kind of thing and they will be followed."

Currie was regaining her composure and the wheels in her mind were spinning. There might be nothing in her weighty rules book about a player being arrested mid-match (so distasteful), but there certainly were rules about forfeiture.

She opened her well-worn copy of *Country Club Tennis Rules,* which she always kept at her side. "Section 9a (5) firmly states that if a player must forfeit a championship match before the completion of said match, the loser of the semi-final will take his or her place."

Allie stared up at Currie in disbelief. "So what, exactly, does that mean?"

"It means that you will be playing Mrs. Shana Jones for the Jones Belle Vista club championship." Currie looked at her watch. "Section 9a (6) states that the rescheduled match will begin exactly one hour after the forfeiture occurs. I suggest you hydrate and stretch. I will speak with Mrs. Jones."

"But she's not even here," Allie sputtered, gesturing at the crowd.

"I'll help find her," said Karen, who'd come over to thank Currie. Allie shot her an evil look. "I'll call her cell phone, but let's all look around. It's so noisy she may not hear."

Fern, Galen and Sage negotiated their way through the festivities, trying to locate Shana.

It was becoming more and more crowded, and Sage was starting to worry that she would never find the woman who might be her mother. Suddenly, she walking arm in arm with a big, tattooed man. Sage tugged on Fern's sleeve and pointed. The three of them walked purposefully across the lawn.

"Excuse me, Ms. Jones?" Sage felt her legs trembling and she smiled weakly. "My name is Sage Silverfox Shapiro. Would you mind if I asked you a question?"

When Shana turned towards the girl, a sob rose in her throat. It was like looking in a mirror. One that erased time, not to mention makeup.

"It's you! Finally, it's you!"

"What are you talking about, baby?" Wayne turned from Shana's shocked face to Sage's. "Man, you two sure look alike. You family from West Virginia?"

"I think I might be," said Sage. She looked back at Shana. "Did you give up a daughter for adoption in Morgantown in May of 1995?" Sage could feel Galen and Fern behind her and it calmed her.

Shana's eyes flooded with tears and she wiped them frantically with the back of her hand, never taking her eyes off of Sage.

"Yes," she said, turning to look at Wayne. "A beautiful baby girl. Not a day has gone by when I haven't thought of her, of you."

Shana dropped her tennis bag, held her arms out and Sage stepped into them. Inside the bag, Shana's phone ran, but she ignored it.

After a long hug, she took Sage and turned her by the shoulders to face Wayne, who stood silently watching.

"This is my husband, Wayne Jones. We have two children, Destiny and Lil Wayne. I can't wait for you to meet them. I never told Wayne about you, but I'm telling him now." She looked up at Wayne. "Wayne, this is my daughter … Sugar."

"That's Sage. Sage Silverfox Shapiro."

"Now this is what I call a GOOD secret, a lot nicer surprise than the one I just gave you," said Wayne, giving Shana a hug. "The more the merrier!"

He winked at Sage and she smiled back at him.

"Now don't you want to introduce us to…?"

"I'm Galen Shapiro and this is my wife, Fern Shapiro. We are Sage's parents. We drove down from Brooklyn this morning."

Galen waited for the uncomfortable silence she expected to follow this introduction, but it didn't come.

"You've raised such a beautiful daughter," Shana gushed. "You must be so proud of her."

"Yes, we are," Galen said, beaming at Sage. "She is such a gift. A gift, apparently, we owe to you."

"Maybe it's too soon for me to ask you this, but do you know where my father is?"

Shana pulled gently away from Wayne. "Oh honey, your daddy died before you were born. He was bit by a timber rattler. His name was Levi, and he was raised in the snake handling tradition of the Pentecostal Church. His daddy, Pastor John, also died from a snake bite, and his mama died of grief, so you've got no kin left on that side. Mark 16:18 says 'They shall take up serpents,' and Levi's family truly believed that. I'm sorry."

Fern and Galen, despite being followers of Wicca, looked a bit taken aback.

"Honey, that's a lot of news for this little one," said Big Wayne, who noticed that Sage had gone a bit pale. "Maybe we should find somewhere quite where you two can talk."

Sage nodded. She felt a bit dizzy. None of the many scenarios she'd imagined involving her birth parents had included a fundamentalist snake-handling father, and the only people in her neighborhood who looked like Shana, in her heavy makeup and tiara, were drag queens.

But the warmth of Shana's smile and embrace helped Sage erase all earlier visions of her mother. Shana, in her own way, was just perfect, and to be fair, Sage knew her family had not figured in any of Shana's imaginings either. The important thing was that her birth mother wanted her and had been looking for her.

Shana finished wiping a Dolly Partonesque amount of mascara on the sleeve of Big Wayne's lilac golf shirt with the embroidered Jones Belle Vista crest. She seemed to be getting control of herself.

"We were just on our way home, would you like to come and visit with us?" Shana asked Galen and Fern. Her phone was still buzzing, and across the lawn she saw Karen, who was waving and pointing at her own phone. She ignored her.

Then she spotted Allie, slightly off to the side, with Currie Holmes. Allie caught sight of her with Sage, froze, and then turned away. A notion, a very unpleasant one, dawned on Shana.

"Sug…Sage, honey, can I ask you one little thing? How on earth did you track me to Jones Belle Vista? And why did you come today?" Shana asked, although she didn't really need her suspicions confirmed. Allie Beech, that conniving, heartless *bitch*.

"Someone named Pippa found my Facebook page and emailed that she knew you, and that you might be my mother. She wrote that I should come here today and if I thought so too, I should introduce myself."

"Pippa!" Big Wayne turned pale. Mountain people took their ghosts seriously. "Honey, when was this?"

"A few weeks ago."

"Well that ain't, uh, likely. You see Pippa, she used to live here a long time ago, and then there was a storm on this boat and well…" Wayne sputtered as Galen and Fern looked on curiously. Shana, however, knew that the only ghost involved in this was the ghost of Allie's long-dead decency.

She also realized Rex, Jamal and the rest of the Vixen crew were filming whatever nonsense was going on with Allie and the tournament. Although she knew in her heart that being on television wasn't *really* important, the thought that they'd failed to record her reunion with her long-lost daughter rankled her. Thousands, maybe millions of people would have seen her and Sage together at last. And Shana herself could have watched it over and over again.

"Sage, sweetie, the woman who emailed you wasn't Pippa, Pippa's passed," Shana explained as kindly as she could.

"Passed what?" asked Fern, completely confused.

"Probably passed out," mumbled Galen, looking disapprovingly at the one-percenters staggering merrily around the Belle Vista lawn.

"She's no longer with us," Shana said, and then gave up when she saw the befuddled glances of Galen and Sage. Shana had no idea what religion they were, but clearly they didn't talk about the departed a whole lot.

"Anyway, that don't matter, what matters is you're here! I got just one little thing to clear up before we go get to know each other," Shana handed her tennis bag to Wayne and gave Sage a quick hug. Then she marched off towards the tennis courts, leaving her husband standing with his wife's surprise teenage daughter and her two moms.

Fortunately, a life of working in bars had given Wayne a knack for rolling with the situation. He'd once spent an entire afternoon talking religion with a Maori surfer, his Scientologist girlfriend and the Yiddish-speaking parrot they'd bought from a rabbi.

"What say I get us all some lemonade," Wayne said cheerfully, using his big arms to shepherd the group toward the tables on the edge of the lawn. "Look here, some folks just cleared out of this table, we can wait for Shana right here. You know, we make Belle Vista lemonade from fresh lemons right in the kitchen."

"Organic lemons?" asked Fern.

"Yes ma'am," said Big Wayne proudly. "Our friend Judy, she got me into organics and what you call locavore food. At first I thought that meant crazy food, you know, like loco – well, when you meet Judy you'll understand. But most everything here at Jones, I mean Belle Vista, is now organic and locally grown."

"Really? We run an organic bakery," exclaimed Galen. And to Sage's dismay, her moms and Big Wayne started gabbing about *produce* of all things. On one of the most important days of her life. Middle-aged people, whether Wiccan or redneck, were just not cool.

She excused herself, saying she had to use the ladies' room, and crept toward the tennis court where Shana and a dark-haired woman in tennis whites were having animated conversation. Amazingly, a film crew was recording the entire thing. She wanted to text Jasper, but she was afraid that she'd miss something.

When she got closer she realized that it was more like an argument, and she felt her pulse start to race. Fern and Galen had vowed never to argue in front of Sage and she was expected to remain calm too. Whenever one of them got angry, that person would retreat to her room to meditate. Sage was amazed when she was at Jasper's for dinner and he and his mom, an editor at the New York Times, got into a full-blown shouting match over the Occupy movement. She was ashamed to admit she found arguing a bit exhilarating, like eating a BLT on the sneak.

"Don't bother to lie to me, Allie Beech," said Shana, leaning in toward Allie. "You found my daughter and brought her here as some sort of party stunt, trying to embarrass me and Wayne. Well, we're not embarrassed. We're thrilled."

"Oh, really" said Allie, pulling back slightly as if she might catch something from Shana. Sage thought she looked beautiful, but cold, like the Evil Queen in fairy tales.

"You have absolutely no proof that is true; this girl said she spoke with Pippa. Maybe she's a so-called psychic just like you. Or just plain crazy. And as for being thrilled, perhaps you'd be equally thrilled to learn that this is your last day at this club. Your husband has sold it back to us. He's apparently in some sort of financial difficulty. In words you can understand, you are broke and no longer welcome here."

"I know that," spat Shana. "And I can't get outta here fast enough now that I know what you are really like. You should be ashamed."

"Ashamed," scoffed Allie. "I'm not the one who had a secret illegitimate child I abandoned and never even tried to find."

"That's not true," exclaimed Shana, pain evident in her voice. "I tried and tried to find her."

"Well, she was very easy to find, she had a Facebook page dedicated to finding *you*," Allie retorted.

"And how do you know all that if you're not the one who emailed her, *Pippa*?" said Shana. "Maybe if you spent half as much time with your own children, instead of looking for mine, you'd know that you are not exactly in the running for mother of the year."

"Well, my children were conceived in wedlock, not in the parking lot of some substandard high school in the back of a Chevy," said Allie, moving in close to face Shana.

"I'll have you know Sage was conceived behind a church, so get your mind out of the gutter," Shana yelled.

Sage noticed that while most of the party guests had evacuated the area immediately around the feuding pair, three women in tennis outfits had materialized behind Shana, and Byron was with them. His eyes went wide when he saw her, and he looked from her to Shana and back again. Sage just nodded, and Byron gave her a big smile and a thumbs up.

"I've done a lot of shitty things," said a tall, model-gorgeous blonde who was obviously drunk. "But man, Allie, this has all of them beaten hands down."

"I can't believe you took a chance of traumatizing an innocent young girl," said a pale woman with dark hair and a serious look. She wore no makeup and jewelry, and if it weren't for the tennis dress would have fit right in Park Slope.

"Allie, I will *never* make you paella," added a Reubenesque blonde with dark roots, who, weirdly, seemed to be holding some kind of pan instead of a tennis racquet.

Sage wondered if these were Shana's friends. They seemed an odd group, even by Brooklyn's flexible standards.

At that point an older, gray-haired woman in white Bermuda shorts, a white polo, and a giant visor walked over to the table. Sage almost giggled – she looked like a WASP version of Fern's mother Gilda, who had retired to Florida and played golf every day until her skin had turned the color of her vintage Coach bag. Gilda always told her friends that Fern was married to a Jewish male podiatrist.

"Excuse me," said the older woman. "This might not be a good time, as you appear to be having a personal discussion, but as Elena Walinsky will be unable to continue play…"

"Because she was arrested! And her name's not Walinsky, it's Dragon Offal, and she's a polygamist!" interjected the big blonde.

"Bigamist," corrected the serious brunette.

"Yes, um, well, in any case, she has forfeited her position, which, as I informed Allison, makes Mrs. Shana Jones our other finalist," said the older woman. "Mrs. Jones, you will be playing Mrs. Beech on court one, with warm-ups to begin in ten minutes."

"Currie," said Allie, "I believe Mrs. Jones was on her way out."

"Well, in that case, Allison, you win the tournament by default."

"No! Wait!" said the brunette. "Shana, don't let her get away with this. This is what she wants."

"Karen," said Shana, putting her hand on the brunette's arm. "I don't care about this silly old tournament any more. I'm gonna go home and get to know my daughter and her family."

The word daughter gave Sage a warm feeling, which was immediately erased by the triumphant smirk on that Allie's face. She was looking at Shana as if she'd just squashed a bug. Sage felt something boil inside her, and she was in no mood to control it with meditation. She got up and bolted over to where Shana and the others stood.

"Shana, please play in the tournament. I'd love to watch you play tennis. It's my favorite sport." Sage felt herself color a little as she told this white lie. "We can go back to your house and talk after. If it's okay, my moms and I can even stay over. We have plenty of time."

Shana grabbed Sage and gave her the biggest bear hug she'd ever had. It would have felt like being wrapped in a sweaty perfumed blanket, except for those fake boobs poking Sage in the chest.

When she broke away Shana turned to Currie.

"Mrs. Holmes, this is my daughter, Sage. Seems she wants to see her mama play some tennis, and I am not gonna disappoint her."

She then swiveled to face Allie. "I will meet you on court one in ten minutes. Bring your A game, Allie Beech, because I'm in the mood to leave one permanent reminder of me at Belle Vista – my name engraved on that Edgemoor Cup." And with that she grabbed Sage's hand and pulled her towards the locker room.

"Mrs. J," cried Byron. "Make sure you leave time for me to do some hair and makeup. You too, Sage sweetie. I'll wait for you in the tennis shop."

He walked over to Allie.

"Sorry, I only have time to work on Shana and her daughter. But may I suggest a little blush since shame doesn't seem to bring any color to your face."

27

When Shana and Sage emerged from the tennis shop, they found Judy waiting outside.

"Wayne told me you wanted to see me," she said. "But first things first."

Judy put her hands on Sage's shoulders and backed her toward the white wall of the clubhouse. This might have freaked some people out, but Sage was used to having her aura read.

"Hmmm. Electric blue, do you have telepathic abilities? I also see green for healing and turquoise for energy – a very mature aura for such a young person. I'd have to say Shana's daughter has a very old and wise soul, like her mother."

She gave Sage a hug.

"Why don't you run on down to that table over there," she pointed toward the lawn where Wayne sat with Sage's mothers and Destiny and Lil Wayne. "You can meet your new sibs."

Sage left, trailed by Jamal. He turned as he passed Shana.

"I'm so sorry I missed you meeting your daughter, Shana. If it's okay I'd like to come over to your house later and get some footage of your family. Even if we don't put it on the show, I'd like you to have it."

Shana smiled and nodded, then turned to Judy.

"Oh Judy, I am so sorry for how I treated you earlier! I acted just like Allie and every other bitchy woman at this club. You are my dear friend and I don't know what I'd do without you."

"Mrs. J, your apology is officially accepted. And with relief. I was afraid you'd gone over to the dark side. Wayne has done a lot to change the negative energy in this place." She waved her hands in a motion that encompassed all Belle Vista. "But all those decades of greed, deception and just plain evil can seep into your soul. Don't forget I grew up here. You may find it hard to believe now, but I was quite the socialite in training, stealing other girls' boyfriends and writing nasty stuff about them in slam books. I even put Ben Gay in Taffy Dandridge's bra before cheerleading practice."

"Yes, but you're reformed." said Shana.

"Well, not completely, Mrs. J, which is why it's easy for me to be forgiving. If you see ol' Mrs. Dandridge jumping around later, all I have to say is that Icy Hot is a far superior product to Ben Gay. Really makes you feel the burn. Now go win yourself a tennis match."

Shana headed out to court one. She knew Allie would bring her best game, but she felt confident. She just hoped she could win quickly and get back to Sage.

More than three hours later, those hopes had faded with the setting sun. Shana and Allie were deep into a bitterly contested third set, having split sets 6-4 Shana in the first and 7-5 Allie in the second. Heat seemed to settle on the court as night fell and the lights switched on, drawing moths and gnats to swirl around the players.

Shana, a sheen of sweat making her spray tan glow orange in the fluorescent brightness, returned Allie's serve with a deep forehand, pushing Allie back behind the baseline. She ran forward to volley an angle winner that made the usually restrained Allie curse audibly.

"Second profanity offense for Mrs. Beech. A point to Mrs. Jones," said Currie Holmes, looking a bit worse for wear as she sat in the official's chair fanning herself with her rules booklet.

"Well, unlike some people, I don't want to win using forfeits, fake points and such. So fuck that! Twice!" replied Shana with an emphasis on the F bomb that made Currie flinch.

"Point to Mrs. Beech for language violation by Mrs. Jones," said Currie, shaking her head. "Game to Mrs. Beech. Mrs. Jones will serve."

The women were tied 5-5 in the third set, and while their strokes had lost some edge, their attitudes had not. The Founder's Day ladies' final usually drew a small, polite crowd of tennis enthusiasts and family members. But the antipathy between opponents, the whiff of scandal surrounding the Jones' bankruptcy, Elena's public disgrace and the chance to be on a reality show had packed the terraces and patio surrounding the courts.

Despite themselves, the very proper Belle Vista members were thoroughly enjoying a Founder's Day which had already featured not one, but two, people being hauled off in handcuffs, screaming in foreign languages, as a camera crew got it all on tape. The club's reputation might be damaged, but the Pimm's Cup was especially potent this year, and for once, there was something more exciting to watch than the Senior Men's Golf Association's attempt at barbershop quartet.

The sky above Belle Vista suddenly exploded in a sparkling shower of red, white and blue as the fireworks began, illuminating the fortunate and the beautiful below, not to mention a troupe of freelance acrobats filched from Cirque de Soliel cavorting on Founder's Fountain.

"Those two loathe each other," said one socialite to another as Shana, her tiara still tangled in teased golden red hair matted with sweat, tossed a ball skyward to serve.

But the ball dropped straight to the ground with a plop as the terrible, grinding noise of an earth mover split the air. All heads, including Shana's, turned toward the golf course. Vixen's cameras swung toward the noise, focusing on a huge yellow earth mover churning up the ninth green and lurching toward the crowded patio like a defective extra from *Transformers*.

"Daddy," yelled Lil Wayne from the cab, "I'm tryin' to stop but the brake won't work!"

A red-faced Big Wayne chugged helplessly after the wayward piece of machinery, followed closely by Judy, Galen and Fern, trailing various scarves behind them.

"Dear Lord, that man Jones is being pursued by some sort of coven," exclaimed Currie with alarm. On this particular Founder's Day, it did not seem outside of the realm of possibility.

On court, Shana erupted into an impressive display of maternal hysteria. "Oh my God," she screamed, dropping her racquet. "That's my little boy! He's six, and he only knows how to drive ATVs, dirt bikes and his daddy's truck!" Across the net, Allie stood completely rigid.

"Holy shit," said Bethany to Enrique, Sage and Quint. An hour into the match they'd ended up at the same courtside table after Wayne offered to take Galen and Fern on a tour of the kitchens, and Judy and the kids headed back to the pool. Enrique had walked Bethany over and forced her to confess to swiping Sage's poem. Sage had been remarkably unbothered, saying poetry belonged to the universe and plagiarism was "a meaningless establishment construct".

"Not if your teacher uses Turnitin.com," Quint assured her. He'd fallen in love with Sage the moment he spotted her flame-colored curls, and had been glued to her side for hours. Bethany repeatedly texted him that Sage was way too cool for him. She *so* wanted to copy Sage's style. Thrift shop chic, why had she never thought of it?

Sage's eyes widened in horror as the earth mover pushed toward them.

"Will Lil Wayne get hurt?"

"Nah," said Bethany and Enrique at the same time.

"Lil Wayne specializes in hurting other people," said Enrique, "which means we'd better run."

The crowd parted like a posh Red Sea before a sunburned, snot-nosed Moses. Acrobats tumbled off Founder's Fountain and raced toward the safety of the lawn and clubhouse alongside members, staff and guests.

Fortunately for the drunkest evacuees, Lil Wayne was a slow-moving storm. Karen, Byron and Caroline had to half drag Taylor out of danger, as she'd passed out sometime during the second set.

"I wish Sean and Patrick were here," said Karen, "They'd know what to do."

"Apparently, an arrest assisted by a feral cat requires a lot of explanatory paperwork," said Byron, huffing as he picked up Taylor's feet. "Patrick says he's never leaving Brooklyn for this hell hole again."

"Ha. They're probably at Finnegan's Pub across from the courthouse drinking pints as we speak."

The earth mover careened onto the stone patio and picked up speed as Lil Wayne whooped inside. It headed straight towards the cast bronze fountain, where water spouted from the five iron of club founder Thomas Jardine Edgemoor in perpetuity.

"Not Founder's Fountain," shrieked Lavinia. To the amazement of onlookers and the delight of Rex Range, she seemed willing to sacrifice herself to save the hideous bronze relic, posing in front of it like the iconic Tiananmen Square protestor (if he'd worn linen and pearls). But she leapt to safety at the last moment, losing one gold Ferragamo sandal, and much of her starchy dignity, in the process.

The earth mover wrenched the statue from the ground, platform and all, like an old tree stump. The groaning and screeching of metal on metal made it seem as if old Edgemoor were screaming in pain as he tumbled head first onto the patio, his driver bent beyond repair. Where the fountain had stood there was now only a gaping hole in the artfully patterned flagstones.

His work done for the day, Lil Wayne ground the gears, brought the machine to a stop and looked down.

"Hey, Mama, Daddy, look what I done! I dug up a skeleton!"

Jamal rushed to the crater left by the upended fountain, followed by Shana, Big Wayne and his aging hippie posse. They gasped in unison. This was not a product of Lil Wayne's imagination, fueled by Skittles and three liters of Coke.

Embedded in the red Virginia clay, lay a human skull.

"Holy Shit," exclaimed Jamal as he filmed. "The kid really dug up a body."

Lavinia, who'd just pulled herself up onto her elbows, groaned and fainted.

Unbothered by the commotion, Smokey Joe crept up to the edge of the newly gouged crater, jumped lightly on top of the unearthed skull, sat down and began cleaning yellow paint off his paws.

Shana and Wayne crossed themselves, while Fern and Galen grasped the pentagrams they wore to ward off evil.

Judy walked to the edge, put her hands on her hips and stared down.

"You just couldn't leave well enough alone, could you?" she said.

"Who's she talkin' to?" whispered Shana, clutching Lil Wayne to her.

"I don't know," said Big Wayne, shaken. "But I hope to hell it's the cat."

28

"That was really freaky, but kind of exciting," said Sage as she sat on the big sectional in Shana's living room. Destiny and Lil Wayne were asleep on either side of her, Hound Dog at her feet and Hello Kitty curled in a ball on her lap. Fern and Galen sat adjacent to them watching Sage anxiously, while Shana beamed from an overstuffed chair across the room.

Even the shocking discovery of the body, not to mention both Lavinia and Judy being hauled off to the police station after Judy spoke with police, could dim Shana's exuberance at having her daughter home.

"Do they have to keep filming?" asked Galen with annoyance, as Jamal, trying to be as unobtrusive as possible, trained his camera on them. He'd sent a film crew off to the police station to film the action there, and thank God Rex had gone to supervise.

"Mom, it's not a big deal," said Sage. Sometimes she thought her moms were more Amish than Wiccan, they were so anti-technology. She wondered how much they'd freak if they knew her friend Saskia had a twenty-four hour webcam, and even Jasper had his own video blog that featured him eating at every hotdog stand in the five boroughs. So far, he'd gained five pounds and been mugged in Washington Heights, which had gotten him a lot of hits.

"Mrs. and Mrs. Shapiro, this is definitely not the welcome I would have planned for Sage. I agree with her about the freaky part, but ya'll are here now and I'd love to have you stay. After all, it's nearly midnight," said Shana plaintively. "And Sage and me haven't had hardly any time to talk."

"We're booked in a hostel in Del Ray," said Galen. "I think it's time we all head over there." Galen was not about to stay – or leave Sage – in a McMansion filled with meat-eating rednecks, reality television people and, once Wayne brought Judy back from the police station, a possible killer. It was unclear what Judy and that Winter woman had to do with that body in the hole, but they had been at the police station for a *long* time, long enough for Galen to be suspicious. She'd said as much to Fern as they'd driven to Shana's in the Prius. Sage had insisted on riding back with Shana and her brood in their gas-guzzling red Suburban, the one with "TennisMama" on the vanity plate.

"Is this the same Galen who volunteers at The Innocence Project and protests police brutality?" Fern replied testily. "Judy seems wonderful. She keeps bees *and* feeds feral cats. Clearly she and that Lavinia person knew the deceased and just have helpful information."

"I'm sure that's why that Karen, the lawyer, went down to the station with Judy. Because you need a lawyer to provide 'helpful information'," Galen huffed. "I don't want our Sage involved with these people, any of them."

"Well," Fern said philosophically, "one of these people is her biological mother, and she turns eighteen next year. We can prevent her from seeing Shana now, but next May she can just take off and live with her if she wants. I think our role here is the same as it has always been, to be supportive. If we create a climate of negativity toward Shana, aren't we really saying we don't love what Sage *is*, only what we have made her *into*? Because she is part Shana."

"I wish you wouldn't make sense when I'm upset," Galen said. But she'd agreed to try and be supportive. To a point.

"Mom, I really want to stay," pleaded Sage. "Shana has a special room all made up for me."

Fern squeezed Galen's forearm, her signal for Galen to back down and take a deep breath.

"Alright," said Galen resignedly. She just hoped the "special room" wasn't the one with antlers and fish mounted on the walls. She shivered involuntarily.

As if reading her mind (and Galen did get a weird vibe from Shana), Shana said, "Sage's room is upstairs, and it's very girly and very cozy. You are welcome to have a look."

"No," said Fern, leaning over Destiny and kissing Sage on the cheek. "I'm sure it's lovely, but it's time we got going."

Jamal shut off his camera, came over and gave Shana a hug. "Rex is going to kill me, but I'm leaving too. You and Sage deserve some privacy."

"See, he's quite respectful for a member of the exploitative commercial media," Fern whispered to Galen.

After she left, towing a reluctant Galen by the arm, Shana and Sage took Lil Wayne and Destiny upstairs and tucked them in. Then Shana showed Sage to the guest room.

It was clearly Shana's vision of the ideal girl room. Frothy lavender curtains and a duvet to match, complete with a mountain of pillows and bolsters in floral chintz and a pile of stuffed animals. On the walls were framed reproductions of Degas dancers and a large Justin Bieber poster.

"You and Wayne have guests stay here?" asked Sage dubiously.

"Wayne's guests are big redneck guys and I make them stay in the basement," said Shana. "Actually, I told Wayne this was a guestroom, but I've never let anyone stay here, even my mama. I decorated this just for you."

Sage didn't know what to say. Her little room in Brooklyn was all earth tones and Indian fabrics, with cinderblock and plank bookcases, although her books overflowed onto the floor and into the corners. Justin Bieber! Her only poster was the iconic red and black Che Guevara. Still, she was touched.

"I always had a room for you. Even in our little townhouse, I made sure Destiny's room had twin beds."

"I know you said you looked for me, but why didn't you start earlier?" Sage turned and faced Shana, who was busily turning down the duvet and fluffing pillows.

Shana sat down and patted the bed. Sage sat next to her.

"Sage, you are actually older than I was when I found out I was pregnant with you. And your daddy had already died. Try to imagine what that might feel like. Now my family would have welcomed you, but then you would have been just one more kid in our town with a teenage mama and no daddy. I didn't want that for you. So I asked a lawyer to find you parents who'd gone to college and could give you the kind of life I couldn't."

"Then, after I gave you up, I was so sad. I headed up here. I guess I thought I might be able to finish school, then work my way through college, or maybe hairdressing school. I thought once I got on my way, I could find you and at least be in your life."

"But you didn't try to find me back then, did you?" asked Sage, a hint of accusation creeping into her voice. "Fern and Galen, they never would have lied to me about that."

Shana shook her head.

"I was naïve about how hard the world is on a seventeen year-old runaway. I ended up working in a gentlemen's club. I never stopped thinking about you, but I didn't want that world to touch the nice, safe life I was sure you had. Now once I met Wayne, got married and had Destiny and Lil Wayne, that changed and I wanted us to be family."

Shana took Sage's hand.

"But I am ashamed to say I was afraid. Afraid if Wayne found out about you, about me getting pregnant so young and giving up my very own child, maybe he wouldn't love me anymore. So until this year, I tried to put it out of my mind. But I always kept your room for you, and hoped in my heart that even if I was afraid to look for you, you would somehow find me."

"But Wayne has been awesome about the whole thing," said Sage.

A fat, shiny tear rolled out of one of Shana's eyes, followed by another. Sage saw that her false eyelashes were coming unglued, but didn't want to interrupt.

"Oh, I know. I sinned against Wayne and his good heart, and against you. He woulda helped me find you, and I lost all those years with you for no reason!"

Shana began to sob vigorously, which was a little alarming to Sage (like anger and makeup, hysterics were discouraged in the Shapiro household). But she did her best, allowing Shana to cry her makeup off on the shoulder of her favorite Free People tank as she patted her back.

"It's okay, Shana. The important thing is we're together now. And I can get to know Destiny and Lil Wayne while they're still kids," she said.

Shana sat up and gave a little sniffling snort. She smiled through her tears. "Look at you, comforting me when I'm your mama, well, birth mama or whatever. You are so mature and lovely. You're everything I've ever dreamed of." Shana gave Sage a warm hug. "Now you settle down for the night and get some sleep and we can talk more in the morning. You have your own powder room right here, and it's got all the face creams and bubble baths a young lady could want."

She gave Sage a big hug and kiss and walked toward the door. Before she closed it she turned back. "I can't wait to go through all your moms' scrapbooks and go over every single minute of your life. Recitals, dance classes, birthday parties – everything."

After Shana left, Sage wondered how she was going to break it to her that Wiccans weren't known for their scrapbooking.

Shana had just shut the door to Sage's room when she heard the front door open. She hurried downstairs just in time to greet an exhausted Big Wayne, who was followed in by Judy, Karen and Sean. Karen wore her navy courtroom suit, which looked more than a little worse for wear, and lugged a large attorney's briefcase.

"Oh, Judy, I'm so glad you're back," cried Shana, hugging her around the neck. "It must have been horrible, bein' a witness and all."

Karen dropped her briefcase with a thunk, went to the bar and poured herself a large scotch.

"I'm afraid our Judy's a bit more than a witness, Shana. She's being charged with conspiracy in Phillipa Edgemoor's murder."

"*Pippa Edgemoor*," said Shana, going pale. "But she drowned falling off some sailboat in the South Pacific. They sent Lavinia her necklace to prove it."

"Oh, no," said Karen, glaring at Judy. "That was a fake Judy had made up by some Internet jewelry seller. The real necklace was on the real Pippa in that hole, which is where Lavinia and Judy dumped her forty years ago."

"Oh, Judy," wailed Shana.

"Look," said Judy. "I'm really sorry to have caused you good people any trouble. But I have to tell you that while Karen has the facts, she doesn't know the truth."

"I haven't even touched on the theft and extortion charges. Judy's being arraigned Monday, along with Lavinia, who's being charged with murder one," said Karen, ignoring Judy's little speech. "At least they agreed to Wayne posting bail for her. If I were the judge, I would have declared her a flight risk and slapped her in jail with Caroline and Taylor."

"Caroline and Taylor!"

Karen nodded. "Taylor didn't want the police to see her drunk, so she filched Byron's keys and tried to drive out of the parking lot. Where, naturally, she rear ended a police cruiser."

Shana gasped, gripping Judy's arm so tightly that she couldn't move, no matter how badly she longed to flee upstairs and escape Karen's judgmental glare.

"When they arrested her," Karen continued wearily, "Caroline rushed over and kept insisting that she was Chef Caroline Walinsky, a noted QVC personality, who could vouch for Taylor's good character. The arresting officer got tired of her bullshit and ran her name. Guess what? Chef Caroline is also a noted check bouncer. They're repeat offenders, so no bail."

"That's our system," Karen added, looking at the ceiling as if asking for a divine explanation. "You kill someone, you go home, you write a few bad checks, you get locked up."

"Vinnie and I are innocent until proven guilty," said Judy, gently loosening Shana's grip and heading up the stairs. She paused and turned one last time. "Thank you for your help, Karen, you're a good lawyer. And that broomstick up your ass makes you look extremely upright and trustworthy in court. I'll just pack a few things, call a cab and go to a motel."

"Uh uh," said Karen, shaking her finger in Judy's direction. "Wayne's money and my reputation say you stay right here where we can keep an eye on you until the arraignment."

Shana tilted her head up toward Judy. "I don't care about that. But you are family. Whatever you've done, we'll stand by you. Now you go get some sleep, you can tell me all about it in the morning."

Sean and Wayne had cracked a couple of beers, turned on ESPN and collapsed on the sectional. Shana thanked Karen profusely, and curled up next to Wayne.

"You are the most wonderful man," she said. "You didn't bat an eye when Sage showed up, and you rescued Judy."

"Karen rescued Judy. I just signed for her bail," Wayne gave Shana a kiss on the cheek. "As for Sage, well honey, she's the spittin' image of you, how could I not love her?"

To Sean and Karen's embarrassment, Shana began to sob loudly.

"Don't cry. I just feel bad you couldn't trust me, but I understand. Now cheer up, I actually got some good news. After the whole event with the fountain, Bob Dandridge came over to talk to me. I thought it was about damages from Lil Wayne and all. But instead, the board offered me a job as general manager of the club. Oh, it ain't the same as owning the place, but the money's real good, and we get to stay members. You know I've got a lotta pride in how I got that place outta the red."

"Oh honey, that's wonderful," said Shana, kissing him again. "But like I said, I'd love you just as much if we were back in a trailer."

Wayne chuckled. "I don't think we could find a trailer that would fit all your shoes, darlin'."

"Well, thank God for a little silver lining," said Karen, plopping down on the sofa next to Sean, who draped his arm protectively around her shoulders. "Frankly, I'm very worried about how things are going to come out in court."

"But you're such a good lawyer," said Wayne. "Shana, you shoulda seen her, just like one of them lawyers on *Law and Order*."

Karen gulped the rest of her scotch. "Not to sound like an egotist, but yes, I am a damned good lawyer. The problem is all my current clients appear to be guilty."

Fox Weekend News

Kelley Morgan adjusted her chair and prepared to read the news. True, it was only a weekend anchor position, but it was a start. And she'd beaten out that prick Max Mavis for the job.

Kelley Morgan: ***"Tonight we have more on the body unearthed earlier this weekend on the grounds of the exclusive Belle Vista Country Club. The remains have been tentatively identified as those of heiress Phillipa Howland Edgemoor, and two women have been charged in her murder. This gruesome discovery sent shock waves through one of the area's wealthiest, most well-connected communities. We go to Max Mavis live at Belle Vista for the details."***

Max stood in the pouring rain outside Belle Vista looking into the mud-filled hole that had, until yesterday, been the unofficial resting place of Pippa Edgemoor. His slicker did not quite keep the rain out of his gelled hair, which would be nice and dry if he'd gotten that weekend anchor spot. That bitch Morgan, she was probably screwing the producer.

Max Mavis: ***"Kelley, a sordid tale of mayhem, murder, deception and blackmail is unfolding here in this bastion of elitism and privilege."***

Oh, brother, thought Kelley. He's been watching Nancy Grace again.

Max Mavis: ***"Police sources report Phillippa Edgemoor was brutally murdered here over forty years ago and dumped in this pit by fellow socialites Lavinia Endicott Winter and Judith Simpson, both now sixty-nine. The women admitted being present at Edgemoor's death, but claim that it was an accident."***

Kelley Morgan: ***"Which is what all killers say!"***

Max Mavis: ***"You can stop interrupting me any time now, Kelley. These cold-blooded murderers didn't realize the foundation of the fountain, which served as the beautiful former debutante's tomb, preserved the crime scene perfectly. Now the evidence speaks for an innocent victim who can no longer speak for herself."***

"Miss Edgemoor, a philanthropist and talented amateur golfer known to her many friends as Pippa, was identified by an

engraved graduation pendant found on the body. A similar pendant, belonging to Lavinia Winter, was found wrapped around the deceased's skeletal hand. Investigators believe the unfortunate victim tore it off her assailant's neck while fighting for her life."

Kelley Morgan: *"Oh my!"*

Oh my? Max fumed. His dog could do better commentary.

Max Mavis: *"Police allege that Winter, motivated by jealousy, ambushed Pippa Edgemoor and killed her. My sources in the coroner's office say her death was caused by blunt force trauma to the skull. Simpson, a cult member and drug abuser, helped bury the corpse and escaped with the victim's car, cash and sable coat. They conspired to conceal the death for more than four decades while Winter played tennis and socialized around the grave of her rival. My sources also report that Simpson, now a nanny for strip-club mogul and former outlaw biker Wayne Jones, was blackmailing Winter."*

Kelley Morgan: *"How horrible!"*

Max Mavis: *"Insightful, Kelley. Is that legal terminology?"*

Wait until the next hurricane, asshole, Kelley thought. You're going to be reporting live from a shaky pier at Rehoboth Beach.

Kelley Morgan: *"I understand this terrible murder is just one of several crimes recently linked to this haven for the rich and powerful."*

Max Mavis: *"On Saturday, Belle Vista was the scene of an armed assault by suspected gang leader Hector Ortiz, as well as the arrest of former tennis pro Elena Dragunova for immigration fraud."*

"Also, accused murderer Lavinia Winter is the mother-in-law of congressional candidate Roy Forrest Beech IV. Beech was recruited to run after Belle Vista member Dan Butts resigned his seat in the wake of the Here Kitty Kitty massage parlor scandal. Didn't you intern there, Kelley? Just joking."

Kelley Morgan: *"Ha ha. Thank you, Max. Try to stay dry. It looks like your spray tan is starting to run. We now go to Beech for Congress Headquarters, where campaign manager Ian Thorne has just announced that Roy Beech will withdraw from the race. Oh my, what's wrong with Ian Thorne's forehead? It looks like he's bleeding!"*

29

"Oh my God, it's like the O.J. Simpson trial combined with the Royal Wedding," said Shana excitedly, pressing her face up against the passenger window of Big Wayne's Cadillac, although her disguise of oversized Chanel sunglasses made it difficult. She'd bought identical pairs for both Karen and Judy, but Karen nixed the idea. Entering court looking like the Jackie O triplets wouldn't help Judy's case. At least not in the court of public opinion, which had been in continuous session during the three weeks since the body was discovered.

"The media has been hyping this as the case of the Country Club Killers, the Grave-Golfing Grannies or my favorite, the Deadly Dowagers," said Karen from the back seat, surveying the mass of cameras, satellite trucks and milling reporters surrounding the courthouse. "That jerk Max Mavis from Fox News is making Lavinia and Judy sound like a high society Manson Family, and apparently now Judy's trending on Twitter, whatever that means. I don't think, in this context, it's a good thing."

Next to Karen in the Cadillac's backseat, Judy harrumphed. "You know, I didn't kill anybody, I don't golf and to my knowledge, I'm no one's granny."

"Stow the attitude before we get in front of Judge Singh," Karen warned as her phone chimed. "It's Ellen DeFarges. Wayne, can you just pull over for a minute? If we go into the garage I'll lose her."

Assistant Commonwealth's Attorney Ellen DeFarges was leading the prosecution against Lavinia and Judy, and in Karen's complimentary words was "one tough bitch". She was also sixty and from a leading local family that chose not to join Belle Vista. Judy and Lavinia would get no mileage out of age or lineage from her.

"Uh huh. Yes. You've confirmed with Judge Singh? Okay, give us ten minutes to get through the media zoo and we'll be in your office."

"Ellen DeFarges says something has come up and the hearing is postponed," said Karen, slipping her phone into her briefcase side pocket. "She wants us to meet with her and Lavinia's legal team in her conference room now. I think she may offer Judy a plea deal."

"No deal that includes time in the Big House," said Judy with alarm. Taffy Dandridge had sent her a boxed set of classic women in prison films to cheer her up.

Karen sighed. "My plan, hopefully, is to return you to Shana's Big House in the Enclave. And if you keep your mouth shut – no rants about the pigs and brutality like at the arraignment – we just might be able to do that. I know there's pressure on DeFarges. Judge Singh has a backlog and is very attached to his vacation time. He's more worried about this circus going to trial than you are."

"Somehow I doubt that," said Judy.

The Commonwealth's Attorney's conference room was spacious by government standards and included a sizeable rectangular cherry conference table, but Lavinia's phalanx of attorneys made it seem cramped and crowded. On the left side of the table sat the prosecutor, her second chair Nate Armour, and a drab middle-aged woman in a rumpled khaki suit. Karen didn't recognize her.

That left Karen and Judy no option but to squeeze in on the left with Lavinia, pale but composed in a dove grey silk suit and the triple-strand Endicott family pearls, her four attorneys and an investigator. Considering all the weighty briefcases brimming with folders, and equally weighty egos, it was a tight fit.

Ellen DeFarges immediately got to the point.

"As you all know, the prosecution's case is based on the theory that Lavinia Winter and Judy Simpson conspired to murder Phillippa Edgemoor on the afternoon of December 26, 1972. They allegedly lured her under false pretenses to Belle Vista Country Club and bludgeoned her to death, presumably with one of her own golf clubs, the motive being jealousy on the part of Mrs. Winter and profit on the part of Ms. Simpson. However, certain evidence has come to our attention that tends, instead, to corroborate an alternate theory of Ms. Edgemoor's death. One that does not support murder or manslaughter charges."

"I told you...owww!" Judy started to speak, but Karen stomped on her foot under the table.

Farrell Katz, lead attorney on Lavinia's legal team, smiled and folded his hands in front of him. "So you have discovery to share with us, and are now considering Ms. Winter's claim of self defense?" Katz was a pit bull of a criminal attorney who'd spent twenty years as a public defender and now ran his own shop, Katz, Telemakis and Gargulio. The staid white shoe firm of Peregrine et al called on Katz when their waspy clients engaged in malfeasance beyond standard white collar crime. Lavinia detested Katz's sharp European-cut brown suit, the hair on the back of his sweaty hands and his tendency to end conversations with "Alrighty then!". But Edgar Chastain had assured her that he was top drawer, and it was not as if he'd be escorting her to a tea dance.

"Based on this new information, yes, I'm open to considering that theory," said Ellen DeFarges reluctantly. Lavinia had been beastly to her oldest sister at Merrywood, and she'd looked forward to sending her off to maximum security boarding school for the rest of her life. "I've had copies of the reports efaxed to everyone, but I thought it would be simpler if Clare Buxton, a private investigator, explained her findings directly. Then perhaps we could save the court some time, expense and unnecessary media exposure by arriving at a sensible solution in these chambers."

"Plea agreement! Alrighty then!" interjected Katz, earning one of DeFarges searing looks, not to mention a disapproving sniff from his client.

Clare Buxton stood up, ran her fingers through hair that could use another wash, then pulled a sheaf of papers from an L. L. Bean boat tote.

"Um, I was hired a few months ago by Mrs. Winter's daughter, Mrs. Allison Beech, to discover the whereabouts of Ms. Phillippa Edgemoor. In the process, I did quite a bit of research on Ms. Edgemoor and discovered her to be associated with a disturbing pattern of suspicious deaths dating all the way back to her childhood. When Mrs. Beech terminated my services, I continued to investigate on my own because, as a former law enforcement officer, I felt compelled to discover the truth behind these deaths." Clare took a breath. "Then, when Mrs. Winter and Ms. Simpson were arrested, I realized that this information might prove exculpatory. So, although my research was not quite complete, I brought it to the police and the Commonwealth's Attorney's office."

"Would have been nice to be in the loop," murmured Katz.

"No kidding," echoed Karen.

Clare ignored them and passed copies of her report around the table. Clearly, she could have made a tidy sum bringing her research to Lavinia's team, but she felt strongly that Pippa Edgemoor's file belonged with police first and foremost.

"The details are in here, but basically, Phillippa Edgemoor may be responsible for at least three deaths. First, it is likely that she drowned a classmate, Betsy Greig, in 1957. Then there was her fiancé, who jilted her and was found with a bullet in his head a week later, the death ruled a suicide. And finally, there was her stepmother, former showgirl Candy Cotton, who supposedly strangled to death accidentally when her scarf caught in an electric fan while she and Pippa were alone at the Edgemoor mansion. The details are in my report, but in each case jealousy turned to rage, which led to murder. As a psychopath, Pippa was able to conceal her crimes."

Lavinia gasped.

"Really, Vinnie? You're still shocked? After she tried to kill you? Why, because she was on Cotillion Court?" erupted Judy as Karen stomped again. "Owww!"

Clare looked down at her copy of the report.

"I've turned this information over to the cold case squads in the jurisdictions where the deaths occurred, and they've found corroborating evidence in two cases already."

"So, if my client was confronted by a serial murderer, self defense becomes not only a likely scenario, but *the* most likely scenario; in fact, it is the only plausible scenario. Alrighty then!" interjected Katz, looking pleased.

"Save your closing arguments for Fox News, please, Farrell," said DeFarges.

"What about the conspiracy charges against Ms. Simpson?" asked Karen.

"I didn't find the idea of those two teaming up likely," said Clare. "So I went through some of the old Belle Vista records I'd copied when I was investigating Phillipa Edgemoor's disappearance. There's a complaint by the security guard that Ms. Simpson had been sneaking into the club for most of December, feeding the club's cats and sleeping on a library sofa. So, in other words, she didn't show up on the 26th specifically to meet Mrs. Winter and Ms. Edgemoor; she was squatting there."

Katz smiled like a man who'd just won the lottery. "So, Ms. DeFarges, we're looking at a dismissal here, no charges? A public apology to Mrs. Winter would also be nice. Her reputation has suffered."

"Not so fast," said Ellen DeFarges, raising her slender, elegant palm. "The statute of limitations may have run out on concealing a body and not reporting a death. However, Ms. Simpson, with the aid of Mrs. Winter, absconded with a Jaguar, a sable coat and enough cash for a felony theft charge, which is still prosecutable. Then she proceeded to impersonate Ms. Edgemoor in Las Vegas, and sent a false communication in Ms. Edgemoor's name to her attorneys to cover up her death."

"Ms. Simpson at the time was under the influence of the Universal Family of Truth, and most of that property was turned over to cult leader Sheldon Bernstein, also known as Father Yaweh Galileo," said Karen. "I have affidavits from other former cult members attesting to that. I have an expert witness who can testify."

"Father loved that car," interrupted Judy, "and the coat. He used it as a bedspread. Why I remember...owww."

Ellen DeFarges raised her palm again. "I'm not interested in the disgusting details of Ms. Simpson's 'Life with Father,' or your expert witness. We're clearly not going to trial. I'm just pointing out that we cannot have a complete dismissal here. After all, there are also the recent matters of the forged death certificate, forged Merrywood medallion and the false presentation of Ms. Edgemoor's death to her estate lawyers."

"Neither profited from that," said Katz quickly.

"And the extortion of money by Ms. Simpson from Mrs. Winter," Ellen continued.

"Mrs. Winter has said she was merely demonstrating generosity toward an old friend," said Karen.

Ellen DeFarges's lips narrowed into a thin line. She was done with courtroom etiquette.

"Cut the crap everyone. These ladies, albeit accidentally, bumped off their esteemed former debutante colleague, dumped her body in a hole like a rat carcass and ran off with a fair number of her prized possessions. Then, for forty plus years, they conspired to keep it all secret. Now anyone who thinks I'm going to let them just walk out of here really does *not* know me."

"First, as part of this plea, I'm going to need detailed statements from both Mrs. Winter and Ms. Simpson describing exactly what happened to Phillipa Edgemoor. *Today. Now. Before they leave this room.* Then, all of these brilliant legal minds are going to reach an agreement on charges and a sentencing recommendation I can present without shame to Judge Singh, who has non-refundable tickets to Italy next week and is anxious to wrap this up. I'm not talking pointless prison time, but they've got to plead guilty to *something*."

"Jaywalking?" suggested Judy. "Owwwww!"

From the official statements of Lavinia Endicott Winter and Judith Simpson, AKA Sister Sunshine Galileo.

Tuesday, December 26, 1972, 4:45 PM. Belle Vista Country Club:

Lavinia felt queasy. She licked her lips and picked up the neatly typed pages stacked on the passenger seat of her Mercedes. She took a deep breath and opened the car door. Lavinia was Secretary of the Rules Committee and she was always prompt when submitting her meeting minutes, no matter what time of year. She would not make an exception for the holiday. The club was quiet that afternoon and the temperature unseasonably warm. Mist rose off of the golf course and a flock of black birds screeched through the pale sky. Lavinia shivered as she walked towards the deserted clubhouse, clutching her notes. She hoped she wouldn't throw up.

Yesterday had been a wonderful Christmas. Lavinia had told her husband Prescott that she was expecting their first child and he was thrilled. Her morning sickness, which was really all day sickness, had subsided for most of the holiday. They had gone to her parents' house for dinner and she had shared the happy news. She smiled at the memory of her mother's ecstatic face as she slid the minutes through the mail slot of the Officer of the Rules Committee, Julia Hallowell. Lavinia shut the door behind her softly.

Judy Simpson had fled the Universal Family of Truth after a fight with Father Yaweh, who had taken a fourteenth wife after deciding having only thirteen was unlucky. She'd hitchhiked cross country and surprised her family, just as they were putting their tasteful Williamsburg-style fruit and magnolia Christmas decorations over the front door.

But not only did her parents refuse to give her money, they wouldn't even let her in the house. Judy had been sleeping at Belle Vista for two weeks, unbeknownst to the staff. She made herself quite comfortable on an ancient leather sofa in the Whitehall Room at night and ate meals courtesy of her father's club number as she contemplated going back to the Family, where at least she was wanted.

That afternoon, Judy was getting ready to slip out of Belle Vista for good. She had stuffed her ragged knapsack with stolen food, a bottle of Jim Beam and twenty bucks some drunken reveler had dropped the night of the club Christmas party. As she grabbed her tattered scarf and wrapped it around her neck, something caught her eye.

Judy watched her Merrywood classmate, Lavinia Winter, put something through Julia Hallowell's mail slot. As Lavinia walked out the door, Judy followed stealthily behind. She was going to ask Vinnie for some money for old time's sake. Vinnie wasn't particularly charitable, but she wouldn't want a ragged Judy following her home.

Lavinia stopped in the parking lot and took a deep breath, watching a graceful family of deer on the tenth tee. One of those filthy feral cats that haunted the club also watched them intently. She picked up a rock and threw it towards the cat. The deer ran off, but the cat didn't move. He stared back at Lavinia and hissed loudly. "Scat!" she yelled.

"Leave that poor creature alone."

Lavinia turned around, startled.

Pippa Edgemoor, wearing a smart grey wool pleated skirt and pale yellow cashmere twin set, walked purposefully toward Lavinia pulling a golf bag, a handbag slung over her shoulder. In the rays of the setting sun, a pair of large diamond studs sparkled in her ears.

Judy ducked behind one of the club's massive air conditioning units, unseen by either woman. She did not want to run into Pippa, who'd probably call the cops and report her for vagrancy.

"You scared me," Lavinia turned to face Pippa. "What are you doing here?"

"What am *I* doing here? As if I don't have a right to be here? Please!" Pippa laughed, throwing her head back and opening her red lips. "I came to get my clubs. I'm driving cross country to spend a month in Palm Springs, as I do every year." She studied Lavinia, cocking her head to the side. And then she said it. "But this year, Prescott will be joining me. Did you know that, dear little Vinnie? He's going to leave you."

Pippa waited for a reaction. When one didn't come, she pressed on.

"Do you like the earrings he gave me for Christmas?" She pointed to her ears triumphantly. Her earrings gleamed in the setting sun. They appeared to be several carats larger than the ones Prescott had proudly presented Lavinia in front of the tree yesterday morning.

"That's not true," Lavinia whimpered. She placed her right hand over her stomach protectively. Prescott *was* scheduled to fly to Palm Springs next week, *on business.*

"He's always preferred me, ever since high school." Pippa smiled. "In every way."

Lavinia dropped her car keys to the pavement. A cold sweat washed over her and her pulse quickened. She began to breathe rapidly.

Pippa turned and walked slowly toward her shiny red Jaguar XKE at the edge of the lot, near the construction site for the new Founder's Fountain. Without thinking, Lavinia broke into a run. She grabbed Pippa's arm as she caught up with her, and almost swung her back around. Pippa let go of her golf bag and stumbled, but did not fall.

"Grow up Vinnie! Face facts!"

Pippa dropped her purse to the ground, reached into her golf bag and pulled out her seven iron, swinging it above her head like the lacrosse stick she'd wielded as captain of the Merrywood Fighting Virgins.

"You want to fight? Let's fight, then. I always win."

"Not this time," said Lavinia, despite her terror. "You couldn't take the Cotillion Crown from me, and you can't take Prescott."

Pippa took a swing at Lavinia, who ducked just in time. Pippa swung again, her eyes black and cold. She reached for Lavinia's neck with her left hand, and her fingers grasped Lavinia's Merrywood School pendant. She jerked violently on the chain, which snapped as Lavinia defensively pushed her attacker.

"Whoa, girls. It's the season of peace!" shouted Judy, as she stepped out of her hiding place. She'd been enjoying the catfight until she realized that Pippa truly seemed intent on grievous bodily harm.

But Judy was too late. Pippa lost her footing and tumbled backwards. The back of her head hit a stone retaining wall with a sickening crack.

Lavinia stood frozen, watching a thin line of blood trickle out of Pippa's parted lips. Her neck was bent at an odd angle, and she did not move.

"Oh shit. You've really done it now, Vinnie," Judy said, walking up to stand beside her. She knelt down and put two fingers on Lavinia's neck just under her chin. No pulse. "You've killed the bitch."

"Judy!" Lavinia's heart was racing. "You saw it?" Tears were streaming down her cheeks. "She attacked me! She said horrible things! She swung a golf club at my head!"

"Yeah, I saw it." Judy put her hand on Lavinia's shoulder. "Was she really screwing Prescott?"

"I have no idea!" Lavinia wailed. "I just came here to turn in my minutes. Oh Judy, what am I going to do? Will I have to go prison? I'm pregnant."

Judy silently chewed on her lower lip for a minute. She scanned the parking lot, making sure there were no witnesses.

Her eyes rested on the big hole in the ground that was to serve as the foundation for Founder's Fountain. She pointed to the construction site like the ghost of Christmas Future.

"You want to just dump her in the ground?" Lavinia wiped the tears off her face with the back of her hand. "That doesn't seem right. We should call the police. You can tell them what you saw."

"After smoking pot and drinking half a bottle of bourbon? Vinnie, she was having an affair with your husband. The cops call that motive." Judy sighed. "Just look at it as a burial without a coffin. Pippa loved Belle Vista. It's only fitting that she rest here for eternity. Now, pull yourself together. We have work to do."

Together they lifted Pippa off the pavement by her shoulders and feet, and carried her to the edge of the construction pit.

"On three," said Judy, prompting a sob from Lavinia. "One, two, three."

They swung her body and dropped it in the hole as darkness fell. The feral cat Tecumseh watched from the tenth tee. Judy got a shovel from the groundskeeper's shed and covered the body with a layer of red Virginia clay.

"I heard Charlie say that they were pouring the foundation for the fountain tomorrow morning. No one will ever find her. Rest in peace, Pippa. It's more than you deserve."

Judy wiped her hands on her flowing skirt, picked up Pippa's Hermes handbag and fished out her keys. She returned the seven iron to Pippa's bag and hoisted the bag into the trunk of the Jag.

"I'll write a letter to Prescott from Pippa, breaking off the relationship," Judy said. "I'll tell him that I, meaning Pippa, want to travel for awhile, and I'll send her lawyers the same message. Everyone will be so glad she's gone, no one will dig too deeply. No pun intended."

"Thank you," Lavinia said softly. "What am I going to do? How can I possibly behave normally after this?"

"You have no choice, Vinnie. Pretend it never happened. You're a WASP. It's your nature."

Judy looked at the darkened clubhouse.

"Good riddance, Belle Vista. I'm outta here!"

She opened the door of the car and slid in.

"Hey, there's a sable on the passenger seat. Cool. Fur is murder, but given the circumstances…"

With that, she started the Jaguar, kicked it into gear and, with a wave at Lavinia, sped off into the night.

A gentle rain began to fall and Tecumseh crept into the groundskeeper's shed and sniffed the shovel used to bury Pippa. Unlike her human peers, he would miss her. In the shallow grave, Lavinia's monogrammed Merrywood School pendant lay cradled in Pippa's cold palm, the fine silver chain threaded through her slender fingers.

30

Allie cowered in the restroom nearest Judge Singh's courtroom. When the postponement was announced, she'd walked out of the courtroom and straight into the maw of the media horde. She fled through the nearest door, leaving the rest of her family behind.

A sympathetic guard was keeping the female reporters out, but she knew she'd have to leave at some point and somehow make it down to the parking garage, where Roy and the twins were waiting. She literally could not take one more camera pushed in her face – if the case against Mother went to trial, Allie was going to need to ransack Taylor's tennis locker for medication.

She jumped as the door eased open an inch and the noise of the mob outside came flooding in, instinctively backing up against the ancient radiator under the only dingy window.

"Allie?" A tanned foot with five lavender toenails in a four-inch cork-soled platform slid inside the door and pushed it open a bit farther. The rest of Shana Jones, in a bright purple silk jersey dress, slipped in, closing the door firmly behind her.

"Here to deliver me to the media?" said Allie.

"Well, no," said Shana. "I actually thought maybe I could help you get outta here."

"Why on earth would you want to help me?" Allie asked, still backed up against the far wall.

To Allie's surprise, Shana laughed out loud.

"Why, Allie, that's a good question! I really don't know."

Allie shocked herself by laughing as well, a laugh that nearly ended in tears.

"I would think this was a trick to humiliate me, but you're not like that, are you Shana? I was right all along. You are different from the rest of us. I was just wrong about how you're different. You are a better person in a tackier package."

"Hmmm. I think that's supposed to be a compliment, so I'll take it. Now I have an idea, but for it to work, you're gonna to have to strip." Shana laughed again. "If you don't know how, I can show you."

The media mob pounced when Allie Winter Beech, in a navy St. John suit and Tory Burch sunglasses, a red and navy patterned Hermes scarf covering her hair, emerged from the restroom. They swarmed her, shouting questions as two guards held them back and cleared a path to the elevator.

"Mrs. Beech, does this postponement mean your mother has pled guilty?"

"Mrs. Beech, has your mother's murder case destroyed your husband's political career? How about your marriage?"

"How does it feel to find out your mother is a killer?"

Just as the elevator doors opened, "Allie" removed her scarf and shook out a mane of bright, wavy red hair.

"Surprise!" said Shana with a smile as she stepped into the elevator and the doors closed behind her.

By that time, the real Allie Beech, in gaudy purple silk and cork platforms, had already escaped down the stairwell to the garage and the shelter of her waiting Mercedes.

Shana dressed carefully in her best white tennis dress, the one she had bought because it looked so "Allie" back when she was trying to fit in. Then she packed her tennis bag with her racquet, a towel, sunscreen and a new can of balls. Finally, she picked up the plate of carrot cake muffins she'd baked earlier, and headed out to the Suburban parked in the driveway.

The two weeks since the sentencing had passed in a blur for Shana. Sage, back in Brooklyn, had promised to visit Labor Day weekend before she started school. Judy and Lavinia were both serving probation for concealing Pippa's death, but to Judy's chagrin, the arraigning judge placed her on house arrest with an ankle monitor for six months, while Lavinia, the actual killer, was required only to surrender her passport. Both women were sentenced to a hundred hours of community service and fined three thousand dollars.

"Well, Judy, honey, you do have a history of fleeing the scene," Shana had reminded her gently this morning over coffee. "Anyways, the bees need you."

Judy was busy harvesting her honey, to be sold at The Moon Goddess for a nice profit. Karen wryly noted that should be enough to keep Judy from resorting to blackmail.

"Although, God knows, if she did there are probably enough people at Belle Vista with secrets to keep her comfortable for a century," she'd added.

Shana couldn't believe that Karen had been so generous, handling Judy's case for free. Pro bono she called it. She believed that Karen and Judy secretly liked each other, despite their comments to the contrary. Judy said she'd agreed to be Karen's client because "the price was right". Karen insisted that a high profile case like Judy's was the best way to jump start her new private practice, even if it meant representing "a culty flake who'd smoked way too much ganga".

Spencer had been happy to pay for Taylor's defense, but he and Karen agreed with the judge that a month of rehab was in her best interest. Taylor, judging by the scene she pitched in court and the choice names she called Karen, disagreed. It cost Spencer an extra thousand dollars to get the contempt charges dismissed.

Karen was not worried. "Oh, Taylor is all hot air," she'd said to Shana. "Besides, I did fight off a pack of Jamaican drug dealers with my tennis racquet."

Shana tuned the radio to WMZQ as she headed out of The Enclave. She waved at Kim Jennings, who was supervising her small army of gardeners, but as usual Kim pretended not to see her. Shana frowned.

She rolled down the window and shouted, "Hey, Kim! Kim! How you doin'?" forcing Kim into a wave and a frozen smile. Shana rolled the window back up, satisfied. She had decided, among other things, not to put up with being ignored and snubbed.

Fifteen minutes later, she pulled onto Belle Vista Boulevard and wound her way up the tree-lined drive toward the top of the hill. Halfway up, she passed Caroline's house, where a pale, muscular, blonde man was mowing the front yard as Caroline's neighbor stared, pretending to trim her roses.

Okay, Shana admitted it was a little weird to see Yuri Dragunov gardening for Caroline, and even weirder that he and Elena were living in Caroline's pool house. But according to Karen, the FBI had all Caroline's and Elena's charges dismissed in exchange for testimony against Jack Walinsky. Jack was still on the lam and presumed living in Europe on money he'd bilked from Wayne and his other clients. Karen also said that Elena had gone ballistic when FBI agents showed her photos of Jack with an even younger Slavic blonde at the Bucharest café where Interpol had almost nabbed him. Apparently, even bigamists get jealous.

Yuri and Elena had even gotten green cards once Caroline agreed to give them a place to live in exchange for Yuri being her handyman and Elena cleaning house. Shana did have to chuckle at the thought of Elena as Caroline's maid.

"I send her to Coin Star every week with all my change," Caroline told Shana gleefully during tennis last week. "I'm trying to teach her some American thriftiness."

Best of all, since the charges had been dropped, Caroline had been able to take the job at QVC, although Shana hoped she started selling something else soon. She'd already bought three paella pans, and while she didn't know exactly what paella was, it didn't sound like something Big Wayne would eat.

She finally reached Washington Circle, the oldest and most exclusive part of Belle Vista, parking in front of 117, a restored 1920s Tudor so dreary Shana knew it must be tasteful. She walked up the flagstone walkway lined with boxwoods, balanced her plate of muffins on her left hand and rang the bell.

"Hey Mrs. J," said Quint as he answered the door. "Come on in. I was just texting Sage about plans for when she comes back."

Shana smiled as she entered the dim, cool foyer. From what Sage told her, Quint texted her every day. Sometimes every hour. Sage was trying to decide if he was an "over-privileged preppie stoner doofus" or "kind of cute".

"Well, honey, he can be both," Shana had advised. "Just remember if he asks you to go to church, bring a condom."

"So how is Mr. Jones?" asked Quint.

"Oh he's loving life. Good thing for us he got to keep his new job and the club got to keep Mrs. Edgemoor's trust money. Apparently, she just has to be dead, doesn't matter how or when. So Quint, honey, I brought these muffins over for y'all." She held up the plate. "How is everybody here?"

"Well, I guess you know Dad's campaign tanked 'cause of Grandmama knocking off Mrs. Edgemoor and all. Enrique started classes and is working with Ian on some other political thing, so Bethany's crying her mascara off because she never sees him. And Mom, well, she's cleaned and organized everything in the house, including my sock drawer, which was unfortunate," he said, thinking about all that good weed swirling down the toilet bowl.

Quint lowered his voice.

"You know, Mom hasn't left the house since the sentencing. I mean, not just like she hasn't been anywhere, she hasn't even gone outside, like, on the patio. She's white as a ghost. Bethany can't even get her to use self-tanner. Plus, she won't see Grandmama or speak to her."

Shana put the plate of muffins on the hall table and took Quint's hand.

"Well, you know, your mama was traumatized by all this."

"Yeah, but it's weird. Grandmama is back at Belle Vista playing tennis and bridge like nothing happened."

"Well, Quint I think in a way getting rid of that terrible secret has been a relief for her."

"I kinda think she's just really good at pretending everything is normal, even when it's not," offered Quint. "All those old ladies are. But I'm really worried about Mom."

Shana smiled. "Well, I think I can help her break out of her funk. Where is she?"

"The breakfast room. I'll take you."

Allie sat in her charming, sun-filled breakfast room, scanning the newspaper for scandals that were worse than hers. It had become her daily obsession. She was still in her white terry robe, bleached to immaculate cleanliness by daily washes.

"Hi Allie, I brought muffins over," said Shana cheerily, putting the plate down on the glass-topped table between them. She spoke as if this were a regular occurrence, ignoring the fact she'd never been invited to the Beech home.

Allie looked up dully.

"I hope you got my thank you note, Shana. I'm sure the wording was somewhat vague, but in etiquette class they neglected to teach us how to thank someone for helping with an escape from a courthouse restroom."

"It was a lovely note. I framed it," said Shana. "But I'm here to get you up and out. Allie, it's time you faced Belle Vista."

"I don't care about Belle Vista." Tears shone in Allie's eyes. "My life has been a joke. I went to Vassar, you know. I graduated with honors and a degree in art history. I could have done something with my life. Instead I've spent it trying to be my mother, a killer who, as the media so helpfully pointed out, has played tennis atop her rival for decades. I've ruined my husband's political career. A career he didn't even want. I forced him into it so he'd be good enough for me and the lofty Winter family," Allie sniffed. "What a sham. I lied and cheated to make my children look good while letting them run wild. Bethany with her ridiculous story about a royal boyfriend, and Quint..."

"Now Allie, Quint is a good boy who loves you and Bethany is a real smart girl, with a little guidance from you they'll be fine. As for Lavinia, well Allie, she was fighting for you when she accidently killed Pippa, and she covered it up for your sake. That don't make it right, but your mother was trying to protect you, and you owe her something for that. We all make mistakes; I'm a testament to that."

"Again, as I asked you in the courthouse bathroom, why do you care? I did terrible things to you, because I felt you weren't fit to be a member of our club – a club filled with liars, killers, swindlers and alcoholics. And hypocrites like me."

Shana pulled out a white wicker chair and sat down.

"I'm not gonna say that's not true, because it is. But Allie, you can't change the past. You can only change the future, and you're not gonna change it sitting' around in your robe feeling sorry for yourself. I know you want a new life, but first you gotta go fix the one you've got. You can start by doing something for me. You owe me a tennis match."

Allie looked at her, aghast. "Surely you're kidding?"

"Nope," said Shana. "We were tied 5-5 in the third set and I was about to serve. I worked hard to win the Edgemoor Cup, and I want to finish the championship match on camera for *Queen of the Court.*"

Allie groaned and put her head in her hands. "Shana, ask me anything but that. Can't I just write a check to some charity you're fond of, like something for unwed trailer park mothers?"

"No. I need to finish this for my own sake, and you need to hold your head up high and face Belle Vista and the world. I've got my car outside."

"But look at me," said Allie gesturing to her pale, naked face and threadbare robe.

"Oh, we can fix that. I already texted an SOS."

"You called?" asked Byron as he stepped into the room, makeup cases in hand. Quint followed, his arms draped with designer tennis whites.

"Oh God," said Byron looking at Allie. "Thank heavens I brought my aerosol spray tanner!"

Allie could hear the pseudo whispers as she and Shana headed to Court one, where Rex, Jamal and the rest of the crew were set up.

"I can't believe she's showing her face here," said a ferret-faced blonde in a tight Nike ensemble who was seated at a courtside table, sipping Diet Coke.

"Like mother, like daughter," replied her companion, a petite brunette in a pique L'Etoile tennis dress. "No shame. Better make sure we don't offend her, or we might end up under a water fountain or something."

"She does look fabulous," admitted the blonde. "Positively skeletal. You know I've heard emotional trauma is the best diet."

"Eyes straight ahead," said Shana, squeezing Allie's arm. "And don't expect any breaks because you haven't been practicing."

"I hardly think I need *breaks*, Shana. I've played tennis on these courts all my life."

Shana had been right; she needed to come back to Belle Vista. Like it or not, it was part of who she was. Out of the corner of her eye she saw Lavinia take a seat, iced tea in hand.

"Now that's the Allie Beech I remember," said Shana as they walked on court and Rex's assistant came over to fix their mics. "Let's play ball!"

"That is a baseball expression, Mrs. Jones. We prefer 'Let us commence play'," said Currie Holmes, who'd been persuaded, against her better judgment, to officiate once more. Since this would decide the winner of the Edgemoor Cup she felt she had no choice.

The remainder of the match lasted a mere fifteen minutes, with the women trading impressive ground strokes, overheads and volleys. Currie was pleased to note that there were more winners than errors.

Shana was up 6-5, 40-30 when she lunged at a backhand approach shot and lofted to the ball to Allie for an easy overhead smash, a shot Allie rarely missed. To the shock of the substantial crowd now gathered around the courts, Allie mishit the ball badly, sending it at least three feet wide of the ad court alley.

"Out!" shouted Currie Holmes. "Game, set and match to Mrs. Shana Jones."

Shana and Allie walked to the net and shook hands with Currie, then each other. A quizzical expression crossed Shana's face.

"I hope you didn't miss that shot on purpose."

"Does that seem like something I would do?" replied Allie.

"Let's have Lavinia on court for the presentation of the cup," said Currie, who hoped her large visor would disguise her face as she posed next to her old friend, the killer.

Lavinia walked on court handed the large silver cup to Shana, smiling for the official picture. Then she turned to Allie.

"You played beautifully, Allison. You always play beautifully."

The two women stood there staring at each other until Shana handed the trophy to Currie and embraced them both in a tight, sweaty, very un-Belle Vista group hug.

Rex motioned to Jamal to move in for a close up.

"I think that's a wrap."

Epilogue

Queen of the Court

Reunion Show

Max Mavis, who had left Fox abruptly after an undisclosed incident with an intern, attached his microphone and settled into an overstuffed chair on stage. Thanks to the deal with HWN (Hog Wild Network), Vixen Video could film its first *Queen of the Court* reunion show on a real stage set, complete with two tan ultra suede sofas just large enough to force the participants uncomfortably close together.

Taylor, Caroline, and Elena sat on one sofa facing Karen, Allie and Shana on the other, all decked out in their designer best. Max had a hard time taking his eyes off Shana's substantial cleavage, but he forced himself to focus on the cue cards in his hands. They were full of questions emailed and tweeted from around the country.

Max Mavis: *"Hello, I'm your host Max Mavis. Welcome to the first reunion show for Queen of the Court, the only reality series to combine tennis, high society and true crime. Our first viewer question is for Taylor. Amanda from Buffalo asks; 'Taylor, are you sober?'"*

Taylor, in a white leather Jason Wu skirt, smiled, crossing and uncrossing her tanned legs a la *Basic Instinct*. ["Too bad we're going to need to blur that," said Jamal to Rex off camera.]

Taylor: *"Great question! I am happy to report that since completing rehab, I have been clean and sober, not to mention newly single. Next month, Vixen Books will publish my book, Virgin Cocktails: You Don't Have to Be One to Drink One."*

Max Mavis: *"That's fabulous Taylor! I can't wait to get my hands on … your book. Quick question, if you wanted to, could you add alcohol to these drinks? Just kidding! Our next question is for Caroline. Stephanie from Philadelphia writes; 'Was your ex-husband*

Jack ever arrested, and are you and Elena really friends? She was so mean to you during Season One.'"

Elena and Caroline scooted a bit further apart.

Caroline: *"Jack is still at large, but I'm happy to report he's moved up five spots on the FBI Most Wanted list, and we expect him to make the top ten."*

Caroline pulled a paella pan from behind her back and lifted it into the air.

Caroline: *"I am enjoying a very successful career with QVC selling these wonderful and moderately priced paella pans!" She shoved the pan towards the camera.*

Max Mavis: *"What about your relationship with Elena? Things got pretty nasty with all the threats and so on. Elena, are you treating Caroline better?"*

Elena: *"Ex-wife has been most generous opening home to me and Yuri, even though pool house is small and damp, so I am practicing false politeness to her most days."*

Elena shot Caroline a hard look, adjusting her lime green micro-mini.

Elena: *"Also, since Yuri is better at making hot sex than good money, I must teach tennis to pay rent on moldy pool house."*

Caroline: *"Elena runs the men's tennis program at Belle Vista now. She's made lessons longer and harder, so the program just keeps getting bigger and bigger."*

Max Mavis: *"Who wouldn't like a long, hard workout with Elena? Next question. Karen, Abby from Illinois asks; 'Why aren't you returning to the show next season?'"*

Karen: *"I decided to go back to work, plus Sean and I got married last month and are in the process of adopting a baby girl from Malawi."*

Karen blinked uncomfortably. Byron had insisted on false eyelashes. She felt like Bambi in a black Pucci sheath, but she was almost out of here.

Max Mavis: ***"Of course we've had many, many questions for Shana, who's so popular with our viewers. But we've had to pick just two. Frank from Tucson writes; 'Shana, I've always had a soft spot for strippers. Great season. How is your daughter Sage doing?'"***

Shana sat up straight and smiled at the camera. She looked stunning in her plunging green Roberto Cavalli dress.

Shana: ***"Thanks, Frank, I guess. Sage is such a lovely young woman. She'll be attending Brown University in the fall. We're all so proud of her. She's the first person in my family to go to college."***

Max Mavis: ***"Here's a tough one from Deena from Tolerence, Arkansas: 'As a Christian I was disappointed that you accepted your daughter being raised by gay Satanists. My Bible study is praying for you and Sage.'"***

Shana: ***"Deena, honey, Wiccans worship nature, like the birds and bees. Or I guess in the case of Galen and Fern, bees and bees. They've been great moms to Sage, and maybe your Bible study should pray that God opens your hearts to his love."***

Shana threw her arms open wide, which caused Byron to say his own little prayer that the tape on her boobs would hold.

Max Mavis: ***"You preach it, Shana. Now for Allie, who viewers of HWN voted their top reality-show villain. Rita from Carson City, Nevada, writes: 'How shocked were you when your mother was arrested for murder? Did it ruin your husband's political prospects? How about your marriage?'"***

Allie felt ridiculous with her sprayed hair and form-fitting red Diana Von Furstenberg, and she found Max's questions offensive.

Allie: ***"Roy was actually quite relieved to get back into real estate and our marriage is just fine. I've opened my own interior design***

business, Beech House, and I've decided not to return for Season Two. My daughter Bethany is going to take my place, since she's taking a gap year off before college."

Max Mavis: *"What about your mother and that whole body beneath the fountain thing?"*

Allie: *"It was an accident and Mother was cleared. I think she's been more than sufficiently punished. The Social Register dropped our entire family."*

Max Mavis: *"Out of the Social Register. Wow, that's the high society death penalty."*

Max did not give Allie, who looked like she might commit murder herself, a chance to respond.

Max Mavis: *"Ladies, two dead bodies in one season. How are you gonna top that? Well here are two people that I think will keep viewers very interested. I want to introduce our two new Queens of the Court: Miss Bethany Beech, and Mrs. F. Brand Lippert!"*

Taylor: *"What the fuck?* ["We're going to have to bleep that," Rex noted.] *How did Lauren Lippert get on the show? I heard that old bastard* ["Bleep!"] *was divorcing that fucking bitch.* ["Bleep! Bleep!"] *She doesn't even belong to Belle Vista!"*

Max gestured to the curtain on the side of the stage and it parted. Out walked Bethany Beech and … *Shontae Briggs*. Bethany did a little curtsey to show off her flouncy pink Shoshona skirt, and Shontae waved to the audience. She wore a tight red leather dress and rhinestone boots. In her arms she carried a contented Smokey Joe, all dolled up in a matching red rhinestone-studded collar and leash.

Allie: *"Ah, that's not Lauren Lippert."*

Shana squealed and jumped up, hugging Shontae. A slightly squashed Smokey Joe let out a warning hiss.

Max Mavis: *"No, that's not Lauren Lippert. That's Shontae Lippert,*

recently married and now a full member of Belle Vista, thanks to the generosity of her billionaire husband. Wow, look at that ring!"

Shontae held up her left hand for the camera, displaying a significant sapphire surrounded by diamonds.

Max Mavis: ***"That thing is huge, and Season Two is going to be huge! Game, set, match! I can't wait to see what happens on and off the court!"***

{"Neither can I," Rex whispered to Jamal. "Neither can I."}

Acknowledgements

We would like to thank our families and friends for their support and encouragement, in particular Jody Leidolf for his excellent cover design, Elizabeth Desio for her editing and her lovely poem, Abby Lantz and Emily Leidolf for their copyediting skills and Lee Hathaway for her careful reading and insightful comments.

About the Authors

Melanie Howard is an award-winning writer whose work has appeared in *SELF*, *Cosmopolitan*, *Glamour* and other major magazines. She is a graduate of the University of Virginia and lives in Alexandria, Virginia with her husband and children.

Andrea Rider Leidolf is a graduate of the University of California , Berkeley, and the University of Virginia. She was the Washington correspondent for *Spy* magazine and currently works as a reading specialist in the public school system. She lives in Alexandria, Virginia with her husband and children.